The Darkness Dwellers

Also by Kirsten Miller

KiKi STRiKe

Inside the Shadow City
The Empress's Tomb

Kiki Strike

The Darkness Dwellers

Kirsten Miller

BLOOMSBURY

NEW YORK   LONDON   NEW DELHI   SYDNEY

First published in the United States of America in January 2013
by Bloomsbury Children's Books
www.bloomsbury.com

For information about permission to reproduce selections from this book,
write to Permissions, Bloomsbury Children's Books,
175 Fifth Avenue, New York, New York 10010

Library of Congress Cataloging-in-Publication Data
Miller, Kirsten.
Kiki Strike : the darkness dwellers / by Kirsten Miller. — 1st U.S. ed.
         p.   cm.
Summary: While Kiki Strike is in Paris trying to stop her evil cousin,
the princess Sidonia, from all sorts of terrible deeds, it is up to Ananka and the
other Irregulars to help Kiki find the cure for baldness, foil the evil plans of Oona's
twin, and keep Ananka herself from falling in love with the wrong young man.
ISBN 978-1-59990-736-9 (hardcover)
[1. Crime—Fiction.   2. Identity—Fiction.   3. New York (N.Y.)—Fiction.
4. Paris (France)—Fiction.   5. France—Fiction.]   I. Title.   II. Title:
Darkness dwellers.
PZ7.M6223Kip 2013   [Fic]—dc23   2012023303

Book design by Regina Roff
Typeset by Westchester Book Composition
Printed in the U.S.A. by Thomson-Shore, Dexter, Michigan
2 4 6 8 10 9 7 5 3 1

All papers used by Bloomsbury Publishing, Inc., are natural, recyclable products
made from wood grown in well-managed forests. The manufacturing processes
conform to the environmental regulations of the country of origin.
Manufactured by Thomson-Shore, Dexter, MI (USA); RMA587LS120, December, 2012

*For Georgia, my wild child. May you grow
to be the person you're meant to be*

The Darkness Dwellers

Preface

There are plenty of impatient people in this world who will pick up a book and thumb past its preface. You should be proud you're not one of them. The point of a preface is to prepare you for the story you're about to read. And when it comes to the dark and dangerous tale that's written on these pages, you'll need all the preparation you can get.

But before I begin, allow me to introduce myself. My name is Ananka Fishbein. If you haven't heard of me, I won't hold it against you. Perhaps the name Kiki Strike rings a bell? If not, I congratulate you on your recent release from prison. You see, a few years back, Kiki's name was on the cover of every newspaper in the country. The first part of her story has already been written. But if you're just joining us, sit back and make yourself comfortable. You've arrived at the very best moment.

Here's what you need to know so far. . . .

Kiki Strike and I have been members of a secret band of girl geniuses known as the Irregulars for the past six years, and our mission has been to protect the Shadow City—a network of forgotten tunnels beneath downtown New York. We've battled greedy smugglers, hungry ghosts, and several well-known society figures in the process. But our most important mission—the one described on these very pages—was the mission that determined the future of a small kingdom in Eastern Europe and the fate of our illustrious leader.

There's no time to waste getting started, so I've taken the liberty of preparing a short dossier on a few key figures.

Ananka Fishbein

Known as the most brilliant and talented girl in Manhattan, with a face so lovely . . . Okay, I'm kidding. I don't really have any remarkable gifts. I was invited to join the Irregulars because my parents possess an enormous library, and I've read most of it. (Before I turned twelve, I had a lot of time on my hands.) My areas of expertise include (but are not limited to): rats, maps, the history of New York, alien abduction, Bigfoot-like creatures around the world, and giant squid.

Betty Bent

The Irregulars' sweet-tempered master of disguise, Betty rarely leaves the house without first concealing her identity. As a result, only close friends and relatives know what she really looks like. (Or do we?)

Kaspar (aka Phineas Parker)

A graffiti artist, squirrel lover, and former vigilante, Kaspar is now a trusted associate of the Irregulars. He's also Betty's boyfriend.

DeeDee Morlock

DeeDee is a chemistry prodigy and co-creator of *Fille Fiable,* the only perfume proven to make its wearer appear more trustworthy. She's responsible for the Irregulars' potions, antidotes, and explosive devices. *Most* of the time they work.

Iris McLeod

Formerly the Irregulars' mascot, Iris is now our youngest member. By the time she was twelve years old, she had developed the rat-repelling potion that saved the Irregulars from a gruesome fate and helped DeeDee concoct *Fille Fiable.*

Luz Lopez

In the market for a skin-searing laser security system or surveillance camera concealed inside a stuffed pigeon? Luz Lopez is your girl. The Irregulars' engineering expert can craft any gadget you desire. If only she could work the same wonders on her rather *challenging* attitude.

Oona Wong
Computer hacker, lock picker, former forger, and a usually trustworthy member of the Irregulars. Only three months before this story began, Oona's father tried to have us all killed. Having been raised an only child by Mrs. Ning Fei, Oona was shocked to learn that she might have an identical twin sister named Lili. (An *evil* twin sister, naturally.)

Kiki Strike (aka Princess Katarina of Pokrovia)
Life-threatening allergies and a startling lack of pigment didn't prevent the vertically challenged founder of the Irregulars from becoming a world-class kicker of bad-guy butt. Kiki's biggest challenge? The one she now faces: avenging her parents' death.

Livia Galatzina
Kiki's aunt, Livia, became queen of Pokrovia after murdering Kiki's mother, the most beloved princess in Pokrovia's history. When Livia turned out to be one of the world's worst rulers, she was banished from her native land. She and her

daughter fled to New York, never realizing that one of the diamond rings she'd packed for the trip was engraved with a secret message that could expose her crimes. That ring is now in the possession of her niece, Kiki Strike.

Sidonia Galatzina
Livia's daughter and a nasty little sociopath, Sidonia was New York's "It Girl" until she tried to murder Kiki Strike. That's when the Irregulars forced her to flee to Russia. Unfortunately, she chose not to stay.

Sergei Molotov
Livia's henchman, Sergei thinks he's funny and wears waaaay too much cologne. He looks and acts like a cartoon villain, but Sergei's weapons are real and he's never afraid to use them.

Verushka Kozlova
A former member of the Pokrovian Royal Guard and Kiki Strike's beloved guardian, Verushka rescued Kiki from her homicidal relatives and trained her in the martial arts. Before this story began, Verushka had recently recovered from an assassination attempt. But only the Irregulars knew she was still alive.

Lester Liu
A genuine bad guy, Lester Liu is Oona
Wong's father and the head of a vicious
Chinatown smuggling gang known as the
Fu-Tsang. After the Irregulars got in his
way, he joined forces with Livia Galatzina
to kill us. Lester is currently serving a
forty-year prison sentence.

Lili Liu
A girl who looks enough like Oona Wong
to be her twin sister.

Molly Donovan
My friend and former classmate at the
Atalanta School for Girls, Molly is the most
famous delinquent in Manhattan. She now
attends the Boreland Academy, a school for
young people with behavioral problems or
a tendency toward violence.

Principal Theodora Wickham
Principal of the Atalanta School for Girls,
my mentor, and quite possibly the coolest
lady on Earth.

Consider yourself briefed. Are you ready for a little
adventure?

Chapter 1

A Tale of Two Princesses

i, Ananka Fishbein, have an embarrassing secret I'd like to share with you. When I was younger (much, *much* younger), I used to dream of being a princess. Go ahead. Giggle all you want. But at the time, I thought it sounded like a job with some excellent perks. Fabulous clothes, all the caviar you can eat, and the ability to have your enemies shipped off to prison. (Or beheaded, if you were *really* ticked off.) Now that I've gotten to know a few princesses, I realize just how foolish I was. These days, I'd rather take a job scrubbing Porta-Potties than go anywhere near a *royal* throne.

In the immortal words of one Madame Amelia Beauregard, I'm as common as they come. (More on *her* later.) And I'm happy to be the product of a long line of peasants. Unlike princesses, female Fishbeins have never been forced to marry their cousins—or had their heads lopped off when they failed to produce heirs to the Fishbein throne. Of course, one might argue that princesses are rarely beheaded these days. But the job is as deadly as it's ever been. For those who find this hard to believe, I offer as proof Princess A and Princess B.

One of the very first royals I've had the pleasure of meeting, Princess A was nearly murdered when she was little more than an infant. She survived the assassination attempt. Her mother and father did not. Princess A spent the following fifteen years running from relatives who wanted to kill her—and trying to avenge her parents' deaths. Sounds like a barrel of laughs, right?

Princess B lives in fear of a "curse." From what I've read, every royal family has one. Members of the Austrian royal family (including the notorious Marie Antoinette) were often born with pronounced underbites. French nobility possessed enormous noses, and the British royal family is famed for Dumbo-like ears. But the princesses of a certain Eastern European kingdom are said to be burdened with the worse curse of all—incurable baldness. Princess B worries that one morning she'll wake up as hairless as a mole rat. Just as her mother did the day she turned seventeen.

I should add that these two particular princesses are first cousins—and sworn enemies. One would do anything to rule the tiny country of Pokrovia. The other would do anything to stop her. Those of you who've been following my adventures know that Princess A is none other than Kiki Strike, founder of the Irregulars. Princess B is her cousin—the beautiful, enchanting, despicable Sidonia Galatzina. And *this* is the story of which princess prevailed.

It all began on a Valentine's Day not long ago when I arrived unannounced at the Soma Inn in lower Manhattan, where Kiki Strike had taken temporary lodgings. The term "fleabag hotel" doesn't do justice to the variety of vermin that scuttled down the halls and snuggled up under the bedsheets. The Irregulars had been forced to spend an entire weekend wrangling herds of giant cockroaches before Kiki's room was fit for human habitation.

Of course, the Soma Inn was the last place anyone would expect to encounter the heir to the throne of Pokrovia, which was exactly why Kiki had chosen it. The whole world was searching for the pale little princess who'd come back from the dead. Kiki Strike had one final task to complete before she let anyone find her.

When I reached the hotel, a black town car was already idling at the curb. The trunk popped open as I passed, and an enormous man jumped out from behind the wheel.

"You need some help with that?" He hurried toward a tiny creature who had emerged from the hotel lobby with a giant suitcase in each hand.

"Knock yourself out," the girl said, setting her luggage down in the snow. When the man grabbed the handles and lifted, his eyes nearly crossed from the strain.

"You got bricks in here, honey?" he asked.

"Just a few supplies, *precious*," Kiki Strike replied flatly.

Her colorless hair was tucked beneath an ebony wig. Dark sunglasses hid her icy blue eyes. She wore a black overcoat, tall black boots, and black leather gloves. As always, Kiki looked like an assassin on assignment at a fashion show.

"Ananka! You have come to see us off?" A short nun with a thick Russian accent appeared at Kiki's side.

"I think this outfit may be my favorite," I said with a giggle. In the months since she had staged her own death, Verushka hadn't left the house without one of Betty Bent's ingenious disguises.

"Yes, I never knew habits were so practical," replied Kiki's beloved guardian in a hushed voice. "I can hide almost anything under these robes. You would not believe what I have strapped to my ankle!"

"I can only imagine," I told her.

"Okay, Ananka, enough with the small talk," Kiki announced. "Our flight leaves in two hours. So why don't you just go ahead and tell us why you're here. I assume something has gone seriously wrong, because I believe I made it clear that we wouldn't need a formal farewell. Verushka and I will be back before you even realize we're gone."

"I know," I said. "But I've been thinking."

"Uh-oh," Kiki groaned.

According to Kiki, her trip to Pokrovia would take no more than three days. There would be just enough time to meet with the country's prime minister—and use the clues engraved in the band of a pink diamond ring to find a treasure Kiki had been seeking for years. In less than a week she would return to New York with evidence that her only aunt had murdered her parents. It sounded like a simple-enough plan. But when it came to the royal family of Pokrovia, nothing was ever simple.

"It's about your aunt," I said. "I'm worried she might cause trouble for you and Verushka."

Kiki sighed. "Ananka, *you* were the one who took charge of getting Livia and Sidonia out of my hair. All reports place them both in a castle in the middle of Loch Leven in Scotland right now. So admit it. You did a fantastic job."

She was right about that. My idea to "persuade" a well-known movie director to cast Sidonia as the lead in his film about Mary Queen of Scots had been nothing short of sheer genius.

"Yeah, but *you* were the one who taught me to always have a backup plan," I pointed out. "If Livia shows up in Pokrovia and tries to get in your way, you may need something to bargain with. And we both know there's nothing baldie wants more than a full head of hair. So I'm going to tell the Irregulars to keep working on the cure for the Pokrovian royal curse."

"That won't be necessary," Kiki persisted. "And just between us, I'm getting worried about DeeDee. Every time she invents some new drug or ointment, she always ends up testing the stuff on herself. She's going to poison herself someday."

"I'll tell DeeDee to be more careful," I said. "But I'm afraid I'm going to have to insist. You may end up needing the cure. So we're going to make it. End of story."

Not long before I first met Kiki Strike, I won the only award of my academic career. I was named the seventh grade's "Best Conversationalist." Even back then, I could hold forth on a wide range of topics—from Egyptian embalming techniques to reported Yeti attacks in the mountains of Nepal. But I've always been hopeless when it comes to expressing the things that matter most. My mouth takes my heartfelt emotions and spits them out in some kind of code. Luckily, the people who know me best usually figure out how to crack it.

Standing outside the Soma Inn, I couldn't utter the words I needed to say. And Kiki might have squirmed if she'd heard them. Neither of us has ever qualified as the warm, fuzzy type. But we both knew that I couldn't bear the thought of anything happening to her. She had rescued me from a dull, drab existence and showed me how thrilling the world could be. I owed Kiki Strike everything, and I wasn't about to lose her.

"Okay," Kiki finally agreed. "You guys go ahead and cook up the cure. I'll call you as soon as Verushka and I land in Pokrovia."

"Good luck," I told her.

"Luck is for the ill-prepared," Kiki said, ducking into the car. "But thanks anyway."

I watched the town car pull away from the snow-covered curb with Kiki and Verushka inside.

✶   ✶   ✶

Kiki had promised she'd be back in New York in three short days. But it would be months before I'd see her again.

Chapter 2

A Cure for the Royal Curse

Chinatown was silent but for the crunch of boots on ice. Snow banks rose on either side of me, their dingy walls speckled black, brown, and yellow. Two days had passed since a blizzard had slammed the city, but the streets and sidewalks of Manhattan had yet to be cleared. Now the sky threatened more snow. The clouds that brushed past the church steeples were dark gray and faintly furry. At times they dipped so low that you could have almost reached up to pet them.

When I finally arrived at Oona Wong's apartment, I found that the Irregulars hadn't bothered to wait for me. DeeDee Morlock, our chemist, was busy adjusting a portable lab she'd set up on the dining room table. Luz Lopez, mechanic and engineer, was assembling something that resembled a medieval torture device. Neither girl glanced up to greet me.

"Hi, Ananka." Betty Bent was moping on the living room couch. Aside from her bright red wig and miserable expression, she was the spitting image of Jackie O. "Luz said they don't need me." She touched a hankie to the corner of one eye.

"You might not be in demand today," I tried to console her. "But masters of disguise don't stay unemployed for long. Where are Oona and Iris? I want to talk to everyone together."

"Oona's in the kitchen with her grandmother," Betty said. "Mrs. Fei sent Iris out to get some supplies. I volunteered, but they said I'd be too nice to haggle with the shopkeeper!"

It was a wise call, in my opinion. Betty would have paid twice the price and left a generous tip. But I changed the subject rather than say so. "What's Mrs. Fei cooking?" I asked, sniffing at the air.

"I don't know." Betty's nose wrinkled with disgust. "But from the smell of it, I'd say death."

I followed the stench of burned hair and cocoa butter to the kitchen. There, I found Oona's honorary grandmother, Mrs. Fei, sitting on a wooden stool in front of the stove, stirring something inside a cast-iron pot. Her silver hair was pulled back in a bun, and a gas mask covered her nose and mouth. The kitchen windows had fogged with steam, and condensation dripped from the ceiling.

"Whatcha making?" I asked, peeking over the rim of the cauldron. The gooey brown substance inside was bubbling and spitting like molten manure.

"Don't come too close!" the old woman barked at me through the gas mask. "You think I wear this to look sexy? This stuff could be poison. If we get lucky, it will grow hair."

I hopped back a few feet and watched her muscular arms continue to churn the concoction. Although she'd never had a chance to earn an MD, Mrs. Fei was one of the most respected physicians in Chinatown, and her homemade potions had saved hundreds of lives.

"So that's the cure? Is it done already?" I asked.

"Not yet," Mrs. Fei said with a shake of her head. "This is just an old recipe. It needs to be adjusted. And we are missing the most important ingredient—*dong chong xia cao*."

"*Ewwww.*" Oona stuck her head out of the kitchen's pantry. "Is *that* what you told Iris to get? I hope you don't expect *me* to be your guinea pig."

"Why? What is it?" I asked.

Mrs. Fei placed the lid on her cauldron and winked at me over one shoulder. "Caterpillar fungus," she said. "From the Himalaya Mountains."

"Got it!" Twelve-year-old Iris McLeod had arrived, bearing a small brown paper bag. Dressed in pink snow boots and a pink ski jacket, she looked much younger than twelve—an impression reinforced by the fact that she chose to skip all the way across the kitchen.

Mrs. Fei took the bag. She dumped its contents into one hand and sorted through the shriveled caterpillar carcasses with a finger.

"Where did you get *those*?" I asked Iris, expecting to hear that they'd been found alongside a mummified yak—or discovered in the ancient medicine cabinet of a long-dead Tibetan doctor. Iris's parents were archaeologists, and her house on Bethune Street was packed with bizarre treasures they'd brought back from their expeditions.

"The corner store," Iris sang merrily. "They usually charge $259 a pound. I got 'em down to $159!" Then she proceeded to twirl through the kitchen as if a waltz were playing inside her head.

"What's wrong with you?" I asked. "Did you slip and get brain damage on the way back here?"

"Nothing's *wrong* with me," replied the tiny blond girl. "I had a date last night."

"Tricking another delivery boy into your house doesn't count as a date, Iris," Oona yelled from the pantry. "It's called *kidnapping.*"

"I didn't *trick* him," Iris shouted back. "He came in on his own!"

"Quiet!" Mrs. Fei ordered through her gas mask. "You want bad energy to destroy all my hard work?"

"Okay, ladies, let's go," I said, shooing everyone under the age of sixty out of the kitchen. "I want to talk to the Irregulars in the living room right now."

"Bossy, bossy . . . Kiki should leave *me* in charge for a change," I heard Oona grumbling as she emerged from the pantry.

"What was that?" I demanded.

"Nothing!" Oona insisted.

★   ★   ★

Finally, all six girls gathered in Oona's opulent dining room. Only our well-dressed hostess fit in with the scenery. Oona lived like an heiress from another age, and it was easy to forget that she hadn't been born into great wealth. Her apartment's museum-worthy antiques and stunning Chinese scrolls were the rewards of her hard work and cunning. As a little girl, Oona had often been forced to Dumpster dive for her dinner. Now she ate her meals at a table that had once belonged to an empress—the same table where a meeting of the Irregulars was about to be called to order.

I grabbed the only remaining chair. DeeDee, dressed in her white lab coat, was clearly impatient to get started. Luz Lopez was making a few last-minute tweaks to her invention while Oona, Betty, and Iris debated the legal definition of kidnapping.

"Kiki's at the airport," I announced, and everyone fell silent. "Before she left, she agreed to let us send her the cure."

"Yay!" cried Iris.

"It's about time!" DeeDee huffed. It had been her idea to develop a cure for female baldness. "If Livia and Sidonia ever get their hands on Kiki, it could be her only bargaining chip. I don't know why she refused to postpone her trip until I had something ready to give her!"

"She doesn't think she'll need the cure. The most reliable gossip pages continue to place Livia and Sidonia Galatzina on that island in Scotland," I said. "Just yesterday there was a report from the set of *The One True Queen*. Apparently Sidonia has locked herself in her room until the writers give the movie a happier ending."

"Here we go again," Luz Lopez muttered under her breath. "You really think they're stuck on that island? Don't you know they have boats in Scotland?"

"Your optimism has been duly noted, Miss Lopez,"

I said. "Now let's talk hair. DeeDee? Can you give us a debrief? Tell us what Mrs. Fei's cooking in the kitchen?"

"Sure." DeeDee sat up straight. She'd cut her own dreadlocks again, and they sprang from her scalp like miniature snakes. "Kiki told us that her aunt went bald at age seventeen. Setting aside all the superstitions about bald Pokrovian queens . . ."

"What superstitions?" chirped Iris.

"Pokrovians believe witches shed their hair when they reach adulthood. They say a bald woman should never be queen," I explained.

"Yes, well, I think there may be a more scientific explanation for Livia's baldness," DeeDee continued. "I believe she suffers from androgenetic alopecia. It's a hereditary disorder that causes the hair to thin. It's not particularly common among women, but it's not unheard of, either."

"You say it causes the hair to *thin*?" I butted in. "That time I pulled the wig off Livia's head, she was as bald as a bowling ball. Are you sure alopecia is the problem here?"

"No," DeeDee admitted. "We'll just have to keep our fingers crossed."

"Great. *That* always works out," said Luz. This time everyone ignored her.

"Where are you at with the cure?" I asked DeeDee.

"Iris and I have been studying an old recipe that Mrs. Fei found. That's what she's cooking in the kitchen. We're going to update it—add a couple of modern ingredients and run it through the new filtration equipment

Luz made for us. I think there's a good chance the cure could work."

"How will we know if it does?" Betty asked.

"Well—" DeeDee started to say.

"No!" I interrupted when I noticed DeeDee running her fingers over her dreadlocks. "No experimenting on yourself this time! That was Kiki's only condition."

"Anyone know a bald guy who'd be willing to try it out?" Luz asked.

"If I can't test it on myself, I'm not going to test it on some innocent person!" DeeDee argued. "Which means there won't be any way to know if it works. At least until Livia tries it."

"Hold on. Hold on," Oona jumped in. "Let me get this straight. You're making a cure for Livia's baldness. But we're not even sure if this crud's gonna work, and we haven't even discussed how we'll get it to Pokrovia. Is that right?"

"Pretty much," DeeDee said with a shrug.

"Good to know." Oona crossed her arms and warily watched the rest of us as if we'd gone completely insane.

"Look, no one is claiming that the plan is perfect," I said. "But we're all going to pitch in and help. DeeDee, you and Luz seem pretty busy. What can the rest of us do?"

DeeDee and Luz leaned together and consulted. When they were finished, Luz smiled. "Go out and get us some lunch?" she suggested.

"It's way too cold outside," Oona declared. "Send the munchkin."

"Hey!" Iris shouted. "I *told* you not to call me that!"

"We need Iris," Luz said. "She's DeeDee's assistant. What we don't need right now is a computer hacker, Jackie Kennedy, or a girl who's read too many books about Bigfoot."

"No offense," DeeDee added.

"None taken," I said.

"Speak for yourself," Oona mumbled.

Chapter 3

The Prettiest Thief in New York

i led the way along the treacherous path to the grocery store. Ahead of me, a professional dog walker swaddled in multiple coats, scarves, and mittens slipped and slid around the corner, dragging two beagles and a pit bull behind her. I silently thanked Betty Bent for my custom-made snow boots. The metal spikes that covered their soles gripped the ice like tiny talons.

"Mmai mhunt mahliv mha mhay mi mha!" I heard behind me. Oona Wong was grumbling again.

"Mwa?" Betty replied.

The scarves wrapped around Oona's face muffled her words, but nothing short of a gag would have kept her from complaining. Betty and I weren't exactly thrilled to be demoted to lunch ladies, either. But unlike Oona, we knew when to stay quiet.

Finally our destination appeared, beckoning us like a tropical oasis. The sidewalk surrounding Chu's Fruit and Fish was clear and dry, as if the storm had steered around the store. Tall pyramids of brightly colored fruit rose behind the windows, and perfect puffs of hot steam floated into the atmosphere every time the front door swung open. Inside, we found Mr. Chu at the register, dressed in the same spotless white tank top he wore every day. None of us had ever seen him step out from behind the counter, and Oona liked to speculate that he might not wear any pants.

"Good afternoon!" he greeted us cheerfully. I mutely lifted one heavy arm in response.

"*Mmho mmoo mhay* think I am, their *maid*? It's *my* house!" Oona fumed as she unwound her scarf and snatched the hat off her head. "Luz and DeeDee have some nerve! I've got *seniority*."

"Give it a rest, would you?" I sighed. "Who's got the shopping list?"

"I do." Betty searched through the pockets of her sleek black overcoat.

"*You!*" someone said with a growl. Mr. Chu's sunny smile had shriveled into an angry pucker. "I told you to never come back here!"

I scanned the shop. Aside from a skinny stock boy who was cowering behind the bok choy, we were the only people around.

"Excuse me?" Betty inquired politely. "Are you talking to *us*?"

"I'm talking to her!" Mr. Chu shouted with one crooked finger pointed just to the left of Oona. "She comes in here and tries to sneak money out of my register, and then she thinks she can come back the very next day?"

"*What?*" Oona blurted, two round red patches growing

on her cheeks. Oona had never been anyone's idea of an upstanding citizen, but I had to admit—her shock looked genuine.

"Call the cops, dummy!" Mr. Chu ordered the stock boy as he ducked around the counter. "I caught the thief!" When he appeared in front of us, I was briefly relieved to see that his lower half was clothed in cut-off dress pants, knee-high socks, and rubber sandals. "No more Mr. Nice Guy!" he yelled at Oona. "You're going to jail, girlie!"

Mr. Chu started to stomp toward Oona, and I had a split second to act before he could reach her. I plucked a giant grapefruit from the base of a five-foot fruit pyramid, hoping to bury him up to his knees in an avalanche of citrus. When the pyramid proved solid, Betty took over, shoving a tower of pineapples into his path.

"Sorry, Mr. Chu!" she cried as the man howled in fury.

"Move it!" I shouted, grabbing a still-stunned Oona by the arm and dragging her out the door. We were barely half a block down the street when Mr. Chu came barreling out of his shop.

★　★　★

I think it's fair to say that most people, when chased, usually have a good idea *why* they're being chased. Perhaps they've robbed a bank, egged the mayor's house, or winked at a lady wrestler's boyfriend. As far as I knew, it had been at least three days since I'd done anything worthy of a sprint. But as a member of the Irregulars, you learn to run first and ask questions later. When you've made as many enemies as we have, sometimes answers are a luxury you have to live without.

Our snow boots should have given us a clear advantage over Mr. Chu's sandals, but our layers of winter clothing were no match for the shopkeeper's sporty ensemble. He stayed right behind us for a half-dozen blocks. When we reached Chatham Square, I glanced over my shoulder and saw the middle-aged man fly over a fire hydrant with the perfect form of an Olympic hurdler. A few seconds later, I tried to turn onto Catherine Street, but one of my legs remained behind, and I flopped face-first into a grimy snowbank. Oona and Betty slowed to watch as I wrenched my boot free from a crack in the sidewalk.

"Go!" I shouted at them, and the two girls disappeared down the street. Just as I started to follow, I felt someone grab the back of my coat with one hand and whip my hat off with another.

"Humph!" Mr. Chu exclaimed at the sight of my mousy brown hair. He spun me around and shook a finger in my face. "You tell your Chinese friend I mean business. If I see any of you again, I will send you all to prison! You understand?"

"Yes, sir," I said, figuring it was best to play along. I could have unleashed one of my new kung-fu moves, but Mr. Chu had suffered enough for one day.

"Good," he huffed. He dropped my arm and left me standing on the street corner, listening to the sound of his sandals slapping against his heels.

I had almost reached Oona's house when I saw the doors of a graffiti-covered delivery van pop open. Betty and Oona leaped from the back of the parked vehicle.

"Is he gone?" Betty asked nervously.

"Yeah, he's gone," I told them. "What was *that* about?"

"I have no idea," Oona insisted. "I shop at Chu's all the time. I never stole a thing."

"Not even a grape or two?"

"*Everybody* takes a grape or two," Oona snapped. "How else would you know if they're any good?"

"I'm *kidding*," I assured her.

"Maybe it was a case of mistaken identity," Betty offered. "I wonder who Mr. Chu thought you were."

"Mistaken identity? How many people out there are as gorgeous as . . ." Oona stopped mid-boast, and her eyes grew large. We all knew there was one person (other than herself) whom Oona deemed "gorgeous." A girl by the name of Lili Liu.

The Irregulars had only glimpsed Lili once, at the Metropolitan Museum of Art. That was when we learned that Oona Wong might have a twin. Oona's mother had died in childbirth, and her criminally inclined father had shown no interest in raising a daughter. Lester Liu had given Oona to Mrs. Fei, who worked in one of the sweatshops he owned. While her father grew wealthy, Oona and her honorary grandmother suffered in terrible poverty. And for fifteen years, that had been our friend's sad, shameful story. She didn't know that her mother had given birth to a second child in the hours before she died. Mrs. Fei knew about the baby named Lili, but she'd always believed that Oona's twin sister had been too weak to survive.

Then Oona's double appeared at a museum gala, and Lester Liu had introduced the girl to the world as his daughter Lillian. She looked coddled and spoiled—like the only child of a very rich man. As jealous as Oona might have been, I had a hunch that she would have welcomed a sister. But Lili disappeared the same night Lester Liu was arrested. As far as we knew, she hadn't even visited the jail where he was serving a forty-year sentence for kidnapping, forgery, art theft—and the attempted murder of Oona Wong.

"Don't make a big deal out of this until we know for sure that it's Lili," Oona warned us.

"So you really think someone might be impersonating you?" I asked.

"I wasn't going to say anything, but I got kicked out of the dim sum place on Baxter Street yesterday," Oona admitted. "The manager claimed I'd been dining and dashing. I figured all that e-coli had finally eaten her brain, but now . . ." Oona shrugged helplessly, and my heart flooded with pity. Less than three months had passed since she'd sent her own father to jail. The last thing Oona needed now was more family drama.

"Come on," Betty said softly, wrapping an arm halfway around Oona. "Let's pick up lunch and get you home. Don't worry. We'll find a way to fix all of this." The look she shot at me behind Oona's back wasn't as confident as her words.

Chapter 4

The Case of the Snow-White Lilies

When we reached the next grocery store, Oona refused to go inside. She hid around the corner instead, behind a multicolored mountain of snow and uncollected garbage. By the time Betty and I finished shopping, Oona's teeth were chattering and her nose had turned purple. The three of us trudged silently back to her house, where we found a delivery man scaling the icy stairs to the front door.

"You girls live in this building?" the man asked between the blooms of three dozen red roses.

"I do!" Oona instantly perked up.

"Your name Gertrude Sing?"

"No." When Oona sighed, her face disappeared behind a cloud of frozen breath. "Gertrude's on the fourth floor. Up the stairs to the right." Oona opened the front door for the delivery man, and then turned back to us with a miserable expression. "You know your life sucks when

your ninety-year-old neighbor gets Valentine's flowers
and you don't get squat."

"Is today really Valentine's Day?" I asked.

"Yeah, Fishbein. February fourteenth. Same day every
year," Oona said.

"Save the sarcasm, Wong. I just had an idea. Do you
guys know what happens on Valentine's Day?"

"You really need us to explain it to you, Ananka? Have
you ever *met* a member of the opposite sex?"

"Okay, Oona," Betty said. "That's enough. Let Ananka
talk."

"Would you guys be up for a little trip to the Marble
Cemetery?" I asked.

Oona looked confused, but Betty's eyes lit up. "We
can find out who leaves the lilies every Valentine's Day!"

"Oh yeah. I remember now," Oona said with much less
enthusiasm.

"I'll go! I'll go!" Betty exclaimed.

"You guys have fun," Oona told us. "I'm not freezing my
butt off just to see what kind of person wastes flowers on
dead people."

"It'll be more entertaining than watching the other
Irregulars work," I promised Oona.

"But not quite as exciting as taking a nap," she said, lift-
ing the bag of groceries out of my arms. "See you tomorrow. I hope you still have all your toes."

★   ★   ★

The Irregulars had been regularly visiting the hidden
graveyard known as the Marble Cemetery for almost three
years. We knew about its underground vaults and the

tunnel that connected them to the subterranean Shadow City. But the walled enclosure just off Second Avenue was still keeping one secret from us. Though we'd never encountered another visitor in the cemetery, every February 14, a dozen white calla lilies mysteriously appeared near one of the tombs. There was always the same poem on the card attached to the bouquet.

I will not ask where thou liest low,
Nor gaze upon the spot;
There flowers or weeds at will may grow,
So I behold them not:
It is enough for me to prove
That what I lov'd, and long must love,
Like common earth can rot;
To me there needs no stone to tell,
'T is Nothing that I lov'd so well.

ILEMA

I might have found it terribly romantic, if I'd known the first thing about romance. While most of my friends had already booted a boyfriend or two, I was in serious danger of becoming—*shudder*—a late bloomer. It wasn't really my fault. As a student at the Atalanta School for Girls, I was more likely to have a close encounter with an extraterrestrial than a member of the opposite sex. I knew only one crush-worthy boy—and I'd been repeatedly informed that he was completely off-limits. Fourteen Valentine's Days had already passed without so much as a corny e-card. My fifteenth would be spent staking out a snow-covered graveyard. It cheered me a little to know that sweet, pretty Betty Bent would be there by my side. If she was with me on Valentine's Day, it meant she wouldn't be spending it with Kaspar—her handsome beau and the boy of my dreams.

☆   ☆   ☆

Betty kept watch while I picked the lock on the Marble Cemetery's gate. Once inside, we realized we must have just missed the caretaker. A shoveled path began at the entrance and ran along the southernmost wall. The rest of the graveyard remained a seamless stretch of white. No tombstones rose from the snow—the names of those buried beneath the frozen ground were chiseled into plaques set in the cemetery's walls.

We followed the caretaker's path to its end, then waded through the snow until we reached the shelter of one of the graveyard's trees. The afternoon light was growing dim, and the tree's skeletal branches cast enough of a shadow to hide us from view. We carved out a hole in the two-foot-deep snow and settled in to wait for our guest.

"I really wish Kiki was here," Betty whispered.

I'd been thinking the very same thing. Kiki was the one who'd first spotted the flowers. It felt a bit wrong to uncover their secret without her.

Betty pulled out her phone and checked the clock. "Do we know what time the lilies usually show up?"

"Why? Are you in a hurry? You got big plans tonight?" I teased her. Kaspar attended an art academy outside the city, and he hadn't made it to town in weeks. Part of me hoped that Betty would end up looking for love a little closer to home.

"Sort of," Betty admitted shyly. "Kaspar said he's going to have something delivered to my house at six o'clock. I should probably be there when it arrives."

"What is it?" I asked, trying not to sound jealous.

"He wouldn't tell me." I knew Betty was blushing underneath her fuzzy scarf. "It's supposed to be a surprise."

Just as fresh flakes began to fall, the wrought-iron gate that hid the graveyard from the rest of the city opened with an unpleasant creak, and an elegant figure appeared. She was tall, thin, and dressed in a charcoal-gray coat that swung about her boot-clad ankles. A dark hat concealed her face. In her arms, she cradled a bundle of calla lilies, their blooms whiter than any snow that has ever fallen in New York City. The woman stopped in front of one of the plaques on the wall and placed the lilies on the ground beneath it. From her pocket she retrieved a white handkerchief, which she used to dust the city soot from the name engraved in the stone. Then she stood back and stared straight ahead, as though she'd been transported to another place, leaving only a lifeless body behind.

"This isn't right," Betty whispered. "We made a mistake coming here. We shouldn't be watching this."

I was feeling the same remorse, but I wasn't about to admit it. "Come on—aren't you curious?" I tried to convince both of us.

"Not anymore," said Betty stiffly. Before I could stop her, she rose from our hiding place and started toward the cemetery's exit. I had no choice but to follow her. My sense of horror grew when I saw Betty stop at the woman's side.

The lady peered down at the two of us, and I realized she was much older than her perfect posture suggested. Her attractive features had been hardened by time, and her thin lips were so tight that a smile would have cracked them. The eyes that studied us were steel gray and just as cold.

"My name is Amelia Beauregard. Whom do I have the pleasure of addressing?" The woman's crisp, upper-crust accent was a holdover from an era of gaslights and horseless carriages.

Betty held out a hand. "How do you do? I'm Betty Bent. And this is my friend Ananka Fishbein. Sorry for interrupting you, ma'am. We were just leaving."

Amelia Beauregard's eyes scanned my coat, which was still covered in gutter muck from my earlier fall. Something about her expression told me she suspected I was descended from donkeys and wearing dirty underwear. She turned to Betty but didn't take her hand.

"A young lady must wait for the older person to offer her hand first."

"I'm sorry," Betty said, taken aback. I didn't blame her. No one had corrected *my* manners in years.

"No, you *apologize*. Now, would you girls care to tell me why you choose to spend your afternoons spying on old ladies in cemeteries?"

"We didn't know you'd be an old lady." Somehow the words hadn't come out right.

"What Ananka is *trying* to say," Betty translated, "is that we spend a lot of time in this cemetery, and we've noticed the beautiful flowers you bring every year. We didn't think many other people knew about the graveyard, so we were curious to see who left the lilies. We really didn't intend to spy on you."

Something flickered in Amelia Beauregard's eyes. "You make a convincing case," she said, examining Betty a bit closer.

"Thank you, ma'am."

"And you have an impressive sense of style. It's been years since I've seen a young lady dress so well. You said your family name is Bent?"

Betty nodded.

"Any relation to Franklin and Eloise?"

"They're my parents."

"I admire the work they do at the Metropolitan Opera. The costumes they designed for *The Magic Flute* were remarkable. You're quite lovely, too. My hair was once that very same shade of red."

Betty lifted one hand to her hairdo. "It's just a wig," she admitted.

"It suits you," Amelia noted. "You know, Miss Bent, I've been searching for someone like you . . ." She drifted off, her brain calculating unknown possibilities. "What I mean to say is that I run several schools. I've been looking for a young assistant. Someone with potential. A girl who could use a little polish. A diamond in the rough, if you will."

She opened her handbag, fished out a silver cardholder, and handed each of us a business card.

AMELIA BEAUREGARD
HEADMISTRESS
L'INSTITUT BEAUREGARD
NEW YORK · PARIS · ROUGEMONT

Just a glance at the card turned my spine to ice. L'Institut Beauregard was an etiquette academy, and it was infamous among my fellow students at the Atalanta School for Girls. Every September, at least one of my schoolmates was enrolled in after-school classes at the institute. By the time she returned from Christmas vacation, her transition from sassy schoolgirl to well-behaved robot was almost always complete.

"I'm very flattered, Madame Beauregard," Betty told her. "But I'm afraid I'm too busy with school to consider taking a job."

Amelia Beauregard was not easily deterred. "Why not sleep on it, my dear?" she suggested. "I leave for Paris in a few days, and I could use some help while I'm there. A trip might be a pleasant way to begin your employment. Do you happen to speak any French?"

"A little," Betty replied.

"Betty's too modest. She's practically fluent," I said.

"Humility is a rare and precious quality," Madame Beauregard noted, the sides of her mouth curling up ever so slightly. "If you are interested in the position, Miss Bent, please stop by the institute. Now, if you'll kindly excuse me, I have some thinking to do. Good day, ladies." Having thus dismissed us, Amelia Beauregard turned her attention back to the plaque on the wall. Before Betty could pull me away, I caught a glimpse of what was written there.

GORDON GRANT
BORN JANUARY 18, 1920
MISSING IN ACTION AUGUST 1944

THE FISHBEIN GUIDE TO . . . BEING A LADY

I know exactly what you're thinking. What does it take to be a *lady*? And why on earth would I want to be one? (This is a question most male readers are probably asking right now. Please substitute the word *gentleman,* sirs. You'll find it works equally well.)

Not long ago, being a lady meant presenting a certain face to the world. A lady never used a fish fork to eat steak. She kept her nails filed and her appearance tidy. And she never wore white shoes after Labor Day. This was the sort of person that girls were told they should strive to be. That's all fine and dandy, of course. Wearing dirty clothes can be quite unsanitary. And when used correctly, fish forks are genuinely handy utensils. But times have changed. In the twenty-first century, I think we can all aim a *little bit* higher, don't you?

A Twenty-First-Century Lady (Or Gentleman) . . .

1. Meets challenges with grace, cunning, and courage. (And occasionally a mean right hook.)
2. Knows how to defend herself—in an argument, a sporting match, or a dark alley.
3. Is a champion of all who are younger, weaker, and less fortunate than herself.
4. Knows you catch more flies with honey than vinegar. (Though she's prepared to whip out the vinegar in case of emergency.)
5. Chews with her mouth closed. (For many reasons, including the prevalence of flying insects.)
6. Is comfortable in her own skin. (No matter how many times her parents drag her to the dermatologist.)
7. Is always open to learning and trying new things. (Never turn down an opportunity to ride a pig. Trust me.)
8. Chooses her allies wisely. And while she never sets out to make enemies, she knows they're not always avoidable.
9. Is too busy to worry about what other people may think of her.

Ch𝔸P𝕋E̦R 5

Institutionalized

A young woman is judged every time she leaves her home. Her posture, her attire—even her table manners—speak volumes about a girl's background and upbringing. Parents today are eager to give their daughters every advantage. They spare no expense when it comes to tutors and tuition. And yet most neglect to provide their offspring with the most fundamental of skills.

The world is watching your daughters. A refined appearance and an understanding of etiquette will act as a shield against loose tongues and cruel eyes. For almost a century, L'Institut Beauregard has transformed Manhattan's girls into refined young ladies. You will notice a difference in less than a week—and so will everyone else.

—Amelia Beauregard, Headmistress,
L'Institut Beauregard

That night, I stayed up late, waiting for Kiki to call from Pokrovia. Rather than address my ever-growing pile of homework, I decided to engage in a bit of wholesome cyberstalking. The website for L'Institut Beauregard was a sickening shade of pink, with text written in a florid cursive font. Unable to bear the sight of the fake smiles plastered on the faces of the Institute's poster children, I hastily clicked the link for "Parent Testimonials."

> *"Before L'Institut Beauregard, my daughter and I were at war. Since she graduated, we've become the best of friends. Yesterday she even asked to borrow my pearls! A year ago, I would have been terrified that she'd pawn them and run away. But now I know I can trust her."*

> *"Just six months ago, my daughter was a slovenly oaf. Thanks to L'Institut Beauregard, her personal hygiene has improved significantly! Yesterday, a neighbor even complimented me on her appearance. The woman was only being nice, of course, but it wasn't so long ago that such a sentiment would have been too ludicrous to utter!"*

> *"My little **** went through a horrifying stage when she wanted to be a writer. She would spend all day moping around the house and scribbling in a notebook. It was depressing to watch! Thank goodness for L'Institut Beauregard. Now my precious darling loves nothing more than*

shopping. Just two months of instruction, and she's a whole new girl!"

There were more, of course. Girls who'd had "potty mouths," girls who'd stumbled over their own two feet, girls who'd shown a preference for boys from bad homes. Amelia Beauregard had cured each and every one of them. According to the wealthy mothers of Manhattan, she was a miracle worker. Her character was irreproachable, her own background pristine.

"Ananka, would you *please* take your clothes out of the dryer when they're done?" My mother dumped a load of unfolded laundry on my bed and readjusted the pencil that pinned her curly black hair into an untidy bun. "I'm not your maid." She caught sight of my computer screen and gasped. "Why on earth are you looking at *that*?"

"What?" I asked, wondering if she'd seen something I hadn't. It was as if she'd caught me surfing for smut. "It's just the website for L'Institut Beauregard. It's an etiquette academy."

I noticed that my mother's posture had suddenly improved. "I know what it is. And I know all about that horrible woman who runs it."

"Amelia Beauregard?" I asked. "What'd *she* ever do to you?"

"For your information, she and her institute ruined my sophomore year of high school."

"Wow. She was ruining people's lives back in the dark ages?" I asked.

"*Not* funny," my mother replied. "That woman and her

so-called *school* turned half the girls in my class into mind-less zombies. I lost my two best friends thanks to her."

"Really?" A personal connection tends to make any investigation more intriguing. My fingers scuttled back to the computer keys, eager to dig up a little more dirt.

"Yes, and then your grandmother decided to sign me up for classes when she found out our trust fund would cover the fees. She said I was a little 'rough around the edges.'"

"At least Grandma didn't threaten to send you to a boarding school in West Virginia."

"You're never going to forgive me for that, are you?" my mother asked.

"It was just a joke, Mom. So, if you went to the institute, how come you ended up being so normal?"

"I got myself kicked out."

"*You?*" I snorted. This was the same woman who'd once demanded that a traffic cop write her a ticket after she'd accidentally parked in a handicap zone. "How did you manage *that*?"

"It's none of your business," my mother said slyly. "I don't want to give you any ideas. But let's just say you're not the only one in the family with a rebellious streak."

"I wouldn't tease me if I were you," I warned her. "Don't think that I can't find out what you did."

"Go ahead. Give it your best shot," my mother said. "But you might have more fun turning your detective skills on Amelia Beauregard. Back in my day, they said Madame had a secret. No one knew what it was, but there was something behind all the gossip. I'd swear to it."

"Might it have had something to do with a mysterious

gentleman friend?" I said, mimicking Amelia Beauregard's manner of speaking.

"It might," my mother said. "Do you know something I don't?"

"Maybe," I said with a smile, just to torture her.

"Well, I expect a full report soon," my mother quipped on her way out the door. "Or I'll have to send you to the institute to do some firsthand research."

When I was certain my mother wasn't spying over my shoulder, I clicked out of the institute's website and called up Google. In the search box, I typed, "Gordon Grant MIA 1944." The first listing was a page from a site titled *Benedict Arnolds: Little-Known American Turncoats.* I clicked through and found myself staring at a black-and-white photo of a young man in a uniform. I could see how his good looks and rakish grin might have warmed the cockles of Amelia Beauregard's icy heart. "Gordon Mackenzie Grant," the headline read. "Nazi Collaborator and Saboteur." Jackpot.

> *Raised in Shacklesville, Alabama, Gordon Grant was a recognized mathematical genius by the age of ten. At age twenty-two, he was a respected professor at New York's Columbia University. During World War II, he joined the Army's Office of Strategic Services, a precursor to today's CIA. For most of the conflict, Grant worked as a cryptographer. Then in 1944, he volunteered for a dangerous assignment—one that required parachuting into Nazi-occupied France.*

With the liberation of Paris looming, Hitler ordered the German army to leave the city in ruins upon its retreat. Hidden in the catacombs beneath Paris, Gordon Grant's unit was tasked with intercepting Nazi communications, decoding them on-site, and protecting the town from destruction. However, it is now believed that Gordon Grant was operating as a double agent.

When French and American forces arrived in Paris, they discovered that the men in Grant's unit had been slaughtered. The tunnels beneath Paris were rigged with explosives that, fortunately, had failed to detonate. Despite an extensive search, Gordon Grant's body was never discovered. Reports claimed he had escaped the city with the German army—and the femme fatale who had turned him against his own country.

I leaned back in my chair and wondered what Madame Beauregard's fancy friends would think if they knew she still had the hots for a saboteur.

Chapter 6

The Great Switcheroo

The human brain is a devious little organ. Spend all night cramming your head with facts and figures, and you'll discover it's empty the next morning at test time. Beg it for a clever comeback during a spat, and it will finally deliver four hours later when you're alone in the bathtub with a face full of soap. It's almost as if our brains like playing tricks on us. They enjoy knowing things that we don't. Even when we sleep, our brains tease us with riddles. Sometimes we can solve them. More often than not, they just drive us nuts.

That night I dreamed I was standing outside a grand ballroom. A benefit for the Royal Society for the Prevention of Cruelty to Children was about to begin. Everyone was eagerly awaiting the guest of honor. I was about to join the festivities, when a woman pushed past me. I couldn't see her face, but I recognized the wig she was wearing. In one gloved hand the woman carried a golden cage. She stepped into the ballroom, and the crowd turned to face her. When Livia Galatzina held up the cage for all to see, I noticed that it contained a tiny white mouse. The guests went wild, and the ballroom doors slammed in my face.

✶ ✶ ✶

"Gee, that looks comfortable."

Every inch of my body ached. I forced my eyes open and saw nothing but wood. It wasn't the first time I'd fallen asleep facedown on my desk. I let my head flop to one side. A man was standing outside my room, chewing on a piece of toast.

"Hi, Dad."

"What were you studying that kept you up so late?" my father asked.

"Etiquette," I mumbled.

"Fine, don't tell me." My parents rarely believed a word I said. "There's coffee in the kitchen."

"What time is it? Am I late for school?"

"It's Sunday, Ananka. Drool on your desk all day if you like." He disappeared, humming the "Anvil Chorus" on his way down the hall.

There was some reason I needed to get up, but I couldn't remember what it was. Sleep was beckoning me back into blissful oblivion, when I was jolted to consciousness by the sound of my phone ringing. It was Luz Lopez.

"Hey," I answered, my eyelids drooping.

"Have you heard from Kiki?" No *hello*. No *how are ya?* Some people might have called Luz brusque. Others would have preferred the word *rude*.

"Kiki," I repeated, now completely awake. How could I have forgotten about *Kiki*?

"You said she was going to call you when she got to Pokrovia," Luz said.

Another dose of adrenaline shot through my system. "She didn't."

"Yeah, I figured," Luz said. "We need to meet. I've got something to show you."

"What is it?"

"Like I said, Fishbein, it's something I need to *show* you."

"Okay." I sighed. "Send a text to the other girls. I'll meet you all at Fat Frankie's in thirty minutes."

As usual, Fat Frankie's diner was packed with police officers. I could see Oona peeking out from our regular booth at the back of the restaurant. She appeared to have her eye on a handsome young recruit who was sitting at the counter munching on a giant cruller. No crisis, however large, could keep Oona from flirting.

"I'm here," I announced, sliding in next to Betty. "Let's get started."

Luz pulled a sheet of paper from her army-issue backpack. "Can I just state for the record that I thought it was crazy for Kiki to go to Pokrovia without taking proper precautions?"

"What have you found?" Thanks to my growing anxiety and the odor of vaporized lard in the air, I was beginning to feel slightly nauseous.

"I get e-mail alerts whenever anything about Kiki or

the Irregulars is posted online. This picture showed up on a French gossip blog this morning." Luz passed around a photo of a girl with white hair emerging from a black limousine. She was dressed all in black, with a scarf hiding her face below the nose and sunglasses concealing her eyes. Kiki Strike.

"Wow. Is that Pokrovia in the background? It sure looks fancy," Iris marveled.

"That picture was taken in *Paris*," Luz corrected her. "Last night. In front of the Prince Albert Hotel."

"What is Kiki doing in France?" Betty asked.

"Didn't her plane have a layover in Paris?" DeeDee asked. "Maybe they had to deal with some mechanical trouble. Or maybe Kiki just decided to stop off in France for a café au lait. She always complains that you can't get a good one in New York."

"I have no idea if Kiki's in France or not," Luz responded. "The only thing I know for sure is that the girl in this picture is *not* Kiki Strike."

"What do you mean, Lopez?" Oona leaned forward across the table and snatched the photo out of Iris's hands.

"It can't be Kiki," Luz stated. "I took some measurements and made a few calculations. The girl in the photo is at least five foot seven. What's Kiki? Four foot ten?"

Oona examined the photo more closely.

"Are you sure?" I asked.

"According to the blog, there was an incident last night at the hotel. The Princess of Pokrovia slapped a bellhop for denting one of her Louis Vuitton suitcases. Sounds like she made quite a scene."

"Well, it's not *our* Princess of Pokrovia," Betty insisted. "Louis Vuitton luggage is way too conspicuous for Kiki. And she'd never slap a bellhop. Or make a scene."

"Of course Kiki wouldn't," Luz said. "But it *does* sound a lot like another princess I know."

"Sidonia," I said with a groan.

"Exactly," Luz said. "So, let's take a moment to examine the evidence. Kiki disappeared sometime last night. Then her deranged cousin showed up in Paris that very same evening wearing a white wig. I don't know how they managed it, but Livia and Sidonia must have gotten their hands on Kiki. Except for the white hair, no one really knows what Kiki looks like. I think Sidonia is going to pretend to be the true heir to the throne."

"But what about the movie?" Betty asked. "I thought Livia and Sidonia were supposed to be in Scotland!"

"I called the set this morning," Luz said. "The director thinks Livia and Sidonia are still locked up in their suite, waiting for the script to be rewritten. But no one has actually *seen* them in days."

"What are we going to do?" DeeDee asked, and everyone at the table immediately looked at me.

"Anyone feel like a trip to Paris?" I asked, just as a bear-sized man covered in curly black fur approached our table. It was Fat Frankie himself, making a rare appearance among his patrons. The bloody stains on his apron made me wonder if he'd been butchering meat for the lunch special or disposing of an unnecessary employee.

"Hey, what's up, Frankie?" Oona asked. She had introduced the Irregulars to Fat Frankie's the previous summer, but according to Kiki, Oona and the owner had been friends for ages—ever since the day Frankie discovered an eight-year-old Oona sifting through the restaurant's garbage cans and brought her inside for a hamburger on the house.

"My waiter just told me you were here," said the man, his big, sad eyes focused only on Oona. "After all these years . . . I just can't believe it."

"Believe what?" Oona said, the smile still stuck on her face.

"That you would run away without paying for your food. I let it pass the first time 'cause we're friends and all. But three times? My waiters have families, Oona. They depend on the money they make here at the diner!"

"No! Frankie! It wasn't me!" Oona insisted.

The denial seemed to break Frankie's heart. "That's what *I* said when they told me. I said it couldn't be her! But then I looked at the security tapes. I thought you were a nice girl now."

"I am!" Oona yelped, but Fat Frankie dragged her from the booth and frog-marched her out to the snow-covered sidewalk. The policemen having breakfast at the counter turned to stare at the pretty girl with the bright red face. By the time the rest of us caught up with her, Oona was almost in tears.

"What's going on, Oona?" DeeDee demanded.

"Did you really skip out on your bills?" Iris asked.

Oona opened her mouth, but no words came out. Silently, she spun around in the sidewalk slush and stomped off down the street.

"Why would she do something so stupid?" Luz asked. "This was her favorite restaurant."

"Boy, you guys never cut Oona a bit of slack, do you?" I said.

"Why should we?" Iris asked. "You know what Oona's like. She was nice for about ten minutes after we saved her life. Then she went right back to being a pain in the butt."

"Oona's difficult, but she's also incredibly loyal," Betty argued. "She would never steal from Fat Frankie."

"Yeah, but Fat Frankie watched the tapes . . . ," Luz began.

"Fat Frankie saw someone who *looked* like Oona," I explained. "Doesn't mean it was actually her."

"Who else could it . . . ?" DeeDee stopped and sighed. "Lili Liu is still in town, isn't she?"

"Yeah," I confirmed. "This is the third time Lili's gotten Oona in trouble. She's been stealing from restaurants and stores all over Chinatown."

"How come our relatives are such pains in the butt?" Luz groaned. "Kiki's aunt. Lester Liu. And now Oona's identical twin?"

"They're *not* identical," DeeDee insisted for the millionth time. She was the only one who thought the two girls weren't a perfect match. "I'd say they're fraternal twins at best."

"We have to stop Lili before she gets Oona sent to jail," Iris said.

"Couldn't we have one crisis at a time?" Luz asked. "We haven't even figured out what to do about Kiki yet!"

"We'll deal with Lili in a day or two. Here's what we're going to do now," I told her, taking charge. "You, Iris, and DeeDee are going over to Oona's house. You'll all apologize nicely and then finish working the baldness cure. Betty and I are going to pay a visit to Amelia Beauregard."

"Who's that?" Luz asked.

"The woman who leaves the lilies in the Marble Cemetery every Valentine's Day," I said.

"Why are you going to see *her*?" DeeDee asked.

"Because she might just be our ticket to Paris," I said.

Chapter 7

What Happened
to Kiki

i t makes no difference whether you're Manhattan's stealthiest cat burglar, the fastest safecracker in Queens, or the brawniest bandit in all of the Bronx. There's one place on Earth you'll never break into. No matter how hard you try—or what surgical tools you possess—you can never break into another person's mind. Which makes the task before me particularly difficult. For now I must describe events as they happened to someone else—and try to see the world as it looked through her icy blue eyes. It would be easier if I were allowed to tap my imagination from time to time or add a few embellishments. But Kiki Strike is a stickler for the truth, and she's promised to "inform me" if I get my facts wrong.

The first thing Kiki says she remembers is waking up freezing. The cramped room was octagonal, its walls stone and its tall, arched windows boarded over. Outside, the wind battered the building, and frigid breezes crept through its cracks. A rotting rope hung from the center of the ceiling. At the top of the rope was a large metal bell. Kiki was inside a bell tower, but the church it belonged to could have been in Pokrovia or Poughkeepsie. There was simply no way to tell.

Hoping to make a racket, Kiki grabbed the rope and pulled with all her strength, but the bell wouldn't budge. She tried to pry a board off the windows, but it refused to give. She yelled until her voice grew hoarse, but no one came to her rescue. Finally, there was nothing to do but sit down with her back to the wall and try to make some sense of the situation.

That's when she saw it—a small black book that blended in with the floorboards. The cover was filthy, and the spine had crumbled away. Kiki flipped to the first page, where she found a title, *The Two Little Princes,* and a short inscription written in fresh black ink: *For my beloved niece.* It was a cruel joke, Kiki realized at once. Like all royal children, she had always been haunted by the tale of the Princes in the Tower—two little English heirs to the throne who were locked away in the Tower of London so that their evil uncle Richard could become King of England. No one knew how long they'd survived after their imprisonment. But they were last seen in 1483, when the elder was twelve and his brother just ten. Their whereabouts remained unknown for almost two hundred years—until the day their bones were discovered at last, buried beneath an ancient staircase. The thought of their final hours, alone in a dark, rat-infested prison cell, was enough to make your average princess tremble in terror. And a book on the subject was the sort of twisted gift that only Livia Galatzina would be evil enough to give.

As soon as she'd finished ripping the book into a million little pieces, Kiki tried to recall what had happened. The last thing she remembered was dinner service on the plane to Pokrovia by way of Paris. As the flight attendant delivered the disturbingly pink salmon entrée to the passengers, she'd paused at Kiki's seat just long enough to refill Kiki's coffee cup. Across the aisle sat Verushka Kozlova, disguised in her nun's habit. She, too, had only a cup of coffee. Yet somewhere over the Atlantic, Kiki had felt her eyelids grow heavy. A second cup of coffee did nothing to help. The sound of snoring drew her attention across the aisle. Verushka's head was tilted back at an unusual angle, and the sounds that came from her throat made Kiki think of a dying goat. Suddenly, a herd of goats stormed down the aisle past her chair. Dizzy and disoriented, Kiki rose and followed them as they hurled themselves from the emergency exit into the darkness. She felt herself falling and falling. . . .

And now she had landed.

Chapter 8

The Lady Factory

L'Institut Beauregard was located in a prim four-story townhouse on West Tenth Street in Greenwich Village. Its bricks were all the perfect shade of red, and its shutters were painted a tasteful forest green. The slush that splattered the rest of the city had miraculously spared the building. Its stairs were cleaner than the floors of an operating room.

Betty followed as I opened the front door and entered a lovely waiting room. A homey blaze crackled in the fireplace, and plush velvet armchairs were arranged around a gently worn Oriental carpet.

"You're not students." The voice was too young to sound so haughty. A girl only a few years our senior was sitting at an antique writing desk in the corner. She had pearl-laden ears and straight blond hair that had never known a tangle. A gold pin bore the name Taylor Lourde.

"How did you figure *that* out?" I asked. "Was it the life in our eyes?"

The girl showed no sign that she'd heard my joke. "Students arrive through the side entrance. Girls with bad ideas come through the front door. If you're here to 'rescue' some friend of yours, you might as well leave right now."

"We're here to see Madame Beauregard," Betty said.

"And what makes you think Madame Beauregard will see *you*?"

"What's up with the attitude, Taylor?" I said, leaning across her desk, my face inches from hers. "I thought this school was supposed to teach you to be *polite*."

"It teaches girls how to be *ladies*. There's a difference."

"I'd say."

The girl opened her mouth to bite back, and then snapped it shut at the sound of footsteps.

"Miss Bent. Miss Fishbein. How nice of you to pay us a visit." Amelia Beauregard glided into the room. Once again, she was dressed in gray—from the gray silk blouse buttoned up to her chin to the gray stockings that made her legs look cadaverous. Even her few bits of exposed flesh were almost grayish in color, as though the women were slowly turning to stone. She checked her watch. "It's four o'clock. Would you care to join me for tea?"

"Yes. Thank you, Madame Beauregard," said Betty. "That would be lovely."

As soon as the woman's back was turned, I stuck out my tongue at Taylor Lourde and received a snooty snarl in response.

❖   ❖   ❖

Amelia Beauregard led us through the building, past a large room with an observation window that faced the hall. A class was in session, and a man in an argyle sweater was teaching ten young women how to curtsy. Outside the window stood an anxious mother, watching nine of the girls dip in unison while the tenth repeatedly fell flat on her butt.

"Mrs. Underwood." Our hostess acknowledged the woman with a nod.

"Oh, Madame Beauregard!" the woman moaned miserably, grabbing and clinging to Amelia Beauregard's elbow. "Ivy's hopeless! I've been watching for fifteen minutes, and she hasn't managed a single curtsy!"

"You must have patience, Mrs. Underwood," Amelia Beauregard counseled as she peeled the woman's fingers from her arm. "Poise cannot be purchased overnight. Ivy wasn't gifted with grace, but neither are most girls. She simply needs more practice. I find the curtsy comes more naturally once the bottom is bruised from falling."

I watched Ivy giving it an honest effort and wondered why she would bother. She was dressed in the same gray yoga outfit as the other girls, but her black nails, hair, and eyeliner were all evidence of an undercover Goth girl. Every time she fell, a tiny skull on the end of a chain bounced out of the top of her sports bra. She seemed to be the only real person in the group of bland Barbies.

"She looks kind of interesting," I told Betty.

Amelia Beauregard laughed, and Mrs. Underwood followed suit, though it was clear she had no idea what was amusing.

"No one under thirty is *interesting*," Amelia Beauregard corrected me. "The most you can hope for is *inoffensive*. Now, if you'll excuse me, Mrs. Underwood, I must tend to these young ladies. Come," she ordered as if we were a pair of corgis.

⚓ ⚓ ⚓

Amelia Beauregard's office was painted Wedgwood blue and furnished in the manner of a Victorian sitting room, with overstuffed chairs and tasteful *objets* perched everywhere the eye might land. Above the fireplace was a portrait of a rather severe-looking gentleman in a 1940s-style three-piece suit.

"Please, have a seat," said Madame, and Betty and I chose a settee upholstered in ivory silk. I saw the old woman glance down at my legs, which were crossed at the knee and fidgeting wildly, and shake her head. I looked over at Betty and noticed that hers were crossed daintily at the ankle, just like Madame Beauregard's. I felt myself blush as I corrected my pose. Two maids entered the room, one carrying an enormous silver tower stacked with finger sandwiches and cakes. The other servant bore a tray with tea and cream.

I pointed at the painting above the fireplace. "Who's the guy in the picture?" I asked, trying to make pleasant conversation as the maids set to work serving the food.

"The *gentleman* is my father, Humphrey Beauregard III. His friends and family knew him as Trip. *You* may refer to him as Mr. Beauregard. He founded this institute almost one hundred years ago."

"He looks like a very serious man," Betty noted.

"He was," Amelia confirmed. "He was a serious man with serious ideas. Unlike the weak-willed parents of today, he didn't believe in coddling children. The young are dangers to themselves, he would tell me. Unless their wild instincts are tamed, they risk bringing shame upon themselves and their families. My father saved generations of New York girls from social suicide. I, too, was rescued by his institute." She glanced up at the portrait. "I shudder to imagine what Papa might have said if one of his girls had ever been caught spying on elderly ladies."

"We apologize for what happened in the Marble Cemetery," Betty said as I took the opportunity to pile my plate high with finger sandwiches. "We don't usually do things like that."

"We were just curious about the lilies," I jumped in. "Was the person who died a friend of yours?"

This time, it was Betty who looked horrified. "Ananka!" she whispered.

Surprisingly, Amelia Beauregard was willing to talk. "He was someone who sacrificed several lives for his country," she said. "It was a very long time ago."

"I thought the Marble Cemetery stopped accepting burials in the 1930s," I remarked.

"You've obviously done your research, Miss Fishbein," Amelia Beauregard said with a hint of respect in her voice. "He wasn't buried there. His body was never recovered. My family had connections to the Marble Cemetery, and they allowed me to put up the plaque. His own family couldn't afford a memorial. But that's enough about me for now. I've done a little digging myself, ladies. I read about the Underground Railroad site you discovered, Miss Fishbein. And I know that you were both involved in foiling the heist at the Metropolitan Museum of Art last November."

"The point is?" I asked with my mouth still half full of cucumber sandwich and my ankles no longer crossed.

"The point is . . . ," Amelia Beauregard began. Then she stopped, and her entire body spasmed as if she'd taken a sip of poisoned tea. "No, no, no. This isn't any good! I can't hold a conversation with someone who insists on displaying such atrocious manners. You should never speak with your mouth full, Miss Fishbein. Your napkin should be in your lap, not wadded up in your left hand. And please sit up straight with your legs together. Your posture makes you look like someone who should be painting buffalo on the side of a cave, and I'm certain your mother has told you that nice girls don't lounge around with their underwear on full display."

I was about to teach Madame Amelia Beauregard a thing or two when I felt Betty's cool hand on my arm and heard her whisper in my ear, "Remember Kiki." Trying not to gag on my pride, I dutifully straightened my posture and folded my napkin in my lap.

"Much better," said Amelia with a smug smile. "I wouldn't be surprised if one day you turned out to be human, Miss Fishbein."

The hand Betty kept on my arm was the only thing between Amelia Beauregard and a verbal smackdown. "Would you mind if we discussed your job offer, Madame Beauregard?" Betty inquired.

"Not at all," the old lady said, taking a dainty sip of her tea. "But I'm afraid you'll find my conditions have changed."

"I don't understand," said Betty. "Why would they change?"

"As I mentioned, I did a little reading about you and your friends. And whatever your reasons for coming here today, I'm quite confident they have nothing to do with employment or etiquette. I have a feeling there's a reason you need to travel to Paris. Am I right?"

Betty looked at me. Neither of us had anticipated this.

"Don't worry, my dear. I don't need to know your secrets any more than you need to know mine. The job is yours if you want it, Miss Bent. And I shall be happy to take you with me to Paris. But while you're gone, I'll need Miss Fishbein's assistance with a little project of mine."

"My assistance?" I asked. My back ached from remaining so rigid. "What can *I* do?"

"I've heard that you attend the Atalanta School for Girls—is that correct?"

"Yes," I cautiously confirmed.

"Excellent. You see, Miss Fishbein, L'Institut Beauregard doesn't advertise. We rely on word of mouth to bring in new faces. That's why every year or two, I like to offer a scholarship to a particularly difficult student. A girl they say can't be tamed. It keeps my teachers on their toes, and it's an invaluable public relations tool. The following season, the applications pour in."

"I'm not enrolling in your school," I said. There was only so far I was willing to go. We could find another way to get to Paris.

"Oh, I'm afraid you wouldn't pose much of a challenge, Miss Fishbein. I merely uttered a few sharp words to you, and now you're posed on that loveseat like a perfect little lady. Give me a few weeks and your manners would outshine those of the Queen of England. No, I'm not interested in you, Miss Fishbein. I'm interested in one of your classmates."

"Who?" I asked.

Madame Beauregard rose and opened a desk drawer. When she returned, she was holding a sheet of pale blue notepaper. "Do you recognize any of the names on this list?"

I took the paper and my eyes began to run down the alphabetized list of forty names. When I reached the *D* names, I came to a halt.

Francesca Daly
Marley Donald
Molly Donovan

I couldn't help it. I started to howl with laughter. "You want to recruit *Molly Donovan*?"

"What's so funny?" Madame Beauregard snapped. "I take it you're acquainted with Miss Donovan?"

"Sure. She's a friend of mine. But have *you* ever met Molly Donovan?" I asked.

"No," the lady admitted. "I've only heard stories. They say she's rather wild."

"Wild doesn't begin to describe Molly. She's practically a force of nature. She held the Atalanta record for detention by the eighth grade. She set off twenty-four smoke bombs in a single morning. I *wish* I could convince her to enroll in your school. She'd *destroy* it."

Betty pinched me, but I have a feeling Madame never

caught that last part. "What do you mean, you *wish* you could convince her?" she demanded.

"Molly isn't at Atalanta anymore. She was expelled last semester. Now she attends a boarding school for troubled children in West Virginia."

"She does?" For a moment, Madame Beauregard looked horrified. Then she shook it off. "I presume she returns to the city each summer?"

I shrugged. "Dunno. She's pretty happy raising her pigs."

Amelia Beauregard clasped a hand over her heart. "Pigs?" she asked weakly.

"Yes, *pigs*. The school she goes to is also a working farm. Molly won second prize in the Pig Rodeo a couple of months ago."

"Well," said Madame Beauregard. "It sounds as though this will be quite a challenge. I look forward to turning Miss Donovan into an upstanding young lady."

"I just *told* you. There's no way she'll do it."

"And I just told *you*, Miss Fishbein. Either Molly Donovan enrolls in the institute's summer program or Miss Bent will have to find her own way to Paris. I suggest you act quickly. My flight leaves the day after tomorrow."

THE FISHBEIN GUIDE TO . . . TEA PARTIES

Think tea parties are for preschoolers, Mad Hatters, and prissy old ladies? Think again. A famous author once wrote, "Love and scandal are the best sweeteners of tea." So, if you decide to throw a party, invite only people you know well—and those you'd like to know a bit better. It doesn't matter whether you offer your guests scones, cucumber sandwiches, or pigs in a blanket. The most delectable tidbits served at afternoon tea should always be *secrets*.

- Afternoon tea (often called high tea by people who want to sound fancy and don't really know what they're talking about) is usually served around 4:00—the perfect hour for plotting, when school is out but parents (and most nosy adults) are still at work.

- Tea has always been the detective's beverage of choice. Why? Tea contains a substance known as L-theanine. When combined with caffeine, it produces a state of mind that's both relaxed and alert. (But you'll need to drink three or more cups to get there.)

- Don't like caffeine? There are herbal teas that may enhance vision, put you to sleep, improve your memory, cure depression, protect you from colds, and kill harmful bacteria.

- Does one of your guests have a secret you'd like her to share? The Pokrovians say, *When the belly is full, the mouth opens wide*. So don't be stingy with the finger sandwiches and cake.

- Forget all the rules and have a good time. But don't lift your pinky finger when you sip your tea. (Not because Amelia Beauregard wouldn't approve. It just looks ridiculous.)

- Should something go horribly wrong at your party, you'll be happy to know that black tea can be used to ease pain, stop bleeding, and soothe sunburns. It can also treat smelly breath and stinky feet.

- Skip the tea bags and serve loose-leaf tea. Once you're done, the leaves left behind in your cup can reveal the future. Look for symbols like a cabbage, which means someone will envy you, or a parrot, which warns you to be wary of gossip.

CHAPTER 9

The Boreland Academy

The next morning, I was chugging coffee on a five a.m. train bound for West Virginia—home of the infamous Boreland Academy. Technology was forbidden at Molly Donovan's school, so if I was going to convince her to learn how to curtsy, I would need to do it in person. It was a task I didn't relish. Some girls spend their childhoods dreaming of all things pretty and pink. I had a hunch that Molly's fondest fantasies were more likely to feature a flamethrower.

I was excited to see her, though. We'd grown to be friends in the months before she was shipped off to boarding school, and our friendship had proven to be mutually beneficial. She'd supplied me with confidential information, and when Molly had wanted to be expelled from the Atalanta School for Girls, I'd designed the stunt that had done the trick.

☆ ☆ ☆

For the first few hours of my journey, I sent e-mails and surfed the Internet. Then, around eight a.m., my phone lost coverage. With nothing else to do, I turned to gaze out the window at the Pennsylvania wilderness. The sight brought back a half-forgotten memory—a flash from the past that left a smile on my lips.

When I was eleven years old, my parents and I had taken a camping trip to the same woods that were now speeding past my window. My mother kept the portable radio tuned to NPR because she couldn't stand the sound of silence. I spent most of the trip on the lookout for werewolves and nearly fainted when I found a tick burrowed into my armpit. And my father wasted an entire night searching the forest for a cricket that was keeping him from falling asleep. That trip had been the Fishbein family's last excursion into the great outdoors.

From the safety and comfort of my train seat, I could almost see nature's appeal. It was quite lovely, after all. Even scrub brush looks charming beneath a thick February snow. But for better or worse I was born a Fishbein, and I was already itching to get back to the city.

✮ ✮ ✮

An hour after we passed through the village of Burp, West Virginia, I spotted the Boreland Academy perched on a sunny hillside. Snow-covered pastures surrounded white clapboard buildings that must have served as both barns and classrooms. To the west, nearly hidden in the trees, were six bare-bones barracks. It looked as though the Army had commandeered Old McDonald's farm.

I was the only person to disembark at Boreland, and I

found the station empty. A handwritten sign that said TAXI pointed out the front door, but the snow piled up in the parking lot hadn't been shoveled for weeks. Even the road beyond the station was empty. Faced with the prospect of freezing to death while waiting for a ride, I shoved my hat on my head and my mittens on my fingers and started off for the school on the hill.

The road was still covered with several inches of pristine snow. There were no tire tracks. Aside from myself, the only creature to have made the journey in recent days was a giant cat with paw prints the size of pie tins. I followed its footsteps for half a mile, until they jumped the bank at the side of the road and disappeared across a field. A few hundred yards from the school, the only sound was the wind shifting the snow. Then the peace was broken by the howl of a furious beast. I saw a black-haired boy in a straight jacket being led to an unmarked van in the academy's parking lot. Suddenly, he jerked out of his keepers' hands and made a run for it across the pasture. He was halfway to the woods when he stumbled and fell face-first in the snow. As they dragged him upright, I could hear him cackling.

A burly orderly pointed me in the direction of the school administrator's office. It was inside a long, narrow building that might once have been a chicken coop. Past the office, the roads were blocked, and there was a sign that read, ABSOLUTELY NO VISITORS BEYOND THIS POINT. SNIPERS ARE ON DUTY. TRESPASSERS WILL BE SHOT. I stepped into the office. The lady at the front desk wore a red gingham shirt and a beehive hairdo. On the wall behind her head, within arm's reach, were three hunting rifles. I could tell by the way she greeted me she wasn't afraid to use them.

"Yes?" asked the woman, her eyes narrowed and her muscles tensed.

"I'm here to see one of your students," I said. "Molly Donovan."

"Why?" she asked, and I knew "for a friendly visit" wasn't the right answer.

"Her grandmother died," I said, opting for a classic. "Her parents sent me to break the news. They would have come themselves, but they're too busy arranging the funeral. Molly's grandmother requested a coffin in the shape of a Budweiser bottle, and they're waiting for it to arrive from Ghana."

The woman didn't blink. "Do you have a copy of the death certificate?"

"No," I admitted. "The coroner is still trying to determine the cause of Ms. Donovan's death. Her refrigerator fell on top of her—but they're not sure if it was an accident or foul play."

"All right, over here," the woman snapped impatiently, pointing to a spot on the floor in front of her. "Arms over your head." She patted me down from head to toe and yanked my phone from my pocket. "You'll get this back when you leave," she said. "Take a seat." I started to sit in the metal folding chair on one side of her desk. "Not there!" the woman exclaimed. "In the cage!"

Across from her desk was a large Plexiglas barrier with a door. Beyond the barrier were four chairs and a coffee table. I was being quarantined, as if I might infect the students of the Boreland Academy.

"Really?" I asked. "Is that necessary?"

"Do I look like the kind of lady who likes to joke

around?" the woman asked. I had to admit that she didn't. Not even remotely. "Have a seat, and I'll page Molly Donovan."

🏵 🏵 🏵

Ten minutes later, Molly barged into the office, her cheeks ruddy and her Wellington boots coated with what must have been pig manure.

"Ananka!" she shouted. Inside the cage, she wrapped me in a smelly hug. "What are you doing here!"

"Your parents sent me to talk to you," I said solemnly, winking at her when the secretary wasn't looking.

"Oh no," Molly whispered theatrically. She caught on quickly.

"I'm afraid so," I told her.

"Not Grandma!" Molly sobbed on cue. Her anguish was so realistic and her wails so loud that the receptionist finally had to intervene.

"Why don't you take her outside for some fresh air?" she suggested irritably.

"Good idea," I said. I took Molly by the shoulders and guided her through the door. Once we were outside, Molly promptly switched off the waterworks. "Nice job," I told her. "I see you inherited your mom's talent." Molly's mother had won two Oscars and was hailed for her ability to master the most obscure accents. Molly's father was Manhattan's most successful plastic surgeon.

"That must be the only thing I inherited from my mother. You have no idea how many people think I'm adopted. So I'm guessing you want to talk in private," Molly said, ducking under the barricades and heading for one of the white clapboard buildings. "Come on. I'll take you to visit Ananka Jr."

"What about the snipers?" I asked.

"There's only one, and he's stationed on the other side of the farm. You'll be fine."

As we trudged down a muddy path toward the ever-stronger odor of pig poo, Molly brought me up to date. In the past few months, she'd taught herself how to whittle, designed her own line of outdoorsy apparel, and started writing her memoirs.

"How do you find time to do it all?" I marveled. "Have you figured out how to go without sleep or something?"

"Naw," said Molly. "It's this place. They don't let us have cell phones or computers. You'd be amazed by how much you can accomplish if you don't waste time on celebrity gossip. Here we go." We had arrived at the source of the stench—a barn big enough to house a herd of dinosaurs. Molly opened a wooden door and stood back to let me pass. Inside was a series of stalls, each filled with one enormous pig. Molly's was the size of a Volkswagen Beetle. The sow snorted with glee when she spotted Molly's red ringlets.

"Ananka, meet Ananka Jr.," Molly said.

"It's a pleasure," I told my namesake.

"So, what's the story?" Molly asked as she nuzzled the giant porker. "Why are you here?"

"Do you know a woman named Amelia Beauregard?"

"No," said Molly. "Should I?"

"She knows you."

"Really?" Molly grinned. "Do tell."

"She's the head of a place called L'Institut Beauregard. Have you ever heard of it?"

"The finishing school? The one that lobotomizes half of Atalanta every year?"

"That's the one. She wants to offer you a scholarship."

"Me!" Molly snorted. "Why *me*? I'm loaded. She should give her stupid scholarship to some girl who needs it."

"She's not offering the scholarship because you need financial help. She's offering it because she thinks you're special."

"Here we go again." Molly rolled her eyes. "Everybody thinks I'm *special*."

"It's not that," I assured her. Molly was very prickly when it came to her impressive math skills. She'd once told me that her parents treated her like a sideshow freak, dragging her out at parties to impress their friends. "Madame Beauregard doesn't care that you're a math genius. I don't even think she knows. She just cares that you're a delinquent. She wants to reform you."

"So she's trying to get my friends to recruit me? Look, Ananka. I have no interest in going home to live with Mommy Dearest just so I can attend charm school every evening. Tell this Beauregard lady I said it's not going to happen."

"I would. It's just that . . ."

"What?" Molly demanded.

"Well, she's kind of blackmailing me."

"Some prissy old lady?" Molly asked with a look of new-found respect.

"Yeah, a friend of mine applied for a job with her. But

she won't give my friend the position unless I convince you to take summer classes at the institute."

"You're kidding! I'm starting to like this crazy broad. So she thinks she can turn me around, does she?"

That's when I began to get nervous. Molly was far too confident. "Look, you don't really have to go. Just say you will now, and back out later. That's all I'm asking."

"No way," Molly said. "I'm a woman of her word. If I say I'm going to go, I'm going to go. I'll teach Amelia Beauregard a thing or two."

"This isn't some sweet old grandma, Molly."

"I certainly hope not! Besides, I don't have any weird ideas about old people. I never knew my grandparents. Nobody ever tried to buy my love with candy or presents. As far as I'm concerned, being old doesn't make you any sweeter or weaker than the next person."

"But Amelia Beauregard . . . ," I started.

"I get it, Ananka. She's tough." Molly shrugged. "I'm tougher. And I still owe you a favor for getting me kicked out of Atalanta. So tell Madame B. that I'll see her this summer. Now what do you say, want to give Ananka Jr. a ride?"

★ ★ ★

At two o'clock, I caught the train out of Boreland. The other passengers stared at my coat, which was filthy after a day spent with Molly and Ananka Jr. I must have reeked of sow, because no one on the crowded train chose to sit by my side. So I stretched out across two seats and enjoyed my first decent sleep in days. Three hours later, I was woken by the sensation of my cell phone vibrating inside my jeans pocket. Only then did I realize that I'd managed to go nearly an entire day without access to technology. I dug under my layers of clothes like a desperate addict and pulled the phone out.

"We've heard from Kiki," read the first text message.

CHAPTER 10

Kiki Strike and the
Darkness Dwellers

LOCATION ON THE VERGE OF DISCOVERY:
MONDAY, FEBRUARY 16

a s the light that squeezed between the boards began
to fade, Kiki heard footsteps outside her cell. A key
scratched at the lock and the door opened. A pudgy man
dressed in black, his face hidden beneath a plastic mime's
mask, stepped into the room. In one hand he had a gun.
The other hand held a bucket and a bag. With the gun
aimed at his captive, he slowly placed the bucket on the
floor. Water slopped over its side, soaking the bottom of
the brown paper bag.

"I want to speak with my aunt," Kiki demanded. "Tell
her I have a proposition for her."

The man stared at the pale elfin girl. Behind his mask,
his eyes were wide.

She tried the same sentences in twelve different lan-
guages. When she didn't receive a response, Kiki took a
step toward the man, and he flinched. The hand that
held the gun was shaking wildly, and his trigger finger

twitched. Obviously word of Kiki's martial arts skills had preceded her.

"Relax," Kiki tried, but the man backed out the door and slammed it shut. Kiki heard the key rattling in the lock, then the sound of someone scurrying down the stairs.

She squatted to examine the items he'd left behind. The bucket was filled with nothing but icy water and a rag. Inside the bag was a pink polyester dress with a white lace collar and a note. Kiki took the letter and examined it under one of the weak beams of light.

> Dear Princess,
> Your aunt will be paying you a visit soon. Please bathe so you do not offend her royal nose with your beastly odor. In the meantime, enjoy your visit to the tower. It won't last long. And should you try to escape, please remember that we have your old servant. Her health depends on your good behavior.
> Love and kisses,
> Sergei

Kiki crumpled up the note from her aunt's favorite henchman and pulled the pink dress over her black sweater and pants. However hideous the ensemble might be, any extra warmth would be welcome during the night. Then she sat on the floor and wondered what Livia had planned. Now that the world knew Princess Katarina was alive, how would Livia explain Kiki's disappearance to the Pokrovian ambassador? What would the *New York*

Times report? Huddled against the wall, Kiki played a game of mental chess with her aunt, while all around her the cold February wind wailed. Later, when the rats came out, she stayed as still as a statue, letting them crawl across her, sniff at her mouth, and even nibble on her fingers. She hadn't eaten in over twenty-four hours, and if it hadn't been for her life-threatening allergies, she might have been tempted to make a quick meal of her furry guests.

☆ ☆ ☆

Unable to sleep, Kiki had almost lost track of time when she heard the sound of people scaling the stairs outside her cell. She could make out the footsteps of two individuals—both significantly lighter than the man who'd visited earlier in the day. She stood up, removed the pink dress, and prepared to meet her aunt face-to-face. While she waited, she listened more closely. The movements outside sounded slow and furtive. It wasn't Livia Galatzina who had come to see her. The ousted Queen of Pokrovia never deigned to creep.

Kiki slid to the left of the entrance, her back against the wall. On the other side of the door, she heard male voices whispering in French and the sound of a lock pick in the keyhole. She was certain that her gentlemen callers had no idea that they weren't alone in the tower. The element of surprise was on Kiki's side, and she waited to ambush the intruders.

The door opened and two flashlight beams danced across the walls. Kiki hesitated.

"There it is. Isn't it beautiful?" One of the beams came to rest on the bell above their heads.

"You're joking, no?" a second male voice scoffed. "*This* is our project? It's a hunk of rusting metal!"

"It's a national treasure!" the first whispered angrily. "Now shut the door, Marcel. The guard will be back soon."

The door swung closed, and one of Kiki's guests lit a lantern. He carefully placed it beneath the bell and shrugged off a black backpack filled with heavy equipment. When he was finished, he took in his surroundings. That's when his eyes landed on the ghostly creature still pressed against the wall.

Those of you who've seen Kiki Strike know that her brand of beauty is something of an acquired taste. And until you acquire that particular taste, the sight of a girl with translucent skin and hair the color of spiderwebs is liable to scare your pants off. The boy stumbled backward, one hand over his mouth as if to stifle a scream.

"What's wrong with you?" his friend asked. Then his eyes followed the finger that pointed directly at Kiki. "*Mon Dieu!*" the second boy exclaimed with his eyes squeezed shut. "Make it go away!"

"I think I'll stay if you don't mind," Kiki said pleasantly in perfect French. "After all, I *was* here first."

"It speaks!" cried the first boy.

"*Mon Dieu!*" repeated the second.

"Would you both *stop*?" Kiki was growing annoyed. "I'm not a ghost."

"V-vampire?" one of them stuttered.

"No, I'm not a vampire, either. I'm one hundred percent human. And if you don't mind me saying so, you're both acting like a couple of ninnies."

Sometimes one well-chosen word is all you need. The

dark-haired boy rose to his feet and swept the dust from his pants. "If you're just a girl, how did you get up here?" He was a bit too thin and a little too pale. A most attractive combination, Kiki noted.

"Where's *here*?" she asked.

"The bell tower of St. Maurice*," the boy replied.

"In Paris?" Kiki asked.

"Of course it's in Paris! What's going on? Who are you?"

"You first," Kiki insisted.

"We came to fix the hunk of junk hanging over your head," said the second boy. He was taller and burlier than his companion, with shaggy blond hair and a cocky expression. And he didn't seem to take the task at hand very seriously at all.

"Marcel!" the first boy scolded. "It's a secret!"

"Don't worry," Kiki assured him. "I'm not in any position to gossip. So, do you two make a habit of repairing rusty old bells in the middle of the night?"

"It's not just *old*," the first boy grumbled. "It's one of the most famous bells in France. It hasn't been heard in a hundred years. We want everyone in Paris to enjoy it again."

"Sounds like a project for the Darkness Dwellers," Kiki said.

"What would *you* know about the Darkness Dwellers?" blurted the dark-haired boy, unaware that he was addressing someone with a photographic memory and a penchant for reading several online newspapers each morning.

---

*This church does not exist. The Darkness Dwellers do not believe in taking credit for their works, and they have requested I change key elements of my story. I didn't bother to argue. After all, you probably think this is a work of fiction, anyway.

Kiki tapped her temple with an index finger. "Hmmm. Let's see. According to the Paris police, the Darkness Dwellers are a mythical organization. There's no solid evidence that any group by that name has ever existed. However, many Parisians believe that the organization was formed to protect the catacombs—a network of bone-filled tunnels deep beneath this city. The Darkness Dwellers' fans claim the group secretly repairs national treasures aboveground as well." Kiki paused to point at the bell before continuing her lecture.

"But not everyone thinks they're so wonderful. Some people believe that the Darkness Dwellers exploit the catacombs for their own amusement. A while back, a police officer reported that the group had used stolen electricity to build themselves an underground movie theater. And earlier this year, a shipment of old skeletons on its way to New York was intercepted by French customs officials. Some think that the bones had been pilfered from the catacombs, and that the Darkness Dwellers were selling them to finance their adventures.

"But the police still insist that the Darkness Dwellers are just figments of the public imagination. I suspect that the truth in this case is much more interesting. In my experience, it usually is."

The two boys looked like they'd been walloped with a *saucisson sec*.

"How . . . ?" one started to ask.

"I read *Le Monde,* and I pay attention."

At last, the dark-haired boy stepped forward and offered Kiki a hand to shake. "Truly impressive. My name is Etienne," he said. "My friend is Marcel."

"You can call me Kiki. So, *are* you members of the Darkness Dwellers?"

"No," Etienne admitted. "They never invite anyone under eighteen to join. Marcel and I don't want to wait another two years, so we've been trying to prove ourselves worthy of the honor."

"And give them a little good press," Marcel added.

"Yes," said Etienne. "The Darkness Dwellers' reputation has suffered since those skeletons were seized by customs. Marcel and I want to fix something beautiful so Paris will love them again. But our last project was a terrible disaster. There was an accident, and we almost destroyed a tenth-century crypt. My father had to pay a fortune to repair the damage, but the body inside the crypt . . . Well, let's just say that this project could be our last chance to prove that we're not completely incompetent."

"So, you're intending to break into this tower every night to work on the bell?" The beginnings of a plan were forming inside Kiki's head.

"That was the idea," said Etienne. "I go to an engineering school, and we studied this church in class. The city has never raised enough money to fix the bell, and the whole building has been abandoned for years. I thought Marcel and I would be able to come and go as we pleased. Then on Saturday, we discovered a night watchman stationed downstairs. I've spent the last two evenings studying the man's movements. He heads to the café across the street for his dinner at ten and for breakfast at five. We can slip in and out of the church while he eats. If you don't mind my asking, is the man guarding *you*? Did someone lock you up in here?"

"Yes." Kiki sighed. "But the less you know about it, the longer you're likely to live."

"So, you're a damsel in distress, eh?" Marcel said, doing a rather poor impersonation of a swashbuckler. "Good thing we showed up to save you."

"Did I *say* I need saving?" Kiki snipped.

"You must excuse my friend," Etienne apologized. "He's not known for his tact. Look, the door is open now if you'd like to go. We won't tell anyone that we saw you."

"I'd love to leave, but I can't," Kiki replied. Livia claimed to have kidnapped Verushka. If Kiki tried to escape, her beloved guardian might die. "And you two can't stay here. I'm expecting visitors soon. They won't be amused if they discover I have company. You'll have to come back some other time."

"What will happen to you if we go?" Etienne asked.

"I'm sure I'll live," Kiki said. "I have something my captors might want. I just need a chance to propose a trade."

"But you could freeze to death in the night!"

Etienne's concern was so charming that Kiki almost laughed. "I come from a very cold country. I know how to survive in weather like this."

"Do you have any food? I brought a sandwich. . . ."

"You're very kind, but I can't accept it."

"Are you *sure* you don't want to come with us?" Etienne urged. "Is there any way we can be of assistance?"

Kiki considered the offer. "Yes. I suppose there is one thing you can do. You can send a message to my friends in New York."

"You're an American?" Marcel scoffed. "How is that possible? Your accent is perfect!"

"Who said I was American?" Kiki examined the tall blond boy. There was something *off* about Marcel. Kiki considered herself to be an excellent judge of character, and as far as she could tell, Marcel didn't have much. Etienne was dedicated to fixing the bell, but Marcel didn't appear quite so committed. He had other reasons for visiting the tower, Kiki guessed—reasons he may not have shared with his friend.

"Will you please excuse us for a moment, Marcel?" Kiki asked as politely as she could. "I would prefer to speak to Etienne alone."

THE FISHBEIN GUIDE TO . . . FRIENDS & ENEMIES

A twenty-first-century lady or gentleman knows how difficult it is to choose the right allies. Loyal friends can be massive pains in the butt. Smooth-talking comrades can be snakes in disguise. And everyone makes mistakes. So how do you know whom to keep close—and whom to keep tabs on? Simply take the quiz below. If the person in question scores more than 200 points, she or he's a true friend. Anything less and you might want to consider recruiting a new BFF.

(When you're done, find out from your friends what *your* score would be. Then do your best to improve it.)

1.	Would your friend defend you if you couldn't defend yourself? (For instance, if you were injured, out of the room, or on the toilet.)	+100
2.	Has she ever made you laugh so hard that you peed your pants?	+50
3.	Does she litter?	−25
4.	Can she be trusted with your secrets? (No matter how frivolous or twisted they might seem to her.)	+100

5.	Or would she sell you out for popularity/a plea bargain/a stick of gum?	−150
6.	Is she pretty and/or popular?	0
7.	Does she have skills you admire?	+75
8.	Does she have hair you admire?	0
9.	Is she rude to waiters?	−100
10.	Is she cruel to animals, small children, or people who are different?	−200
11.	Does she give good advice?	+100
12.	Is her advice likely to get you arrested/grounded/ beaten up/excommunicated?	−100
13.	Do your parents like her? (This is a trick question. Only *you* know if your parents can be trusted.)	0
14.	Is she imaginary?	−25
15.	Does she make you feel superior?	−50
16.	Does she make you feel inadequate?	−50
17.	Would she go to jail for you? (Don't let her.)	+100

Chapter 11

Things Get Hairy

NEW YORK CITY: MONDAY, FEBRUARY 16

if you're a woman of means and you live in Manhattan, there is only one place to go for a manicure. The salon doesn't advertise. There's no name on the door. But if you know the right people—and they like knowing you—eventually someone will whisper these words in your ear: *Look for the Golden Lotus on Seventeenth Street.* Make an appointment, but leave your secrets at home. The ladies employed by the Golden Lotus have an ear for gossip—and a boss who's made a fortune collecting rich women's scandalous stories.

I was pounding on a door that opened night or day for the wealthy, famous, and indiscreet. But that evening, the blinds were pulled at Oona Wong's exclusive nail salon, and a CLOSED sign had been hung in the window. Behind the locked door, someone was moaning in pain.

"What's going on?" Betty appeared behind me. "Who are they torturing in there?" For some reason, she was sporting a UPS uniform. I let the disguise pass without comment.

"Beats me. I was on the train back from West Virginia when I picked up a message from Oona. She says she's heard from Kiki."

"I know! I'm so relieved!" Betty gushed. "How was your trip to Boreland?"

"Educational, to say the least. Molly agreed to go along with the plan."

"She did?"

"Yeah. With a little too much enthusiasm, if you ask me."

"Well, if we've found Kiki, maybe we won't need Molly's help after all," Betty noted as Iris opened the door and peeked through the crack.

"There you are!" the tiny blond girl whispered. "Come in! Come in!"

☆ ☆ ☆

The salon was furnished with plush chairs and state-of-the-art manicure tables. At the far end of the enormous room, three white-smocked cosmetologists huddled around a reclining chair. All I could see of their patient was two twitching feet.

"*Arrrrrrgh!*" came a groan.

"Geez, Oona, is it really supposed to hurt *that* much?" Luz grimaced. Both girls were watching the action from a safe distance.

"There usually isn't this much hair to remove," Oona said with a shrug. "We've never lasered a real bearded lady before."

"Maybe we should give her a break," Luz suggested squeamishly.

"Ladies!" Oona called out to her employees. "Take ten. Get some coffee. This could be a *very* long night."

"What's going on?" I asked. "Are you guys training for jobs with the Spanish Inquisition?"

"Hey, Ananka. Hey, Betty," Oona said. "Take a look at this."

The white-smocked women had vanished into the break room, leaving their patient behind in her chair. Slowly, DeeDee pulled herself upright, hiding one half of her face with a hand.

"Don't laugh!" she warned.

"We won't," Betty promised prematurely, because when DeeDee dropped her hand, I began to cackle. Half of her face was covered in thick black hair.

"Ananka!" Luz chided me as she attempted to keep a straight face. "It's *not* funny."

"How . . . how . . . ?" I gasped, hoping the contents of my bladder wouldn't start trickling down my leg.

"Clearly, Miss Morlock ignored your orders and sampled some of her own medicine," Oona said, biting her cheeks to keep the grin off her face.

"DeeDee! I told you not to experiment on yourself! Why didn't you listen?" I couldn't stop laughing long enough to give her a proper lecture.

"You know I don't believe in animal testing," DeeDee replied sheepishly. "And it would have been unethical to give the cure to another human being without making sure it wasn't totally toxic. So I put a little of the stuff on my cheek, just to see if it did anything."

"Well, I guess we know it works," Betty remarked. "But how do we know it's not eating your insides?"

"That's just what my mom said. She and my dad hauled me to the hospital as soon as they saw the beard. I spent all day getting tested. The doctor says I'm totally fine."

"How did you explain your condition?" I wasn't laughing anymore. "I really hope you were careful."

"Of course I was!" DeeDee insisted. "I told the doctor I was working on a science fair project and it got out of control."

"How many times are you going to use *that* tired excuse?" Oona asked. In the three years since she'd joined the Irregulars, DeeDee had been injured in dozens of "science fair" experiments.

"It usually works like a charm," DeeDee said. "No one wants to hear some kid ramble on about her silly little science fair project. But the doctor today asked more questions than most. For a second, I think he hoped I might be his ticket to fame and fortune. But I played dumb and told him I didn't even remember which chemicals I'd used."

"And he believed you?" I asked.

"I think so," DeeDee replied.

"Good." I exhaled with relief. "But *please,* let's all try to be a little more careful from now on, okay? We're already down an Irregular. Speaking of which, what's this about a message from Kiki? And why didn't she send it to *me*?"

"It came to the Golden Lotus e-mail address," Oona said. "I guess Kiki was being careful. She didn't want to give the boy any of our names."

"The boy?"

"The message wasn't sent straight from Kiki," Luz informed me. "It was from some French kid who said he'd found Kiki locked in a bell tower."

"What?"

"He claims she's fine," Oona said. "But she needs the cure ASAP."

"What did I tell you?" Luz gloated. "Livia must have kidnapped Kiki. Now she wants something to bargain with."

"Did our French friend give us any delivery instructions?" I asked.

"No," Luz said. "He just told us Kiki would be back in touch soon."

"Well?" Oona asked DeeDee. "Do we have something to give her?"

"I'd say the cure works pretty well," DeeDee said, stroking the remains of her lustrous beard. "But how are we going to get it to Paris? I'm assuming the US mail isn't an option."

"We have a way," I announced. "Want to tell them, Betty?"

"I've been offered a job at L'Institut Beauregard," Betty began to explain to the group.

"The school for robots in training?" Oona broke in. "Do you have any idea what they *do* to girls there? I've heard some terrible things, Betty. Two women came in for a pedicure the other day, and one was bragging that her kid just graduated with honors from the institute. Now mommy and her little snuggle bunny enjoy wearing matching outfits and collecting commemorative plates. Thing is, I *know* the girl they were talking about. She used to be one of my favorite clients. Until a few months ago, she was a first-class delinquent. If that Beauregard woman can turn *her* into a dream child, imagine what she'll do to someone like *you*!"

"Someone like me?" Betty repeated. "I'm not even going to *ask* what that means."

Oona cocked her head and caught my eye. "*You* know what I'm talking about, don't you, Ananka?"

I did. But I'd been so focused on getting an Irregular to France that I hadn't considered whether sweet Betty Bent was really up to the job.

"Here's the deal, you guys," Betty announced with a huff. "Madame Beauregard is going to Paris. She wants me to go with her. If I'm there, I can deliver the cure to Kiki. It's as simple as that."

"You really think your parents will let you go?" Luz asked.

"Let me? When they heard, they practically *insisted* I take the job," Betty said. "Madame Beauregard is good friends with their boss at the opera."

"But you *can't* go to Paris!" Iris squealed. "Kaspar just got here!"

"Wait. Kaspar's here? In New York?" I practically stammered, and Iris gave me the evil eye.

"That was his Valentine's Day present," Betty told me. "He got someone to take care of his pet squirrels, and he's staying here with his friend Howard for the rest of the week."

"Maybe one of us could go to Paris in your place?" Iris asked.

"Are you kidding?" Luz scoffed. "Have you *met* my

mother?" There was no way Mrs. Lopez would ever give her daughter permission for a jaunt across the Atlantic.

"I can't use my passport until I'm hair-free," said DeeDee. "The girl in the photo doesn't have a beard."

"Don't look at *me*," Oona said. "I've got a business to run and a twin sister to hunt down."

"I'm *twelve*," said Iris.

"Kiki put me in charge while she's gone," I reminded them all. "I have to stay here to oversee everything."

"Well, then, I guess that settles it," Betty declared. "I'll accept Madame Beauregard's offer tomorrow."

"Are you *sure*?" DeeDee asked her.

"What if she tries to brainwash you?" Oona asked.

"Maybe I should ask my mom after all," Luz mumbled.

"Thanks for the vote of confidence," Betty finally snapped. "For your information, I'm a lot tougher than you think."

CHAPTER 12

Ananka's Story Hour

In her world-renowned etiquette manual, *Savoir Faire*, author Amelia Beauregard states:

> *Unless you were raised by a pack of feral dogs, you know there is no excuse for tardiness. A lady is on time for all appointments and engagements. Should a true emergency prevent her from reaching her destination at the appointed hour, a lady will always telephone ahead. True emergencies include earthquakes, appendicitis, and civil war. They do not include broken heels, fashion dilemmas, or faulty alarm clocks.*

It's too bad that *Savoir Faire* was the only book in existence that my mother had never allowed in her house.

I figured I was in trouble when I arrived home from the Golden Lotus and picked up the scent of massaman curry wafting down the stairs of my apartment building. It was my father's signature dish, and the only meal either of my parents cooked well enough to serve to unsuspecting guests. The problem was—it wasn't *their* guest they were feeding.

"I'm sorry, I'm sorry, I'm so sorry, so sorry," I chanted as I burst through the door. When it slammed behind me, a thousand piles of books wobbled like Jell-O. Seated across from each other at the dining room table were my father and Theodora Wickham, principal of the Atalanta School for Girls. "Did I miss dinner?" I slid into a chair with my coat still on.

"It's only seven thirty," my father informed me, pointing to a clock on the fireplace mantel. He was wearing his very best corduroy jacket, and he might even have combed his hair. It was a sign of just how far my parents were willing to go to help my academic career. "Dinner hasn't been served yet."

"Oh good," I said, slumping back in my chair and breathing a sigh of relief.

"Now that you've made it home, perhaps you can explain why you missed school today?" The principal put on her glasses and examined me closely. "You don't *look* ill. Perhaps you've sustained some sort of internal injury? Or maybe you've developed a painful boil that prevents you from sitting still and learning your lessons?"

"It's a long story," I told her.

"One we all look forward to hearing over dinner," my father said. "Now go help your mother get everything ready while I finish talking to Theodora."

☆ ☆ ☆

I know what you're thinking. How many fifteen-year-olds hang out with their high school principals? Perhaps you're picturing me with a pocket protector, a brown nose, and an unctuous smile. I'd be the first to admit I'm a bit of a geek, but I'm not *entirely* hopeless. And Principal Wickham was never your average authority figure. Despite my disastrous grades and risible attendance record, she had decided to make me her personal protégé. Girls who had previously held my position had grown up to be the most powerful women in New York City.

In return for Theodora Wickham's personal guidance, I had agreed to a single condition. Every month I would sit down for a meal with my parents and the principal. Over dinner, I would provide a detailed account of my activities—both academic and extracurricular. The principal knew about the Irregulars, and she insisted I stick to the truth, the whole truth, and nothing but the truth. So I did. I never fibbed or exaggerated. I always told all three adults in my life *exactly* what the Irregulars were doing. Principal Wickham believed every word. My parents called it "Ananka's Story Hour."

I set a heaping platter of rice on the table and took my seat next to Principal Wickham. Once I had straightened my silverware and rearranged it into the proper order, I carefully folded my napkin into my lap. I looked up to find my fellow diners staring at me as if I had dipped my fingers into the curry and used it to finger-paint dirty pictures on the walls.

"Ananka?" my father asked. "Are you all right?"

"Yep," I assured him.

"Was there something wrong with the silverware?" my mother inquired.

"No. You just had the positions of the spoon and the knife mixed up. But don't worry about it. It was probably just an accident."

"I'll *try* not to worry," my mother snipped.

"I never knew that you were such an expert on etiquette, Ananka," Principal Wickham noted wryly.

"I'm not. . . ."

"She's fallen in with a bad crowd," my mother butted in. "The girls at L'Institut Beauregard."

"I have *not*," I argued. "I just helped Betty get a job there. That's all. I've only met Amelia Beauregard twice."

"So, you've met Amelia?" the principal asked. "May I ask what you thought of her?"

"You really want to know?"

"Certainly! I've always valued your opinion, Ananka."

I set my fork down, wiped my lips, and prepared to let loose my honest opinion. "Amelia Beauregard has the personality of a pit viper," I told everyone at the table. "And she isn't teaching her students how to be 'ladies.' She's training them to be mean little zombies. She's brainwashing them to believe that there's only one right way to dress or behave. Madame Beauregard thinks that if you cross your legs at the knee or chew gum in public, then you should be treated like you're some sort of cave dweller. I don't know much about etiquette, but I never realized that the point of having good manners was to make other people feel like dirt."

My mother beamed. My father nodded thoughtfully. But Principal Wickham only sighed.

"Yes, it's sad," she said. I could tell by the look on the principal's face that it wasn't a meaningless turn of phrase. "Amelia wasn't always so stuffy."

"You know the Wicked Witch of Tenth Street?" my mother asked.

Principal Wickham's eyes twinkled, and for the briefest of moments, she could have passed for someone sixty years younger. "She and I were best friends growing up. Back then, she was the last person I would have expected to run an etiquette academy. If anything, Amelia was known for being a bit wild."

"Oh, do tell!" my mother exclaimed. I'd never seen her so excited outside of a rare book store. Usually Lillian Fishbein had no time for gossip.

"Amelia was quite attractive and terribly smart," Principal Wickham began. "She did things that the rest of us only dreamed of doing. She took flying lessons and raced cars with boys from bad neighborhoods. Once, during a blizzard, she made it to a New Year's party by skiing across Central Park in her ball gown. All the girls were terribly jealous of her. Amelia had a wonderful boyfriend, too, a handsome army officer. Her parents didn't approve of the match, but the two of them were engaged to be married when he returned from the war. Unfortunately, he never came back. His name was . . ." She made a show of trying to remember. I had a sneaking suspicion that she hadn't forgotten.

"Gordon Grant?" I offered.

"I do believe that's it!" she exclaimed, lurching backward a bit, as if the name had hit her with the force of a rubber bullet. "How did you . . . oh, you *are* a good detective, aren't you? How did you find out?"

"I met Madame Beauregard at the Marble Cemetery. She was leaving flowers in front of a plaque with his name on it."

"That's odd," said the principal, pausing with a spoonful of curry three inches from her mouth, "because . . ."

"There's nobody in the grave. She told us so herself."

"So, where's the corpse?" my dad asked.

"The army never found Gordon's body," Principal Wickham explained. "And there were some who claimed there was no body to find."

"I don't understand," said my mother.

"Gordon Grant may not have died during the war. There were whispers at the time—only rumors, of course. People said Gordon fell in love with a spy—a femme fatale—who persuaded him to betray his country. After the war, he stayed in Europe with her. Who knows? Perhaps he's still there."

"He abandoned Amelia?"

The principal nodded. "When she realized he wasn't coming back, Amelia went mad with grief. Her parents were forced to send her away for a while. She spent several months at a mental hospital upstate. By the time she came back, she'd changed for good. I remember visiting Amelia's house the day she returned. There was no life left in her. She refused to acknowledge that Gordon might still be alive, and it was as if she'd died with him."

"How terrible. Are you still friends?" my mother asked.

"No. I tried to keep in touch with her, of course, but Amelia broke all connections to her life before the war. I still see her now and then at museum galas and charity events. But even though it's been sixty-five years, she still avoids me." The principal took in a deep breath and seemed to pull herself out of the past.

"Now, how did I allow you to get me so sidetracked, Ananka? I believe you were about to tell us where you were today. I thought we had a deal. You're supposed to inform me if you need to miss school."

"I'm sorry," I said. "It was a last-minute crisis. I had to visit Molly Donovan."

"At the Boreland Academy?" the principal asked.

"In West *Virginia*?" my mother added.

"I told you it was a long story." I sighed.

My father checked his watch. "Well, it's eight o'clock now. I think we've got time to hear it."

"No more secrets, remember?" the principal added when I hesitated.

"Make the story as long as you want, Ananka. The last one you told was *quite* entertaining," my mother said.

"Okay," I muttered. I could already tell that my parents wouldn't believe a word of what I said. "You know how Kiki Strike left to claim the throne of Pokrovia?" All three adults nodded gamely. "Well, the Irregulars have been working on something she might be able to use as a bargaining chip if she got captured by her enemies. It's a cure for female baldness—androgenetic alopecia to be exact. DeeDee says it's almost ready. . . ."

"I think this story has already gotten a *little* far-fetched," my mother scoffed.

"Your friend has developed a cure for female baldness?" My father laughed.

"That sort of thing would be worth a great deal of money," the principal remarked. She always took me seriously, and I loved her for it.

"If it *worked*," my mother added sarcastically.

"See? This is why I prefer to keep my mouth shut," I complained. "Either you want to hear the story or you don't."

"We apologize, Ananka," my father said. "Please. Continue. You're an excellent storyteller. Maybe you've finally found your calling. It might be nice to have a novelist in the family someday."

With that meager encouragement, I took a deep breath and began my tale. I told them about Kiki's disappearance, DeeDee's experiments, and Betty's trip to Paris. When I'd finished, my parents' eyebrows were frozen in arches of surprise.

"What a fascinating story," said the principal, as if nothing she'd heard had shocked her. "But what does all of this have to do with your trip to see Miss Donovan?"

"Molly was part of the deal we made with Amelia Beauregard. She refused to give Betty the job unless I talked Molly into taking classes at L'Institut Beauregard."

"Molly Donovan? At Amelia's Institute?" Principal Wickham didn't seem too fond of the idea. "Why Molly? Did she say?"

"Madame Beauregard keeps a list of girls that she wants to tame. She does it for the publicity. Every time she turns a notorious delinquent into another little robot, half the mothers in Manhattan sign their daughters up for classes. She showed me the list, and Molly was the only girl on it that I knew."

"And Molly agreed to go to the institute, did she?"

"She thinks it will be fun," I said. "I don't think she understands what she's getting herself into."

"No," the principal agreed. "I don't suppose she does."

THE FISHBEIN GUIDE TO . . . DELIGHTFUL DINNERS

If you've ever skimmed an etiquette manual, you may have reached the conclusion that evening meals are fraught with peril. But the truth is, table manners are pretty obvious. Is it disgusting? (*Blowing your nose on the tablecloth. Drinking straight from the gravy boat.*) THEN DON'T DO IT. Will it make a big mess for someone else to clean up? (*Putting your butter-covered knife back down on the table. Sticking your uneaten beets under the chair cushion.*) THEN DON'T DO IT. See what I mean?

So, let's all loosen up a bit and start enjoying our meals. Here are a few *Fishbein* tips. . . .

Seating Your Guests

If you're American, you probably throw at least one dinner party a year. And with a little forethought, your next Thanksgiving meal can be *extremely* entertaining. Simply offer to organize the seating arrangements. Then make a list of the people you've invited and ask yourself the following questions: Which guests are likely to hurl mashed potatoes at each other? Which will have the most scandalous gossip to share? Which need to kiss and make up? With a little planning you can start battles, end wars, or uncover your family's juiciest secrets. Just place name cards at the appropriate seats and watch the fun begin!

Knives, Forks, and Spoons

At some point in your life, you will sit down to a fancy dinner and find yourself faced with more forks, knives, and spoons than you ever knew existed. Once again, there's a simple solution to this dilemma. Every time a new course arrives, choose the fork and knife farthest away from the plate. Should you forget this simple rule, distract your fellow diners with fascinating facts. I like to discuss the dark histories of the utensils being used. (Did you know forks were once condemned by the Catholic Church?)

Servers and Waiters
Never, ever be rude to the people serving your food. (Whether it's your dad, your butler, or a harried waiter.) Not only is such behavior a sure sign of bad character, it's incredibly stupid. Give your waiter a hard time, and he may add a little something "special" to your spaghetti. Your dad is less likely to get his revenge in this way, but then again—you never know.

Proposing a Toast
Toasting began in ancient Greece as a way for hosts to prove they weren't poisoning the guests. (Greeks and Romans, it seems, were *very* fond of poison.) These days, a toast is an excellent way to get something off your chest. All you need to do is stand up and get everyone's attention. (Use a clean spoon to ding the side of your water glass if necessary.) Make sure you've practiced your speech—then let 'er rip. A well-delivered toast can express your gratitude, expose a rat, draw attention away from the liver you tried to hide under your plate, or explain how you arrived at the conclusion that one of your guests is guilty of murder.

The Heimlich Maneuver
Know it. Don't practice the technique on small children or animals.

ChAPTER 13

Kiki Visits the Catacombs

Kiki sat in her frilly pink dress and watched a strip of sunlight slowly slide across the floor of her cell until it dimmed and disappeared. Finally she closed her eyes. Another day had come and gone. She'd waited for Livia's visit, but now it seemed clear that her aunt wouldn't be making an appearance. Which meant that somewhere in Paris, Verushka would be forced to spend another night in captivity. Kiki prayed that her guardian's quarters weren't as grim as her own. Verushka was growing older and frailer each day. She wouldn't last long in an abandoned bell tower.

Still, there was one thought that offered some hope. Verushka Kozlova hadn't been executed. Livia was too smart to kill the old woman while the true heir to the throne of Pokrovia was breathing French air. Verushka was Livia's insurance that Kiki wouldn't attempt an escape. And for the first time, she had read her niece well. In fact, there was little need for locked doors or guards. If Kiki saw the slimmest chance to keep Verushka alive, she would stay in the bell tower as long as it took.

Fortunately, Kiki's confinement wouldn't be solitary for long. If Etienne was true to his word, the two French boys would return as soon as the guard downstairs left for his dinner at ten. Kiki might have been too worried to realize it, but she was looking forward to seeing Etienne again.*

It was so dark inside the tower that Kiki barely knew she'd been napping. But the moment she heard footsteps on the stairs, her eyes popped open. Half a minute later, Etienne arrived with a large shopping bag. Marcel followed close behind, his lips wearing a goofy grin while his eyes carefully scanned the room.

"Did you get word to my friends?" Kiki asked Etienne in French, not bothering with hellos.

"Yes—they said to tell you that they'll have the cure to you tomorrow."

"A cure for what?" Marcel inquired.

"Nosiness," Kiki replied. "I just hope we can treat it before it kills you." She was glad she hadn't trusted Marcel with any secrets. He seemed even shiftier than the first time they'd met.

"What's in the bag?" she asked Etienne.

"I brought you a few things." He crouched next to Kiki and began pulling items from the sack. A baguette. A bottle of Evian. A hunk of pungent cheese.

"Thank you." Kiki tore off the top of the Evian bottle

---

*You're taking liberties with the story, Miss Fishbein. —KS

and gulped down the contents. "Why don't you two share the rest when you need a snack? I'm afraid I have allergies."

"That's American for 'I only eat hamburgers,'" Marcel snorted.

"Surely you can eat *something* here," Etienne pleaded. "You must get some food into your stomach. The cheese tastes much better than it smells, I promise."

"I'm sorry," Kiki said. Just the aroma wafting up from the cheese was enough to give her a case of hives. "I'm on a strict diet."

"I'll eat it," Marcel offered. "No reason to let it go to waste."

"Well, then, at the very least you can use these." Etienne ignored his friend and pulled out a coat, scarf, and gloves. "They belong to my little sister. She's ten, but I think you may be the same size."

"You're very kind." Kiki was genuinely touched. "But if I keep that clothing, the people who put me here will know I've had guests."

"Ah. I hadn't thought of that." Etienne sighed. Then his spirits seemed to rebound. "I have an idea. No one is going to pay you a visit before morning. So there's no reason for you to sit here and stew. Put the coat on, and we'll take you out for a night on the town. The guard downstairs won't be back from his dinner yet. We still have a few minutes to sneak you out. Have you seen Paris at night before?"

"Mais bien sur," Kiki said. "Many times."

Etienne remained undeterred. "Have you seen the *catacombs*?" He let the word dangle like a carrot in front of her.

"No," Kiki replied with a grin. "I haven't."

"The Darkness Dwellers are throwing a little get-together this evening. Perhaps you'd like to crash it?"

"They are?" Marcel sounded outraged. "I've been begging you to introduce me for months! Why didn't you tell me they were having a party?"

"Because I thought we would be working tonight," Etienne explained before turning back to Kiki. "So what do you think?"

"I suppose I *could* use some fresh air," she said.

"Well, there's not much of that in the catacombs. But I suspect you might enjoy yourself anyway. We'll wait outside while you change," Etienne said, pointing to the dress Kiki was wearing over her own clothes. "The catacombs are no place for pink."

⚜ ⚜ ⚜

They sat outdoors on the Boulevard St. Germain and guzzled café au laits as the traffic zipped past in front of them. It took three cups before Kiki felt her strength begin to return. As soon as she was ready, Etienne led the way to a shadowy side street that was littered with dead pigeons and dog droppings. While blasé pedestrians sauntered past, he and Marcel lifted a round metal manhole cover. A ladder led into the darkness. Without further discussion, Etienne began to descend.

"Ladies first," Marcel smirked. Kiki knew he was expecting to see some sign of fear, and she had no intention of humoring him. Without a second's hesitation, she followed Etienne down the ladder. A few moments later, she heard Marcel sliding the cover back into place and the sound of his boots stomping on the ladder's metal rungs.

At the bottom, Etienne trained a flashlight on the brick tunnel that stretched out before them. It was perfectly round, roughly six feet in diameter, with a thin stream of chocolate-colored liquid trickling along its floor. Whatever the stuff was, it smelled nothing like chocolate. Hanging from a makeshift hook hammered into the mortar was a large black bag.

"This isn't the catacombs. It's a sewer," Kiki observed.

"You just figured that out?" Etienne asked, unzipping the bag. "I was wondering if you'd lost your sense of smell as well as your appetite. There used to be entrances to the catacombs all over the city. My favorite was a few blocks away, but the police sealed it off last week. So we'll just have to go through the sewers until I find a more hygienic approach."

"You're aware this is extremely dangerous, right?" Kiki inquired matter-of-factly.

Marcel hopped off the last rung of the ladder. "Just like a girl," he said. "Afraid of a little *merde*?"

"You must not have met many girls," Kiki responded. "I was referring to sewer gasses. They're difficult to detect and they can kill a person in minutes. Even a big oaf like you."

Etienne laughed. He seemed more lighthearted now that they were underground. "That's why I always offer my guests one of these." He passed Kiki a gas mask.

"Impressive." Kiki turned the equipment over in her hands. "These are manufactured for the COS and the

French special forces. They're state-of-the-art—no more than a few months old."

"You know a lot about military equipment."

"I was raised by a soldier. Which also means I know how much this kind of equipment can cost. I doubt most sixteen-year-olds could afford masks like these."

"And *I* doubt most girls are able to tell a gas mask from a hair dryer."

Kiki's left eyebrow rose. "Next time you're in New York, I'll introduce you to some girls who can teach *you* a few things."

Once the gas masks were fitted securely over their noses and mouths, the trio trudged through the sewers. Rats scampered by while toilets flushed, sending streams of fresh filth gushing toward their feet. Etienne turned a corner, and Kiki followed, only to find the way blocked by a rusty metal gate. She watched as he pulled the gate out just far enough for the others to pass. Once they were all on the other side, he carefully pushed it back into place. They were inside a cramped, dry space. There didn't seem to be anywhere to go until Etienne and Marcel lifted a thick sheet of metal from the floor, revealing a hole. At the bottom of the hole lay the catacombs.

As the world's greatest unsung expert on the subject of underground worlds, I feel it's my duty to pause here for a brief history lesson. (One that's filled with corpses, implosions, and hard-partying kings, of course.) The tunnels beneath Paris are far more ancient than New York's

Shadow City. Some may be more than seven hundred years old. Originally they were quarries where thousands of men labored in the darkness, cutting the stones that built France's greatest monuments. At the time no one worried that those stones were being chiseled out of the very same rock that supported the city. Once the work was done, the maze of mines might have shared the same fate as New York's subterranean world, forgotten by all but a handful of intrepid explorers. But in the eighteenth century, the tunnels began to collapse. Aboveground, entire streets disappeared. Houses plunged hundreds of feet into the earth. Worried that much of the city might be destroyed, King Louis XVI sent engineers into the old tunnels to keep them from crumbling. He also dreamed up a new use for the old quarries. The city's graveyards had been overflowing for years. So millions of dead Parisians were exhumed and their bones given a new home. That's when the tunnels beneath the city began to be called the catacombs.

At least one king threw raucous parties in the tunnels. Criminals often used them to elude the police. Invading armies turned them into bunkers. By the time of Kiki Strike's visit, the catacombs' rough-hewn walls bore marks left by countless visitors. A blue-and-white sign identified the street far above her head. Multicolored arrows pointed in every direction. Black stenciled letters demanded SILENCE! in German. It was a dark, dank, airless world, but Kiki could tell it had never been empty.

"I thought I'd at least get to see a few bones," she joked as she took off her gas mask.

"I'm afraid they're all in a part of the tunnels called the ossuary," Etienne replied. "I hope you're not disappointed. I can take you to the ossuary some other time—or you can visit on your own. It's the only part of the catacombs that is open to the public. The section we're in now never housed any human remains, but it does have a rather interesting history. During World War II, the Nazis built bunkers just to our left. The French Resistance was hiding not far to the right. At times the two groups were less than a meter apart." He pointed down another passage, but Kiki could see nothing but a pile of rubble. "In fact, I know an interesting story. . . ."

They heard a thump in the distance that sounded as if someone had stumbled.

"Let's go." Etienne lowered his voice to a whisper. "I'll tell you the story another time."

"Who did we hear?" Kiki whispered.

"It could be anyone, but it's probably the police. They patrol the catacombs, looking for trespassers. It's easy to avoid them if you know your way around."

Kiki followed as Etienne slinked through the tunnel, passing a dozen forks as if he were following a familiar path. Behind them, Marcel seemed to be scribbling directions on a piece of paper.

"You don't need a map?" she asked Etienne once it felt safe to talk.

"Maps are discouraged," the boy replied. "They can fall into the wrong hands."

"No joke," Kiki agreed. "So why is your friend making one?"

Etienne glanced back over his shoulder. "It's only

temporary. Marcel will study it and then throw it away. He's learning the tunnels. He needs to know them by heart if he wants to be a Darkness Dweller."

"They expect you to memorize the catacombs? Aren't there miles of tunnels down here?"

"One hundred and seventy-seven to be exact, and the Darkness Dwellers keep a complete map of the passages in their heads. One of the English members calls it the Knowledge."

"So how did *you* come to know the catacombs?" Kiki asked.

Etienne grinned. "I found an entrance to the tunnels in the basement of my grade school," he said. "Back in the seventeenth century, the building had been a monastery, and the monks stored their beer in the cavities. When I was eleven, I formed a group called *Les Taupes* to explore the tunnels."

"That sounds familiar," Kiki muttered. "So what happened to the rest of Les Taupes?"

"We are no longer friends," Etienne said sullenly. "Once when I was sick with the flu, they decided to visit the catacombs without me. They were reckless, and they all got caught by the patrol. Our school decided to destroy the entrance to the tunnels. Exploring was all I lived for in those days, and it took months to find another way underground. When I did, I refused to take my former friends with me. For years, I came to the catacombs on my own. It may have been lonely, but it was easier that way."

They stomped along in silence until a ghostly figure came into sight.

"What's that?" Kiki asked. The figure painted on the

tunnel wall resembled an enormous white artist's dummy. Its spindly legs danced a jig while a question mark floated above its head.

"It's *Le Corps Blanc*—the White Corpse. He's all over the catacombs. He's meant to confuse tourists and lead them astray. Never follow his directions. But never go the opposite way, either. It's best to just ignore him."

"There are a lot of tourists down here?"

Etienne chuckled. "That's just what we call people who don't know what they're doing. They're tourists; we're *cataphiles*."

"And how many cataphiles are there?"

"No one knows." Etienne came to a stop and focused his flashlight on a mural painted on the wall. It showed a figure in dark robes forging through a dreary forest. Vines crept around his ankles while tree branches reached down to snatch him. The man had paused to peer over his shoulder. The painting didn't reveal what he saw behind him— just the fear that made the man's eyes bulge from their sockets.

"Wow," Kiki marveled. "That's pretty twisted. As much as I admire the art, I'm not sure I'd want to run into the artist down here."

"There are similar paintings in every section of the catacombs," Etienne informed her. "I've seen sculptures and mosaics as well. Some of the art is quite good, and most of it is a little disturbing. A few pieces are sick enough to make *me* worry about meeting their creators."

"Don't worry, *mon petit cher,* I'll protect you," Marcel said. Kiki grimaced at the sound of his voice. She'd almost forgotten the big lug was trailing behind them. "How much longer before we get to the party?"

"I have no idea," Etienne confessed.

"You have no idea?" Kiki asked.

"I haven't picked up the directions yet," Etienne said. He faced the mural and let his fingers pass lightly over the wall. They appeared to dip inside what looked like a hole in a tree trunk and emerged with a piece of blue paper, which he unfolded and examined. "Okay," he told his two companions. "You're in for a treat. We're going to the grotto."

"What did you just do?" Kiki asked.

"That's how we communicate down here," Etienne told her. "Every group has a set of secret drop points. We leave messages for each other inside holes in the walls. The leader of the Darkness Dwellers knows I spend a lot of time in this part of the catacombs. He left the note for me."

"But I thought you weren't a member," Kiki noted. "How do you know where the Darkness Dwellers' drop points are? And why do they leave messages for you?"

"They won't let him join, but they're happy to let him act as their mascot," Marcel said with a snicker.

Etienne blushed. "They still think of me as a kid," he explained. "That's why I'm trying to prove myself by fixing . . ." He froze and flipped off his flashlight. The darkness embraced them. In the distance, they could hear someone approaching.

"Sounds like we're being tailed. Follow me," he whispered in Kiki's ear. "My hideout isn't far away."

Kiki felt herself being guided down the tunnel and then through a narrow passage. The walls brushed her shoulders on both sides, and she tried to step as softly as possible.

When they reached an open space, Etienne turned Kiki to face a tiny opening in a wall. "We're safe now. Look. You can see the passage we just left."

Outside in the tunnel, the beam of a flashlight grew brighter. A mustachioed man wearing a navy Macintosh and knee-high boots passed their hiding place, then paused as if confused. After a minute of contemplation, he continued in the same direction, and the light gradually faded away.

"Was that him?" Marcel asked softly.

"Yes," Etienne confirmed. "Let's make sure he's gone before we turn on the lights."

"Who was it?" Kiki inquired.

"A man named Fitzroy," Etienne said. "I met him down here a few months ago. He told me he was searching the catacombs for his father's corpse. He claimed the man died in the tunnels during World War II, but his body was never recovered."

"Lies," Marcel spat.

"Unfortunately, I believed him. I'm lucky I brought the man back to the hideout to meet Marcel. He recognized Fitzroy at once."

"Louis Fitzroy used to work for my father," Marcel explained.

"Marcel's father is a policeman," Etienne added. "As a matter of fact, he's head of the force that patrols the catacombs."

"Interesting," Kiki said, regarding Marcel through new

and narrowed eyes. "And that man who just passed was once one of his subordinates?"

"Yes," Marcel said. "Do you remember the police officer who discovered a movie theater inside the tunnels? That was Fitzroy—he was the man who tried to convince the world that the Darkness Dwellers exist. My father humiliated him, and now he's looking for a way to repair his reputation."

"What do you think Fitzroy's really after?" Kiki asked.

"Proof that the Darkness Dwellers are real!" Marcel exclaimed. "Proof that he's not an idiot as my father claims!"

"Fitzroy must think that Marcel and I can help him," Etienne added. "He's been snooping around, trying to find his way back to my hideout."

"Where *is* your hideout?" Kiki asked.

"You're in it." Etienne flipped on his flashlight.

It was a small, egg-shaped space. The domed ceiling was just high enough for Marcel to stand without stooping. The walls were perfectly smooth and covered in a reflective paint that made the entire room glow. There was a comfortable sofa, several bookshelves, and an Oriental rug.

"Remarkable," Kiki said.

"I've been working on it for years," Etienne explained. "I was twelve when I found the room. I knew it would make the perfect hideout. There are three narrow entrances, so it's easy to come and go. The first thing I did was camouflage all of them. And then I cut windows through the rock so I can see who's in the tunnels nearby." He lifted a wooden flap to reveal one of the tiny holes he'd bored into the walls. "I think the next step will be electricity. It would

be nice to have a small fridge and a television down here."
He suddenly stopped, blushing at the way Kiki was watching him. "You must find this all very silly."

"Not at all," Kiki replied. "I think it's fantastic." She couldn't seem to pull her eyes away from the thin, dark-haired boy.

"Well, I'm bored," Marcel announced. "Isn't there a party we should be attending?"

✠   ✠   ✠

It felt as though they had walked for hours before the sound of music reached their ears. Soon, a faint glow appeared in the tunnel ahead, and they followed the light to its source. The enormous room was oval in shape, with a row of theater seats along its perimeter. A web of wires clung to the ceiling and dozens of naked bulbs dangled from cords like luminous spiders. Black-and-white movies lit up the walls while a three-piece band played at maximum volume. The guests represented every walk of life. There were young men with dreadlocks and older men wearing ties. Women in camouflage jumpsuits and others dressed in designer heels. The only thing they all shared in common was a love of the dark, dangerous tunnels beneath Paris.

A fierce-looking guard stopped Kiki and her friends at the entrance. He and Etienne took turns shouting into each other's ears, and it seemed for a moment that the trio might not be welcomed inside.

At last Etienne caught the attention of a lanky man dressed in jeans, a T-shirt, and a dinner jacket. He could have grown a garden in the dirt caked under his fingernails, and his wild hair and woolly goatee gave him the appearance of a middle-aged faun. The man came up and pinched Etienne's cheek playfully. Then he exchanged a few words with the guard before leading his three guests into the party just as the band decided to take a break.

"You're out late," the man teased Etienne. "I didn't expect you to come. Don't you have school in the morning? Who are your friends?"

"Marcel and Kiki," Etienne told him.

"Welcome. My name is Phlegyas."

"Phlegyas is the leader of the Darkness Dwellers," Etienne added.

"I am merely one of the founders. We have no leader," Phlegyas corrected as he shook Kiki's hand. He seemed to be a patient man, but Kiki could tell that it wasn't the first time he'd had to set Etienne straight.

When Phlegyas offered his hand to Marcel, the boy could only grin stupidly.

"He's been asking to meet you for months," Etienne explained when Marcel failed to find his tongue.

"I'm flattered," Phlegyas said. "I hear your father doesn't believe we exist."

"You know who I am?" Marcel sputtered. "You know about my father?"

"The Darkness Dwellers judge people on their own merits. It makes no difference to us who your father is. If Etienne trusts you, I see no reason why we shouldn't do the same. He told me that you two have been working on another project somewhere in Paris. I'm looking forward to reading about it in the newspapers."

"The news will be good, this time," Etienne promised.

"I'm sure it will. For now, I'm pleased that you have work that will keep you away from the catacombs. I'm afraid they are not safe at the moment."

"Were they ever safe?" Kiki asked.

"No," Phlegyas admitted. "But until recently, most of the people who disappeared in the tunnels were victims of their own carelessness. Now it seems there may be something more sinister at work."

"What do you mean?" Marcel asked.

"You've heard about the bones that were stolen from the ossuary and shipped to New York? The ones that were seized by French customs officials?" Phlegyas asked, and the three young people nodded. "The Darkness Dwellers have been investigating the thefts. After all, we are the guardians of the catacombs."

"*You* are?" Marcel blurted out. "What about the police?"

"Please do not take this as an insult to your father, Marcel, but the catacomb police are incompetent," Phlegyas said. "When we learned that skeletons had been seized by customs officials, the Darkness Dwellers sent members to patrol the ossuary. They discovered strange symbols on the walls. A test tube. A joker's hat. A house. The paint was almost invisible to the naked eye. It appeared clearly only under a black light."

"Who do you think drew the symbols?" Etienne asked.

"I wish I knew. The bones have always attracted strange sorts. As long as they aren't vandals or thieves, the Darkness Dwellers usually let them go about their business. But the people responsible for the symbols may have attacked one of our members last week. The man left for night duty in the ossuary and was discovered unconscious the next morning. He says he never saw the person who assaulted him."

"Did he file a report?" Marcel asked.

"With your father? What should he have told the head of the Catacomb Patrol? That he belongs to a group that the police insist are an urban legend? That he broke the law by visiting the tunnels and was attacked by a man he never saw? The Darkness Dwellers must handle this on our own."

"But isn't the ossuary open to the public?" Kiki asked. "Shouldn't everyone in Paris be warned of the danger?"

"As luck would have it, the ossuary was closed to visitors earlier this week. A species of beetle has infested the area, and the authorities must send in exterminators. So for the moment, the public is not at risk. Until the mystery is solved, however, I would like the three of you to avoid the ossuary at all costs."

"We will," Etienne promised.

"I'm just here as a tourist," Kiki assured the woolly man. As much as she would have enjoyed a little detective work, she had far more pressing matters to consider.

"And you?" Phlegyas asked Marcel. "Will you stay out of the ossuary?"

"Sure, I guess," Marcel replied, as if his mind were elsewhere.

"Excellent. In return for your cooperation, Monsieur Roche, let me show you around and introduce you to a few of our members." He took the blond boy by the shoulder and led him through the party.

Marcel glanced back at Etienne as if there were something he desperately needed to say.

"It sounds like you might have a real problem down here," Kiki remarked once the others were gone.

"Whatever it is, Phlegyas will handle it," Etienne replied.

"You admire him a great deal," Kiki observed. "How did the two of you first meet?"

"Four years ago, Les Taupes and I found Phlegyas trapped in one of the tunnels. Part of the ceiling had collapsed and a rock had broken his ankle. A couple of us helped him get to the hospital, and since then he's been like an older brother to me."

"A brother who won't let you join his club."

"Well . . ." Etienne sighed. "He says I'm not ready yet. You know how brothers can be. Sometimes they're the last people to take you seriously." He led Kiki over to the chairs that circled the perimeter of the room. When they sat down, the room turned into a forest of limbs. It almost felt like they were alone.

"Why doesn't Phlegyas think you're ready?"

"He says I'm too much of a loner, and he wasn't happy with the way I dealt with my old gang, Les Taupes. He thought I should have forgiven them for getting caught in the catacombs. He told me that one day I'd discover that I need other people just as much as they need me. I think that's why he was so pleased to see I brought friends tonight."

"Which brings us to the subject of Marcel," Kiki said. "How did you end up friends with the son of the man in charge of the Catacomb Patrol?"

"I met Marcel for the first time about a year ago. He was always lurking around the entrances to the catacombs. It was obvious he was hoping someone would take him inside. Most of the people he approached weren't very nice to him. I suppose I don't blame them. Everyone who visits the catacombs is breaking the law, and word got out that Marcel's father works for the police. But after a while, I began to feel sorry for him, so I finally offered to give him a tour. The whole time he wouldn't stop talking about the Darkness Dwellers and how much he dreamed of being a member. When he told me he was good with his hands, I thought he might be the perfect person to help me repair one of Paris's old treasures. Unfortunately, Marcel exaggerated his skills. As always, I would have been better off on my own."

"So, you and Marcel haven't known each other that long?"

"No. We don't exactly run in the same circles. Marcel is lucky—he's just an ordinary guy."

"And you're not?"

Etienne shook his head sadly. "I was born with obligations."

"For instance?" Kiki probed.

"For instance, I may not have the pleasure of your company tomorrow night. There's an event that my mother tells me I must attend."

"An event?"

Etienne grimaced. "A ball thrown for a horrible girl. The sort of person who would slap a bellhop for denting her luggage. But because she's a princess, my mother insists that I introduce myself. She would love nothing better than to make a match between us. Now perhaps you can understand why I prefer to live life underground."

"Do you usually spend a great deal of time with royalty?" Kiki inquired.

"Unfortunately, I cannot escape them," Etienne said. "My full name is Etienne Antoine. My father is the Duc de Lutèce*†. Someday I will inherit his title."

"So that's how you managed to pay for those gas masks," Kiki replied with a grin. "And your princess? Who's she?"

"Katarina," Etienne spat out the name. "Katarina, Princess of Pokrovia."

If Kiki could have turned any whiter, she would have. "And you're supposed to meet her tomorrow night? At a ball here in Paris? That's impossible."

"I wish it were," Etienne said. "But her aunt had tea with my mother just yesterday, and my attendance was requested. I'm afraid I can't back out now."

"No, that's not what I—"

"*There* you are!" They looked up to find Marcel looming over them, and Kiki's mouth clamped shut. Marcel clearly had a bone he wanted to pick.

"Hello, Marcel," Etienne said with a weary sigh. "Did you manage to meet everyone?"

Marcel ignored the question. "Were you listening the other day when I told you about the two tourists?"

"Tourists?" Etienne droned.

"I told you I heard my father talking to one of his men.

_____

*At Kiki's rather annoying request, I have given her "friend" a new name and title.
†Annoying? How do you think I feel about all this "innuendo." Stick to the story, Fishbein. —KS

He said two tourists have disappeared down here in the last three weeks."

"Yes, I remember you mentioned something about that," Etienne replied.

"And you don't think there's any connection?" Marcel demanded.

"To what?"

"To the things that are going on in the ossuary! That's where the tourists were when they vanished!"

"It's tragic, Marcel," Etienne said. "But we both know people lose their way down here all the time."

"One of the tourists was with two friends. They said she walked a few meters ahead and was never seen again."

"If there's someone kidnapping people in the ossuary, the Darkness Dwellers will catch them," Etienne said.

"The tunnels are no place for vigilantes!" Marcel insisted.

"Vigilantes?" Etienne replied coldly. "For some reason I thought we were discussing your *heroes*."

Chapter 14

The Stalker in the Mercedes-Benz

DeeDee Morlock lived in a brownstone on 106th Street, not far from Columbia University. My apartment was located on the opposite end of the island of Manhattan—sixteen subway stops and over a hundred traffic lights away. Yet of all the Irregulars who might have volunteered for the job, I was the one knocking on DeeDee's door at the crack of dawn. The baldness cure was finally finished and bottled. As soon as school was out, I'd be rushing back downtown to deliver it to Betty Bent before she hopped on the plane to Paris.

I'd asked Luz to run the errand, but she *swore* she would be performing community service until six in the evening. (There had been a little *incident* involving Luz's sister, a rude neighbor, a handmade Taser, and a carton of rotten eggs.) Oona also refused to help. She was going to skip school and stake out Chinatown restaurants, in the hope of ambushing Lili Liu. So I was the one who crawled out of bed while the city was still dark and slogged uptown to get the goods.

One knock on the Morlocks' front door and a scrawny, burn-speckled arm reached out and dragged me into the living room.

"Look out the window," DeeDee ordered, pulling the curtains aside. "D'you see her?"

"See *who*?" I almost snapped. I'd had to skip my morning coffee in order to make it to the Morlocks' on schedule.

"The woman in the Mercedes!" DeeDee exclaimed.

I scanned the line of cars across from DeeDee's house. Sure enough, there was a fortyish blonde in a pin-striped suit sitting behind the wheel of a black Mercedes-Benz.

"Who is she?"

"Dunno," DeeDee said. "But I'm pretty sure she was watching me yesterday when I got home from the Golden Lotus."

"I wouldn't worry. She doesn't look all that dangerous." It was a stupid thing to say.

"Most dangerous people don't," DeeDee wisely pointed out. "What if she works for Livia? Or Con Edison? Or the FBI?"

"Is there any reason the FBI might have you under surveillance?" I wasn't joking. You never knew with the Irregulars.

"Not anymore," DeeDee said. "Unless it has something to do with Kiki."

"Okay. We'll deal with your stalker. But first things first. Where's the cure?"

I followed as DeeDee bounded up the stairs to her

bedroom laboratory, her dreadlocks bouncing like springs. Though a nasty smell still lingered in the air, the room itself was immaculate. Even the glass bottles filled with DeeDee's various chemicals and concoctions were lined up in neat rows.

"Wow, you cleaned!" I exclaimed. DeeDee's room was usually filthy, and her idea of tidying up was to sweep everything under the bed. (And I do mean *everything*. Oona once discovered a take-out container filled with something that looked like rice—until it started to wriggle.) But when I bent down for a quick peek beneath the box spring, I spotted nothing but a solitary dust bunny.

"Yeah, the parents weren't happy to find out I was experimenting on myself again. I thought tidying up might earn me a few brownie points, but they haven't even noticed."

"At least you got rid of your beard," I noted.

"Most of it," DeeDee confessed. "I had a little shave this morning. I guess I'll pay another visit to the Golden Lotus after school. Anyway, here you go." She plucked a glass jar off the lab counter. The goop inside was a rather unappealing shade of brown. "I call it Lots O' Locks."

"Catchy." DeeDee always gave her formulas cheesy names.

She looked disappointed by my reaction. "Don't you get it? It's LOL for short. As in, the joke's on Livia."

"Clever. I gotta tell you, DeeDee, this stuff looks just like . . ."

"Yeah, and it smells like it, too. But I'm proof that the goop really works," DeeDee said. "The instructions are printed on the label. If Livia doesn't follow them carefully, she'll need electrolysis on her palms."

"Wouldn't that be *terrible*?" I giggled.

"I doubt I'd lose sleep over it. But listen, I need Betty to get Kiki's promise about something. As soon as she's done with Livia, Kiki has to find a way to get the stuff back to me. It hasn't been properly tested, and I couldn't live with myself if it fell into some innocent person's hands. You never know what the side effects might be."

"You mean they could be worse than full-on facial hair?"

"It's possible," DeeDee admitted. "Even medicine you can buy at a deli can have some pretty weird side effects. Amnesia, black urine, hallucinations, sleepwalking, loss of bowel control . . ."

"Eww. Enough said." I gingerly placed the jar in my backpack and wiped my hands on my jeans. Then I checked the clock on my phone. "Gotta go," I announced. "I promised my principal I wouldn't miss any more classes this week. I'll drop the cure off at Betty's house this afternoon before she leaves for the airport."

"Are we still sure Betty's the right girl for the job?" DeeDee asked. "She's so . . ."

"What?"

"*Sweet.*" DeeDee made it sound like a dirty word. "And remember when Betty was kidnapped at the Bannerman Ball? She was trying to be helpful, and she almost got herself killed."

The memory made me shudder. "I know. Betty's not ideal. I wish we could send someone else, but it's not possible. All Betty has to do this time is get the cure to Kiki. We'll just have to hope nothing goes wrong."

"But something *always* goes wrong," DeeDee said.

She had a point. "Look, I'll stay in constant touch with Betty while she's overseas. If there's a problem, I'll deal with it when the time comes. But right now, I need to get to school, or I'll be in stuck in detention for the rest of the week."

"So, you're just going to leave?" DeeDee was wringing her hands. There was something else she wanted from me. A leader's work is never done.

"What's wrong now?"

"The woman in the Mercedes-Benz, remember? You were going to help me find out if she's really following me."

"Right. Sorry, I almost forgot." I sighed. "Your parents have any surgical supplies lying around?" DeeDee's father was a chemistry professor and her mother was a doctor. The house was stocked with all sorts of goodies. A single Morlock family medicine cabinet contained all the supplies you'd need to perform emergency brain surgery.

"Sure."

"I'm going to need two pairs of thin latex gloves and some super-greasy salad dressing."

"Why?" DeeDee asked with an uncharacteristically wicked grin. "Are we going to be doing some probing?"

"You'll see," I told her.

★   ★   ★

No one could impersonate innocent schoolgirls like DeeDee and me—we'd been wearing that particular disguise for years. We charged down the front stairs of the

Morlocks' brownstone, whispering and giggling. A few yards past the black car parked at the curb, I fished a compact out of my coat pocket, puckered up my lips, and pretended to check my lip gloss in the mirror.

"The Mercedes just pulled out behind us," I told DeeDee.

"I knew it!" DeeDee whispered.

"Let's make sure we're being tailed before we take evasive action," I said. "As soon as we get to the end of the block, bend down and tie your shoelaces."

The traffic light was green when we reached the corner. The Mercedes should have sped past. But it was still lurking behind us. As DeeDee paused to tie her shoes, the car came to a complete halt.

"Well, there's our proof," I said. "But if it makes you feel any better, she's not a professional detective. Whoever this chick is, she's never tailed anyone before."

"Nope," DeeDee replied with a shake of her head. "That doesn't make me feel any better at all."

"Maybe this will." I unzipped my backpack, and each of us took out two hand-shaped balloons filled with salad dressing. "Aim for the windshield."

DeeDee's first balloon splattered across the Mercedes' hood, but our other three missiles found their mark. Just as I'd expected, the woman in the driver's seat immediately switched on the windshield wipers, smearing salad dressing across the glass. I almost wished I could have seen the surprise on her face, but she'd disappeared behind a thick film of grease.

"You're right," DeeDee said. "That did feel good."

"See you later," I told her before we bolted off in

opposite directions. "Let me know if she has the guts to come back!"

❄　　❄　　❄

I caught a bus across Central Park and hopped out on the corner of Sixty-Eighth Street and Lexington Avenue. I had less than three minutes to get to class, but I already could see the snow-covered spires of the Atalanta School for Girls in the middle of the next block. As I waited for a light to change, two of my classmates appeared beside me. Though I normally found Dylan Handworthy and Ginger Altschul about as fascinating as dung beetles, I couldn't peel my eyes away from them. They both seemed different somehow. The miniskirts and painful-looking heels they'd once favored had been replaced by prim ensembles that were better suited for a tea party than a high school classroom.

"I hear she'll be on the throne of Pokrovia by May," Dylan confided.

"I *do* hope the coronation will be televised," Ginger gushed in an accent that sounded vaguely British. "I would love to see what Princess Katarina looks like. She must be stunning if she's Sidonia Galatzina's cousin."

"I'm not so sure about that." She may have been dressed like a goody two-shoes, but Dylan hadn't lost her taste for gossip. "I have a feeling there's a very good reason that Sidonia never bothered to mentioned any relatives."

"Oh no!" Ginger gasped. "What if Princess Katarina is horribly deformed? You know, I read somewhere that she has weird white hair. What if she was born with one of those disorders you get from too much inbreeding? My mother told me there are royals who are so hideous that they've been banned from showing their faces in public!"

"No, I don't think that's it," Dylan said. "You can work wonders with plastic surgery these days. But I *did* hear one of the girls at the institute say that Princess Katarina was raised by some old peasant woman. She's probably just incredibly vulgar."

"*Poor* Sidonia. She must be *so* embarrassed to have a cousin like that!" Ginger said. "Do you think there's still time to train the princess to be queen?"

"Why do you suppose Princess Katarina is in Paris? Do you think it's a coincidence that she and Madame Beauregard are visiting the same city at the very same time? I suspect Madame has been called in for emergency damage repair."

"Oh, thank heavens! If anyone can fix the princess, Madame can!"

The light changed and the two girls left me frozen behind on the curb. I watched the way they glided across the street. There was no doubt about it. That rigid posture and those dainty steps were the undeniable marks of a very familiar beast.

✡ ✡ ✡

For the first time in weeks, I walked down the halls of the Atalanta School for Girls with my eyes open. And I saw them—*everywhere*. Students walking as though they were balancing invisible books on their heads. Girls with naturally booming voices speaking in ladylike whispers.

Classmates whose formerly untamed tresses had been straightened or set. If I hadn't known better, I would have wondered if their bodies had been snatched by unusually prissy aliens. But now I realized I was dealing with a far more sinister force than extraterrestrials. I was dealing with Amelia Beauregard.

"It's not polite to stare," a freshman chided me.

A friend of hers joined in. "A lady doesn't let her mouth hang open."

"I used to wear jeans like that before I knew any better." They were ganging up on me. I'd battled evil princesses, smugglers, and man-eating rats. But I had never expected to find myself faced with a zombie invasion. I took one clumsy step backward and bumped into someone standing behind me.

"Get to class, ladies," ordered the principal.

"Yes, Principal Wickham," the zombies all sang in unison.

"Did you see that?" I gasped once the girls were gone. "Did you see what Madame Beauregard has done to them? She's stolen their souls!"

"It's happened every year for as long as I've been at Atalanta," Principal Wickham confided. "Two or three girls enroll in after-school classes and by winter break they're wearing their mother's pearls. But it seems Amelia's institute has grown quite popular among the Atalanta student body this year. Hopefully some of Amelia's pupils will forget their training over summer vacation."

"And the rest?" I asked.

"The rest will send *their* daughters to the institute."

I thought of Betty. In a few hours she'd be leaving for Paris with Amelia Beauregard. Would she be the same person when she returned to New York? Or would Madame work her black magic on Betty as well?

"I've got to warn her," I muttered.

"I was thinking the very same thing," Principal Wickham agreed.

THE FISHBEIN GUIDE TO . . . FLOWER ARRANGING

Are you the sort of person who has a hard time saying "I'm sorry"? (Or "I was wrong to accuse you of murder at dinner the other night." Or "I had no idea that a hamster could be such a dangerous gift.") Then don't say it. Send flowers instead! They're the perfect way to express all of those ooey-gooey emotions that your mouth refuses to utter.

If you are looking for handy tips that will help you create stunning arrangements, please enroll in classes at your local finishing school. I like pretty things as much as the next person, but I'm here to dispense only *useful* advice.

Express Your Feelings with Flowers

A bouquet can express many lovely sentiments. But not all flowers are as sweet as they smell. Ask a florist to teach you the secret language of flowers (or look it up online), and you'll discover that every bloom has a hidden meaning. A flower arrangement can say exactly how much you care—or it can warn the recipient that she's cruising for a bruising.

Add the Perfect Touch

In my opinion, no flower arrangement is complete without a bug or two. I'm not referring to the six-legged sort. (Though a few of those could be amusing additions to the right arrangement.) Tiny listening devices are difficult to detect when hidden among petals and leaves. A simple centerpiece on the dining room table can provide a few days of beauty—and hours of priceless entertainment.

Always Choose the Right Vase

Whenever I receive flowers, I sincerely thank the person who sent them. Then I remove the arrangement from its vase and take a quick peek inside. I'm not just searching for bugs. Practically anything can be smuggled inside an opaque flower vase. If the bouquet is particularly fragrant, even the smelliest of substances might be hidden within.

Repel Unwanted Pests

There are certain flowers you wouldn't want to sniff. They can fill a room with the delightful aromas of smelly socks, skunk juice, rotting meat, or putrid corpse. Put a bunch of these blooms together in a lovely arrangement, and you have an ideal pest repellant. Some will keep flies or mosquitoes away. Others are certain to send unwanted guests fleeing for fresh air.

Survive in the Wild

Flowers aren't just pretty, of course. Some are edible. Some have medicinal properties. And some are poisonous enough to kill an elephant. Don't set off into the wilderness (or hide out in a florist's shop) until you know which is which.

CHAPTER 15

The Doppelgänger

Betty was dressed like a secretary from the 1950s. Cashmere sweater, tweed pencil skirt, sensible heels, and horn-rimmed glasses. She took the cure from me and carefully tucked the jar inside her large, faux-alligator suitcase.

"What if they stop you at customs? What are you going to tell them?" Kaspar didn't seem pleased to see Betty setting off for a trip with Amelia Beauregard. The worry written on his face made him even more appealing than usual. I tried my best not to stare.

"I'll just say it's homemade hair gel," Betty replied.

"Hair gel that smells like sewage?" Kaspar asked. "Who's going to believe *that*?"

Betty shrugged and reached for her coat. "Does it matter if they believe it? Are there any laws against taking a jar of poop to France?"

"Betty, are you *sure* you're up for this trip?" I inquired for the twentieth time.

"Yes!" Being asked the same question twenty times was enough to exasperate even the nicest girl in the world. "You know, Ananka, you and the other Irregulars take risks all the time. Nobody ever asks DeeDee whether she's *sure* she wants to cook up a new batch of explosives. Or asks Luz if she's *sure* it's a good idea to make a laser-shooting robot. Why is everyone so worried about *me*? I didn't sign up for the Irregulars so I could sit back and watch my friends have all the fun. So, please, just step aside and let me do my job, will you?"

"Okay, okay!" I held up my hands. "Don't go nuts. No one's gonna confiscate your passport!"

"Good." Betty huffed as she buttoned her coat. "The only thing that bothers me is having to go to France while Kaspar is in town on school break. I know you're going to be busy, Ananka, but will you do me one favor? Will you try to keep Kaspar entertained until I get back?"

I glanced over at Kaspar, and he smiled back at me. Perfect teeth, twinkling green eyes, delightfully tousled auburn hair . . . I forced my gaze down to the floor.

"Sure," I muttered. "No problem."

A horn honked on the street outside Betty's basement apartment.

"That must be Madame Beauregard," Betty said. "Wish me luck!"

✮ ✮ ✮

A black limousine sat idling outside the body-piercing shop next to Betty's building. Two ferocious-looking boys crouched on the sidewalk with their backs to the wall. One had a bright blue Mohawk that rose half a foot from his scalp. The other boy had a four-letter word inscribed on his forehead. With its tattoo parlors and punk supply stores, St. Mark's Place must have been the sort of street Amelia Beauregard walked in her nightmares. I had a feeling she'd never voluntarily ventured so close to the grungy East Village during her waking hours.

"Betty!" one of the young punks called out. They both jumped up when they spotted her suitcases. "You want some help with that stuff?"

"No thanks, Ralph," Betty replied. "I've got it all under control. You guys better be good while I'm gone! No scaring the tourists, you hear!" She turned to me and whispered, "They're such sweeties."

Keeping a careful eye on the natives, Amelia Beauregard's chauffeur helped Kaspar pack Betty's four heavy bags into the trunk. Then he opened the door to the backseat and waited for Betty to slide inside. Madame Beauregard was already seated by the opposite window, dressed in her standard gray uniform. She gave me a brusque nod. Then her attention was captured by something behind me, and her face seemed to soften. I glanced over my shoulder and saw Betty kissing Kaspar good-bye. I expected the scene to inspire a lecture on vulgar displays of affection, but for once, Amelia Beauregard looked more wistful than outraged.

"Wanna grab a cup of coffee?" I asked Kaspar after the limo rode away with Betty inside.

"Why not?" he replied.

And that, I'm sad to report, was the last thing that was said for five whole blocks. I tried to recall a single story or shocking fact that I might be able to share with him.

Anything would have worked—even one of Luz's horribly dirty jokes—but my brain simply refused to function in the presence of the boy beside me, and it was Kaspar who finally broke the silence.

"I really hope it wasn't a mistake sending Betty to Paris."

"Yeah, me too," I replied. "Betty's a great master of disguise, but she might be a little too sweet for a job like this." Maybe he'd noticed it too. Maybe Kaspar was ready to date a girl with a little more edge.

"I'm not worried because Betty's *sweet*," Kaspar said. "That Beauregard woman would be a match for me, you, or *any* of the Irregulars. And from what Betty's told me, it sounds like there might be a little more to Madame than we realize. Don't you think it's a bit strange? The woman must know a thousand girls, but she decided to hire the one she met in a graveyard. I suspect Amelia Beauregard has something hidden up her prissy silk sleeve."

This was an angle I hadn't considered. I'd worried about what the woman might *do* to Betty. But I'd never asked myself why she'd chosen Betty Bent in the first place.

"Did you say anything to Betty?" I asked.

"Sure. And she promised to be careful, but I wish one of us could have talked her out of going."

"When Betty calls to check in, I'll tell her to put on a disguise and disappear the second she thinks there might be trouble," I said. "She must have packed a few costumes in those suitcases. The girl took enough luggage for a three-month trip."

"Yeah, she said she wanted to be prepared."

"To do *what*—stage an impromptu production of *Les*

Miserables?" The joke popped out of my mouth and took us both by surprise. Not only did Kaspar get it, he actually laughed! I took a moment to give myself a mental high five. Unfortunately, a moment was all I got.

"Hey, isn't that Oona?" Kaspar suddenly asked, pointing to the other side of Third Avenue. "Should we invite her to join us for coffee?"

"It can't be. Oona's staking out restaurants in Chinatown today." A pretty Asian girl was stomping through the snow in high-heeled boots, headed in the direction of St. Mark's Place. Her enormous sunglasses and woolly hat couldn't conceal a startling resemblance to Oona Wong. I was briefly annoyed by the thought of having to add a third wheel to my date with Kaspar. Then I realized what I might be seeing.

"Holy moly," I whispered. "We found Lili Liu!"

"You think that's Oona's sister? Betty told me she was causing trouble all over town. Want me to grab her?" Kaspar offered.

"Not just yet," I replied. "I promised Betty I'd show you a good time. And there's nothing more fun than a little detective work. Let's follow her and find out where she's going."

✯   ✯   ✯

There are billions of people on earth, and all of us share the same few hair, skin, and eye colors. The way I figure it, we all have a double walking around somewhere. But the odds are pretty good that you'll never run across yours. So, if you're strolling down the street one day and you spot a person who looks *exactly* like you, it's quite possible that you haven't found your double. You've seen your *dop-pelgänger*. And it probably means you're in for a whole lot of trouble.

Look-alikes are generally human and often quite amicable, but doppelgängers are invariably evil. It's said that a person who catches a glimpse of a doppelgänger may have illness or insanity in her future. Which is why I was pretty sure *someone* was in danger the moment Kaspar and I found ourselves hot on the trail of Oona Wong's. But I never would have guessed that someone might be *me*.

We followed the girl up Third Avenue. Along the way, I tried to instruct Kaspar in the fine art of tailing suspects. To make ourselves less conspicuous, we tucked our hair under our hats and wrapped scarves around our faces. We let Lili Liu walk half a block in front of us, and whenever she paused, we'd pretend to be whispering sweet nothings into each other's ears. I *might* have gotten a little carried away with my performance, and I *might* have stopped paying attention. We were halfway to midtown when Lili disappeared.

Kaspar ran ahead to see if he could pick up the trail. As he passed a free-standing ATM machine encased in ice, a leg shot out and delivered a powerful blow to his chest. He collapsed on the sidewalk, and a figure in black pounced on him. In less than a second, the heel of a fancy black boot was pressing down on Kaspar's Adam's apple. I rushed to the scene, desperate to rescue the boy of my daydreams.

"Come any closer and I'll crush the kid's windpipe," the girl shouted. She even *sounded* like Oona Wong. "Who are you and what do you want?"

"My name is Ananka," I called out from behind my scarf. "I'm friends with your sister!"

"Ananka? Why are you following me! And who is *this*?" She kicked Kaspar sharply in the ribs.

"I'm *Kaspar*!" he yelped, removing his scarf and revealing his face.

"Oona?" I asked skeptically. "Is that really you?"

"Who else would it be!" she snarled, removing her heel from Kaspar's throat.

"How can I be sure?" I contemplated asking for some sort of ID.

"I don't have to prove anything to you, Fishbein!" the girl barked back. It was Oona, all right. No question about it. "What are you two doing? I could have killed you both just now!"

Only because I was distracted by Kaspar, I thought. *Otherwise, I would have kicked your obnoxious butt.*

"We were sure you were Lili," Kaspar explained as he massaged his throat. "We were trying to follow her back to her lair."

"Oh my God! You thought I was *Lili*?" Oona wailed. "That was the one person I was trying *not* to look like. You really thought it was her—even though I'm wearing sunglasses and a hat?"

Oona had never bothered to learn how to travel incognito. "Yeah," I admitted. "What were you doing this far uptown, anyway? You were supposed to be watching restaurants in Chinatown all day."

"I didn't mean to come all this way. I was heading to Betty's house because I needed a disguise. Then I noticed you guys following me, so I kept walking until I had a chance to ambush you."

"Betty just left for France," I informed her.

"I can't believe I forgot she was leaving today!" Oona moaned. "What am I going to do now? I can't go anywhere in Chinatown without someone chasing me down the street. Thanks to Lili, the whole neighborhood is convinced I'm a thief. Half the stores on Mott Street have Lili's photo up by their registers, and all the clerks shout 'shoplifter' as soon as they see me. I had no idea how much damage Lili's managed to do—she'd already hit every restaurant I tried to stake out today. I had some little old lady pelt me with *bao* the second I stepped through her door. And I'm only wearing this *hideous* hat because the waiter at another place dumped a bowl of cold sesame noodles over my head."

"You really think your sister's doing all of this just to get you in trouble?" Kaspar asked. "Couldn't there be some other explanation?"

"How can you even ask that, Kaspar? You know what my family's like! This is Lili's way of punishing me for putting our dad in jail. She knows the worst thing she could possibly do is force me to move to Cleveland."

"You won't have to move anywhere," I assured her. "We'll find Lili and put an end to her crime spree. Kaspar's going to help, too. He needs a bit of excitement while Betty's gone."

"Does he, now?" Oona smirked, her own worries briefly forgotten. "And I guess *you're* the girl who's going to give it to him?"

If I had been close enough to kick her, I would have.

THE FISHBEIN GUIDE TO . . . GREETINGS & SALUTATIONS

Minutes after you meet a person, your new acquaintance will have formed an opinion of you. She'll have decided whether you're affable, interesting, potentially dangerous, or likely to be carrying a great deal of cash. First impressions are often wrong, but that doesn't mean they're easy to change. So make sure you always show the world the side of yourself you want it to see.

Be the First to Offer Your Hand
It doesn't matter how old you are—or whether you're male or female—a firm handshake can make you seem more confident, trustworthy, and friendly. (A scientifically proven fact!) Simply smile, hold out your hand, introduce yourself, and shake. It really couldn't be any easier.

Have a Little Something to Say
Need to impress, charm, or subtly intimidate a person you're scheduled to meet? Just do a little research! A quick Internet search can reveal a new acquaintance's hobbies, talents, or criminal record—all of which can make for great conversation starters! (Do take care not to creep people out. No one likes to think they've been under surveillance.)

Never Jump to Conclusions
If you're a gifted detective, a person's appearance can tell you a great deal. However, only a fool would assume there wasn't any more to the story. The dainty girl dressed in head-to-toe pink could turn out to be a kung-fu champion. The man with the warm, winning smile works as a professional hit man. The shifty-looking kid may end up being your most loyal friend. But you'd never know any of this unless you bothered to *talk* to them.

Get Your Foot in the Door
Sometimes the people you need to meet aren't terribly interested in meeting *you*. These situations call for a little ingenuity. For instance, an Australian associate of mine recently arranged a "meeting" with a shady dentist who'd been giving her the slip. Hania took a piece of ordinary bubble gum and used a syringe to inject fake blood into the center. Then

she popped the piece into her mouth and strolled into the dentist's office. Before she reached the receptionist's desk, she pretended to fall flat on her face. When the woman spotted the blood gushing from my associate's mouth (and threatening to stain the carpet), the receptionist dragged her back to see the elusive dentist. Rather brilliant, I'd say!

Leave a Memorable Calling Card

Once upon a time, ladies carried "calling cards" to leave behind when they visited the homes of friends or acquaintances. I've recently had a few made with the Irregulars' logo. I use them whenever I need to send a message. Sometimes that message is *I was here.* More often, it's *YOU'VE BEEN WARNED!*

ChAPTER 16

Kiki and the Melting Queen

PARIS: WEDNESDAY, FEBRUARY 18

Kiki could smell him long before she saw him. Sergei Molotov cruised in on a wave of cologne so foul that it could only have been purchased at a flea market in Minsk. He threw open the door to Kiki's cell in the bell tower and held out his long arms. Dressed in a suit that straddled the line between gray and violet, with his black hair slicked back and his handmade Italian shoes polished to perfection, he looked like your basic cartoon villain.

"Give me a hug, you disgusting little she-beast," Sergei demanded as he wrapped his arms around his captive. "I cannot believe this will be our very last meeting!" It was a dangerous move on his part. This, after all, was the same man who had shot Verushka Kozlova and attempted to frame her for murder. Kiki would have killed him for far less than a hug. But it was a day for bargains, not bloodshed. Instead of breaking his neck, she merely slammed Sergei against the wall.

"Where is Livia?" Kiki asked, choking on the stench of Sergei's cologne.

Sergei peeled himself off the wall and smiled. "Queen Livia will be arriving in minutes. I came early to give some air to the room. As usual, you smell like goat. And where is the beautiful pink dress I sent? Is that it? Thrown in the corner like a rag? Go! Put it on! You should want to look pretty on your last day alive!"

Rather than waste time arguing, Kiki pulled the pink polyester dress over her head.

Sergei stood back and studied his model. "I think the outfit is missing something. What could it . . . ah yes!" He reached into a pocket and produced an enormous pink bow, which he clipped to Kiki's hair. "Perfection!" he announced. "I am a fashion genius. The queen will be pleased! I think I hear her now!"

Livia Galatzina tried to make a grand entrance but came to a sudden halt before she could get through the door. Both aunt and niece gasped at the sight of the other. Livia wore a Chanel suit in an arresting shade of purple. The multiple strands of pearls hanging from around her neck could have been mistaken for the world's tackiest lobster bib, and her blond wig would have been right at home in the Dolly Parton collection. But it was Livia's face that rendered Kiki speechless. A gruesome combination of plastic surgery and pancake makeup had given Livia the appearance of a melting wax figure.

"Ha!" A sharp, spiteful laugh jolted Kiki out of her trance. "Look at the elf!" Sidonia Galatzina suddenly pushed past her mother and sidled into the room. She was a stunning girl with ebony hair and golden eyes. A slightly crooked nose was her only obvious flaw. (Months earlier, I'd broken her schnoz with a single punch.) But hidden beneath the guise of a fairy-tale princess was a black-hearted beast.

"I believe pink may be your best color, my dear," Livia observed. "You shall make a somewhat attractive corpse, Katarina."

"And I just *love* what you've done with this place." Sidonia snickered.

"Hello, Aunt Livia," Kiki greeted her relatives politely. "Sidonia. How are my two favorite psychopaths? I was told you were spending the winter in Scotland."

"Making a movie about a queen who couldn't manage to keep her head?" Sidonia replied with a haughty laugh. "*Please.* You should have known better. I was born to play victors, not victims."

"I must admit, I expected better from you, Katarina." Livia tsked. "Did you really believe we wouldn't be watching? You publicly announce that the long-lost Princess of Pokrovia has returned from the dead, and you expect us to exile ourselves in a dreary little country that's filled with nothing but sheep?"

"I thought you might realize the game was over. There's no chance you'll ever be queen again," Kiki retorted. "The whole world knows I'm alive. If I disappear now, people will start asking questions. And my friends will make sure you're the very first person they interrogate."

"Oh, but you won't disappear!" Livia exclaimed. "Haven't you heard? The Princess of Pokrovia has decided to claim her throne after all. The future queen and I have been busy with the preparations all week."

"The future queen?" Kiki asked, playing dumb.

"You probably don't recognize her at the moment," said Livia, stroking Sidonia's smirking face. "But with a white wig and a little makeup, she's unmistakable. Princess Katarina of Pokrovia—back from the dead and ready to rule. It's a good thing you've always gone to such lengths to avoid having your photograph taken. It would have made it more difficult for my beautiful child to impersonate you if the world had seen what an ugly little creature you are."

"Ah." Kiki nodded. "So Sidonia has stolen my identity. I was wondering what you two had in mind."

"That wonderful gentleman Lester Liu was the inspiration. Having one of his daughters impersonate the other. Genius! Sergei, remind me to send Mr. Liu a thank-you gift as soon as we've finished with Katarina."

"I suppose that means you've come to kill me. May I ask what you've done with Verushka?"

"Ms. Kozlova will be joining you in the afterlife," Livia said. "We shall be visiting her next."

"Mother!" Sidonia huffed. "Stop answering the elf's questions. I'm already running late as it is. Can we just get this over with?"

"Darling, you were the one who insisted on seeing your cousin dispatched. The dreadful child would have been dead *days* ago if we hadn't been forced to work around your social schedule."

"I wanted to make sure it was done *right* this time," Sidonia said. "Okay, Sergei. Go ahead. But don't get any blood on my shoes."

Sergei bowed deeply before removing a Russian combat knife from an ankle holster. "Your wish is my command."

"Stop trying to act cute. Of course it is!" Sidonia said, stomping her foot. "Say your last words, Katarina."

Kiki grinned. "I have a proposal for you."

"We're not interested in any of your proposals," Livia replied. "Nothing can save you now."

"I realize that," Kiki said. "I don't intend to bargain for my own life. I would like to barter for Verushka's life instead."

"*Why?*" Sidonia asked. "She's just an old servant."

"Then it should mean nothing to you if she lives," Kiki observed. "But since you ask, Verushka saved my life more than once, and I would like to repay her before I die."

"Forget it," Sidonia said. "Now that I have your title, there's nothing you can possibly give me."

"Perhaps," Kiki replied. "But I know how to save something you wouldn't want to lose."

"Do all the elves talk in riddles?" Sidonia snipped. "Get to the point, Katarina!"

"Your hair," Kiki replied bluntly. "Your mother developed the Pokrovian royal curse at seventeen. And *your* seventeenth birthday is just around the corner, isn't it? Do you ever dream that you'll wake up bald? I know how to keep those nightmares from becoming reality."

Sidonia's face was suddenly as bloodless as Kiki's. "The curse can't be stopped. Mother's been to see the best specialists in the world. Her condition is incurable."

"Perhaps she hasn't met the right experts," Kiki said.

"Do you recall the rat-repelling perfume you once coveted? Or the tonic that renders poisons and drugs ineffective? Well, the same young lady who invented those formulas has developed a cure for your condition."

"Why should I believe you?" Sidonia blustered.

"I don't expect you to believe anything. That's why I'm asking only the life of one lowly servant in return for the cure. I can even have a supply delivered to you right here in Paris. All you'll need to do is release Verushka."

"Don't listen, Princess! This is one of Katarina's tricks," Sergei warned.

"I agree, dear," Livia said. "And wearing wigs isn't as terrible as one might think."

"Did I *ask* for your advice, Mother?" Sidonia barked. "How would we make the trade, Katarina?"

"One of my associates will contact you," Kiki said. "She will exchange the cure for Verushka. Then you will be free to kill me."

"How will you know Verushka is safe if you're locked away in a bell tower?" Sergei asked. He seemed genuinely curious—and more than a little bit wary.

"That's my problem, not yours," Kiki replied. "Do we have a deal?"

Sidonia took a deep breath. "I don't know."

"Then I would recommend investing in some super-glue. I can only imagine what your new subjects might think if your wig should ever fall off. You know how Pokrovians feel about bald queens. It's such a *primitive* superstition, isn't it? People can be *so* cruel."

"You have twenty-four hours," Sidonia announced. "Sergei, get the door."

Chapter 17

Unfortunate
Side Effects

NEW YORK CITY: WEDNESDAY, FEBRUARY 18

Shortly before Hanukah, when I was nine years old, my mother took a job as a cleaning lady at the main branch of the New York Public Library on Forty-Second Street. Having earned three PhDs, she was a bit overqualified for the position. But it wasn't a job my mother intended to keep. After all, we had our own remarkable library, which lined every wall in our home. My mother took the job for *me*. I'd read about the sprawling archives hidden below the library and neighboring park—miles and miles of books, documents, and forgotten treasures— and I dreamed of exploring them. My parents couldn't afford the kind of presents that my Atalanta classmates received for Christmas or Hanukah. My gift that year was an after-hours tour of the semi-secret library archives that are buried beneath Bryant Park.

For much of my childhood, I'd been haunted by the feeling that I was a disappointment to my parents. I never felt unloved or neglected, but at times I'd catch them watching me. And I knew they were wondering how two studious individuals could have produced someone so *strange*. I'd never come close to making straight As, and I spent my free time studying reports of alien abductions and watching videos about giant squid.

The only trait I seemed to have inherited from Bernard and Lillian Fishbein was my love of books. Aside from our shared fear of Mother Nature, that was our family's one little patch of common ground. The evening my mother snuck me into the library's archives, we intended to stay for only an hour. Instead we roamed the aisles all night long, cracking open countless dusty tomes and leafing through the diaries of hard-living luminaries. A guard discovered us in the morning, and my mother was promptly relieved of her duties. We bought hot chocolates from a café in Bryant Park and reveled in our discoveries. It was the first day I really felt like a Fishbein.

It might have been that memory that made me choose Bryant Park as the site of an early-morning Irregulars' meeting to discuss Oona Wong's family troubles. Or maybe it was the park's strategic location—right in the center of Manhattan, an equal distance from the Irregulars' various schools. But it's just as likely that I wanted to make my friends pay. The previous day, I'd been up before dawn, ferrying the cure from one end of town to the other. Now it was the other girls' turn to suffer a little. It was only fair. Right?

"Where's DeeDee? I have to get back uptown to class!" Luz announced. "We all got Betty's e-mail this morning. She made it to Paris just fine. There's nothing any of us can do until she hears from Kiki's French boyfriend. And why are we meeting outside in a park, anyway? I'm freezing my butt off! Can't we go to a diner and get some coffee?"

"All restaurants in Manhattan are off-limits to us right now," I explained.

"Why?" Luz demanded.

"Go ahead, Ananka. Tell them it's all my fault," Oona mumbled miserably. She was wearing one of Mrs. Fei's old coats, and her long, glossy hair was hidden under an unflattering baseball cap.

"Now that Betty is in France with the cure, we need to start focusing on our next project," I said. "Oona's in trouble. Lili Liu is still impersonating her. The girl's been dining and dashing all over town. There's a chance she could get Oona arrested. So we're not going to test our luck at any restaurants until we figure out how to stop this girl."

"Why does that mean we have to meet in the cold? We can still talk on the phone! Or meet at a restaurant in Brooklyn!" Luz argued.

"Brooklyn?" Oona looked confused. "I've never even *been* there."

"Me neither, but I'm pretty sure they have restaurants."

"You've made your point, Luz," I said. "Next subject?"

"I have an idea that might help us find Lili," chirped Iris. "How about a map?

"A map of what?" Oona asked dismissively.

"Well, I was watching a movie called *Silence of the Lambs* last night . . ."

"Isn't that R-rated?" Luz interjected. "Your parents let you watch that sort of stuff?"

"Sure—don't yours?" Iris replied matter-of-factly. The

embarrassment on Luz's face told us not to expect an answer. "Anyway, in the movie, the FBI is searching for a serial killer. They use a map to plot all the places he's dumped bodies. It helps them figure out where the guy lives. So, what if we plotted all the places that Lili's been spotted? It might help us zero in on where she's been staying."

"That's actually a pretty good idea," Oona admitted reluctantly.

"Thanks!" Iris beamed.

Just then, a blast of wind tore through the empty park, shaking great clumps of snow from the tree branches. One landed with a splat a few inches to my left. "So, Iris, you and Oona get started on the map after school. We'll meet again tomorrow."

"Why not tonight?" Oona asked. "It's not going to take that long to make the map. We might even be able to hunt Lili down before Luz's curfew kicks in."

"I have other plans tonight," I said.

"What do you mean you have *plans*?" Oona demanded.

Fortunately, I never got a chance to answer. DeeDee was sprinting toward us, arms flailing and eyes wide.

"Ananka!" she panted. "The blond woman in the black Mercedes! She followed me here! I tried to lose her, but she kept showing up everywhere I went. I swear, it's like she has some sort of tracking device."

"Did you inspect your shoes and bags for devices?" I asked.

"I know the rules! I do a check every morning!" DeeDee insisted.

"You're being followed?" Oona asked.

"Stalked!" DeeDee corrected.

"The fun never stops, does it?" Luz muttered. "Just when I was looking forward to a few minutes of down-time."

"Where is the lady now?" I asked.

"Right across from the subway station." DeeDee pointed toward the corner of Forty-Second Street and Sixth Avenue.

"Did you get her license plate number?"

"Of course I did!" DeeDee said. "I memorized it the first time I saw her. FTSVP01."

"Iris, stay here in the park and call 911," I ordered. "Tell them you're being followed by a black Mercedes, license plate number FTSVP01. Say you think the driver might be armed and dangerous. Try to sound really young and really scared. Have them send a cop right away. The rest of you come with me."

"Where are we going?" DeeDee asked.

"To have a little chat with your stalker," I said.

Crouched down out of sight, the four of us traveled in a single line along a row of parked cars until we reached the Mercedes. The lady inside nearly soiled her beige leather seat when I stood up and rapped twice on the passenger's side window. She was rail thin, immaculately dressed, and her hair was a shade of blond that comes out of bottles that cost five hundred dollars. The woman must have mistaken me for a juvenile panhandler, and her lips were forming the word *scram* when she spotted DeeDee standing to my right.

There's a Pokrovian folk saying that goes a little like this: *Never trust a person who smiles for no reason.* In my experience, the folk of Pokrovia can be a wee bit paranoid, but in this case, they're probably right. There was no reason for the lady in the black Mercedes to be so overjoyed to find a fifteen-year-old chemist peering through her window. And yet here she was, showing more teeth than a crocodile. I wondered if the woman had mistaken DeeDee Morlock for lunch.

"Who are you, and what do you want?" I demanded once the lady had lowered the glass barrier between us.

"I'm sorry?" She kept on smiling, even as she feigned confusion. "Perhaps I should ask the same question of you?"

"You know who I am. You've been following my friend for days. Either you tell us what you're after, or we'll let the cops find out. They're already on the way. So talk fast and don't even think about driving away. We have your license plate number."

My tough talk had zero effect on the woman. She simply passed a crisp white business card through the window. "My name is Faye Durkin. I'm a senior vice president at Fem-Tex Pharmaceuticals. I would like to speak with Miss Morlock about her hair-growing formula."

"How do you know about that?" DeeDee stepped forward.

"Your physician, Dr. Edmonds, and I have been friends since Yale. He was the one who shared the wonderful news about your discovery."

"Don't they teach doctor-patient confidentiality at Yale?" Oona asked. "Or did Dr. Edmonds just skip all the lectures on medical ethics?"

Faye Durkin kept her eyes glued to DeeDee. "When

Dr. Edmonds mentioned Miss Morlock's visit to his office, he believed he was acting for the greater good," she insisted. "Do you know how many people might benefit from a formula like Miss Morlock's? Are you aware that thousands of women in this city alone suffer from life-altering hairlessness?"

"No, but we know how much cash a cure could make for Fem-Tex Pharmaceuticals," Luz said.

"Hey, wait a second. Didn't Fem-Tex come out with a product a while back that was supposed to treat female baldness?" Oona asked.

"Yes, well, that formula had a few unfortunate flaws," Faye Durkin admitted.

"That's right! I remember! It didn't grow hair, and anyone who tried it came down with projectile diarrhea. I lost a fortune on your stock!" Oona growled.

"I'm sorry to hear that, but I think a girl your age might be a little too young to be playing the stock market, anyway."

"Look, I don't think you realize who you're dealing with, lady," Luz jumped in. "We're not little girls, and we're not idiots. We're New Yorkers. *Native* New Yorkers. You need to start taking us seriously."

"Oh, but I *do* take you seriously," Faye replied as if humoring an irate toddler.

"No, you don't. But you're about to," I told her just as a cop car pulled up, its siren wailing.

"These girls bothering you, ma'am?" inquired one of the two officers in the car.

"Excuse me?" Oona was instantly outraged. "She's the one bothering *us*! We were the ones who dialed 911!"

The cop regarded Oona through narrowed eyes. "You look familiar. I've seen you somewhere before. Wait . . . aren't you that girl who got kicked out of Fat Frankie's? The shoplifter whose photo is up all over Chinatown?"

"No," she said, taking a step backward. I slid an arm around Oona's waist—not to comfort her but to keep her from fleeing before it was necessary.

"You girls looking for trouble? You wanna take a ride down to the station?"

"That won't be necessary, officer," Faye Durkin said sweetly. "These delightful young ladies were just giving me directions to Bloomingdale's."

The policeman looked skeptical, but there was always a chance that one of us was a lawyer's kid. "In that case, ma'am, you have a nice day," he said. "And you girls get to school. If I see you on the streets after eight thirty, I'll arrest you for truancy."

Faye Durkin beamed up at us as the cops drove off. "It looks like I just did you a good turn, ladies. Maybe you'd like to return the favor?"

"Where did the police just go?" Iris had joined the group, but now Luz appeared to be missing.

"Apparently the police won't question a rich blond lady who drives a Mercedes," I sneered.

"You can hardly blame them," said Faye Durkin. "Unlike gangs of teenage hoodlums, wealthy blond women don't tend to be terribly dangerous."

"I don't know about dangerous, but you're definitely irritating," DeeDee said. "There's no hair-growing formula, Ms. Durkin. It was just a school science fair project that got out of control. I couldn't replicate the results if I tried."

"And that would be a very plausible excuse, Miss Morlock, if I hadn't taken the trouble to contact your school. The science fair was months ago. I believe you took home first prize for something called Morlock's Miracle Mixture. It sounds delightful, but I'm afraid it would render too many of Fem-Tex's most profitable products obsolete."

DeeDee could only play dumb for so long. "I worked my butt off making the Miracle Mixture. I spent ages testing it before I entered it in the science fair. I haven't even *started* analyzing the hair formula yet. It's not safe. . . ."

"So there *is* a formula!" Faye Durkin clapped her hands together like a performing seal. "Don't worry, our lawyers will address any safety issues."

"Your *lawyers*?" DeeDee asked. "Don't you employ scientists to test all your new products?"

"Sometimes it's less expensive to face a few lawsuits."

"You're not listening to me!" DeeDee snapped. "I just said the formula could be really dangerous!"

"Oh, but I *am* listening. And I'm prepared to offer you a sum of money substantial enough to soothe any pangs of conscience. . . ."

"Forget it, lady. DeeDee doesn't need your dirty cash. We're all independently wealthy." I winced when Oona said it. The Irregulars didn't need anyone looking too closely at our finances.

"Oh really? And who exactly are *we*?" Faye inquired. "Are you some sort of girl gang?"

"We're just a group of teenage hoodlums who are late for school," I said. "We don't have any more time to talk."

Oona stuck her head inside the car. "Don't follow

DeeDee. Don't contact her. Don't even *think* about her. DeeDee's answer was no, and it's final."

"Let's go," I told the others.

"Wait! Miss Morlock!" Faye called. When there wasn't a response, she cranked her car's engine. But as soon as she stepped on the gas, it was clear that she wasn't going anywhere. All four of the Mercedes's tires were flat.

"Did you slash her tires?" I asked Luz once we were out of sight.

"Who, me?" Luz replied as she groomed her nails with the blade of a Swiss Army knife.

"When did you have time to do it?" Iris asked.

"While you guys were talking to the cops," Luz said.

"That fast!" Iris was impressed.

"Well, don't do it again!" I shouted. "We're down two Irregulars, and you're on probation! We can't have you sent to juvie now."

"Would've been worth it," I heard Luz whisper to Oona.

CHAPTER 18

The Perils of
Puppy Love

erhaps the Irregulars should have given Faye Durkin a cure. Not *the* cure, of course. But in retrospect, it might have been smarter to scoop a little something into a jar and let her figure out that it wasn't capable of growing anything other than mold. There's no doubt in my mind that the moment we told her she *couldn't* have the cure, there was nothing in the world Faye Durkin wanted more.

And I knew *exactly* how she felt. Faye Durkin wasn't the only one who wanted something she couldn't have. Standing in the shadows off Second Avenue that evening, watching the traffic go by, I felt like the butt of some cruel cosmic joke. The villain of a pretty pink romance novel. The subject of an after-school special about the perils of puppy love. But when I spotted Kaspar rushing to meet me in front of the gates of the Marble Cemetery, I couldn't stop my heart from dancing. There were thousands upon thousands of good-looking guys in Manhattan, and only one of them was dating Betty Bent. Yet *that* was the boy I desperately wanted to win. Our brains may enjoy playing tricks on us, but it seems our hearts can be downright cruel.

"Hi, Ananka," Kaspar said.

"Hey," I replied, letting my gaze linger on the handsome face half-hidden by the hood of a black sweatshirt. Looking back, I have a hunch that Kaspar's closet was filled with black hoodies, but that evening I would have sworn he was wearing the one he'd had on the first time that I saw him. Was he sending me some sort of secret message?

I tried to think back. Was it possible that Kaspar had known I was watching the night I'd spotted him painting a giant, threatening squirrel on a downtown wall? Maybe he had seen me, scaling the side of a nearby building using nothing more than a few strands of ivy? Had he finally realized that an outlaw graffiti artist guy like him belonged with a vine-climbing, roof-hopping girl like me?

I didn't have the guts to find out. "Are you ready?" I asked instead.

"You kidding? I've been looking forward to this for months!"

My hands were shaking, and it took longer than usual to pick the lock on the cemetery gates. "I can't believe Betty hasn't taken you down to see the Shadow City yet."

"We were planning to go the next time I was in town, but then she got shipped off to France. When you offered to give me a tour, she made me promise to go without her."

My heart sank a little when I realized Betty wasn't worried. Either she knew Kaspar would never be interested in another girl—or she didn't know me well enough to know that I couldn't be trusted.

"I feel kind of bad," Kaspar continued. "Here we are having fun, and Betty's in Paris, bored out of her mind. I talked to her right before I left to meet you. She still hasn't heard a peep from Kiki."

"What about Madame Beauregard?" I asked. "Any news on that front? Last time Betty texted me, she and Madame were on their way to the Paris branch of the institute."

"Yeah, I guess they spent the day watching little French girls tie scarves in new ways."

"Let's hope the kids banded together and made an escape rope," I said, eager to move the conversation away from Kaspar's girlfriend. "Now grab that snow shovel against the wall. We have to uncover the tomb of Augustus Quackenbush."

I was either shoveling snow or daydreaming about my handsome companion when our unexpected guest arrived. In either case, I failed to hear the gate creak open and the sound of footsteps on the icy path through the cemetery.

"Forget anything?" The voice came from behind us.

My guilty conscience had me on edge. I shrieked and almost fell head-first into the hole that lay open in front of me. When I regained my footing, I wheeled around to find Iris watching the scene with her hands on her hips. She looked like a giant snow cone in her pink jacket and white ski pants and boots. A giant *angry* snow cone.

"Iris!" I grumbled. "What are you doing here?"

"Betty sent me a message. She wanted to make sure you guys had everything you needed to explore the Shadow City tonight. She was surprised that I hadn't heard from you. Since there's so much snow in the cemetery, she figured you'd want to use the passage in my basement."

"I didn't want to bother your parents."

Iris may have been the youngest Irregular, but she wasn't a fool. "You mean the same Martin and Henrietta McLeod who've been excavating a Moche tomb in Peru for the past two months? I'm sure they wouldn't have minded a *bit*."

"I guess I forgot they were out of town." I threatened the little girl's life with my eyes.

"I'm starting to think you should see a doctor," said Iris, ignoring my warning. "You've been forgetting a lot of stuff lately. Like this." She held up a small vial of perfume. "Were you planning to feed the rats tonight?"

There was no clever reply to be made. Iris was right. The tunnels of the Shadow City were home to an army of man-eating rats. Without a few dabs of the Irregulars' rodent-repelling perfume, Kaspar and I could have been a two-course dinner. It had been months since I'd made such a stupid mistake, and I was mortified that I'd screwed up in front of the one person on earth that I truly longed to impress.

"Thanks, Iris." I snatched the bottle out of her hands. "I guess you just saved my butt."

"For the third or fourth time," Iris noted. "You know, since I'm already here, I'm thinking it might be fun to see the Shadow City again. I haven't been down there since winter break. You guys mind if I tag along?" The evil little genius directed the question to Kaspar, not me.

"Sure! The more the merrier!" Kaspar said. "As long as Ananka doesn't mind."

"Mind? Why would I mind? You go ahead and take your first look," I said, handing Kaspar my flashlight. "Just wait for us when you get to the bottom of the stairs."

As soon as Kaspar was underground, I linked arms with Iris so she couldn't attempt an escape. "What have you been hinting at?" I hissed in her ear. "Did Oona say something to you?"

"I don't need Oona to tell me you have it bad for Kaspar," Iris answered. "I was born with two eyes and two ears of my own. What exactly do you think you're doing, Ananka?"

"Betty asked me to keep Kaspar entertained while she's gone," I said. "So that's what I'm doing."

"You lied to us today at the park."

"I didn't *lie*. I said I was busy! What's dishonest about that?"

Iris gave me the sort of look it took my mother years to perfect. Fifty percent disappointment, thirty percent exasperation, and twenty percent disgust. "Ananka, nobody's gonna blame you for having a crush on Kaspar. *All* of us have crushes on Kaspar. He's the coolest guy in New York! But promise me you're not going to do anything stupid."

"You know what would really be stupid?" I sneered. "Taking advice from a twelve-year-old. Either go home or mind your own business, munchkin."

I had imagined guiding Kaspar through the underworld that Kiki Strike and I had discovered, showing him the abandoned gambling parlors, opium dens, and dance halls that were built by criminals two hundred years before we were born. I'd introduce him to the skeleton of Percy Leake III and impress him with my knowledge of nineteenth-century river pirates, antique bedpans, and ferocious rodents. Kaspar would be so astonished by my fearlessness and brilliance that he would fall head over heels in love with me. We'd gently break the news to Betty when she returned, only to discover that she'd found a new beau on her trip to France. Then we would all live happily ever after.

But of course, Iris stuck to me like chewing gum to a sneaker. When she wasn't asking ridiculous questions (*What do you think those pirates would have done to people who betrayed them?*), she was praising Betty (*Isn't she just the greatest? I think she may be the nicest, most loyal girl I've ever met!*). And when she wasn't talking about Betty, she was regaling Kaspar with tales of her parents' amazing adventures. (*They once found the tomb of a noble lady who'd been executed and buried without her head. That was the price you paid back then for making the moves on another woman's husband.*) Suffice it to say, I barely got a word in edgewise.

"Look, it's Angus McSwegan! We're already under my house!" Iris exclaimed as we arrived at a room occupied by the century-old remains of a bootlegger. "You guys want to come up and get some dinner? My nanny is making her meat loaf tonight. Luz says it's even better than Fat Frankie's."

My stomach betrayed me by rumbling at the mention of food. I'd been too excited to eat before I left for the cemetery. And that brat Iris *knew* how much I loved Fat Frankie's meat loaf.

"Kaspar?" There was no point in continuing our trek through the tunnels. "You hungry?"

"I'm starving!" he replied with a dazzling smile. The boy was so darn easy to love.

We popped our heads out of the hidden exit in Iris's basement to find the smell of meat loaf already in the air. But Iris's nanny hadn't cooked it. Oona was sitting at the table upstairs with a packet of little red stickers in her hand and a map of New York spread out in front of her. Luz and DeeDee puttered about by the oven, wearing novelty aprons that (according to Iris) said "Kiss the Cook" in ancient Sumerian.

The Irregulars usually steered clear of Iris's kitchen. Kiki called it the world's most dangerous spice cabinet. All four walls were lined with shelves, and each shelf held jars, Baggies, and bottles of herbs and seasonings from around the world. Few of the packages were labeled, however, and Iris was not a careful cook. DeeDee had once spent six hours in the bathroom after Iris served her a bowl of chili that she'd accidentally prepared using *bhut jolokia,* a pepper so hot that some villages in India use it as elephant repellant.

"What's going on here?" I demanded.

"You wanted to meet at Iris's to work on the map, *remember?*" Oona replied, glancing over at Kaspar. "Something make you forget your own orders, Fishbein?"

"Iris told us you wanted meat loaf for dinner," DeeDee added. "We followed her nanny's recipe, but I have no idea if it's done. Is it supposed to look like a brick?"

"Let me take a peek." Kaspar bent down to peer

through the window on the oven door. "I happen to be the world's foremost expert on meat loaf."

"They don't know what you've been doing," Iris whispered behind me. "But this can become an intervention at any moment."

"I'll be right back," I told the three oblivious girls. "Iris, come with me."

We stood in the hallway beneath the McLeods' gruesome collection of ceremonial masks. Angry gods, demons, and devils leered down at us. I'm sure my face at that moment was far more terrifying.

"Are you familiar with the term *insubordination*?" I growled.

"Are you saying that I haven't been submitting to your authority?" Iris responded, glaring back at me. She tried to cross her arms, but the padding of her pink down coat made it impossible. They kept slipping back to her sides.

"Do you know what happens to soldiers who refuse to obey orders in times of war?"

"Do you know what happens to soldiers who let terrible things happen and then claim they were 'just following orders'? It's called the Nuremburg defense. The Nazis were big fans of it and—"

"You've got a lot of nerve comparing a Jewish girl to the *Nazis*, Iris."

"And *that's* what's called a straw man argument," Iris observed. "Instead of addressing the real issue, you've chosen to invent an argument that you believe will be easier to win."

"I don't care what I'm doing or what it's called!" I shouted, then quickly lowered my voice. "Why are you trying to humiliate me, you little turd? I'm supposed to be in charge!"

"I'm not trying to hurt you. I'm trying to help you!" Iris insisted. "And I'm *trying* to save the Irregulars!"

The note of desperation in the smaller girl's voice caught me off guard. Iris wasn't acting out of spite. She really believed she was doing the right thing.

"What do you mean?" I asked.

"Don't you see what's going to happen if you keep throwing yourself at Kaspar? He's going to tell you that he likes Betty, not you. He'll be nice about it. He might not even say anything to Betty. But you'll be embarrassed, and Betty will find out somehow, and then she'll never trust you again. And Kiki will be mad that you've been acting so stupid when she left you in charge. Everyone will end up taking sides, and the Irregulars will break up. It might not happen overnight. But believe me, Ananka, it *will* happen."

"How would *you* know?" I demanded.

"It's obvious! It would be obvious to you, too, if you were thinking clearly right now!"

"I'm thinking clearly enough to know I don't need a lecture from a giant pink snow cone." I gave her my dirtiest look before I spun around. "Enjoy your meat loaf, Iris. I'm going home. And I expect that map to be finished in the morning."

"What should I tell the others?" Iris asked, hurrying after me as I stomped down the hall. "They think *you* called the meeting!"

"Tell them whatever you want," I said, opening the front door. "I don't care what any of you think anymore."

"Please don't go—" The slam cut her off.

THE FISHBEIN GUIDE TO . . . THE BEAUTY OF SCARVES

The designer Coco Chanel is often quoted as saying, "A girl should be two things: classy and fabulous." In private, she would add a third. *Prepared*. That's why the grande dame always took a scarf with her wherever she went. Like all French ladies, she knew that there's no more versatile item of clothing. A simple silk scarf can pull any outfit together—or give it a certain je ne sais quoi.

But I'll leave the fashion tips to Coco. *La mode* has never been the *Fishbein* focus. So let's take a moment to discuss the more practical side of scarves. . . .

Secret Maps and Messages
During World War II, scarves were an essential part of many spies' toolkits. Maps and messages were often printed on silk, which was extremely lightweight, compact, waterproof, and durable. But silk's biggest advantage over paper is the fact that it's difficult to detect when hidden on the body. Paper is not only bulky, it would rustle if a spy were frisked by enemy agents.

A Quick Disguise
We all know how important a quick, easy disguise can be. Centuries of outlaws have used scarves (sometimes called cravats or bandannas) to conceal their features. Unless you're robbing banks or slinking past security cameras, you may not need to cover most of your face. Sometimes disguising your appearance can be as simple as covering your most distinguishing feature—your hair.

An Emergency Change of Clothing
The best adventures are often the messiest, so you'll want to take a change of clothes. But you might not get very far if you're lugging a giant suitcase. I recommend carrying a cute scarf, instead. A few quick twists, and a scarf can become a halter top, a belt, a hair bow, or a turban. Larger scarves make excellent sarongs, which are ideal for seaside adventures.

Bandages, Tourniquets, Restraints, and Blindfolds
These are four things every adventurer should have on hand. A scarf can serve all four purposes, though not at the very same time.

A Flexible Weapon

A scarf may even be able to help you fend off an attacker. (Long, rectangular scarves suit this purpose best.) Simply wrap an end around each hand and pull the scarf taut. The strip of fabric can be used to deflect blows and jabs. It can also be used to strangle an attacker if the situation becomes truly dire.

CHAPTER 19

Le Traître

PARIS: WEDNESDAY, FEBRUARY 18

i have nothing to say in my own defense. After writing
that last chapter, even *I'm* disgusted with Ananka
Fishbein. So let's leave her alone to wrestle with her filthy
little conscience and head back to Paris for a while. I
wish I could promise a relaxing holiday, but while I was
plotting to steal Kaspar's heart, another traitor was at
work in the City of Light.

Kiki sat on the rough wood floor of the bell tower,
waiting for Etienne to arrive with word from the Irregulars. At least twelve hours had passed since she'd made
the deal with Sidonia that morning. In another twelve,
she would have to deliver the cure—or Verushka would
pay with her life. Etienne had promised to stop by after
the ball his mother had forced him to attend. But Kiki
didn't need a watch to know that he was running late.
He had warned her that his mother might keep him at
the party past ten. Kiki told herself that she needed to be
patient. But she couldn't bear the thought that somewhere

in the city below, in a ballroom filled with the fanciest of French people, Etienne might still be dancing with Sidonia Galatzina.

Kiki could have fled the tower at any time. Tucked away between two loose stones was a key Etienne had made for the door. But it was only to be used as a last resort. So Kiki studied the darkness, listened to the patter of rat feet, and hoped her friend hadn't succumbed to her cousin's charms. He wouldn't have been the first young man to be dazzled by the dark-haired princess. Back in New York, Sidonia had often allowed a small pack of lovestruck suitors to follow a few paces behind her. They kept her supplied with nonfat lattes and presented their credit cards whenever Sidonia left a store with a trinket or two that she hadn't bothered to purchase.

Kiki pushed those memories out of her head and tried to think of more pleasant things. So she began making a mental tally of all the royal heirs who had been murdered by family members. It was a very long list, and she was nowhere near finished when she leaped to her feet and pressed one ear to a boarded-up window.

Few noises reached the top of her tower, but ten police cars with sirens wailing tend to make quite a racket. Instinct told Kiki that someone had come to her rescue. And she couldn't allow that to happen. She unlocked the door and was down the stairs in time to see Livia's guard making a run for it. As he sprinted down the dark nave toward the apse of the ancient church, four men with guns and flashlights stayed hot on his heels.

Taking advantage of the diversion, Kiki slid along the wall of the church's western aisle and ducked behind a tomb that was topped with a sculpture of a roly-poly noble-man dressed in the metal suit of a medieval knight. Lying on one side, with his head propped up on one hand, he looked a lot like an armadillo watching TV.

Standing on tiptoe, Kiki peeked over the sculpture's bulging flank. I know better than anyone how hard it is to surprise her. So I would have given just about anything to see Kiki's face when she saw Marcel Roche stroll into the church with a SWAT team behind him.

"The girl is upstairs in the tower," Marcel told the men in French. Gone was the scruffy blond oaf Kiki had met in the tower. Just as she'd suspected, that version of Marcel had been little more than an act. But somehow the bold young man who'd replaced him didn't seem any more genuine.

A half-dozen police officers charged up the stairs with weapons drawn. Kiki heard the wood splinter as they kicked in the door at the top. Not a minute later, the men returned empty-handed.

"There's no one inside the tower," one of the officers reported.

Shaken by the announcement, Marcel's façade began to crack.

"I'm not surprised." A distinguished-looking gentle-man had arrived in the church. He wore his navy suit like a uniform, and his black hair was cut as short as a sol-dier's. Kiki could see he was the sort of man who needed the world to acknowledge his authority. "Did you find any evidence that the tower has been recently occupied?" he asked the officers.

"We found this, sir." One of the officers held up a frilly pink dress and a matching hair bow.

The man took the dress from the officer and rubbed the fabric between his fingers. "Polyester," he announced before he turned to face Marcel. "You told me the girl was someone important."

"She is!" Marcel insisted. "What difference does a dress make? She was important enough to kidnap! And she looks just like that princess who's been in the papers."

"Whoever the girl was, she appears to be gone. I believe you've been fooled, Marcel. Some neighborhood child has played a prank on you."

"But the guard!" Marcel protested.

"Ah yes, the guard—if that's really what he is. I suspect he may be nothing more than a harmless old drunk seeking shelter from the cold. Still, we will hold him on trespassing charges. If we cannot elicit a confession, we will not be able to keep the man in custody."

"Papa," Marcel tried. "We can't wait for the guard to be questioned. We can't wait another moment. Terrible things have been happening in the ossuary. For once, please listen to me!"

Papa? Kiki crouched down behind the tomb when she saw the older man take his son by the elbow and guide the boy toward the church's western aisle for what he thought was a private chat. Once he was certain that no one was listening, the man's tone turned vicious.

"Listen to what, Marcel? I have heard enough of your crazed ramblings for one day. Princesses locked in bell towers? A secret group that builds underground cinemas?

Sinister forces at work in the catacombs? They're nothing but the fantasies of a silly little boy. You've spent months trying to convince me that the Darkness Dwellers are real. Then you said you were *investigating* some bone thefts. And now you change your tune and insist that worse crimes are being committed in the ossuary—right under my nose."

"Someone was attacked! Two girls could be dead! I'm trying to help, Papa!"

"By making me look like an idiot? You say you would like to join the police? This is no way to prove that you deserve such an honor! My men respect me and do as they are told. Those who let their imaginations run wild are dismissed. You're just like your mother, Marcel. Your mind is infected by fancy."

"Everything I've told you is true! I spoke to the leader of the Darkness Dwellers last night! Phlegyas warned me to stay out of the ossuary. He thinks strange rites are being performed there. And *you* were the one who told me about the two girls who vanished in that same part of the catacombs!"

"Yes, and as always, there is a perfectly sensible explanation. The girls were foolish enough to break the law, and they were foolish enough to get lost. We will find them or their bodies eventually."

"What if you're wrong, Papa? What if more people vanish in the ossuary?"

"That portion of the tunnels will be closed to the public for the next three weeks. I've been informed that there's a rather unfortunate bug problem."

"You know that won't keep people out! You can't depend on a group of vigilantes to protect the catacombs!"

Marcel's father let his eyes tour the surroundings, ensuring that no one had heard Marcel's outburst. Then he took a step forward and hissed at his son. "I am Philip Roche, the head of Catacomb Patrol. I alone protect the tunnels! I deal with facts, not fantasies! And there is not one scrap of evidence that you haven't lost your mind. You said there was a girl in this church who would be able to support your story. For once I believed you, and now I look like a fool."

"Then take Etienne in for questioning!" Marcel urged. "Threaten to arrest him, and he will convince you this isn't a fantasy!"

"How many times must I tell you, Marcel? That is not a solution! Your friend comes from a powerful family. His father is the Duc de Lutèce! I cannot question Etienne about a group of people who do not exist. His parents could arrange to have me dismissed from the force. I'm afraid that this has all been a terrible disappointment, Marcel. Let's not prolong the embarrassment. *Allons-y!*" he shouted out to his men.

"But Papa!" Marcel begged.

"Tais-toi!" his father barked, his voice echoing down the aisle. "You say you want to be like me? Then act like a man and take responsibility for your failures!"

The police officers marched out of the building, leaving Marcel all alone. Moonbeams pierced the stained-glass windows and formed puddles of heavenly blue light on the floor of the nave. But Marcel kept to the gloom of the aisle. Sitting on the edge of the nobleman's tomb, his shoulders were hunched and his head hung in shame. Kiki suspected it wasn't the first time that the boy had tried and failed to please his father. But in Kiki's opinion, growing up with a tyrant was no excuse for turning into a snake. Etienne had shown Marcel nothing but kindness, and the boy had repaid him with treachery.

If a close friend or a family member has ever tried to kill you, then loyalty is probably one of the traits you prize most in people. Kiki could be a bit fanatical on that particular subject. She seethed whenever she saw anyone stabbed in the back. Once, after a meeting, the Irregulars had attempted to watch *The Count of Monte Cristo*. The story of the hero's betrayal left Kiki so furious that she'd stormed out of her very own house.

While Marcel sat on the edge of the tomb, it took every ounce of restraint that Kiki could muster to remain hidden behind it. She would have loved to show the boy how she dealt with traitors. But Verushka Kozlova's life expectancy had just been dramatically reduced. The guard the police had taken into custody worked for Livia Galatzina. As soon as he was able to make a phone call from the station, Kiki's beloved guardian would be dead.

She waited, desperate for a chance to slip outside unseen, but unlike Kiki, Marcel wasn't in any hurry to leave. He watched the altar as if awaiting further instructions. He didn't even turn when the door creaked open behind him.

The moonlight followed Etienne through the entrance. Dressed in a classic tuxedo and black overcoat, he wore formal attire as effortlessly as he would a pair of jeans. On his way to the tower, he caught sight of the church's other visitor. "Marcel? I thought I told you we wouldn't be working tonight."

"Your friend is gone," Marcel announced flatly.

"Gone?" Etienne repeated, his dark brows knitting. "What do you mean, she's *gone*?"

Kiki's ghostly white face rose from behind the nobleman's tomb. "He means that I wasn't twiddling my thumbs in the tower when he showed up here with the police," she announced in French.

Marcel gasped. Regardless of the news, Etienne couldn't help but grin when he laid eyes on Kiki. "The police?"

"That's right. Marcel brought his father here to meet me."

Marcel sprang to his feet. "You've been in the church the whole time?"

"Yes, and I heard every word that you said."

"Then why didn't you tell my father I was speaking the truth!"

"I don't help traitors," Kiki spat before turning to Etienne. "Marcel has been using you. He doesn't give a crap about joining the Darkness Dwellers. He wants to be a policeman instead."

"Marcel? A policeman?" Etienne sputtered.

"He thought he could impress *papa* by proving the Darkness Dwellers exist. When that didn't pan out, he told his father about the attack in the ossuary. Marcel wanted me to back up his story, but unfortunately, I wasn't available. So he told his father to arrest you."

"Is this true, Marcel?" Etienne demanded. "You wanted to have me *arrested*?"

"No! I mean yes—but only because you won't listen to reason, Etienne. The police need to know what's going on in the tunnels."

"Excuses, excuses," Kiki said. "Be a man and take responsibility for your failures."

"You agent provocateur!" Marcel snarled as he moved toward Kiki. "I'm taking you to my father right now. You're going to tell him everything you know, or I'll convince him you're dangerous and have him lock you away."

When Marcel grabbed for Kiki's arm, she latched on to his wrist, spun the large boy around, and flipped him over her shoulder. His landing was hard enough to crack two of the tiles beneath his rump.

"You're right about one thing. I *am* dangerous," Kiki announced. "Here's some advice for you. Your father is a jerk. You'll never impress him. Stop trying or you'll end up even worse than he is. Now, if you'll excuse me, I need to clean up the mess you've just made."

☆ ☆ ☆

Kiki says that Paris is breathtaking in the early hours of the morning. The traffic quiets, and the tourists are tucked away in their beds. Golden lights transform ordinary buildings into fairytale castles. The Île-de-France becomes an enchanted island, and the bridges over the Seine seem like gateways to glittering realms. But that morning Kiki couldn't be charmed. She knew an evil queen was slumbering somewhere in the magical kingdom. There were only a few hours left before daylight roused her. And when the queen awoke, Verushka Kozlova would die.

Kiki started running even before she'd settled on a direction. She was almost at the river when she heard someone sprinting down the street behind her. She wheeled around, fists clenched and ready to fight.

"Don't punch me! I believe you!" Etienne kept his voice low. "I know you're in trouble and I want to help. But first, can you please—*please*—tell me who you really are?"

It was a perfectly reasonable question, but it happened to be one that Kiki rarely answered. The Irregulars had known her for years before any of us were trusted with the truth. And yet she decided to share her secret with a French boy whom she'd fancied for less than a week. A crush, it seems, can make even Kiki Strike reckless.

"I am Katarina, Princess of Pokrovia. But my friends call me Kiki Strike."

"That's what I thought," Etienne said. "Now, where are we going?"

THE FISHBEIN GUIDE TO . . . THE RENDEZVOUS

And now we must address a subject that even *I* am still trying to master: How to behave at a rendezvous. (Some people would call these arranged meetings "dates." Others prefer the term "hanging out." But a rendezvous seems much more mysterious, don't you think?)

When you're heading off to meet the person you've had your eye on . . .

Don't Wear a Disguise

Do you find yourself changing into someone you barely recognize the second the person you like struts into the room? Do you act, speak, or eat differently than you usually would? If so . . . STOP IT RIGHT NOW! What's the point? Are you worried you won't be appreciated for who you really are? Maybe you will be—maybe you won't. But no one can wear a disguise forever. Just be the wisecracking, giant-squid-loving, or cheeseburger-wolfing person you are.

Bring Your Wallet, Your Brain, and Your Self-Respect

There is one person on Earth upon whom you can *always* rely. Yourself. Be grateful when others show generosity toward you, but always be prepared to pay your own way, pack your own parachute, or change your own flat tires. Helplessness and greed are not attractive qualities.

Show and Accept Common Courtesy
I once watched a woman freak out in the lobby of a Manhattan office building because a gentleman had held a door open for her. From what I gathered, she seemed to find the gesture old-fashioned and insulting. This is insane. We should *all* open more doors, offer more subway seats, and treat the people we like to a little escargot now and then.

Don't Push It
It doesn't matter how fabulous you are, you're going to have crushes on people who will never like you back. Have a little cry (in private), then move on. Do not argue, plead, or stalk. There's someone better just around the bend.

CHAPTER 20

The Most
Dangerous Game

The sun was inching its way over the horizon. Kiki stood on the quay with the inky black waters of the Seine flowing below, her eyes locked with those of a boy she barely knew. A boy who suddenly possessed the secret she'd once have done almost anything to hide. Perhaps you're thinking that it all sounds quite romantic. Combine sunrise, secrets, and the Seine and you'll probably end up with the world's most powerful love potion. But Kiki wasn't in the mood to swoon. She knew that dawn would turn deadly if she didn't act fast. And it wasn't the intensity of Etienne's gaze that kept her from rushing to Verushka's rescue. Kiki would have left the handsome boy behind in her dust if she'd had any clue where her guardian was being held.

"Your friend screwed everything up," she told Etienne, speaking English without realizing it. "The person I love most in the world may end up dead."

"I'll help you save him," Etienne promised in a flaw-less American accent.

"It's a *her,*" Kiki corrected.

"Thank goodness for that," Etienne said. "But you still haven't told me where we're going."

"We?" Kiki snorted. "*We* aren't going *anywhere,* Eti-enne. I should never have gotten you involved in the first place."

"In that case, I hope you're prepared to travel by foot. The subway doesn't run at this time of night," Etienne informed her. "And I haven't seen any cabs. But my driver can get here in ninety seconds. We'll take you wherever you need to go."

"Is your driver trustworthy?" Kiki asked. "Forgive the question, but you do have rather poor taste in friends."

"He's been with my family for years. He's as loyal to us as we are to him," Etienne said. "Shall I make the call?"

Kiki took a breath, rolled her eyes toward the heavens, and signaled her reluctant approval with a nod.

"How did you manage to figure out who I am?" she asked when Etienne was off the phone and his car was on its way.

"I spent half the night dancing with a girl disguised as you. Apparently no one else in Paris recognizes a wig and contact lenses when they see them."

"She's my cousin. Her real name is Sidonia Galatzina. She's trying to steal the throne of Pokrovia."

"I suspected as much," Etienne replied. "My own family has been marrying, murdering, and cheating each other for five hundred years. Ordinary blood may be thicker than water, but blue blood seems to be thinner than mist."

"So you figured out what Sidonia was up to, and you kept on dancing? You must have been enjoying yourself." A tinge of jealousy had crept into Kiki's voice. "I was beginning to worry that you might stand me up."

"Your cousin is a wonderful dancer and an *atrocious* human being," Etienne observed. "She refused to speak to anyone without a title, she called all the other girls 'monkeys in gowns,' and she tossed a glass of champagne in a waiter's face. I suppose I should feel flattered that someone with such high standards took a shine to me. Unfortunately, Sidonia is *much* too evil for my taste. I would have fled for my life hours ago if it hadn't been for you."

"For *me*?" Kiki arched an eyebrow. The pale, serious boy stared back at her, and Kiki could see why Sidonia had fallen for him.

"I thought you might like to know where your imposter is staying." Etienne broke into a mischievous grin. "So I offered to escort her home."

"And?" Despite the circumstances, Kiki couldn't help but laugh.

"Room 712 of the Prince Albert Hotel. Which is really quite convenient, since your friend Betty Bent happens to be staying on the same floor. She sent me a message a few hours before I left for the party. She's here in Paris, and she has the cure."

"Ananka chose *Betty* to deliver the cure?" Kiki frowned. "That's rather unfortunate. Betty certainly has her talents, but I would have picked Oona Wong for this mission. She's got a wicked roundhouse kick. Or Luz Lopez. Not the best kicker, but she's as mean as a snake."

"Would you be planning to do much kicking tonight?" Etienne inquired as his driver pulled the family car to the curb.

"Where I'm going?" Kiki smirked. "I plan to do as much kicking as possible."

"And where exactly is that? You still haven't told me," Etienne said, opening the car door for his female companion.

"I didn't know until now." Kiki slid into the backseat. "*Bonsoir,* monsieur," she said to the driver. "The Prince Albert Hotel, *s'il vous plaît.*"

"Thank you for getting here so quickly, Jacques," Etienne added. He turned to Kiki. "Are we going to pick up the cure?"

"The cure's useless right now, and I'd rather not have to baby-sit Betty. Would you mind texting her so she knows that the plan is on hold? Don't bother telling Betty this next part, but I'm going to kidnap Sidonia. It's the only way I can keep her mother from killing the woman who raised me."

"*We're* going to kidnap Sidonia," Etienne corrected. "I'm afraid you're stuck with me."

"I thought you said you were a loner," Kiki muttered.

"People change," Etienne replied. "I've come to enjoy your company. And I must repay you for exposing Marcel's treachery."

"So you really never suspected Marcel was a traitor?"

"Not for a moment," Etienne admitted. "I thought he was trying to rebel against his father, not win the man's favor. But it does explain Marcel's behavior at the party in the catacombs last night. I couldn't understand why he kept trying to convince me that the Darkness Dwellers shouldn't be trusted to keep the ossuary safe."

"You know, maybe Marcel had a point," Kiki said. "If people are disappearing in the ossuary, maybe the police *should* get involved."

"It wouldn't do much good. The police don't know the tunnels as well as the Darkness Dwellers. There are passages Marcel's father and his men have never even *seen*. And let's not forget that Philip Roche refuses to believe that the Darkness Dwellers exist. He'll fire any officer who even hints that they might. So why would Roche ever believe there might be *real* criminals at work in the catacombs?"

"I don't understand why the man's so stubborn," Kiki said.

"Because Philip Roche doesn't want people to think that the police aren't in complete control of the catacombs. If it ever came to light that some secret organization had free run of the place, it could cause mass panic. The city of Paris sits on top of the tunnels. A few well-placed explosives, and hundreds of thousands could die. Whoever controls the catacombs controls Paris. The Darkness Dwellers aren't dangerous—but they could be."

"Sounds familiar," Kiki said.

"You've said that before," Etienne observed. "Why does all of this sound so familiar to you?"

"Long story," Kiki said. "Now, please lend me your coat."

Wherever you go, you'll find certain individuals who think they'll look like the biggest fish around if they treat other people like pond scum. These poor, misguided ladies and gentlemen terrorize waiters, scream at their secretaries, and belittle anyone they believe is beneath them. The scientific term for such people is *jerks,* and I would imagine that most hotel employees are quite familiar with the species. But I doubt the desk clerk at the Prince Albert Hotel had ever encountered a specimen quite like the one that was heading his way.

"I can't *believe* you spilled wine all over my dress, you buffoon!" Kiki loudly scolded her escort as they made their way across the lobby. "Do you have any idea how many Pokrovian peasants it took to stitch all those beads? Do you know how hard it is to find bead-stitching peasants these days?"

"Key!" she ordered in French when they reached the front desk.

"Princess!" The clerk looked flustered. "I was certain I saw you go up to your room hours ago."

"You've been spying on me?" Kiki snarled in a perfect impersonation of her unpleasant cousin. "Who do you think you are? Give me my key before I have you fired."

"Yes, Princess. You must mean the spare key? I believe you already have the original. That's why I thought . . ."

"I'll take as many keys as I like. Why am I even talking to you? Can't you see that I'm wearing a man's overcoat? I need to change my dress. *Now!*" She slammed her fist on the desk for emphasis.

"Yes, Princess," the man said, nervously sliding a key

across the counter. He jerked his hand back, as if the girl might bite his fingers.

As soon as they were in the elevator, Kiki returned Etienne's coat.

"Nicely done," the boy remarked.

"The show has only started," Kiki said. "Prepare to be dazzled."

When the duo reached Sidonia's room, Kiki silently slid the key into the lock and opened the door. The chamber was dark, but they could discern a human form tucked beneath the sheets.

"Rise and shine, Princess," Kiki sang softly, clamping one hand over her cousin's mouth as she switched on the bedside lamp.

Sidonia's eyes were blinded by the light. Her arms waved uselessly in the air, and her scream never made it out of her mouth.

"It's probably in your best interest to shut up," Kiki informed her. "Unless you can explain to the police why there are suddenly two Princess Katarinas. All they'd need is a blood test to know which one is real—and which is the imposter."

Sidonia glared back at Kiki, but she stopped attempting to scream.

"You are in *big* trouble," growled Sidonia. "When my mother finds out you're here, she'll shoot Verushka herself."

"That's why we're not staying," Kiki stated. "Get dressed. We're going to take a little ride."

Sidonia's lip curled into a snarl. "I'm not going anywhere, elf—and unless you have a weapon you'd like to show me, you can't make me."

"Wrong again. You're still half asleep, and you're not thinking straight. Here's how it's going to work, Sidonia. If you give us any trouble while we're in this hotel, I'll call the police and have your butt shipped to jail. You give us any trouble once we're *out* of the hotel, and my fist will do things to your pretty face that you never thought possible. Understand?"

Sidonia bared her perfect teeth at Kiki, but she slid out of bed and marched over to the room's massive closet.

"Where are we going?" she demanded. "I need to choose the appropriate attire."

"Just wear something warm and waterproof," Kiki said, winking at Etienne. "And when you're done, pick out something cute for me. And make sure it's black, would you?"

"What are you going to do in *there*?" Sidonia growled as Kiki strolled toward the bathroom.

"What do you think? I'm going to freshen up. You'd better be on your best behavior while I'm gone. Etienne doesn't like you much, either," Kiki said as she closed the door.

"I can't believe you chose *her*," she heard Sidonia whine. "Are you *blind*?"

Once the shower was running, Kiki couldn't make out another word. But she didn't rush, and she didn't worry. There weren't many people she would have trusted to guard Sidonia for so long. And even fewer for whom she'd have bothered to shower.

THE FISHBEIN GUIDE TO . . . THE SPORTING LIFE

As you may have guessed, I'm not the most naturally gifted athlete. Any sport involving a ball is bound to leave me bored or injured. But I do believe that every twenty-first-century lady or gentleman should try to pursue the sporting life. Competition is healthy. Fresh air and exercise are even healthier. And fortunately for me, there are many "sports" that don't require extreme height or huge muscles. A few can even teach you valuable skills.

Clay Pigeon Shooting

I would never dream of shooting a real pigeon. But clay targets are fair game. This sport will train you to have a sharp eye, steely nerves, and a steady hand. It also lets you destroy things, which is always great fun. The downsides? It's expensive, somewhat dangerous, and your family might not be fond of firearms.

Archery

A great alternative to clay pigeon shooting for people who don't like guns. Not only will you improve your focus and concentration while learning a bit about physics, but you'll also look super-cool.

Animal Tracking

This is more of an art than a sport. But you can practice it (for free) in almost any environment, and the skills it will teach you could one day mean the difference between life and death. You'll learn patience, observation, stealth—and the ability to tell fresh wolf dung from two-week-old bear droppings.

Martial Arts

Perhaps you have no desire to compete in a ring—or register your fists as lethal weapons. That's fine. Focus on improving your strength and mental discipline instead. And rest assured knowing that, should you ever find yourself under attack, you'll be able to kick some serious butt.

Poker

Card games don't qualify as sports, of course. But poker players know how to read other people. They also tend to be good with numbers, capable of keeping their emotions under control at all times, and able to make a quick buck when they're on the lam.

Track and Field
If you can't beat them, outrun them.

Fencing
You can now practice this formerly deadly sport without fear of mortal wounds. But if you can get your hands on a sword, your skills are bound to prove dangerous.

Chapter 21

The Bait Bites Back

When the telephone in Betty Bent's room rang at six thirty a.m., she answered it instantly. She had been up most of the night, staring at a little jar labeled LOTS O' LOCKS and waiting for instructions from Kiki Strike. Just before dawn, Betty had briefly dozed off, only to be woken by the sound of hushed voices in the hallway outside her room. She thought she heard someone whisper the name "Katarina," but the corridor was empty when Betty peeked out the door. She picked up her cell phone to get a sense of the time and noticed the message light blinking. A cryptic e-mail had arrived from Kiki's French friend. The cure was no longer needed. Kiki was free, and her plans had changed.

The news was a bitter disappointment. After the frenzy to cook up the hair-growing formula—and after all the dire warnings about Betty's employer—it appeared that the most excitement France had to offer was the opportunity to judge a scarf-tying competition at L'Institut

Beauregard. Betty braced herself for another dull day and answered the ringing telephone.

"Good morning, Miss Bent." The early-morning caller was Amelia Beauregard. "I see you're an early riser. Most teenage girls are such slothful creatures. I'm delighted to discover that my assistant is not one of them. You and I have plenty of work to do today, so we must begin *tout de suite*. I have invited a gentleman to join us for breakfast. We will meet you downstairs at L'Imperatrice in forty-five minutes. Does that give you sufficient time to prepare yourself?"

"Yes, Madame Beauregard," Betty said.

"Excellent. Please wear something fetching but age appropriate, if you don't mind. And no high heels, my dear. You shall be walking a great deal this afternoon."

In every great city there are restaurants designed to intimidate anyone who wasn't born into royalty, celebrity, or an organized crime family. L'Imperatrice, the opulent dining establishment at the Prince Albert Hotel, is one such venue. The main room is decorated in shades of ivory, gold, and gray—colors adored by the same French royal family that later wound up getting the axe. Potted palm trees shade L'Imperatrice's diners, a magnificent chandelier sparkles overhead, and crystal glasses are filled with water from the purest alpine springs. You might spot a supermodel picking at her lunch while she flirts with the President of France—and conclude that L'Imperatrice is no place for mere mortals. But the truth is, it's all just for show. The food on the plates may cost more than most

Parisians earn in a month, but it will eventually reach the same sewer pipes as a four-euro Happy Meal. The crowd may seem impossibly refined, but most can trace their fortunes to dumb luck or dirty deeds. So, if you're ever in the mood for some overpriced French food, pull out a chair at L'Imperatrice and give the waiter your order. Don't ruin your appetite worrying that you might not fit in. Just chew with your mouth closed and follow this advice from the Irregulars' master of disguise: *No matter where you are, the best way to look like you belong is to refuse to believe that you don't.*

Betty Bent scanned the restaurant. Seated beneath a palm tree were Amelia Beauregard and a mustachioed man in a dark gray suit. Betty wove through the tables toward the incongruous pair. She swerved to let a waiter pass, and her handbag thumped another guest's shoulder.

"I'm so sorry!" she exclaimed.

The man swiveled around to give Betty a thorough once-over. His black hair was slicked back, and the fumes of his cologne could have overpowered an ox. "Yes, you are," Sergei Molotov said with a sneer.

He hadn't recognized her. Nor had his heavily made-up companion.

"Where *is* Sidonia?" Livia Galatzina sighed. "She promised she would be down at seven. We have another fitting scheduled for half past eight. Perhaps you could telephone her room and remind her?"

"Yes, Your Highness." Sergei tapped a number into his cell phone.

"Outside the restaurant!" Livia commanded.

"Of course, Your Highness." Sergei rose from his chair

and almost bumped into Betty, who remained frozen behind him. "Are you still here? Move along, peasant."

Betty would have tiptoed out of the restaurant to make a call of her own, but Amelia Beauregard had already laid eyes on her. The mustachioed man jumped up as Betty approached the table and pulled out a chair.

"Miss Bent, please stop staring at the former queen of Pokrovia," Madame Beauregard ordered as Betty took a seat.

"Was I staring?" Betty had tried not to be too obvious.

"Yes, you were making quite a fool of yourself. Whenever you're with me, you will be traveling in rarified circles. Please do not embarrass me by behaving like a rube."

"Have you met Queen Livia, Madame Beauregard?" the mustachioed man inquired politely, clearly trying to shift the attention away from Betty.

"Oh yes, she's a lovely woman. Her daughter was once a star pupil of mine," Amelia Beauregard replied. "A truly gifted girl, one of the lucky few who are born with natural grace and charm. She graduated with top honors in a single semester. Miss Bent, may I ask why you're smirking? Is there something that you find amusing?"

"No, Madame," Betty assured her.

"Good. Shall we get to work? Miss Bent?"

Betty wasn't listening. Sergei Molotov had bolted back into the restaurant, dodging waiters and sideswiping tables. When he reached Livia, he bent down and whispered something in her ear. Whatever it was, the effect was immediate. Livia leaped up, knocking her chair over and spilling orange juice across the table.

"Miss Bent!" Amelia Beauregard hissed. "May I remind

you that you're here on official business. You are *not* in Paris to ogle royalty!"

In an instant, Livia and Sergei were gone, and two waiters were removing all evidence of their meal. Everyone else in the restaurant was whispering, trying to guess what had caused all the commotion.

"Please excuse me," Betty said. "I must make a telephone call." Whatever had just happened, Kiki Strike was most likely involved.

"You are *not* excused, Miss Bent," Madame Beauregard announced. "If you take a single step out of this restaurant, I will have you booked on the next flight back to New York."

One look at the woman's pursed lips, and Betty knew it wasn't an idle threat. She settled back down in her seat and carefully folded her napkin across her lap.

"I apologize, Madame."

"Very well," Amelia said, composing herself. "Detective Fitzroy, I would like to introduce you to Miss Betty Bent."

"*Enchanté,* mademoiselle," the detective said, rising from his seat once more to deliver a bow.

"I must apologize for Miss Bent's behavior this morning," Madame Beauregard said without giving Betty a chance to reply to the detective's greeting. "I'll let you decide whether I have made a mistake bringing her to Paris."

The man had been studying Betty's face since she arrived at the table. Now it was Betty's turn to examine his. Detective Fitzroy was in his mid-forties and had never been handsome. His watery blue eyes bulged and his nose looked a little too narrow. Whiskers sprouted from his nostrils and fanned out across his cheeks. Yet there was something appealing about his appearance. The way the skin crinkled around his eyes told her that Detective Fitzroy was a man who often wore a smile on his face.

"*Au contraire,* Madame, you have made a splendid choice," the detective assured her. He spoke English with a thick accent. "Miss Bent is just as pretty as you described. I think they will find her irresistible."

"Wonderful," Amelia said.

"They?" Betty asked. "Who are *they*?"

The detective addressed the old woman across the table from him. "You have not told her?" There was a distinct note of concern in his voice.

"I assumed she would be more cooperative once we were here on French soil," Madame Beauregard responded tersely.

"Excuse me, but what are you talking about?" Betty demanded.

"Please don't be alarmed," the detective said, though he himself suddenly seemed uncomfortable. "I will explain everything. But first let me ask: Have you heard of the Darkness Dwellers?"

"No," Betty replied, feeling even more on edge.

"Then I must provide you with a bit of background information. Three years ago I was a policeman on the Catacomb Patrol. You are familiar with the Paris catacombs, *oui*?"

This time, Betty nodded.

"The old tunnels are very dangerous. Civilians are forbidden to enter, but many do. They often lose their way,

their flashlight batteries run down, or they injure themselves. In the six months I was on patrol, I rescued three
people inside the catacombs. One was lucky—he had been
missing for only a few hours. Two had been underground
for much longer, and they seemed to have lost their minds
in the darkness. They spoke of a mysterious savior who
had discovered them trapped in one of the catacombs'
deepest passages. The man gave the pair water before
guiding them to a part of the tunnels where the police
were certain to find them.

"I should have listened more closely to their story. I
knew that the police never visited the deepest tunnels.
Anything could have been happening down there. But the
man in charge of the Catacomb Patrol was convinced such
expeditions would be a waste of our time. He believed no
sane visitor would dare venture so far into the underworld.
For months, I never once questioned his wisdom.

"Then one evening, I happened to take a wrong turn,
and I found myself inside a tunnel I had never explored
before. I wandered for hours, trying to find a way out.
There was nothing down there—no sign of human activity. I was on the edge of despair when I discovered it: a
cinema."

"A *movie theater*?" Betty asked.

"That is correct. The subterranean cavern I had stumbled across was wired for electricity and appointed just
like an ordinary theater. A large screen hung from the
ceiling at one end of the room. There were dozens of velvet chairs and even a popcorn machine. They had an old-
fashioned projector and a library of classic films. The
walls of the cavern were decorated with movie posters. I

recall *Journey to the Center of the Earth* and *Land of the Lost.* I must admit, it was a very nice cinema. But it didn't belong in the catacombs. I knew I had made an important discovery. I used the electrical wires to guide myself back to the surface, and I immediately filed a full report.

"The next day, I gathered reinforcements and returned to the catacombs. It took us hours to locate the chamber. When we got there, the cinema was gone. Even the chairs had vanished overnight. The only thing left in the room was a note. It said, *'DO NOT TRY TO FIND US.'* And it was signed, 'the Darkness Dwellers.' Everyone on the police force assumed I had pulled a prank. I was officially reprimanded by my superiors and ridiculed by my colleagues. So I resigned from the force and phoned a reporter I knew. She took my claims seriously, but few people ever read the article she wrote."

"I read it," Madame Beauregard said. "And I knew in an instant that Detective Fitzroy was telling the truth."

"How?" Betty asked. What would someone like Amelia Beauregard know about a group of Parisians who like to watch movies underground?

"Because they call themselves the Darkness Dwellers. It's rather unusual for a French group to take an English name, wouldn't you say? Well, I believe I know how they chose it. You may recall, Miss Bent, the day we met in the Marble Cemetery. I was visiting an old friend of mine, a man by the name of Gordon Grant. He was here in Paris more than sixty years ago, working as a code breaker with a small group of French and American spies who were stationed inside the catacombs. They were intercepting orders from Nazi command, hoping to save Paris from destruction. When I heard that Gordon would be spending weeks underground, I began calling his team the Darkness Dwellers. The name was a private joke between the two of us. As far as I know, neither of us ever shared it with another soul."

"Then how could the French group have heard about it?" Betty asked.

"They must have seen the name somewhere in the catacombs. I need to know where they saw it or what they found."

"Why?" Betty asked.

"For years, I was told that Gordon had vanished during the war. Now I have reason to believe that he never made it out of the tunnels alive. If his body is still down there, these new Darkness Dwellers may know where to find it."

"And what does all of this have to do with me?" Betty asked.

The headmistress let the detective answer. "I have spent the past two years attempting to make contact with the Darkness Dwellers," he said. "Somehow they always manage to elude me. But not long ago, I met a young man your age in the catacombs. He showed me a hideout he had constructed himself, and he claimed he knew many of the Darkness Dwellers personally. Unfortunately, he introduced me to a friend, and the other young man recognized me at once. His father is the leader of the Catacomb Patrol. The boys have been avoiding me ever since. I tried to return to the hideout. I know its general location, but the room itself is well hidden. At times I can feel them watching me, but I cannot draw them out. Madame

Beauregard believes they might emerge if we offered the right bait—perhaps the chance to rescue a pretty girl."

Betty had heard enough to get her blood boiling. She had never allowed herself to get upset when Madame Beauregard corrected her manners. Nor had she resented being ordered about like a trained monkey. But *this* was an insult Betty couldn't ignore.

"So that's why you brought me to Paris? To play a damsel in distress? To be *bait*?" she growled at Amelia Beauregard. "You think I can help you find the Darkness Dwellers because I'm *pretty*? What is this, the nineteenth century? For your information, I happen to know more about subterranean tunnels and underground worlds than most people on Earth. I'm also a master of disguise, and I have a red belt in karate. But you wouldn't know any of that because you never bothered to ask. All you knew about me until this minute is that I'm *pretty*."

Madame Beauregard had not anticipated such a dramatic response. "Miss Bent, I . . ."

"*Please.* Allow me to finish. We researched your background, Madame. We know about your friend Gordon. If you're trying to clear his name, that's all fine and dandy. But you should have told me what you were planning before we left New York City. Instead, you decided to spring it on me over breakfast at some fancy restaurant where you didn't think I'd make a scene."

"Yes, I . . ."

"You paid my way to Paris, and I don't want to be in your debt. And as it turns out, I'm not going to be quite as busy here as I originally thought. So I *am* going to help you, Madame Beauregard. Yes, I'll go to the catacombs. *Tomorrow.* Now, if you'll excuse me, I need to make that phone call."

THE FISHBEIN GUIDE TO . . . TELEPHONE ETIQUETTE

A smartphone is the most essential tool an adventurer can possess. It will allow you to call for reinforcements, plot your next move, and document suspicious activities. But a phone is also a tool that can easily be turned against you.

Here are a few frightening facts to consider . . .

Yes, We Are Listening
Politeness aside, there's a very good reason to avoid using your phone in public places. (These include restaurants, stores, movie theaters, and police stations.) Someone is bound to be listening. Eavesdropping on private conversations happens to be a favorite pastime of mine. You wouldn't *believe* some of the juicy tidbits I've picked up over the years— and on several occasions, those tidbits have concerned people I know. So whenever you need to place a call, search for a private spot.

Yes, Those Photos Will End Up on the Internet
Unless you're willing to change your name and move to a country without Internet access, never, ever let anyone take incriminating photos of you. Not your boyfriend, your best friend, or your sweet baby sister. One little argument, and those photos will be posted where the whole world can see them. For eternity. And that will be the end of your glorious future in politics, investment banking, detective work, or crime.

Yes, You Should Be Paying Attention
If you're busy talking or texting, you're probably not aware of what's happening around you. You might not realize that you're being followed by someone who *really* wants a new smartphone. That the person you've been staking out has just emerged from hiding. That the cherry blossoms are particularly lovely this spring. Or that there's an open manhole two steps in front of you.

Yes, It's Your Duty to Call for Help
If you see someone in trouble, immediately call for help. Do not assume that someone else will take care of it. The other witnesses are probably assuming the very same thing. And yes, it *is* your business.

Yes, You Will Lose Your Phone at Some Point
Keep your phone password protected. Or be prepared to have your e-mails, texts, and photos shared with the world.

Chapter 22

A Declaration
of War

a mouse scurried across my path as I made my way toward the well-lit living room at the end of the hall. I could hear my mother tapping at the computer. For months, she had been slaving away on a scholarly work entitled *Mad, Bad, and Dangerous to Know.* I'd thought it sounded like something worth reading until my mother informed me it was all about poetry. As I approached her desk, she was too immersed to hear my footsteps, so I decided to clear my throat.

My mother screamed and put her hand to her heart, as if that were the only way to keep it inside her chest. "Ananka!" she gasped once she'd caught her breath. "I thought you went to bed hours ago! It's three o'clock in the morning!"

The truth was, I'd never even gotten under the covers. I had come home with Iris's warning burning a hole through my brain and locked myself away in my room to suffer in silence. I was mortified, heartbroken, guilt-ridden, and furious. I raged against fate, love, and cute little blond girls who refuse to mind their own business. When my phone rang, I considered hurling it against the wall on the other side of the room. My shame only grew when I saw who was calling.

And yet it felt surprisingly good to hear Betty Bent's voice. It was eight a.m. on her second day in Paris, and the Irregulars' emissary had big news to report. The previous afternoon, she'd sent a note announcing her arrival in France to the boy who'd e-mailed Kiki's request for the cure. Hours later, Betty had finally received word from the mysterious French kid. Kiki was free and no longer needed the tonic. He gave no explanation, but the very next morning, Betty watched Livia Galatzina and her favorite henchman rush from a restaurant in a state of sheer panic. Somehow, Kiki had managed to twist their knickers into a bunch. Betty planned to wait one more day in case Kiki changed her mind about the hair-growing formula. But on Friday she had to focus on a brand-new assignment. Amelia Beauregard wanted to send Betty down to the catacombs underneath Paris to search for Gordon Grant's body.

The report wasn't exactly what I'd hoped to hear. Even if Kiki had managed to outwit her relatives, another Irregular might have fallen into a trap. I didn't like the idea of Betty trudging through dark passages, searching for a man who had betrayed his own country—a man who might not even be dead.

The time had come for me to focus on my duties. I took an oath to stay away from Kaspar. I'd focus on my work and try to forget my heartbreak. I would find some way to help Betty Bent—and pray that she never discovered just how close I'd come to betraying her.

✦ ✦ ✦

"Couldn't sleep," I told my mother. "Thought I'd come look for a book."

"Well, we certainly have plenty of those," she remarked. "Any subject in particular?"

"The liberation of Paris at the end of World War II and Hitler's plans to destroy the city."

My mother took off her glasses and rubbed her eyes. She could work for hours without so much as a potty break, but just a few seconds with me could leave her exhausted. "You know, Ananka, you should try to start your homework at a more reasonable hour."

"It's not homework," I said. I didn't bother to add that I hadn't done any homework in over a week.

My mother looked briefly puzzled, then her energy seemed to surge. "Would this have something to do with Amelia Beauregard?"

"Maybe, maybe not," I teased.

"The books on WWII are in the bunker, of course," she said, referring to the guest room that contained the fabled Fishbein collection of military literature. "But there are always a few new titles on your father's bedside table."

And that's where I found it. A hefty tome published by an obscure academic press, with a title far too long and dull to repeat. My father, dozing beneath a heap of books, cracked open an eye.

"I haven't gotten to that one yet, but I don't think it has any aliens or giant squid," he said.

"I know."

"Then your taste must be improving." He closed his eye again. "Let me know if you'd like to discuss."

It was a sweet offer, but I doubt my father would have wanted to discuss how close I came to dying of boredom before I finally managed to locate the following passage:

> Paris faced new dangers in the days leading up to the city's liberation. In the summer of 1944, it was widely reported that Hitler intended to destroy the French capital should German troops prove unable to maintain control. A small French and American task force was sent into the Paris catacombs to intercept and decode sabotage plans. Four of France's finest agents, an American cryptographer, and an American engineer worked tirelessly for several weeks, listening for evidence that attacks had been ordered. Just two days before the German retreat, all contact was lost with the team in the tunnels. It wasn't until the war ended that investigators began to search for the missing spies. What they discovered in the catacombs shocked even the most battle-hardened officers. Over five miles of subterranean tunnels had been rigged with explosives. Had the bombs been detonated, much of Paris would have collapsed.
>
> Six spies had been stationed in the catacombs, but only five bodies were discovered. The American engineer had been felled by a single bullet. Three of the French agents appeared to have

been ambushed and slaughtered. Two were found murdered in their beds. The third had been strangled as he sat at his desk. The remaining French spy had escaped the carnage, only to die of dehydration before he found a way to the streets above.

The sixth man's body was never recovered, and he has remained at the center of a mystery for over sixty years. Gordon Grant was the team's leader. A brilliant American cryptographer who had won praise for his work cracking enemy codes, he had bravely volunteered for the mission. His superiors remained convinced of his innocence until the bullet that killed the American engineer was traced to Gordon Grant's gun.

Though his guilt remains unproven, it is now widely believed that Gordon Grant murdered four of his colleagues. There had been rumors suggesting the young man was hiding a terrible secret during the weeks before his disappearance. At least one close acquaintance was convinced that Grant had been engaged in an illicit love affair, perhaps with a German spy.

The truth may not remain hidden forever. The French spy who died wandering the catacombs was found in possession of an unusual envelope. The document within contained a coded letter written in Gordon Grant's hand. For sixty years, the message was kept secret by the US military. It has only

*recently been declassified, and this book is the
first to publish it. Perhaps someday soon, the
code will be broken.*

A short message followed. I counted one hundred fifty-nine characters. A jumble of letters that made no sense. Ripping a page from the book would have been an unforgivable offense, so I pulled a pencil from my desk drawer and diligently started to copy down the code.

BVYRB WEITW EEROY ORKRI EYHIR
DAWGO DEPUE EVUTM VDUMD TGOHI
IOTVO BBBVU CUORS SRASE LTEEH
HREVN UYEUU REERV OAMKS NYTUE
LONNT IFTVE NSSNE EOHTI NAGAL
HONHL AZNDR TNETI BRRSM EHOER
OHWDE TESE

Since Principal Wickham had named me her protégé, I had really been making an effort to stay awake in class. But let's be honest, if you've been up all night thinking about spies, slaughters, and sabotage, there's nothing like a physics lecture to send you straight to dreamland.

"Ananka. Ananka!" My physics instructor, Mr. Schiffer, was poking me with a piece of chalk, leaving little white polka dots on the sleeve of my black sweater.

"The second law of thermodynamics!" I blurted out, and my classmates tittered. I twisted around to see a room filled with zombies.

"Nice try, Ananka," Mr. Schiffer said. "You're exactly

three weeks behind the rest of the class. Now go to the principal's office."

"Please," I begged, wiping the drool from my chin. "I had a rough night. I promise I'll stay awake." Principal Wickham may have been my mentor, but she never hesitated to sentence me to after-school detention, and I'd already texted Oona and Iris to meet me at four.

"I've given up trying to punish you," said Mr. Schiffer, waving a note in the air. "But apparently Principal Wickham believes that you might not be hopeless. *She's* the one who requested your presence."

Still groggy, I made a pit stop at the bathroom to splash cold water on my face. Standing at the sink, I could hear the sound of weeping coming from one of the stalls. I squatted down and caught sight of an extra-large pair of ladylike pumps. The stall's occupant was applying bandages to the backs of her heels, which were raw and bloody from rubbing against the shoes' stiff leather.

"You okay in there?" I asked. "You want me to get a first-aid kit? Or maybe some morphine? Those wounds look pretty nasty."

"No, thank you," came the polite reply. Then the sobbing commenced once more.

"You sure?" I tried again, but the only response I received was the sound of a nose being blown.

Suit yourself, I thought, my sympathy exhausted. *That's what you get for letting traitor-loving Amelia Beauregard turn you into the walking dead.*

I pushed through the door and headed toward the dimly lit, reputedly haunted section of the building that housed the principal's office. When I arrived, her assistant glanced up at me and then returned to her typing. She shook her head as if to say, *You've done it again.* But the only words that left her mouth were, "Go right inside, Ananka. They're waiting for you."

Hundreds of eyes always stared back at me whenever I entered the principal's dusty office. Her walls were covered with five decades of photos—snapshots of Atalanta's most illustrious graduates. No one knew more senators, brain surgeons, or CEOs than the principal of Manhattan's most exclusive girls' school. At one time or another, they'd all been Theodora Wickham's protégés. If the principal had bothered to call in all the favors she was owed, she could have easily ended up running New York.

But that day, I breezed into the office and found myself greeted by a new set of eyes—a pair that happened to belong to one of the most famous faces in the world. At age twenty, Theresa Donovan had won an Oscar for her portrayal of a shoplifting street urchin who later became one of Sydney's finest citizens. The actress took on her second Oscar-winning role fifteen years later, when she played the infamous French poisoner Madame de Montespan. Many critics considered Theresa Donovan the world's greatest thespian, but I knew her best as Molly Donovan's detestable mother.

"Hey, Ananka." Molly was leaning back in a chair with her filthy work boots propped up on Principal Wickham's desk.

"Molly," I sputtered. "What's going on?"

"Ananka," Principal Wickham addressed me in her most formal tone. "This is Molly's mother, Mrs. Donovan."

"Yeah, I know," I blurted out before I could stop myself. "I'm sorry. Nice to finally meet you, Mrs. Donovan." I waited for the actress to hold out a hand.

"It's a pleasure to meet you, too, Ananka," Mrs. Donovan replied. She was blond, fair, and much more delicate than the characters she played. Her natural voice had a singsong quality, and no camera could ever capture the beauty of her smile. In the movies, Theresa Donovan was pretty. In person, she seemed positively radiant. I had no problem imagining sweet little sparrows fluttering down from the heavens to perch on her shoulders every time she left her house—or a parade of cute, furry creatures trailing behind her whenever she strolled through Central Park.

What I could no longer imagine was the terrible, overbearing woman Molly had described to me. How could *this* Mrs. Donovan be the braggart who treated her daughter like Hans, the Counting Horse, hauling her out at dinner parties to entertain guests? And what was she doing here at Atalanta with Molly? I looked to Principal Wickham for an explanation.

"I received a call from Mrs. Donovan yesterday morning. She wanted my advice on a matter with which you might be familiar. It appears that Molly has been awarded a scholarship to L'Institut Beauregard."

"Congratulations," I told Molly.

"You don't have to pretend, Ananka," Molly informed me. "They both know you're behind the scholarship. And no, I didn't squeal on you."

"Principal Wickham said that this woman—Madame

Beauregard—had Molly's name on some sort of list." The world's most famous actress didn't speak down to me as most adults might.

"That's right," I confirmed. "Amelia Beauregard keeps a list of girls who need to be tamed."

"And *Molly* is on it?" Mrs. Donovan gave me a puzzled smile as though she hoped I'd let her in on the joke. "Why would she think my daughter needs to be *tamed*?"

I could have pointed to Molly's boots, which remained propped up on the principal's desk. Or reminded Mrs. Donovan of her daughter's impressive detention record. Or the smoke bomb incident that had led to Molly's expulsion from the Atalanta School for Girls. But I had a feeling that facts wouldn't make much of an impression on Mrs. Donovan. She seemed blissfully unaware that her daughter was a delinquent of some renown.

"Perhaps it has something to do with Molly's enrollment at the Boreland Academy," Principal Wickham offered diplomatically. "The school has a reputation as the last resort for the parents of unruly children."

"But Molly *chose* Boreland," Theresa Donovan argued. "I never wanted to send her away to school."

"No," Molly butted in. "You wanted to keep me here so you could introduce me to every shrink in the city. And make me entertain your stupid friends with my math tricks."

"Oh, Molly!" Mrs. Donovan gasped. "I was just proud of you! I've always been in awe of your gifts! I thought therapy might help you take advantage of them. I wish I'd had that kind of encouragement when I was your age."

"Maybe you got to be who you are because your

mother never smothered you with 'help.' Or dragged you off to Europe for months at a time."

Mrs. Donovan looked so wounded that I wasn't sure she'd ever recover. "Is that what this is all about? Did you decide to accept the scholarship to L'Institut Beauregard because you don't want to spend the summer in Italy with me?"

"You mean trapped in a hotel room, being coddled twenty-four hours a day? Thanks, but no thanks. I'd rather spend my vacation learning how to curtsy."

"Molly," Principal Wickham interrupted. "I'm not sure that you've given quite enough thought to your decision to spend the summer at L'Institut Beauregard. That's why I asked your mother to bring you here this afternoon. I know Ananka has warned you about the institute's head-mistress, but I think it might be a good idea for you to observe a few of her other pupils."

"Principal Wickham is right, Molly," I said. "You need to see what's going on here at Atalanta. It's gotten much worse than I ever thought it could. I know you accepted the scholarship to help me out, but I'm starting to have second thoughts about the whole arrangement."

Principal Wickham nodded. "Mrs. Donovan, perhaps you and I could have lunch while Molly spends a little time with Ananka. Would you mind?"

"Not at all." Mrs. Donovan tried to send her daughter off with a smile, but Molly was already out of her seat and halfway to the door.

"Your mom seems really great," I observed once the two of us were alone in the hall.

"My mother's like cake," Molly replied. "The first bite

is amazing. But you'll vomit if you have too much. Anyway, thanks for getting me out of there. That whole 'second thoughts' speech was a nice touch."

"I was serious," I said.

"Oh, come on." Molly rolled her eyes.

"Just wait a few minutes," I told her. "I think Italy's going to start looking good to you pretty soon. Besides, I don't understand why you'd rather stay in Manhattan all summer when you could be wreaking havoc across Rome."

"I'd love to go to Rome. I just don't want to go to Rome with *her*. My mother still thinks she can turn me into her little Mini-Me," Molly said. "She tries to give me all the attention she craved back when she was a kid. Buying me pretty things and taking me for pedicures. She doesn't care that I'm different. She's never even bothered to figure out who I am. I don't want pink toenails. I just want to be left *alone*."

"But," I started to argue just as the bell rang, and girls of all sizes flooded the hallway. A few months earlier, the scene would have been utter chaos. Now it was as quiet and orderly as a parade of debutantes. Half the high school students had already been transformed into Proper Little Ladies. The other half looked terrified that the condition might be contagious, and the younger girls just seemed confused. Molly and I stood with our backs to the wall as the Atalanta zombies glided by.

"Ha! I've never seen so many pearls in my life!" Molly cackled. "As soon as I get out of here, I'm buying an oyster farm." I turned just in time to see her face fall into a frown. "Whoa. Is that Rebecca Gruber?" she whispered.

A tall girl was headed in our direction. Stretched

across her broad shoulders was a wrinkle-free white shirt with a frilly collar. She moved slowly, and her muscular calves wobbled, straining to keep the girl upright as she walked in what I was certain was her first pair of heels—the same pumps I'd seen in the bathroom stall. I couldn't help but stare at Rebecca's once-wild eyebrows, which had now been plucked into submission, and her cheeks, which were tastefully dusted with rouge. The girl had done her best to pull herself together, but I could tell from her puffy eyelids that she'd recently been crying. Fortunately, Rebecca was concentrating so hard on the business of walking that she never realized she was being observed.

"Oh my God, Ananka! What happened to her?" Molly gasped in horror. "Rebecca doesn't wear *skirts*. I've never seen her in anything but sweatpants. When we were little, she wanted to be a *bear* when she grew up! And before I left Atalanta, all she could talk about was finding a way to save the orangutans! Her dream is to run the Bronx Zoo, not to throw fabulous dinner parties! I don't give a crap what happens to most of these girls—they were rotten from the start. But Rebecca Gruber used to be cool!"

"You see? That's what Amelia Beauregard does to girls," I said. "She takes future zookeepers and turns them into little princesses."

Molly wheeled around to face me. "And you're just going to let her keep doing it?"

"There's not much I can do to stop her," I said with a shrug.

"Oh really?" Molly's spine straightened and her hands found her hips. I realized I was in for a speech. "Don't you dare tell my mother, but I *have* watched a few of her movies. And I specifically remember one character saying, 'Evil will triumph if good people do nothing.' I always liked that line, but I never thought I'd get a chance to quote it. Thanks for showing me all of this, Ananka. I know exactly what my next step's gonna be."

"What?" I was already cringing at the answer I knew was on the way.

"I'm not going back to Boreland. My parents can get me a tutor for all the academic stuff. I'm coming back to New York. And I'm enrolling in evening classes at the Beauregard Institute—today."

"But Molly!" I tried.

"Save your breath, Ananka. I'm going to destroy that hellhole from the inside."

CHAPTER 23

The Luxurious Lair of Lili Liu

In the Fishbein family apartment, all books on the subject of human psychology can be found in my parents' bedroom closet. I've been avoiding that section of our library for years. It's not that the workings of the human mind don't fascinate me. It's the mirror mounted to the closet door that keeps me away. My mother must have scavenged it from a Coney Island fun house, because every time I venture near, I'm greeted by a girl with a giant head, devious eyes, no bust to speak of, and a shockingly terrible outfit.

But when I was younger, I was convinced that any books hidden away in a closet were the books I needed to read. As I recall, they did not disappoint. I spent many entertaining hours diagnosing my loved ones while I read about Alien Hand Syndrome, the Fregoli Delusion, and Bibliomania (a condition that appears to run in the Fishbein family). In one of the less sensational works, I encountered an intriguing theory that I've come to accept as fact.

Human beings, I'm now convinced, are capable of worrying about only seven things at one time. Here was my list the day Molly Donovan declared war on Amelia Beauregard:

1. Kiki's kidnapping
2. Betty's boss
3. Betty's boyfriend
4. Oona's sister
5. World peace
6. DeeDee's stalker
7. Iris's big mouth
8. The Atalanta zombie invasion
9. The effects of sleep deprivation
10. Molly Donovan's war

So now maybe you can understand why I'd forgotten all about the Donovan dilemma by the time the last bell rang at the Atalanta School for Girls. It didn't help matters that Kaspar was waiting for me outside the school gates. I had ignored the three e-mails and two text messages he'd sent in the hours after Molly Donovan's visit. He knew about Betty's upcoming trip to the catacombs, and he wanted work to take his mind off her troubles. I tried making excuses, but Kaspar refused to listen. He didn't want to help Luz finish her community service. He didn't want to escort DeeDee to the Golden Lotus for her fifth round of laser treatments. No, Kaspar wanted to join the remaining Irregulars on our first organized hunt for Lili Liu.

When he and I arrived together at Oona's house, Iris McLeod almost swallowed her tongue. For the full fifteen minutes I spent in Chinatown, she and Oona watched every move I made. I might have been pleased to see them acting as a team for once, if their camaraderie hadn't come at my expense. It wasn't *my* fault that Kaspar had insisted on crashing the meeting. Now, every time I glanced in his direction, I felt two sets of eyes boring holes through the back of my skull.

"How long did it take you guys to map all the Lili Liu sightings?" I asked.

"A few hours," Oona replied. "Would have gone faster if you'd stuck around last night to help."

"I had other stuff to do," I told her.

"Maybe you should have mentioned that before we cooked you a meat loaf."

"Why don't we show Ananka what we did?" Kaspar suggested, blissfully unaware of the silent war being waged. He unrolled the giant sheet of paper across the top of Oona's table and bent down to study it. He was so cute when he was concentrating that I forced myself to look away.

"The little red dots are places Lili Liu has been spotted over the last two weeks," said Oona, keeping her attention on me instead of the dots.

"And as you can see," Iris jumped in, "there's a cluster of dots in an area just north of Chinatown. We were surprised to see so much activity above Houston Street."

"Hey, that's my neighborhood!" I exclaimed when I finally glanced down at the map.

"Yeah, we thought it'd be good to focus in on the Bowery between Houston and Astor Place," Oona said, referring to an avenue a couple of blocks to the west of my apartment. Once skid row, the Bowery was now home to some of the most expensive hotels in the city.

"Makes sense," I said. "Lili's probably got a room over there."

"That's what I figured. So, come on. Let's go!" Oona grabbed her handbag. "If we can clear my name and put Lili in jail by sunset, I promise I'll buy everyone dinner at Fat Frankie's."

"You're not coming with us to look for Lili," I said, then hurried to explain before Oona had a chance to complain. "We may need to talk to people who work in the area, and we can't waste time getting chased around by your sister's victims. Besides, I have a new project for you." I pulled a slip of paper out of my back pocket and passed it to her.

"It's a code," Oona said, her eyes skimming over the jumble of letters.

"It's a message written by a man named Gordon Grant. He was an American code breaker working in the Paris catacombs during World War II. Most of his colleagues were murdered, and a lot of people think he was the one who killed them. This note was found beside the body of the one man who almost escaped. Army experts were able to identify Gordon Grant's handwriting, but no one has ever cracked the code. I know it's a long shot, but I'd like you to have a go at it."

"Gordon Grant. That's the guy Amelia Beauregard is

looking for," Kaspar said. Handsome *and* brilliant. I was in serious trouble.

"What, so we're digging up dirt on the elderly these days?" Oona complained. "Aren't there more important matters to deal with? I'm not even that good at this stuff. Besides, why do I have to work on it *now*?"

"The code's been waiting sixty years to be cracked," said Iris, taking Oona's side. "Don't you think it can wait a little longer?"

"No. Ananka's right. The code could be important," Kaspar said, and the arguments stopped immediately. I'd taken charge of the Irregulars on several occasions, but I'd never once inspired that kind of respect.

"I spoke with Betty this morning." I stepped in, feeling more than a little annoyed. "She called Kaspar, too. Turns out Madame Beauregard is even trickier than we thought. She's been looking for Gordon Grant's body inside the catacombs, and she needs a pretty girl to charm two boys who might know where to find it. That's the only reason she took Betty to France. I figure it's probably a good idea to start gathering whatever information we can about Gordon Grant before Betty has to start searching for his bones. If we crack that code, we might be able to help Betty find the man faster—or prove that he's not in the catacombs at all."

"You talked to Betty this morning?" Iris asked. "Why didn't you tell us? What's going on with Kiki? Has there been any news?"

"A little," I said. "Betty got a note from the French kid, saying Kiki's free and doesn't need the cure anymore.

And then Betty saw Livia Galatzina rushing around her hotel in a panic. We both think Kiki's managed to turn the tables somehow. But we'll just have to wait until we hear from her."

"So, Betty gets to go to the catacombs, Kiki's fighting the royal family of Pokrovia, you guys are going to chase down my sister—and I have to sit here alone trying to crack some dumb code?" Oona whined.

"You're not going to be alone. Kaspar and I will head down to the Bowery, but Iris is going to stay here and help you." I gave Iris a mean little smirk. "You guys make such a terrific team."

"Ananka!" Iris protested.

"I'm in charge here, Iris," I told her. "This time you'll do as I say."

It had taken me less than a day to break my own oath. Now I was alone with Kaspar, and I worried that my will-power might crumble. I was so busy kicking myself that I didn't bother to point out the sights as Kaspar and I traveled by foot up the Bowery. We passed an ancient white row house that had served as the headquarters of the most bloodthirsty gang in New York, a crumbling brick tenement with an Underground Railroad stop hidden in its basement, and the site of a theater once known—for very good reason—as the Slaughterhouse. I'd always considered the Bowery to be the most fascinating street in Manhattan, but for once I kept my lips sealed and my lectures to myself.

"Something wrong, Ananka?" Kaspar asked. "I was

hoping to get a walking tour of the dark and dangerous Bowery."

I'd been longing to hear those words for years. Fate was cruel to put them in the mouth of a boy I could never have. "Sorry. I'm just tired. I haven't been getting much sleep lately."

"What's been on your mind?"

Did he really want to know? "Oh, let's see. Kiki's kidnapping. Betty's new job. The Atalanta zombie brigade. Oona's evil twin. DeeDee's stalker . . . and believe me, that's just the start of it," I said, conveniently leaving off number three on my list.

"It must be hard being left in charge," Kaspar commiserated. "I hate to add to your troubles, Ananka, but there is something I want to discuss with you."

My heart started thumping, and I wished I could rip the traitor right out of my chest.

"I'm worried about Betty," he continued, and my hopes promptly shriveled. "She sounded different when she called me from Paris. I think she was really hurt that you guys weren't taking her seriously before she left. She wants to prove that she's just as tough as the other Irregulars."

"Nobody told her she had to be tough!" As far as I was concerned, the Irregulars already had a surplus of toughness. "We just don't want her to get hurt!"

"I think you're missing the point. Just because Betty doesn't go around beating up bad guys doesn't mean she can't handle herself," Kaspar explained. "She has her own way of doing things. And that way *works*. If she thinks she has to act like the rest of you, she's going get herself into a lot of trouble. Now that we know what Amelia

Beauregard had planned for Betty in Paris, that seems like a pretty real danger."

"What do you want me to do?" I asked.

"The next time you speak to Betty, give her the respect she deserves," Kaspar said. "And make sure the other Irregulars do, too."

I hadn't been expecting a scolding, and I didn't know what to say in response.

"Hey, I'm sorry." Kaspar threw an arm around my shoulders and gave me a squeeze. He smelled wonderful. Like spray paint and bath soap and matzo-ball soup. "I didn't mean to sound so harsh. I wouldn't have said anything at all if I didn't like you so much."

He liked me! I couldn't think about anything but that and the arm around my shoulders. Then it slid away.

"Look over there." Kaspar pointed to a figure in front of us. "That can't be our little friend Lili, can it?"

A thin, fur-clad female, just a few inches too short to be fully grown, had waltzed through the doors of a hotel down the street. Moving with caution, we followed behind her. But before we reached the lobby, the girl came barreling out of the building, a doorman hot on her heels. She was remarkably fast for someone wearing knee-high boots with stiletto heels. She and her pursuer veered east onto Third Street and disappeared from view. When Kaspar and I finally made it to the corner, we found the doorman leaning against a brick wall, casually checking the messages on his phone.

"The girl you were chasing—where did she go?" I panted.

The doorman straightened up and slid his phone into the pocket of his uniform. "I tried to catch her, but she got away."

"You must not have been trying very hard," Kaspar observed.

"Prove it," the doorman challenged. "Besides, she's just a kid."

"Then why were you chasing her down the street in the first place?" I asked.

"Because that's what my boss told me to do. It's either that or call the police. Wait a second. Why am I being grilled by a couple of brats? I need to get back to work."

We'd obviously gotten off on the wrong foot. I dropped the hard-boiled act and tried a little politeness. "I'm sorry if we came across as rude just now," I said. "The girl's name is Lili Liu. She's the sister of a friend of ours. Would you mind telling us what she's done?"

The doorman snorted. "You wanna know what she does? She uses the bathroom in the hotel's lobby."

"To do what?" I asked, imagining Lili robbing guests while their pants were around their ankles.

"Wash up," said the doorman.

"I don't understand," Kaspar said.

The doorman sighed. "She comes to the hotel and uses the sink to bathe. I got a friend who works down the street at the Cooper Square Hotel. She goes there, too, sometimes. I guess some fancy guest must have complained to my boss, 'cause he told me not to let her in anymore. But the girl just keeps trying her luck. This is the third time I've had to chase her away."

"If she shows up again, will you please give me a call?" I asked, searching for a pen. "Her sister would like to speak to her."

"You two really friends with her sister?" the man asked, and I nodded. "Then I don't need your number. I can tell you where to find her. My buddy takes the girl leftovers from his hotel's kitchen sometimes. He feels bad 'cause he's got a kid her age. He told me the girl hangs out in Extra Place—you know that alley off First Street. A super who works in one of the buildings there has a soft spot for her. He lets her hang out in an old maintenance shed that a construction company left behind."

"Thanks for your help," I said, casting a confused look at Kaspar.

"You're very kind not to catch her," Kaspar told the man.

The doorman refused the compliment. "No, I'm not," he said, sounding disgusted with himself. "If I was *kind*, I wouldn't chase her at all."

🏰　🏰　🏰

Kaspar and I had no trouble locating Lili Liu's lair. It was the size of a closet, without heat or electricity. A rolled-up sleeping bag sat in one corner and a camping lantern dangled from a hook. The walls were insulated with pretty dresses on hangers, and a row of shoes was arranged on the ground. The clothing looked well cared for, but it was beginning to show signs of wear and tear. A couple of tattered books written in Chinese waited to be read for the hundredth time.

I took it all in with one hand over my mouth. "I was sure that man had to be wrong, but it looks like Lili really *is* homeless," I whispered between my fingers.

"She's been stealing so she wouldn't starve," Kaspar added.

"But she's the daughter of one of the richest men in New York!"

"So is her sister," Kaspar pointed out. "Didn't seem to do *her* much good."

"We've got to get Oona," I muttered. "She needs to see this."

"Then step aside and let me look," said a voice behind me. I spun around to find Oona and Iris.

"You're here! Does this mean you've been spying on us?" I demanded. "Why?"

"Don't ask questions you wouldn't want answered," Oona replied.

"It was all my idea," Iris confessed.

I resisted the urge to strangle her. "We'll talk about this later," I growled as I left the shed.

Oona stood in the doorway, her eyes taking in every pathetic detail. She didn't utter a single word.

"What do you think we should do, Oona?" Iris finally asked.

"You guys should head home," she said. "I'll wait here for Lili."

"But it's getting dark," Iris argued. "And it's already cold. Don't you want one of us to stay here with you?"

"I'm happy to keep you company," Kaspar offered.

"No," Oona replied in an oddly emotionless voice.

"Thank you all for your help, but I need to deal with this on my own."

I should have put up a fight. But I didn't. My long list of concerns had been replaced by a single desire. Instead of worrying about leaving Oona alone in a cold metal shed, all I could think about was spending a few more minutes with Betty's boyfriend.

Chapter 24

Loose in the Labyrinth

Thirty-two hours can feel like an eternity when you're stuck underground with someone you're dying to smack. Kiki had anticipated spending no more than twelve hours in her odious cousin's company. She'd never imagined Etienne might need longer to convince Livia Galatzina to trade Verushka Kozlova for her only daughter. But if the clock in the underground hideout could be trusted, Kiki and Sidonia had passed more than a day together. If Sidonia hadn't succumbed to exhaustion eight hours earlier, Kiki's fists might have put her to sleep.

Sick with worry, Kiki was pacing the perimeter of the hideout when Sidonia woke. The girl's once perfectly formed nose wrinkled prissily when she recalled where she was. In an instant, the princess was perched bolt upright on the sofa. She sat with her knees together and her hands in her lap, touching as little as possible.

"This place is disgusting, you horrible little troll. The furniture smells like butt, and we've been down here forever. How much longer will I have to wait?" Sidonia demanded. The complaining was about to drive Kiki to homicide.

"Until your delightful mother releases Verushka, and Etienne brings her safely here," Kiki responded. "And then you will be escorted to the most luxurious police station in all of Paris. Now that's the tenth time I've told you. Don't make me say it again. I'm already itching to punch you, and I'm sure you want to look your best for your mug shot."

Less than a minute passed. "I'm starving," Sidonia whined.

"And you honestly think I care?" Kiki shot back. "Thanks to your mother, I've been hungry my entire life."

"You know, it's too bad that poison didn't put you out of your misery. I can't imagine what it must be like to walk around looking like a freak of nature."

"You didn't seem to mind pretending to be me. By the way, Etienne thought that white wig didn't suit you at all."

The princess ran a hand over her ebony locks. "That's the irony! Look at me! I'm exactly what everyone wants a princess to look like, and yet I'm forced to dress up like one of the undead just to claim the crown I deserve."

"I'd stop placing so much importance on looks, if I were you," Kiki warned. "All those princesses you see in the storybooks have a full head of hair."

Sidonia glared at Kiki. "The curse is a myth," she sneered. "I was just being cautious."

"I'm afraid the curse is only too real, dear cousin. If you had ever bothered to study your history, you'd know that baldness has run in our family since at least the twelfth century. Ivana the Cruel was the first queen to lose her hair. Do you know how the people of Pokrovia discovered her secret?"

"How?"

"Her wig fell off when she was beheaded in front of a cheering crowd."

"They chopped off her head?" Sidonia screeched. "I certainly hope those peasants were punished! The thought of putting a queen to death! And cheering about it!"

"Ivana was a tyrant with a serious diamond addiction," Kiki said. "She sold Pokrovia's grain to other countries and used the money to buy herself trinkets. She let her own people starve, and she tortured anyone who spoke out against her."

"Maybe they should have kept their mouths shut," Sidonia snipped.

"That's when our people began to believe that bald women should never be queen," Kiki continued. "It's a stupid superstition, and it would have died out if it hadn't been for your very own mother—Pokrovia's worst ruler since Ivana the Cruel."

"I'll be a much better ruler than my mother was," Sidonia said. "I'll make sure to grease enough palms to keep the right people from turning against me."

"Even if you manage to get yourself out of this mess, you'll still be tested. You'll have to prove that you weren't born with the curse. Anyone who's taken a high school biology class could tell you that the odds aren't in your favor."

"Unless you're a changeling like mother insists, then my odds are as good as yours," Sidonia snarled.

"Perhaps, but I have no intention of claiming the

throne," Kiki said. "Pokrovia is a democracy now, and it should stay that way. You don't deserve to be queen and neither do I. Why should one of *us* get to rule a whole country? Just because we were born into the royal family doesn't mean we'd be any good for Pokrovia. Look at what *your* mother did to the place. That's why I'm going to put an end to the monarchy. There isn't going to be another Queen of Pokrovia. But if I *did* want the crown, at least I'd be able to wear it. Because unlike you, my beloved cousin, *I* have the cure for the curse."

"There is no cure for the royal curse!" Sidonia bellowed. "You made it up! It was all just a trick!"

"I didn't make up a thing," Kiki informed her. "In fact, the cure is already here in Paris. Right down the hall from your room at the Prince Albert Hotel."

"Oh, *please.* A cure for baldness would be worth a billion dollars. There's no way one of your hideous little friends—" Sidonia stopped mid-thought. "Who are *you*?" she demanded rudely.

Marcel Roche had just appeared through one of the hideout's three entrances. Kiki was on her feet in an instant. How long had he been eavesdropping? she wondered. How much had he heard? Whatever information he'd managed to gather, she couldn't possibly allow him to leave. A quick kick to the groin and a chop to the back of his head, and Marcel was on the floor, writhing in pain.

He tried to speak, but the wind had been knocked out of him.

"You have something to say, monsieur? Need some help spitting it out?" Kiki demanded, raising her foot to give him another kick.

"She's gone," the boy wheezed.

Kiki spun around. The sofa was empty. In all the excitement, Sidonia had silently slipped out of the room. Kiki rushed down one of the two passages her cousin might have used as an escape route.

"Sidonia!" she shouted into the silence. "Don't be an idiot! You can't go off on your own! You don't know how to read the signs! You could *die* down here! Sidonia!"

There wasn't an answer.

Far more annoyed than concerned, Kiki sprinted back to the room to get a flashlight. Marcel was still groaning on the floor, but now Etienne and Verushka were standing over him. For a moment, Sidonia Galatzina was completely forgotten as Kiki threw her arms around the old woman still dressed in a nun's habit.

"I'm sorry it took so much longer than expected," Etienne said. "Your aunt kept stalling. She thought the police could find Sidonia. When she finally gave in, we had to stop off and get Verushka some food. Livia hadn't fed her for days."

"Are you okay now?" Kiki asked, pulling back from the embrace and studying her guardian's face.

"I feel strong as a mule," Verushka insisted, patting her stomach. Then she pulled Kiki close and whispered in her ear. "The boy is charming. A good match. Your mother would have liked him very much."

"A match?" Kiki scoffed.

"Excuse me, Kiki," Etienne interrupted. "Where have you put your cousin? And why is Marcel on the floor?"

"Sidonia's gone," Kiki reported. "The moron on the floor was eavesdropping on us. I had to keep him from going back and blabbing everything to his daddy. While I was dealing with him, Sidonia ran off into the tunnels. I don't even know which way she went."

Etienne peered down at Marcel, who was finally beginning to recover. "Do you realize what you've done?" he asked coldly. "This is the second time in two days that you've put others' lives in danger. Why are you here?"

"I couldn't go home," Marcel explained. "I couldn't face my father. I spent last night in the Luxembourg Gardens, but the pigeons wouldn't leave me alone, and I barely got any sleep at all. I was just going to take a quick nap in the hideout."

"This is *my* hideout," Etienne said. "I built it myself. You are no longer welcome here."

"Etienne, I'm sorry! Please forgive me," Marcel pleaded. "I should have never betrayed you."

"It makes no difference if you're sorry or not," Etienne replied mercilessly. "When you told me all the cruel things that your father had said, I felt sorry for you. Now I realize he was right. You're hopeless, Marcel. You're a bumbling idiot who screws everything up."

"No." Marcel looked stricken. "It's not true! I'll show you how useful I am. I'll help you find the girl."

"We don't want your help," Kiki told him.

"Get out," Etienne ordered.

The boy pulled himself to his feet. "*Please,*" he begged. "Let me help."

"Perhaps we should give the boy a chance to speak," Verushka advised.

Etienne seemed too angry to listen. "Get out," he repeated, pointing toward an exit. "Now."

As soon as Marcel had slunk away, Etienne pulled off his backpack. "We need to get to work," he told Kiki. "Your cousin is in terrible trouble."

"Who cares?" Kiki said. "We don't need her anymore now that Verushka is safe. Let Sidonia wander around here for a while. She deserves a good scare."

"I don't think you understand," Etienne told Kiki. "Without a flashlight, Sidonia will never find her way out. Without water, she'll be dead in a couple of days. And if she runs into the wrong people, she might not even last that long."

CHAPTER 25

Betty Bent Gets Tough

There had been no further instructions from Kiki Strike. So at eleven a.m. on Friday, Betty Bent marched through the lobby of the Prince Albert Hotel. Every perfectly coiffed head she passed turned to follow her progress. Gone were her sensible shoes and pretty dress. Betty was sporting a sleek black jumpsuit of her own design, knee-high black boots, and a backpack filled with supplies. A compass. A miner's flashlight. Duct tape. And a small device that resembled a kazoo. Betty had come to Paris prepared.

Amelia Beauregard and Detective Fitzroy were waiting for her by the exit. More than twenty-four hours had passed since Betty had last laid eyes on her employer. Time had only fueled her fury, and the sight of the prim old woman in her gray wool suit made Betty's fists clench.

"Miss Bent!" Madame Beauregard exclaimed. "What on earth are you wearing?"

"You expected me to go to the catacombs dressed like Nancy Drew?" Betty asked. "Listen up, lady. I've spent time underground, and I learned a thing or three while I was down there. It's dark, it's dangerous, and boys who hang out in tunnels aren't interested in girls who wear pearls and pretend to be princesses."

"I'm afraid this new attitude of yours is completely unacceptable," Madame Beauregard announced. "I chose you because I believed—"

"Because you believed I'd do as I was told. Right? You thought a sweet, polite little girl like me would never have the guts to question your authority. Well, you should have picked one of those spineless freaks you create at your institute. I'm not who you thought I was. I'm an *Irregular*. Let's go, Monsieur Fitzroy," she ordered the detective. "We've got a body to find."

"But, Miss Bent . . . ," the detective started to say.

"No buts," Betty snapped. "From this point forward, I'm in charge."

⁎ ⁎ ⁎

Despite the frigid weather, Paris's outdoor cafes were doing a roaring trade. But not a single coffee sipper seemed to notice the unusual pair heading into an abandoned Metro station near the Place de la Republique. The sunken entrance below the sidewalk was barred by a graffiti-covered door. Louis Fitzroy reached into his pocket and withdrew a ring with hundreds of keys.

"I copied a few important keys before I left the force," the man whispered as though he were sharing a delectable secret. He'd tried to start a dozen conversations on their ride across town, and Betty had refused to participate in any of them. Being polite hadn't gotten her anywhere but in trouble.

"Would that be a misdemeanor or a felony in France?" she asked, and the man's smile slid off his face.

The rusty door opened to reveal a set of wide, dusty stairs. The arched ceiling above their heads was low and alive with several species of mold. The soot-smeared subway tiles and rainbow-colored graffiti that lined both sides of the stairwell were the only evidence that they hadn't stumbled upon a passage to Hades. Betty followed Fitzroy down to a platform that hadn't seen a passenger in at least half a century. Somewhere in the distance, subway trains sped through the tunnels that now bypassed the station. Old-fashioned ads shouted out from the walls. The first one that grabbed Betty's eye featured a buxom female silhouette bound by a ribbon inscribed with the names of three perfumes: *Indiscret*, *Passionnement*, and *Scandale*. The next ad sold an insecticide called Flit.

"These ads are all from the 1940s," Betty noted.

"Yes, the city closed this station shortly after the war." Fitzroy seemed thrilled to finally hear Betty speak civilly. "It is off-limits to the public."

"Looks like a lot of other people must have copies of your keys, then." The renegade interior decorators who'd brightened the stairwell had left the platform walls paint-free. But Betty still located a simple logo to prove her point—a pair of interlocking Ds drawn with black chalk on a patch of bare concrete.

"You have a sharp eye. That is the sign of the Darkness Dwellers," Fitzroy said. "This is one of the entrances they employ. We are in their territory now."

The detective walked to the edge of the subway platform and dropped down onto the tracks. He held out both arms to Betty, as if to assist her.

"You've got to be kidding." Betty snorted, spurning his offer and leaping down on her own. "What now?"

"Now we walk," Fitzroy said.

"Are there rats down here?" Betty asked, her eyes scanning the shadows.

"Many," Fitzroy informed her. "But you needn't worry. I've never known rats to attack human beings."

"Then I'd say you don't know much about rats," Betty replied.

They strolled along the tracks in silence. Betty tried to amuse herself by sending the resident rodents scurrying with frequent blasts from her Reverse Pied Piper. But she could see that her companion had something on his mind that he wanted to share. Several times, his lips parted, and Betty thought he might speak. Then his mouth shut without releasing anything more than a sigh.

"What?" Betty finally demanded.

"I'm very sorry, Miss Bent," the detective said. "I wasn't aware that Madame Beauregard brought you to Paris under false pretenses."

"Yeah, who would have guessed an etiquette expert could be so rude?" Betty replied.

"I don't know if I would call her behavior *rude*. Sometimes people act rashly when they feel the pressure of time," the detective said pensively. "I have reason to believe that Madame may not be long for this world. She wants to find Monsieur Grant's body before she dies. Perhaps she intends to be buried beside him."

"How sweet," Betty sneered. "Did *she* tell you that?"

"Certainly not," the detective replied. "Madame Beauregard would never share such information with me. She is a very private person—and she has insisted on secrecy since the day I was hired. Until you came along, I was not permitted to discuss the case with anyone. I must admit, it has made the investigation extremely difficult. The people who know the catacombs best are not the sort who appreciate lies. They might have been more cooperative had I been given permission to tell them the full truth about my quest."

"Maybe you haven't found anything because there's nothing to be found, Monsieur Fitzroy. I have a friend in New York who has been doing a little investigating as well," Betty said. "She told me there was a very good chance that Gordon Grant didn't die in the catacombs. Most people believe he fell in love with a German spy and murdered four of his colleagues."

"Yes, I am familiar with those rumors," Fitzroy said.

"So, what are you going to do if they're true? What if Gordon Grant isn't down here?"

"I'll keep looking," Fitzroy replied.

Betty shook her head. "Either you're crazy or wild-goose chases pay really well these days."

The detective found the notion amusing. "I could make better money. I took this job because I choose to believe in beautiful stories. I would like nothing more than to see Madame and Monsieur reunited at last."

Betty could see the sincerity in the detective's sad smile, and it bothered her to know that such a gentle soul had found himself working for someone so awful. "You seem like a very nice man, Detective Fitzroy, but Amelia Beauregard doesn't deserve your kindness," Betty argued. "She's a horrible old lady who treats people like dirt. You should see what she does to the kids who go to her schools. Why are you so determined to help her?"

The detective paused by an old metal sign that was fixed to the side of the train tunnel. *DANGER DE MORT*, it read.

"Perhaps when you're older you'll understand. Sometimes life turns us into people we were never meant to be. I'm not doing this to help a horrible old lady. I'm doing it for the girl she once was." He waited for Betty to speak, but she was still struggling to imagine Amelia Beauregard as anything but a stuffy old crone.

"So today you and I will search for the Darkness Dwellers," he continued. "It is almost certain we will not find them. But maybe when we return to the surface you can do me one favor? I will tell Madame Beauregard that we made contact with the two boys today, and I will tell her that we have new and promising leads to follow. All I ask is that you don't contradict me."

"Why do we have to lie?" Betty asked.

"Watch Madame's face when I tell her, and you'll know," Fitzroy said. "You'll see the girl we are trying to help."

Betty kicked at one of the tracks with her boot.

"You're hesitant," Fitzroy noted. "May I ask why?"

"Because I've *always* been too nice," Betty said. "I've let people walk all over me my entire life, and I'm sick of it. Even if Madame *is* dying, why should I go out of my way to help her? Why should I let her think I'm weak?"

Detective Fitzroy stroked his whiskers and nodded like a physician presented with a familiar set of symptoms. "After I left the police force, I felt as bitter as you do now. I'd been humiliated by my superiors. My colleagues had called me a fool to my face. For months, I searched for a way to prove to the world that I wasn't an imbecile. Every night, I dreamed of exposing the Darkness Dwellers. Even after I came to see all the good that they do—protecting the tunnels the police won't patrol, preserving Paris's neglected treasures—I still blamed them all for my misfortune.

"And then one day I woke from a terrible dream, and I experienced a revelation of sorts. Finding the Darkness Dwellers wasn't the answer. My colleagues would always call me a fool. But it didn't matter in the slightest—as long as *I* knew I wasn't an idiot. After that, I no longer felt bitter. For the first time in months, I felt free. Do you understand what I'm trying to say?"

"I'm not sure," Betty admitted.

"My point is: What difference does it make what Madame thinks? What difference does it make what *anyone* thinks? Have you ever considered the possibility that your kindness may not be a weakness?" asked the detective. "Perhaps it's a sign of incredible strength. Believe in yourself, Miss Bent. And don't try to be anything but the person you are."

Betty barely knew the man. A single day had passed since they were first introduced. And yet somehow he had found the very words she needed to hear.

"So, can you consider my request, mademoiselle? Will you help me do what I can to make an old woman happy?"

"I suppose." Betty sighed as the last of her anger trickled away. "How much farther do we have to go to get to the catacombs, anyway?"

"We're already here," Fitzroy announced. He turned to the DANGER DE MORT sign and pried one side away from the wall. It opened like a door. Hidden behind it was a hole. "If you're ready, Miss Bent, I'll lead the way."

"Not so fast," the girl told him. "I don't set off on adventures with anyone who won't call me Betty."

"Betty, then," the detective said with a smile.

★ ★ ★

As they crawled on their hands and knees through the wall toward the catacombs, Betty could hear something that sounded like rain. Detective Fitzroy reached an opening and paused.

"The tunnels here have flooded," he said. "You were smart to wear boots." Then he disappeared from view, and Betty heard a splash below. She stuck her head out of the hole. Dirty water dripped from the ceiling and ran down the walls of a rock-lined tunnel. Fitzroy was standing in a murky puddle that looked to be six inches deep. Betty hopped down, and together they waded toward dry ground. Arrows in every imaginable shape, size, and color decorated the walls, but Fitzroy drew Betty's attention to a bird crudely drawn with charcoal. It held a leafy branch in its beak.

"Ignore the arrows. People who have no business in the catacombs use them to mark their paths. If you're in trouble, look for liberty birds instead," he advised. "Their beaks can point you in the direction of the nearest exit."

At last they left the rain behind. The tunnel sloped upward, and the ground was now dry. Betty pulled off her backpack to retrieve her miner's flashlight. The bag brushed against the wall and came away with a smear of green paint on the front pocket. One of the arrows was fresh.

"Someone is just ahead of us," Fitzroy whispered.

"Could it be a Darkness Dweller?" Betty asked.

"It is very unlikely," was the detective's response. "I've never known them to use arrows."

Fitzroy pulled a handkerchief from his pocket and covered the end of his flashlight. The beam grew dim, and they could see no more than a few feet in front of them. They crept down the tunnel. As soon as they spotted a soft glow in the distance and heard the sound of muffled voices, the detective switched his flashlight off altogether.

Ahead, the passage bulged to accommodate a small chamber before branching off in multiple directions. Ghostly white mushrooms sprouted from the floor and scaled the room's walls, their stalks twisting and intertwining. In the darkness beneath their caps lay either death or oblivion. The scene held Betty spellbound until she realized that the forest of giant fungi was nothing more than a mural.

In the center of the chamber, an older man was shining a flashlight on one section of the painting while a younger man ran his fingers over the walls.

"Five minutes, Marcel," the older man announced

gruffly. "I don't know how you heard about the missing persons report, but I won't entertain this nonsense a moment longer."

"There must be a hidden drop point here somewhere!" the younger of the pair insisted. "If there is, I know Etienne will have left a message for the Darkness Dwellers. He'll want their help finding the girl."

"Five minutes, Marcel," the older man repeated.

"No, no, no," Betty heard Detective Fitzroy mutter under his breath. "This is all wrong! Wait here while I get rid of them. Don't let the older man spot you, or you might be arrested."

"Arrested?" Betty whispered.

"That's the head of the Catacomb Patrol," the detective said as he began moving toward the light.

"Philip Roche! I thought I heard your voice!" Fitzroy called out in French.

The boy flinched and the older man trained his flashlight on Fitzroy. Betty slid into a shadow.

The man named Roche regarded the detective with all the respect he'd have shown a rodent. "Louis Fitzroy? What on earth are you doing? You know better than anyone that trespassing in the tunnels is forbidden."

"I'm working on a case," Detective Fitzroy explained. "Searching for a man who may have perished down here during the war."

"You mean searching for a way to repair your reputation," Marcel muttered.

"No, I've come to see the hopelessness of that endeavor," Fitzroy told the boy. "What brings you gentlemen to the catacombs this afternoon?"

The older man sighed wearily. "My son, Marcel, has lost his mind. He's had me chasing phantoms for two full days. Now, here I am indulging him once more. A young woman was recently reported missing, and Marcel claims he saw her here in the tunnels. I'm afraid I must hold you responsible for Marcel's flights of fancy, Louis. He believed all those tall tales you told to the press. He's convinced your Darkness Dwellers exist."

"Ah, but they *did* exist," Fitzroy said. "Unfortunately, I discovered they've been dead for decades. They were a group of spies who worked in the catacombs during the occupation."

"He's lying!" Marcel insisted. "He knows there are still Darkness Dwellers in the catacombs! He's been looking for them! Etienne and I have seen him down here a dozen times."

"You're right, Marcel," Fitzroy conceded. "I am still searching for the Darkness Dwellers. But I'm looking for bones, not breathing bodies."

"Did you hear that, you fool?" the boy's father gloated. "Even the man who started the myth admits now that he was mistaken."

"Fine. So you refuse to believe in the Darkness Dwellers. What about the girls I saw in Etienne's hideout?" Marcel asked, growing increasingly agitated. "Were they figments of my imagination as well?"

Philip Roche grimaced with embarrassment. "My son claims he overheard two princesses fighting over some sort of hair tonic."

Princesses? Betty stopped breathing when she heard the word.

"It was a cure for female baldness!" Marcel almost shouted, and Betty clapped a hand over her own mouth.

"I should never have humored this insanity. Come Marcel, it's time to go home."

"I believe there's an exit just ahead," Fitzroy noted calmly. "Would you like me to lead the way?"

"No!" Marcel returned his attention to the mushroom mural and frantically ran his hands over the paint. Then suddenly his fingers dipped inside a camouflaged crevice. When they emerged, there was a piece of paper pinched between them. "Voilà!" he announced, a victorious smile on his face. He unfolded the tract and began to read.

> ATTENTION ALL DARKNESS DWELLERS.
> ON THE AFTERNOON OF FEBRUARY 20,
> A SIXTEEN-YEAR-OLD GIRL DISAPPEARED
> IN THE TUNNELS. SHE IS WITHOUT FOOD,
> WATER, OR APPROPRIATE ATTIRE.
> SHE HAS NO KNOWLEDGE OF THE
> CATACOMBS AND WILL PERISH WITHOUT
> YOUR ASSISTANCE. AT FIVE P.M., WE WILL
> GATHER IN THE COLISEUM TO FORM A
> SEARCH PARTY. PLEASE JOIN US.
>
> ETIENNE

Marcel glanced up. "There's a response scribbled below. It says, '*We will be there,*' and it's signed by Phlegyas, the leader of the Darkness Dwellers. This is proof, Papa! Proof of everything I've told you!"

"The entire group will be gathering in the same spot

at five?" Philip Roche couldn't quite hide his excitement. He licked his lips like a lion watching a watering hole.

"That's what it says," Marcel confirmed.

"And you know where to find this *coliseum*?"

"Of course. It's in a well-traveled part of the tunnels. Even your men would know how to get there."

"May I take a look?" Detective Fitzroy inquired. He snatched the sheet from the boy's fingers, ripped it into tiny squares, and stuffed the pieces into his mouth. For a moment, both Roches simply stared at him, unable to fathom his actions.

"What did you just do?" Philip Roche demanded.

The detective swallowed. "I did the city of Paris a favor."

Marcel stood stunned. "There is a girl lost in the tunnels, and you just ate the evidence. Don't you realize she'll die if the police don't rescue her soon?"

"Yes, but I'm afraid you've asked the wrong man for help, Marcel," Fitzroy said. "If the girl can be found, the Darkness Dwellers will save her. They are the ones who protect these catacombs and their visitors. Your father knows that, and he's terrified the public will discover the truth. So he buries all evidence of his incompetence. He won't risk his reputation by searching for the missing girl if there's a chance he might not be able to find her."

Marcel seemed to brace himself for a brawl to break out, but all Philip Roche did was laugh.

"Tomorrow morning, no one will care about one missing girl," he informed the detective. "Every newspaper in

France will be trumpeting my latest success. Philip Roche will have single-handedly saved Paris from a gang of subterranean criminals. I'll be a hero. My career will skyrocket. And when it does, I will ensure that you, Louis Fitzroy, never work in this city again."

"What are you talking about, Papa?" Marcel asked, clearly confused.

"Your father is a very lazy man. But now that it won't require much work, it seems he plans to arrest all the Darkness Dwellers," Fitzroy explained.

"For what?" Marcel asked.

"Endangering the city," his father replied. "Such a shadowy group can only be up to no good. I'm sure we'll be able to uncover ample evidence of their plots against Paris. Come along, Louis. It's time for you to escort me to the nearest exit."

"You're leaving?" Marcel cried. "What about the girl? I'm sure I saw her head toward the ossuary. Who knows what could happen if we don't find her soon!"

The older man checked his watch. "It is just past one, Marcel. There is plenty of time for me to arrest Monsieur Fitzroy for trespassing and return to the tunnels with reinforcements. See if you can locate more of these announcements while I'm gone. They will help us prove to the press that the Darkness Dwellers are organized and dangerous."

"What about the girl?" Marcel demanded again.

"We'll send out a search party as soon as the arrests have been made. Good work, my son," said Philip Roche. "Don't do anything to screw it up."

Betty waited until Philip Roche and his prisoner had disappeared into the tunnels. Marcel remained behind, scowling to himself. He was so deep in thought that he didn't hear Betty sneaking up behind him. The handle of her flashlight found the perfect spot on his neck, and he crumpled to the floor without so much as a whimper.

Chapter 26

The Revolt on
Tenth Street

i noticed two things the moment I walked through the door of the Atalanta School for Girls. The zombies were chattering away at an unladylike volume. And Rebecca Gruber was wearing sweatpants. Filthy, hole-ridden, hair-covered sweatpants.

"Oh my God! I was *there*." I heard a girl named Bea Elliot regaling a group of freshmen. "Molly Donovan showed up in my flower-arranging class dressed like Che Guevara. You know—olive-green army pants tucked into combat boots and a red beret on her head."

"A red beret? With *her* hair?" a girl scoffed.

"Actually it looked kinda cute. So, Molly marched up to the instructor and asked if she could say a few words to the class. Ms. Sherman told her to keep quiet and take a seat, but that didn't stop Molly for a second. She stood right there and announced that the institute was turning New York's girls into zombies. She said there was nothing wrong with learning how to use a fish fork, but that you didn't need a lobotomy in order to have good table manners. She asked if anyone in the class had been sent to the institute because their parents wanted them to be someone else. A couple of girls raised their hands, and Molly told them to get up and walk out. It was pretty inspirational. Molly should run for president of something."

"Did anyone actually leave?"

"Yeah! Rebecca Gruber was the first one out the door. Then a girl named Ivy stood up, gave Ms. Sherman a curtsy and the finger—and then she hit the road too."

"*Then* what happened?"

"Molly sat down and stayed for the rest of the class. I gotta say, that girl's got some mad flower-arranging skills."

"The teacher didn't kick her out?"

"No! I heard Molly's got some sort of special scholarship, and the instructors can't do anything until Madame Beauregard gets back from Paris. I can't *wait* to see what happens when she does!"

"Miss Fishbein!" Principal Wickham's voice broke through the din. She'd been observing the action from the other side of the hall. "Will you please join me in my office?"

"Did you hear the good news?" I asked once I was inside. The door slammed behind me, rattling the photos on the office's walls.

"You have misjudged this situation, Ananka," the principal informed me, making it perfectly clear that she was far from pleased. In fact, it had been months since I'd seen her so angry.

"How?" I croaked.

"Sit," she demanded, pointing to a chair. "What exactly

went wrong yesterday afternoon? I was under the impression that you could convince Molly to stay away from Amelia's institute. I thought I could depend on you. Now I hear that Molly has dropped out of the Boreland Academy so she can lead a revolt on Tenth Street."

"I couldn't talk her out of it," I tried to explain. "Molly saw Rebecca Gruber wearing pearls and heels, and it sent her over the edge. But I still don't understand why you're upset, Principal Wickham. I thought you despised L'Institut Beauregard. Why not let Molly have a go at destroying it?"

"Molly doesn't stand a chance. Amelia Beauregard chose her for a reason. She's determined to tame the girl, and there's no doubt in my mind that Amelia will succeed if Molly attends the institute."

"What difference does it make to you if Molly gets tamed? She's not even one of your students anymore! You expelled her!"

It was the wrong thing to say. Principal Wickham looked furious.

"Molly was expelled because she *wanted* to go to another school. She may no longer be a student of mine, but I will *not* abandon a remarkable young girl to a terrible fate. I know what Amelia Beauregard is capable of doing. I've watched bigger spirits be broken by the Beauregard method. You need to speak to Molly Donovan at once and convince her to forget her silly plans before Amelia returns from Paris. Do I make myself clear, Ananka?"

I couldn't seem to find my tongue.

"Do I?" she demanded.

"Yes, Principal Wickham," I mumbled at last.

"Don't disappoint me again," she warned.

"I won't. I promise."

"Good. Then you're excused. I suggest you get started immediately."

When it comes to crying in public, I've always believed that there's one simple rule to be observed: *don't*. Bawl your eyes out in the privacy of your bedroom. Lock yourself in the bathroom and fill the whole tub with tears. I'd rather be seen picking my nose and eating the evidence than be caught crying at school. Still, that morning, I fled the principal's office with tears in my eyes. Somehow I had managed to disappoint the one adult who had always believed in me. My meddling had put Molly Donovan in danger. And if Amelia Beauregard was half as bad as Principal Wickham believed, who knew what she was planning to do to poor Betty Bent. My phone began to vibrate inside my coat pocket. I ducked into the girls' room to wipe my eyes and take the call.

"Have you heard from Oona?"

"Hi, Luz," I said. "Hold on a second." I unrolled some toilet paper and blew my nose.

"That was really gross," Luz said. "You should put the phone down when you do that."

"Sorry. What was that about Oona?"

"Have you heard from her? I've been trying to call her for the last three hours. She isn't picking up her phone."

"I was with her last night. . . . Oh no." I moaned. "Where are you right now?"

"Where do you think I am?" Luz asked. "I'm at school!"

"Can you meet me at First Street and Bowery?"

"Is Oona in trouble? Does this have something to do with Lili?"

"Yeah," I told her. "I'm pretty sure that it does."

Fans of monster movies know that every beast is born with a flaw. The dragon has a scale-free patch somewhere on its belly. The witch can be dissolved with a bucket of water. The gorgon will be turned to stone by the sight of her own face in the mirror. No matter how powerful or invincible the movie monster might seem, there's always a way to bring the beast to its knees. Unfortunately, the same also holds true for everyone in the audience. We all have a weakness—a soft spot we hope will never be hit. If a blow were to find that chink in our armor, even the toughest of characters could crack, crumble, and fall. No one is invincible—not even a tough-talking former delinquent like Oona Wong. Which means I should have been better prepared to pick up the pieces when my friend finally cracked. I'd known for months that Oona's weakness was her family.

I hopped out of a cab on the corner of First Street and Bowery. Luz was waiting, and I brought her up to date as we hurried toward Lili Liu's alley. When the maintenance shed came into view, Luz skidded to a sudden halt.

"You left Oona in there last night?" she shouted. *"Alone?* What were you thinking, Ananka?"

"She said she wanted to deal with Lili by herself!"

"And you just *let* her? You remember what happened the last time Oona refused our help! She ended up wrapped like a mummy and left for dead! You should have made Iris stay with her last night."

"Iris is twelve. She had to get home."

"Then Kaspar could have kept her company. He didn't even have school today!"

"I'm sorry," I said. "I wasn't thinking straight. I've had too many things on my mind."

Luz shook her head in disgust. "This is the last straw, Fishbein. You need to stop mooning over Betty's boyfriend and start acting like you're in charge, or *I'm* going to stage a mutiny."

"You know about Kaspar?"

"*Everyone* knows, Ananka."

"I'm going to kill Iris McLeod," I muttered.

"What does *Iris* have to do with it?" Luz demanded before rushing off toward the shed.

The tiny room was dark and cold. The oil in the camping lantern had burned out. A figure wrapped in a sleeping bag sat in the corner, as still as an Incan mummy. But this wasn't a sacrifice left on a mountain peak to appease an ancient god. The still, silent girl was a victim of my own selfishness and stupidity.

"Oona?" Luz called out, but there wasn't an answer. When she bent down and shook the girl, Oona's head flopped to one side. Her lips were blue.

"Lili?" she mumbled without opening her eyes.

"Hypothermia," Luz diagnosed. "We should call an ambulance."

"No!" Oona groaned. "I'm fine!"

"She's *not* fine," Luz argued.

"Then let's get her back to my house," I said. "It's only a couple of blocks away."

Luz and I each grabbed one of Oona's arms and dragged her out of the shed. When we reached the avenue, she started to struggle. "Let me go, I can walk by myself!" she insisted through chattering teeth.

"Sure you can," Luz said, clutching her arm even tighter.

Thankfully, my parents had classes that afternoon, and unlike me, they never skipped school. The apartment was empty. I wrapped Oona in our warmest comforter and made her sit on the side of the tub while a scalding-hot shower filled the bathroom with steam. A few minutes later, Luz arrived with a cup of hot chamomile tea, and we all waited silently in the thickening fog until Oona finally stopped shivering.

"Thanks," Oona told us. "I tried my best to stay awake last night, but I must have fallen asleep around dawn."

"It's fifteen degrees outside," Luz lectured, furious in the way people get at those they love. "People die all the time in this kind of weather."

"I *know*," Oona said. "That's why I was waiting for Lili. But she never showed up."

"Maybe there's somewhere else she goes when the weather is bad," I offered hopefully.

"Or maybe she fell asleep outside and froze to death." Oona's lips were quivering again, though they'd already returned to a healthy shade of pink. "I'm such a jerk. This whole time I thought Lili was out to destroy me. If I had seen her on the street, I would have hauled her butt straight to the police. I should have guessed that my father had abandoned her, too. My twin sister has been homeless for months, and I haven't lifted a finger to help her."

"If you made a mistake, we have time to fix it. We'll find Lili," I promised, humbled by Oona's unexpected transformation. "And if you want us to, the Irregulars will give your sister all the help she needs."

"Thanks," Oona said. "I'll ask my grandmother to get one of our extra rooms ready for Lili. And she can put a few of my clothes in the closet for her."

"Wow. That's really nice of you, Oona." I never would have dreamed she'd go *that* far.

"Speaking of Mrs. Fei, you should call her as soon as possible," Luz told Oona. "She must be worried to death. You know, the next time you decide to spend the night in an alley, the least you could do is take your phone. I was trying to reach you all morning."

"I *did* take it," Oona said. "I just used up the battery surfing the Internet."

"Surfing the Internet?" I asked.

"Yeah, well, I didn't have anything else to do while I was in that shed, so I cracked your dumb code."

"What code?" Luz asked.

"Amelia Beauregard's old boyfriend wrote a message in code right before he disappeared in 1944. It was kept top secret for years, but no one's ever figured out what it said."

Oona fished a small notebook out of the back pocket of her jeans. Its pages warped as soon as they were exposed to the steam.

"Well, the mystery's over. This is what Gordon Grant wrote." She tapped one perfectly manicured nail on a short, handwritten paragraph.

> I never believed I could love anyone but you. Thyrza has proven me wrong. I'm surrounded by darkness, but the world seems brighter than ever before. I know you have the strength to survive without me.

"It must have been a letter to Amelia Beauregard." As much as I despised the woman, I couldn't help but feel a little bit sorry for her.

"Looks like he was giving her the boot for someone else," Luz remarked with no show of compassion.

"But she never got the letter," I added. "The military kept it secret for sixty years. Now Madame Beauregard's got Betty in the catacombs searching for a man who's not even down there. He's probably in Bavaria sharing a schnitzel with his girlfriend the German spy."

"I'm not so sure about the German spy part," Oona said. "Thyrza is a Hebrew name. It means, 'she's my delight.' I doubt there were too many Nazis with names like that."

"But still, Gordon deserted Amelia, and she doesn't even know it."

"She knows it," Oona said. "I'd bet you anything."

"How would she know?" Luz and I asked simultaneously.

"You said some book published the code last year?" Oona asked me.

"Yeah. So?"

"So you think lovesick old Amelia Beauregard wasn't the first person to read it?"

"But she couldn't have cracked the code by herself," Luz argued.

"*Of course* she cracked the code. It may have taken *me* all night to figure out what the key was, but she knew it all along. Remember the notes on the lilies she leaves at the marble cemetery? Remember what she signs them?"

"ILEMA."

"Exactly. I always *thought* it was a weird name. It's

actually an anagram of the five letters used in the name Amelia. They didn't need two As, so they dropped one."

"Okay, you're losing me," I said.

"ILEMA is a key. Gordon and Amelia must have arranged to use a poem code to communicate. Poem codes were used a lot during World War II. They weren't very sophisticated, but they were really hard to crack if you didn't have the key—or if the same poem wasn't used more than a couple of times."

"So, how did *you* crack it?" I asked.

"I knew which poem Gordon Grant used! The same one Beauregard leaves at the cemetery! You know—*I will not ask where thou liest low . . .*" Oona rolled her eyes when she saw I still didn't understand. "A poem code works like this, Fishbein . . . You memorize part of a poem. You choose five words from that poem at random and string them together, and you use those five words to develop a *cipher.* Then you encrypt your message. To *decipher* the message, you need to know which words were chosen from the poem. The key tells you which ones they were. 'I' is the ninth letter of the alphabet, so the ninth word of the poem was first. 'L' is the twelfth letter of the alphabet, so the twelfth word of the poem was next. 'E' is the fifth letter of the alphabet, and so forth."

"Okay, okay, okay!" Luz sighed, fed up with the explanation. "So, if Amelia knows that Gordon broke up with her in 1944, why is she still searching for his body?"

"That's a very good question," I said.

"Should we be worried about Betty?" Oona asked.

"I already am," I told her. "Even my principal thinks

Amelia Beauregard is dangerous. Someone call Betty and share the news about Gordon. If nothing else, maybe she'll find a way to use it to her advantage. Then get on my computer and see if you can dig up any information about a spy named Thyrza."

"Are you going somewhere?" Luz asked.

"Do you have plans with Kaspar again?" Oona said, glaring at me.

"You're hilarious," I said. "I happen to have a date with a movie star."

THE FISHBEIN GUIDE TO . . . THE WRITTEN WORD

If you really mean it, *write* it. Let's say your favorite aunt just sold her Picasso to send you to spy school. Don't send her a text or an e-mail. For heaven's sake, write the woman a thank-you note! Like love letters, bank-robbery notes, and anonymous crime tips, thank-you cards are always best when handwritten. But there are a few things you should consider before putting pen to paper . . .

Be Sure to Practice Your Handwriting

There are many people who believe that a person's handwriting contains hidden clues about her personality. I'm inclined to agree. A quick course in graphology will help you figure out what it *really* means when someone dots the letter *i* with a heart. (My guess? She's probably dangerously unhinged.)

If You Must Remain Anonymous

Blowing the whistle on a powerful criminal? Writing a love letter to the kid down the street? Then you certainly won't want to send an e-mail. And don't bother with the Hello Kitty stationery, either. Get a sheet of white copy paper and a black pen. Write a draft first. Don't get chatty—get straight to the point. Don't use slang or phrases that you tend to use all the time. And don't dot your *i*'s with hearts.

If You Must Communicate Electronically

There's a little thing called "spell check." Use it. I personally feel that spelling is an overrated skill. (Largely because I can't.) However, a letter filled with spelling errors is unlikely to communicate your impressive intelligence. A flawless note takes only a few clicks. If you can't be bothered to make them, then you probably don't care very much about the person you're e-mailing.

If You Must Preview Your Own Mail

I should remind you that opening other people's mail is a federal offense. And take it from me—you don't want to mess with the PO. However, there are certain situations in which you might want to take a private peek at your own letters before ripping them open in front of an audience. In these cases, there are several methods to consider. Your first option is to steam the seal open. Some people prefer the steam from a tea kettle, but I find this method messy, unreliable, and potentially painful. A steaming iron works much better. Just pass the iron back and forth across the seal until you can slide a butter knife underneath. Make sure the iron doesn't leave a scorch mark! Not confident in your ironing skills? Spraying the back of an envelope with hairspray can make it temporarily transparent. It can also make it a bit smelly. If you're good with your hands, you can fashion your own letter-removal device. (Check out the CIA website for examples.) But the easiest way to crack the seal on a letter may be to place it in the freezer for a few hours.

CHAPTER 27

Catching Flies
with Honey

Betty was examining a map Marcel had made of the catacombs when she heard the boy begin to moan. She had propped him up against a wall, his wrists bound with duct tape and his ankles tied with his own shoelaces. It was exactly what Kiki Strike would have done—karate-chopped first and saved the questions for later. A few of the Irregulars might have done worse. But none of us could have taken down Marcel any better than Betty. Yet after the adrenaline stopped coursing through her system, all Betty felt was remorse. She might need the boy's help to find Kiki, and beating people up isn't the best way to ask for assistance.

"Who are you?" Marcel demanded in French when he found his voice. "And why do I keep getting pummeled by girls?"

"I'm very sorry for hitting you," Betty said sweetly. "I needed to make sure you'd cooperate, but I went too far. Are you feeling okay? Can I get you anything?"

At first she wondered if her French was faulty, because Marcel didn't seem to understand a word she'd said. He gaped at her as if she were babbling away in an unknown tongue.

"I hope you don't mind," Betty continued, trying to enunciate more clearly, "but I borrowed the map you had in your pocket. Is it accurate?"

"What?" Marcel snapped out of his daze. "Of course it's accurate, and of course I mind if you take it! It took months to make that map!" He struggled against his restraints for a moment before finally admitting defeat. "You can't leave me tied up. There are people down here who might do much more than hit me."

"I promise—you'll be just fine if you cooperate," Betty assured him. "If not, your dad said he'd be back in a couple of hours. I'm more worried about the two girls you saw down here in the catacombs. Can you tell me a little bit more about them?"

"Why? So you can try to find them and disappear, too?" Marcel barked. "The police are involved now. They'll locate the missing girl."

"Sure, after they've arrested all the Darkness Dwellers," Betty countered. "But you made it sound as if the search couldn't wait. And you didn't seem too happy when your father announced that he had other plans. Speaking of which, are you really going to let him arrest the Darkness Dwellers? Detective Fitzroy told me they never do anyone any harm."

"Maybe not, but they're breaking the law," Marcel argued without conviction. "Why should they be allowed to control the catacombs? You heard my father. They can't be up to any good. Some of them might even be terrorists."

"You don't believe that," Betty scoffed. "And neither does your dad. If you ask me, you've been bending over backward to impress someone who can't be impressed. Your father seems like a difficult man. It must have been pretty hard growing up with him."

Marcel stayed silent as Betty sat down on the floor across from him. When Kiki first met Marcel, she'd instantly recognized a boy pretending to be someone he wasn't. Betty, on the other hand, saw a boy who was still trying to figure out who he was.

"I'm sorry, this conversation must seem very strange to you," Betty said. "I know the French tend to be much more reserved than Americans. I'm just trying to understand. . . ."

"My father thinks I'm weak," Marcel said, his voice cracking a little. "And stupid and slovenly and undisciplined."

"How do you know? Maybe . . ."

"He's told me every day since I was ten years old."

"Oh," Betty said. There was no arguing with that. "Well, *are* you stupid, slovenly, and undisciplined?"

Marcel appeared to find the question confusing. "No!"

"Then that's all that matters. Let your father think what he likes," Betty said, sharing Detective Fitzroy's wisdom. "I doubt helping him arrest a bunch of innocent people would make him change his mind, anyway. In fact, I still don't understand why you're letting him ambush them. Do you have something personal against the Darkness Dwellers?"

"No!" Marcel exclaimed.

"Then why have you been trying so hard to prove they exist?"

Marcel's head drooped. He seemed too embarrassed to meet Betty's eye. "A few years ago, I overheard my father laughing about an interview that Louis Fitzroy had given to one of the papers. But when I read the article for myself, I thought the Darkness Dwellers sounded like heroes. I told this to my father, and he laughed at me. He insisted the organization didn't exist. He claimed the only people inside the catacombs were graffiti artists, petty criminals, and police officers. He made me feel ridiculous. So I came to the catacombs to find proof that the group was real. I thought that might make him take me more seriously."

"So you wanted to prove that your father could be wrong. Not just about the Darkness Dwellers, but about you, too?"

Marcel shrugged. "I don't know. It does sound stupid, doesn't it?"

"It doesn't sound *stupid*. It was just a bad idea," Betty said. "We've all had them. But I think I may have just had a good one. The two girls you saw in the catacombs— would you mind describing them for me?"

Something he saw in Betty's eyes seemed to give the boy hope. "I can do more than that. I know one of them— her name is Kiki. My friend Etienne and I found her locked in a bell tower. She's tiny, with white hair and pale skin. Etienne thinks she's cute, but she looks just like a vampire to me. The girl who was with Kiki has black hair and the face of a goddess. I'm thinking either she or Kiki might be the Princess of Pokrovia who was reported missing early this morning."

"Which of the girls is lost in the tunnels?"

"When I found them, they were arguing. Kiki jumped up and attacked me, and the beautiful girl ran away."

"The dark-haired girl is alone in the catacombs?" Betty refused to use the word *beautiful* to describe Sidonia. The girl was anything *but* to those who knew her.

"Yes," Marcel said. "Is *she* the Princess?"

"Can I trust you?" Betty asked gravely. The boy nodded. "The girl with black hair is Sidonia Galatzina. She's one of *two* living princesses of Pokrovia. Kiki is Princess Katarina—Sidonia's cousin and the true heir to the throne. I came to Paris to help her."

"You're friends with Kiki?" Marcel grimaced.

"I know this may be hard to believe after she attacked you, but Kiki's the good guy," Betty said. "Sidonia and her mother are the ones who locked her in that bell tower."

"Then you probably won't want to be associated with me. Kiki is convinced I'm a traitor," Marcel admitted, sounding hopeless once again. "And I guess I am. I betrayed my friend Etienne. I used him to help me locate the Darkness Dwellers. Kiki knows all about it. That's one reason she punched me."

"Then I suggest you find a way to prove that you've changed, which brings me back to that good idea I just had. Kiki's cousin is in serious danger. As much as they hate each other, I know Kiki wouldn't want her to die. Help me find Sidonia, and I'll let you take all the credit. I hear rescuing a princess is a tried and true way to look like a hero."

"What about the Darkness Dwellers?"

"We'll figure out a way to let them know what your

father has planned. They don't need to know the role you played in it all."

"Why are you being so nice to me?" Marcel asked.

"I know how it feels to be misunderstood," Betty said. She bent down and untied Marcel's wrists and ankles. When they stood facing each other, Betty could see just how large the boy was. Without the element of surprise, she had no hope of subduing him if he decided to attack.

"I'll take the map back now," he said. Betty passed him the document and wondered whether she'd just made a terrible mistake. Marcel studied the paper for a moment. Then he folded the map and shoved it in his pocket. "I saw which way that princess went when your friend's back was turned. I tried to tell Kiki, but she refused to listen. The girl went in the direction of the ossuary."

"That's what I heard you tell your father. What's the ossuary?"

"Hundreds of years ago, they cleaned out the graveyards in Paris and put the bones in one section of the catacombs. There are six million Parisians down here."

"If that's where Sidonia ended up, she must be scared to death," Betty remarked.

"I'm not so concerned about that," Marcel said. "I'm worried that she might not be alone in there."

CHAPTER 28

Reclaim Your Brain

i've often thought that most New Yorkers would make excellent spies. Even as children we're trained to observe others without making eye contact. We can read a book on the subway while keeping tabs on the strange character three seats to our left. (There's *always* a weirdo a few seats away.) We know our neighbors' juiciest secrets without ever exchanging a word with them. And when it comes to celebrity spotting, New Yorkers are unparalleled masters. We can see through their disguises, register their fashion choices, chart their movements, and text our friends—all while looking world-weary and bored.

I'd never been inside Theresa Donovan's home, but I could have given you directions to her door when I was in the fourth grade. She and her family lived less than a dozen blocks from me, in a redbrick building that had been a firehouse a century earlier. The front entrance was wide enough for a horse-drawn fire engine, and if you peeped through the windows, you could see bronze poles disappearing through the first-floor ceiling into the living quarters above.

I knocked at the Donovans' door, never expecting Molly's mother to answer. When she did, it felt like I'd come face-to-face with every queen, con-woman, and murderess she'd ever portrayed. For a moment, it put me on guard.

"Ananka!" Mrs. Donovan exclaimed with surprise. She actually sounded quite pleased to discover me on her doorstep. "Have you come to see Molly? I'm afraid she's not at home at the moment. She told me she had a few errands to run."

"Principal Wickham insisted I talk to her as soon as possible. Does Molly have a phone with her?"

It was the most innocent of questions, and yet it seemed to break Mrs. Donovan's heart just a little. "Molly hasn't used a phone since she enrolled at the Boreland Academy. My daughter doesn't enjoy staying in touch. Before she came home to attend L'Institut Beauregard, I hadn't heard her voice in almost two months."

"Two *months*?" I was trying to imagine what it would take to avoid *my* mother for that long, when I felt a miniature missile thwack my ear. Another grazed the tip of my nose. I glanced up at the sky and was hit on the forehead by a pea-sized chunk of ice. "I hate to ask, Mrs. Donovan, but would you mind if I wait for Molly inside?"

"Not at all!" Molly's mother said as though she wished the idea had been her own. "Please, come in! They said on the news that there's an ice storm heading in our direction. And I could use a little company myself."

She led the way through the living room of my dreams

to a kitchen at the back of the house. An entire wall along our route was filled with photos of her daughter. A toddler Molly drawing numbers on the furniture with chocolate syrup. A school-age Molly making alterations to one of her mother's ball gowns using a pair of garden shears. A teenage Molly riding a giant sow and proudly holding a second-place trophy. There were no movie posters in sight. No golden statues. No humanitarian awards or honorary Harvard degrees. In fact, there was nothing to suggest that one of the most famous women in the world had ever spent time in the building.

When we reached the kitchen, I settled into a breakfast nook beneath a bay window cluttered with more Molly memorabilia while Theresa Donovan busied herself at the stove.

"You caught me in the act of making cocoa. Don't tell my trainer. Would you like a cup?"

"Yes, thank you." *Cocoa?* I liked Mrs. Donovan, I really did. But I had to wonder how someone with all the edge of Snow White—and the killer instincts of Bambi— could have made it in the cutthroat world of show business. I would have been less surprised to hear that Betty Bent had taken charge of the Gambino crime family.

"So, you say Theodora Wickham sent you to see Molly?" Mrs. Donovan placed a mug of sweet-smelling chocolate in front of me.

"Yes," I confirmed as I stirred my cocoa. "She's furious that I couldn't talk Molly out of enrolling at L'Institut Beauregard. She wants me to give it another shot."

"I'm not sure *why* Theodora is more worried than I am, but I do appreciate her concern," Mrs. Donovan said. "She's always had a soft spot for Molly. And Molly respects Theodora. There must be seventy years between them, yet they seem to understand each other completely."

"Principal Wickham knows Molly is special," I said. "I'm not talking about Molly's math skills. She's one of a kind, and the principal doesn't want Madame Beauregard to turn her into everyone else."

On the silver screen, Theresa Donovan's face could project any emotion. In real life, she was so sweet that she could barely manage a convincing frown. "You've met Amelia Beauregard. Do you really think she's capable of something like that?"

"I don't know," I admitted. "Madame Beauregard is one of a kind too."

Theresa Donovan slid into a seat across from me. "After our discussion with Principal Wickham, I had a peek at L'Institut Beauregard's website, and I think I recognized the headmistress's face. When Molly was three years old, there was a game she liked to play whenever we went out for a walk. She would add up all the numbers she saw on the street. Telephone numbers, license-plate numbers, building addresses. Sometimes she'd get so excited that she'd break away from me and start running. Well, one day, Molly ran right into an old lady and knocked her over. I was *horrified*. When I finally reached them, the woman and Molly were just sitting there *staring* at each other. After I helped the lady to her feet, she announced that a child like mine should be sent to obedience school or kept on a leash. I think she even handed me a business card."

"Yeah, that sounds like something Madame would do," I said.

"I was mortified by the whole incident. I didn't know the first thing about being a parent back then. I suppose I still don't. But I do know that I would never want my daughter to be *obedient*. I don't understand why people send their children to that terrible etiquette academy."

"I know that it's not my place to suggest this, Mrs. Donovan, but why don't you just forbid Molly from going to L'Institut Beauregard?"

"Do you really think that would work?" Molly's mother asked with a hopeless laugh.

"I guess not," I admitted.

"I don't see or talk to Molly enough as it is. To be honest, I'm thrilled to have her home from the Boreland Academy. I don't want us to spend our days arguing. I just wish Molly enjoyed my company a little bit more. My own mother died in an accident when I was very small. I'd give anything for a chance to have known her."

I was hardly qualified to offer parent-child counseling, but I saw real tears in the actress's eyes, and I needed to say something. "Maybe Molly's just going through a difficult phase."

"Molly was five years old when she started telling people she was adopted."

"Was she?" I couldn't resist.

"No," Theresa Donovan said with a sad smile. "She's all mine."

A door slammed just as I lifted my cup to my lips, and cocoa spilled down the front of my sweater. I could hear the sound of heavy boots stomping in our direction. A figure in a long black coat and knee-high Wellingtons appeared in the doorway. Two angry green eyes glared at me from behind a ski mask.

"What is that—*cocoa*?" the intruder sneered, setting down the cardboard box she had been lugging and ripping off the mask. Molly's fiery curls crackled with static electricity.

"Molly!" Theresa Donovan gasped. "Please don't be rude. Ananka is our *guest*."

"I came to talk to you about the institute," I said. "Principal Wickham and I—"

"You can spare me your lecture, Ananka." She turned to her mother. "I may be having a few friends over after school today."

"Well, if you're planning to treat them the way you're treating Ananka . . ."

"I wasn't asking. I was *telling* you," Molly said.

"Geez, Molly," I groaned, embarrassed by her rudeness.

"Gotta go," Molly announced, grabbing her box. "I have very important work to do."

I followed her through the kitchen and out the back of the building. Tucked away in a hidden courtyard was an ivy-covered carriage house. Molly stopped just inside the door and kicked off her boots. I stood in utter shock as my eyes passed from the giant portrait of Ananka Jr. that was hanging above a sofa to the impressive collection of medieval gargoyles mounted to one of the brick walls. Molly Donovan had her own house.

"This is all yours, isn't it?" I asked.

"Yeah," Molly said without bothering to look back at me. "It's time you knew the truth. I'm a spoiled rotten brat."

"That wasn't what I was thinking. But you shouldn't treat your mom like that." I was whispering, even though there was no chance Theresa Donovan could hear us.

"Everyone else kisses Mommy Dearest's famous butt. Why should I?" Molly said.

"That's not the point! And for your information, I don't give a hoot that she's a movie star. She's one of the nicest—"

Molly spun around so suddenly that I braced for an attack. "If you're going to give me the speech about how lucky I am to have a mom like her, believe me, I've heard it a million times. I don't deserve to have a sweet, beautiful, perfect mother. And she doesn't deserve a horrible, redheaded delinquent like me."

"Oh, come on!"

"I don't have time for this, Ananka. I've declared war on L'Institut Beauregard. I'm going to fight for all the girls who didn't turn out right. For the freaks of nature. For the black sheep. For all the girls like Rebecca Gruber, who are too clumsy or too hairy or too wild or too tomboyish. I'm going to fight for the girls who were sent to that institute because *someone* wasn't satisfied with them."

The speech gave me goose bumps. For a moment, I was prepared to follow Molly Donovan into battle. "It's a noble cause," I admitted. "But you've got to see—you're *not* one of those girls. Okay, so maybe your mom doesn't understand you. *My* mother is convinced that I'm a pathological liar. But your mom isn't trying to change anything about you, Molly. She loves you the way you are."

Molly snorted. "Because she's a saint. But every time

anyone sees the two of us together, I always know exactly what they're thinking. How did Theresa Donovan give birth to *that*?"

"Even if that's true—and it's *not*—why would you punish your mom for stuff other people think? You know, she told me you tell people that you were adopted. Can you even imagine how much that might hurt her?"

"Yeah, well do *you* have a better explanation?" Molly asked. "My mother and I look nothing alike. We act nothing alike. You know, one of her stupid actor friends used to call me the changeling whenever my mother left the room. He said it right to my face once when I was four. He didn't think I understood what it meant."

"So what? You're Molly Donovan! You're a legend! A hero to half the girls in Manhattan! You don't care what other people say about you!"

"God, Ananka, you're more annoying than all my old shrinks put together. Look, I don't want to be *rude,* but I really don't have any desire to explore my issues right now."

Molly took an X-ACTO knife from a desk drawer and slashed open the cardboard box she'd just brought home. Inside were stacks of neon-green leaflets.

"What are those?" I asked.

"Ads for my new academy. I'm going to hand them out to all the Beauregard girls." She passed me a page from the top of the pile.

Reclaim Your Brain!
Every night at 8 PM
The Donovan House, Wooster Street

Free instruction in subjects every young lady should master
Hand-to-Hand Combat • Guerilla Warfare
Animal Husbandry • Skeet Shooting
Camouflage • Rodeo Riding • Judo

I had to admit it. Molly's school sounded pretty amazing.

"How are you going to teach these classes? Have you actually been trained to do any of this stuff?"

"No, but I'm filthy rich and I know my way around the Internet. I've hired all the experts I need."

"Amelia Beauregard is going to murder you," I said.

"I can't wait to see her try," Molly said.

That's when my phone began to ring.

ChAPTER 29

The Bombs Below

Good manners are the ultimate sign of good breeding and good parenting.
— Amelia Beauregard, *Savoir Faire*

When I was small, one of the first things my parents tried to teach me was to chew with my mouth closed. The question I always asked (usually without bothering to swallow my Brussels sprouts) was: *Why?* I wasn't really trying to be rude. I truly didn't understand. Who cared if I looked like a little barbarian? Why was everyone watching me, anyway? And why did my parents expect me to put on some kind of show every time we ate a meal in public? More often than not, the frustrated reply I received was, "Just do it, Ananka." As you might imagine, I was hardly convinced.

But there was one response that might have made a difference. My mother could have said something like this: *Imagine a washing machine with a window. Now, fill*

that machine with Brussels sprouts, chicken, mashed pota-
toes, and spit. As you watch the contents begin to churn, sit
down and try to enjoy a meal. Getting a little sick to your
stomach? Well that's how everyone else feels when you
chew with your mouth open.

The point I'm trying to make here is that manners
weren't invented to make you or your parents look good. I
don't really care if adults think I'm sweet, charming, and
well behaved. (In fact, I would question their sanity if they
did.) But I'd rather people not feel sick in my presence.
Manners, I've realized, aren't about impressing people.
They're about being *considerate.* And a four-letter word for
considerate is *kind.*

Which brings me, believe it or not, back to the dark,
dank tunnels beneath Paris. Kiki lingered a few steps
behind as Etienne and Verushka toured the catacombs,
cramming notes into the various cracks and crevices used
as drop points by the Darkness Dwellers. The moment the
trio had left the hideout, the future Duc de Lutèce had
offered his arm to the old soldier, and they'd walked side
by side ever since. Etienne was a gracious host, eager to
answer questions about subterranean Paris and happy
to absorb any wisdom that Verushka wanted to share.
And when Verushka began to show signs of a limp, he
slowed his own pace without saying a word.

Kiki had never known her own mother, but she had
listened closely to Verushka's stories and read every book
ever written about her mother's short, ill-fated life. By all
accounts, the most beloved princess in the history of Pokrovia had shown all of her subjects the utmost kindness.
And she had done so without ever realizing that it might

seem unusual. Princess Sophia had been known to give tours of the palace to children caught trespassing on its grounds. She invited workmen to lunch with the royal family and had her chauffeur offer lifts to anyone walking with a cane, a crutch, or an unwieldy bag of groceries. The heir to the throne treated her maid with the same courtesy she would have offered a grand duchess. Such behavior had scandalized those like her sister, Livia, who insisted that manners needn't be shown to the masses. Those who knew better realized the Princess's kindness had earned her people's love—but more importantly, it had also earned their respect.

And as Kiki watched Etienne and Verushka travel through the catacombs arm in arm, she realized that the woman who'd raised her was right. Sophia would have liked Etienne Antoine very much, indeed.

"Do you mind if we stop here and rest for a few minutes?" she heard Etienne ask the counterfeit nun after he'd stuffed yet another piece of paper into a hole in the tunnel wall.

"I think that's a good idea," Kiki announced when she reached the pair. "Verushka's leg must be hurting by now."

"I am a soldier," Verushka insisted, ready to forge on. "I feel nothing."

"You may be a soldier, but you're a terrible actress," Kiki said.

Etienne checked the time. "It's four fifteen. We should turn back toward the coliseum soon. It will be a long walk, and I could use a break myself."

"Are you sure we've delivered enough of these messages? Are the Darkness Dwellers going to find any of them?" Kiki asked skeptically. "We haven't seen a soul the whole time we've been in the tunnels."

"That doesn't mean there isn't anyone down here," Etienne replied. "All we need is a one member to read our note. A single Darkness Dweller will be able to relay the information to his associates aboveground."

Etienne helped Verushka lower herself down to the dusty ground. Once the weight was off her wounded leg, the old woman exhaled with relief.

"May I ask how you injured your leg?" Etienne inquired. "You don't have to tell me if you'd rather not talk about it."

"I was shot," Verushka replied bluntly.

"Two and a half years ago. By one of Livia Galatzina's men," Kiki added. "The bullet was poisoned. Verushka almost died a few months ago."

"And yet here she is, searching the catacombs for Livia's daughter?" Etienne marveled.

"If it was Livia who was lost underground, I would not strike a match to look for her," Verushka explained. "Sidonia is only a child."

"A cruel, evil, despicable child," Kiki said.

Verushka raised an eyebrow. "Or perhaps a weak, confused child who was trained to behave like her mother."

"Sidonia is almost *seventeen,* Verushka. She's not a little girl. She's not going to change."

"I am almost sixty-one. To me, Sidonia is a child. And even *I* am not too old to change."

Kiki huffed. "I think you've been wearing that nun's habit too long. You're going soft."

"If that's what you prefer to believe, Katarina, then perhaps we should talk of other things," Verushka said. "I have wanted to visit these tunnels since I was a very young woman. I do not want the experience to be ruined by bickering."

"Why don't you tell Kiki the story you told me?" Etienne jumped in. "I'm sure she would like to hear about the mystery of the catacomb bombs."

"When were there bombs in the catacombs?" Kiki asked. "And why haven't I heard anything about them?"

"People forget bombs that never exploded," said Verushka. "But when I was training for the Royal Guard of Pokrovia, my favorite instructor was an expert on sabotage. He worked with the French during World War II and arrived in Paris the day the Germans retreated. He could not believe his eyes when he saw that the city was standing. It was known to all that Hitler had ordered his troops to leave nothing but a pile of debris. Some time later, a German general took credit for saving the capital. He claimed Hitler had given the order to bomb Paris, but that he had refused to comply. My instructor never believed the man was telling the truth. He was convinced there was another explanation. He knew that explosives had been found throughout the catacombs. They must have been part of a plot to destroy Paris, but for some reason it did not succeed."

"You have to admit, it was a remarkable plan," Etienne said. "Everyone expected the Germans to bomb Paris from the air, but they were going to destroy it from below."

"Had you heard this story before?" Kiki asked him.

"No," Etienne said. "I knew the Germans had bunkers down here, of course, and that the French Resistance also used the tunnels. I think there were other groups as well. In fact, I've started to wonder if the original Darkness Dwellers might have been English spies."

"The original Darkness Dwellers?" Kiki asked.

"English spies?" Verushka added.

Etienne turned to Kiki. "Do you recall the rubble I pointed out the other day when we were on our way to the party?"

"You said you knew a story about it," Kiki recalled. "But then we were interrupted."

"I once asked Phlegyas why he had given the Darkness Dwellers an English name. He told me he pulled it out of that rubble on his very first trip to the catacombs."

"He enjoys being cryptic, doesn't he?" Kiki remarked.

"I always assumed it meant that Phlegyas discovered something among the rocks. A tract or a message of some sort with the name written on it. Then, a few months ago, I was working on an essay for school about Paris during the Nazi occupation, and I had the idea to create a map of important sites. According to my research, there was a very important location right above the rubble in the tunnels. The Lutetia Hotel—Nazi headquarters."

"The Darkness Dwellers were spying on the Nazis," Verushka said.

"That's exactly what I think!" Etienne exclaimed. "Maybe the Darkness Dwellers were English-speaking spies. Who knows? Maybe they were the ones who prevented the bombs in the tunnels from exploding."

"Perhaps you should do a little digging. Find out what lies behind all the rubble," Verushka advised.

"Yeah, I bet if you solved the mystery, the Darkness Dwellers would finally invite you to join their precious club," Kiki said.

"That may not be a bad idea," Etienne mused.

"Although I still don't understand why they haven't made you a member."

"That's a question for Phlegyas." Etienne checked his watch. "You'll have your chance to ask him in about thirty minutes. It's time for us to meet up with the Darkness Dwellers."

CHAPTER 30

You're Not So Tough

Where are you, Fishbein?" Luz demanded the moment I answered the phone. Someone was screaming bloody murder in the background.

"Right where I said I'd be! At the Donovans' house!" It was becoming clear that nobody trusted me anymore.

"You need to get to Chinatown as fast as you can." I heard crashing, crunching, and cursing. "Ouch! Oona! You just hit me with that!"

"Why are you in *Chinatown*? I thought you guys were at my house researching Thyrza."

"We couldn't get Mrs. Fei on the phone, so we walked down to Catherine Street to let her know that Oona was okay. We found out why Mrs. Fei didn't answer the phone. Lili Liu stole it."

"She *what*?"

"That's where Lili was last night. Stealing all of Oona's stuff."

"How did she figure out where Oona lives? How did she get in?"

"Look, I'm too busy ducking to explain, Ananka. You need to get here before Oona kills someone. Like *me,* for instance!"

"Okay, just give me a few minutes. I'm on my way."

"I'll try to hold out as long as I can," Luz said, "but if anything happens, please don't let my mom bury me in a dress."

"Looks like you're off the hook for the moment," I told Molly as I switched off my phone. "I've got a five-alarm fire to put out in Chinatown."

"Who's Thyrza?" Molly asked.

"What? Oh, some World War II femme fatale. Amelia Beauregard's boyfriend ran away with her."

"That was my grandmother's name," Molly said. "I've never heard of anyone else named Thyrza before. Except for the girl from the poem, of course."

A strange chill tickled my spine. "What was your grandmother up to during the war?" I asked.

"No idea," Molly said. "She died way before I was born. Are you thinking my grandma was the woman who stole Amelia Beauregard's boyfriend? How awesome would that be? You think the old lady's trying to get her revenge by turning me into a zombie?"

"Knowing this particular old lady, I'd say anything's possible," I ventured. "Listen, Molly, I realize you're still angry at me, but can you do me one little favor? Could you please talk to your mom and ask her if she knows where Thyrza was during World War II?"

"I *told* you, I'm busy destroying the institute."

"Fine. You know what could be the coup de grâce? If it turns out Amelia Beauregard has been luring young women into her academy under false pretenses."

"Not bad," Molly conceded. "Not bad at all. Nice to know you haven't gone completely yellow, Ananka."

"Gee, thanks," I muttered.

☆   ☆   ☆

The world and the weather had both turned against me. I called DeeDee and Iris before I sprinted across town to Oona's house, pelted by hail the size of gumballs. I fell four times, ruined my shoes, and nearly got flattened by a careening taxi. I was beginning to feel like the slow-moving target at a shooting range. Wherever I went, I seemed to be under constant attack.

I arrived at Oona Wong's house to find her elegant living room in shambles. The carpet was littered with shards of pottery, overturned plants, ripped-up fashion magazines, and a manicurist's tools. The walls bore several shoe-shaped holes. Someone's lunch was splattered across the kitchen door. Mrs. Fei was sucking up the noodles with a vacuum cleaner.

"Oh my God!" I shouted over the roar. "Lili did this?"

I couldn't hear Mrs. Fei's voice, but I read her lips. "No," she informed me. "*Oona* did this."

"Where is she?" I asked, and the old lady pointed down the hallway toward the bedrooms.

Oona's room was in even worse shape than the living room. Every single article of clothing she owned had been ripped off its hanger and kicked across the floor. The bed's mattress had been picked up and flung against the wall.

Fortunately, Oona's frenzy appeared to have reached its conclusion. She was slumped in a chair, her face buried in her hands. A frazzled Luz was keeping watch over her—from a safe distance.

"What happened?" I asked.

Oona didn't move, so Luz answered for her. "Lili stole her computers, all of her jewelry, her phones, and her ID."

"You forgot three pairs of Prada shoes," Oona added with her hands still hiding her face.

"Basically anything she could fit into Oona's suitcase," Luz said.

"My *limited edition* Louis Vuitton suitcase."

"I know this isn't what you want to hear, Oona, but people get robbed all the time. How do we know it was Lili?" I asked.

Luz picked a seemingly random piece of paper from the mess on the floor and handed it to me. "Lili left a note."

I peered down at the page. It had been ripped out of a Chinese book. Scrawled on one side was a message: *YOU'RE NOT SO TOUGH.*

"Should we call the police?" I asked.

"Why? So they can arrest me for making false reports?" Oona moaned. "One of the neighbors let Lili in the front door last night. Another watched her break into the apartment while Mrs. Fei was asleep. They both swear it was me that they saw."

"Oh, Oona!" DeeDee and Iris had just arrived. As DeeDee gaped at the destruction, Iris marched toward the girl in the chair and wrapped her little arms around her. I expected Oona to push Iris away. Instead she instantly broke into tears.

"Please don't cry," I pleaded. It still scared me to see that someone like Oona could be crushed just like anyone else. "I know how hard you worked to buy all of this stuff, but it's only *stuff*. We have plenty of money. We'll all chip in and replace everything in a couple of days."

Oona only sobbed harder.

"She doesn't care about the things that were stolen," said Iris.

"Then what's the problem?" DeeDee asked.

"Geez." Iris huffed. "Sometimes I think you guys must be robots. Oona just lost her *sister*."

"How could she lose Lili?" I asked. "She never even knew her."

"I thought I did," Oona managed to say. We had to wait another minute for her to be able to continue. "When I saw that shed, I thought I'd finally found someone who knew exactly what it's like to go through life as Lester Liu's daughter. I thought she understood how it felt to be used and abandoned. I wanted to help her—the way Mrs. Fei and the Irregulars have helped me. But Lili doesn't want my help. She's just out to get me. *This*"—Oona gestured to the room around her—"*this* is what I get for trying to be nice. From now on, it's war."

"No, Oona," I groaned. There were too many wars being waged in New York City. I couldn't handle more than one at a time.

"I'm serious, Ananka. Get your coat back on. We're going out to find Lili and haul her little butt to jail."

"I hate to tell you this, Oona, but we're not going anywhere right now," DeeDee said. "Have you looked outside?"

Five heads swiveled toward the window. The sky was

dark and a pile of ice pebbles was growing against the pane.

"They sent us home from school two hours early," DeeDee explained. "We're in the middle of an ice storm."

"Great," Oona growled. "I hope my evil twin freezes to death in that shed."

"You don't really mean that," Iris said.

"You wanna bet?" That's when I knew Oona was on the road to recovery.

"Lili won't be going back to that shed anyway," Luz noted. "I'm sure she made enough money off your stuff to keep herself nice and toasty for a while."

While the other girls gave Luz the evil eye, I silently gave thanks to Mother Nature. The weather hadn't turned against me. Instead, it had given me the one thing I needed the most. *Time.* The Irregulars all appeared harried and haggard. And if I looked half as bad as I felt, then I was the sorriest one of the bunch. My friends deserved a few hours to recuperate. And I needed those hours to restore some of their faith in me. Now, thanks to an unforeseen ice storm, Molly Donovan would be stuck at home with her fliers. Lili Liu would be hiding out from the weather. For a single night, the Irregulars' wars had been put on hold.

"Everyone call your parents," I ordered. "We're all sleeping at Oona's tonight. We'll spend the evening getting this place back in order. Tomorrow is Saturday, and we'll have the whole day. Weather permitting, we can hunt down Lili Liu."

"I don't know if it's safe for me to stay here," Iris told me. "You've probably been plotting my murder for days."

I'd almost forgotten I'd ever been angry with the little

brat. "Against my better judgment, I've decided to let you live," I informed Iris. "In fact, now that we're all together, I have something to confess to all of you. I'm sorry. I let a silly little crush interfere with my duties. I swear it won't happen again."

"Does this mean you're not in love with Kaspar anymore?" DeeDee teased me.

"Iris told *you*, too?" I moaned.

"No one needed to *tell* us," Oona said. "You're not exactly subtle."

"Yeah, well I'm not stupid, either," I said. "I've realized that no boy is worth losing six friends."

"Are you sure?" Luz asked with a grin. "Kaspar *is* pretty awesome."

"Yeah," I agreed. "And that's why he belongs with Betty. So, I'll keep my distance from him and start kidnapping delivery boys the way Iris does."

"I told you before, it isn't kidnapping!" Iris protested.

The laughter in the room trailed off as my phone started to ring. I grimaced at the sound. No one ever called unless there was a problem to report.

"Hello?" I said.

"Hello, Miss Fishbein, this is Amelia Beauregard."

I felt my spine stiffen. "Hello, Madame Beauregard," I said, and the Irregulars snapped to attention. "To what do I owe this pleasure?"

"I'm calling to ask if you have spoken with Miss Bent today."

"She texted me around five a.m. New York time," I said. "I haven't heard from her since."

"I see. Well, I'm afraid I sent Miss Bent on a little

errand this morning. It's now seven p.m. in Paris and my assistant has yet to return."

"A little *errand*? To the catacombs to search for your boyfriend's body? Listen to me, Madame Beauregard. I suggest you do everything in your power to find Betty. Because if anything has happened to her, my friends and I will make it our *mission* in life to destroy you. We know there's something fishy going on over there. A friend of mine cracked the last code Gordon Grant wrote. We know about *Thyrza*."

There was silence on the other end of the phone.

"Do you understand what I'm saying, Madame?" I demanded.

Amelia Beauregard cleared her throat. "I understand," she assured me. "And I will do everything in my power to find Miss Bent."

The line went dead.

THE FISHBEIN GUIDE TO . . . BULLIES

Bullies are the lowest form of life, and at some point, you may have to deal with one. If you end up a target, don't take it too personally. Write it off as bad luck, and make good use of the following tips . . .

Refuse to Give Bullies What They Want
Bullies want to see you sweat, cry, and beg for mercy. It may take a great deal of self-control, but try not to give them the satisfaction. (This is one of the many ways a good poker face can come in handy.) Stand your ground. Practice a blank stare. Think like a jujitsu master, and use your opponent's energy against her.

Fight the Forces of Evil
Don't stand on the sidelines. If a classmate is being bullied, give him your support. And if you ever see a younger, smaller, or less fortunate kid

being tormented, it is YOUR DUTY as a twenty-first-century lady/gentle-man to do whatever you can to help. Do it because it's the right thing to do, but feel free to accept an ambassadorship to France when the kid you helped grows up to be the President of the United States.

Don't Look Like an Idiot

Bullies make fun of things their victims are helpless to change. The size of a kid's bank account. The size of a kid's brain. The size of a kid's pants. Why do they choose to focus on such things? Because bullies are not very clever. So do your best to never look equally dumb. Want to give someone a hard time for being a jerk? Be my guest. But don't crack jokes about a person's weight, hair color, acne, or background. Unless *you* want to look like an idiot.

Be Prepared to Defend Yourself

When dealing with bullies, you may need more than a good poker face. If you are blessed with a rapier wit, feel free to turn it on your opponents. But very few of us are able to cut a bully down to size with well-chosen words. So I suggest some classes in the martial art of your choosing. The confidence you build may ensure that you never need to use your new skills.

Do a Little Detective Work

Some bullies are injured souls who lash out at the world because their own lives are difficult. But a lot of people are just *mean*. Fortunately, if you've read my other books, you should have the skills to figure out which kind of bully is on your case. (These skills include—but aren't limited to—tailing, eavesdropping, and trash-can archaeology.) If you should uncover a painful secret, keep it to yourself. If you discover a not-so-painful secret, discreetly use it to your advantage.

Make a Documentary

Have a trusted colleague film your bully in action. (Or find a way to secretly film a confrontation yourself.) Post the video online, where it will remain *forever*. And it won't go unnoticed. Future employers, teachers, boyfriends, and college admissions committees will all be able to watch your bully in action. Now, that's what I call *justice*.

Chapter 31

Les Frères Corbeaux

The walls of the ossuary were lined with brown bones. Millions of femurs, tibias, and skulls had been neatly stacked from floor to ceiling. In some of the passages, they formed strangely artistic patterns. But Betty and Marcel also passed rooms filled with haphazard heaps of discarded remains. It was as though a gluttonous giant had enjoyed a meal nearby, picked the bones clean, and tossed them over his shoulder.

The atmosphere felt ominous to Betty. The dead had not intended to spend eternity trapped in an ancient quarry. Many had lain undisturbed for centuries only to have their remains brutally ripped from the ground. The bones of princes and paupers now mingled together. Even the most brilliant doctor couldn't have distinguished the mistresses from their maids. Betty understood why the ossuary might beckon to the morbid, the disturbed, and the deranged, who all came to spend time with the dead. This was a place of incredible power.

"I don't know this part of the tunnels very well," Marcel whispered. "I came here a few times when they were still open to the public, but I haven't been back in months."

"I don't blame you," Betty replied, keeping her voice low. Marcel had warned her that flesh-and-blood beings might be lurking among the old bones. He'd told her about the Darkness Dweller who'd been attacked by an unseen assailant—and the signs that bizarre rites were being performed in the darkest corners of the ossuary. Freshly painted symbols had appeared on the walls, and strange marks had been found on the floor.

"Look," Marcel said. He bent down beside a tower of skulls and traced a faint image with his finger. It would have been almost invisible to anyone who wasn't looking carefully—a hat with three floppy points and a ball dangling from each. "They use ultraviolet paint."

"Is that a *jester's hat*?" Betty asked.

"That's what it looks like. Phlegyas said the Darkness Dwellers have found other icons as well. Test tubes. Strange religious symbols. Even little houses."

"What do you think the signs mean?" Betty asked.

"No one knows," Marcel replied. "Not even the Darkness Dwellers."

A pair of beetles scurried up Betty's right boot. She flicked them off with a finger. "What's up with the bugs?" she asked.

"There's an infestation," the boy told her. "Look around you. They're everywhere."

Betty shivered when she saw them. Thousands upon thousands of small black and brown beetles had made their homes in the spaces between the bones. Well camouflaged, they could have remained out of sight. Instead, they peeked out at their guests, waving their antennae to get a good whiff of them.

They must have liked what they smelled. As Betty and Marcel continued, more beetles appeared. Most stayed on the sidelines, like spectators at a parade. A few bold individuals rushed out from the piles and tried to keep pace with the humans. By the time Marcel and Betty turned a blind corner and found themselves at a dead end, a long line of beetles was trailing behind them.

"Shhh," Marcel whispered, brushing a bug from his pants leg. He pointed to a spot next to a mound of dirt and human remains. There, a large hole in the floor offered access to a lower level of the catacombs. The boy turned off his flashlight and dropped to his knees at the edge of the opening. Betty quickly followed his lead, and she caught the sound of voices in the distance. There were three of them, all male, and they slowly grew closer and closer until the men couldn't have been more than a few feet from the hole. Yet Betty could see nothing in the murky darkness below. Suddenly, there was the sound of someone falling and a muffled howl of pain.

"Oh dear," said a man in French. "I do wish she would be more careful. We simply cannot allow her to break any of those lovely bones."

"Perhaps we should use our flashlights, Guillaume," a second man replied. "Just this once, so she can see where she's going."

"I'll need light for my work tonight, anyway," the third added.

"It *is* a risk," the one named Guillaume said. "But I suppose our reward justifies it."

The hole became a pool of light. Betty and Marcel inched backward when a man stepped into sight. He removed a pair of night-vision goggles and opened a leather-bound notebook. His wool pants and waistcoat seemed to have been salvaged from another era, and the copper-colored tweed had been professionally pressed. The collar of the man's white shirt remained spotless, and his sleeves had been neatly folded above the elbow. Even the part in his sandy blond hair appeared to have been created with laser-like precision.

"We still need a leprous femur, the pelvis of a woman who died childless, one skull fit for a production of *Hamlet* in Moscow, and a second skull with a set of cavity-free white teeth," Guillaume announced, reading aloud from a list in his notebook. His voice was crisp, serious, and trustworthy. He could have been a surgeon—or an actor who played one on television.

"Who ordered the teeth?" the second man asked.

"A dentist in Belleville," Guillaume replied.

"Ah, well I hope you charged handsomely," the third man said. "It may take quite a while to fill that order. The toothbrush wasn't invented until 1780."

"Thankfully we're not in a rush *now*, are we, François? We have plenty of time to search for a suitable skull. I was worried it might take weeks to procure the first item on our list. A complete female skeleton is always a tricky order, but fortune deigned to send a beauty our way."

"She is magnificent, isn't she?" François replied. The

statement was followed by a rather inhuman grunt. "Monsieur Segal should be most pleased. When do you imagine we'll be able to deliver? He sounded quite impatient when I took the order over the phone."

"Tell him two weeks, Pierre. We will deflesh the bones this evening. The Dermestidae should have them cleaned by this time tomorrow. But then the skeleton will need to be bleached and dried. If Monsieur Segal complains, be sure to let him know that we have acquired bones of exceptional quality and provenance."

"Should I tell him they belonged to a European princess?"

"No, no. That's far too specific. Aristocracy, perhaps . . . or maybe an actress?"

One of the men yelped with pain. "Our donor does not appear to be very fond of that idea. She just kicked me in the shin."

"Fine, then," Guillaume said, making a diligent note in his journal. "Tell Monsieur Segal that he'll soon have a princess to decorate his powder room. Now let's tend to our other customers. I can see a test tube painted on the floor ahead. I believe there were some fine-looking lepers in that section the last time we visited."

The man standing below the hole disappeared down the passage. A second gentleman appeared briefly in the opening, wearing an almost identical tweed suit in a darker shade of brown. The third man was the largest of the trio. His pants and waistcoat were a burnt orange, and he held a rope in one hand. It led to the wrists of a girl trailing behind him like an obstinate mule. A strip of fabric torn

from the hem of her coat functioned as a gag. It was Sidonia Galatzina.

"Oh my God," Betty whispered to Marcel. "They're
body snatchers! Bone thieves! They're going to kill Sidonia and sell her skeleton!"

"I knew it!" Marcel jumped to his feet. "I *knew* people
were dying down here! But I never imagined anything as
horrible as this! Those poor tourists . . . we need to get
help!"

"There's not enough time," Betty told him. "We'll have
to rescue Sidonia on our own." She tightened the straps
of her backpack and positioned her fingers on the edge of
the hole. She dangled for a moment, then dropped. Marcel cursed softly before he landed beside her.

The pair crept along in the darkness, searching for the
light shed by the men's flashlights. Finally, they spotted a
dim glow. The man in the dark brown suit was sorting
through a pile of pelvises, holding each up to the light,
looking for evidence of childbirth.

"They must have split up," Marcel said a little too
loudly. The man froze and listened for a moment before
he returned to his work.

"Stay here," Betty whispered, carefully plucking a
femur from a nearby pile. She kept to the shadows, slinking softly around the man. Her black jumpsuit rendered
her almost invisible. Her boots had been specially chosen
for stealth. She may not have had Oona's roundhouse
kick or Luz's right hook, but the skills she possessed were
all Betty needed to get close enough to deliver a blow to
the base of the man's neck. He never suspected a thing.

Marcel hurried over, bringing Betty's backpack. Together, they quickly wrapped the man's wrists and ankles with duct tape. Another strip was placed over his mouth. Betty searched the pockets of the man's dark brown suit. She found a roll of mints, a money clip, and a business card.

LES FRÈRES CORBEAUX

FRANÇOIS CORBEAUX, OSTEOLOGIST

Anatomical Supplies and Curiosities

Theatrical Productions, Interior Decoration,
Religious Rites, Homeopathic Cures*

They dragged François's body to a nearby room and hid it beneath a pile of skull shards. They continued onward in search of the remaining Corbeaux brothers and found Guillaume scouring a tall tower of femurs, looking for a leg bone that was riddled with the pockmarks left by leprosy. He was so engrossed in his work that Marcel easily clobbered him from behind. Betty whipped the leather-bound notebook from the man's vest pocket. Listed inside were months' worth of orders, customer names, and prices. The businessmen had been plundering the catacombs—and not all of their victims had been dead when the Corbeaux brothers had first encountered them. She thumbed through the pages while Marcel bound the man's legs. As they worked, the beetles formed a writhing, wriggling circle around them.

"You have a lovely zygomaticus, mademoiselle,"

**The card was in French, of course, but I think we can trust Betty's translation.*

François Corbeaux unexpectedly announced. He'd regained
consciousness before Marcel could seal his mouth. "Perhaps the nicest I've seen."

"Thanks," Betty replied. "Marcel, would you mind passing the duct tape?"

"You're an American. I recognize the accent."

Betty didn't respond.

"If you leave me immobilized, I'll be dead in less than
a day." The casual way he said it made it sound as if he
didn't really mind.

"Then you should tell us where to find the girl you captured. The longer we have to look, the longer you'll have
to wait," Betty said.

"She's with my youngest brother. When you see Pierre,
please tell him I said to treat you gently. I know an American collector who's been looking for a girl like you. Do
you happen to have any Cherokee blood? No? Perhaps
Choctaw?"

"Maybe you should shut up," Marcel said as he slapped
a strip of tape across the man's lips. "Sorry," he told Betty.
"I should have done that as soon as he started talking. I
hope he didn't upset you."

"I've heard a lot worse," Betty replied with a shrug.

The third Corbeaux brother had occupied a vacant chamber off a main passage. A large plastic tarp had been
spread across the floor, but by the time Betty and Marcel
arrived, it was covered by a thick carpet of beetles. Three
of the walls were black with bugs as millions of insects
crept ever closer to the two human beings at the far end

of the room. Oblivious to the infestation, Pierre Corbeaux knelt with a black doctor's bag open in front of him. Sidonia Galatzina stood with her back pressed against the stone. Her arms and legs were bound, and she watched helplessly as her captor chose a scalpel from a leather case and began to examine the blade.

The man clearly knew what he was doing. He never once turned his back to the entrance. And even if he were to change position, there was no way to sneak up behind him. The crunch of bugs beneath boots would warn him that intruders were near. Betty and Marcel would need to confront this man face-to-face.

"You must let me do it," Marcel insisted.

"He's armed," Betty said with a shake of her head. "I'll go in first and distract him. When you see the opportunity, attack from behind."

"What if he attacks you first? You won't stand a chance!" Marcel hissed. "You're only a girl!"

"That's probably the only reason I *will* stand a chance," Betty said.

"You think that beast is less likely to hurt you because you're a girl? He's getting ready to carve up your friend in there!"

"Corbeaux won't consider me a threat, and the Irregulars love it when people underestimate our abilities. It gives us an automatic advantage. If the man in there thinks I'm harmless he'll let down his guard."

"Who are these Irregulars? Are you sure you know what you're doing?" Marcel asked, looking both scared and skeptical.

"I kicked *your* butt, didn't I?" Betty said. "Stay here.

When his back is turned toward you, that's the time to jump in."

Betty sauntered into the improvised operating room in which Sidonia Galatzina was about to be freed of her skeleton. The princess's eyes grew wide when she caught sight of Betty. Pierre Corbeaux glanced up from his work.

"Good morning, mademoiselle." His greeting was chillingly pleasant. Showing no sign of alarm, he reached into his doctor's bag, pulled out a syringe, squirted a few drops into the air, and gently placed the needle in the pocket of his jacket.

"Hello!" Betty replied as if she'd encountered an old friend on the street. "I was just out for a walk through the tunnels when I saw your light. Looks like you have quite an exciting operation planned!"

"Yes," Pierre agreed, playing his part in the surreal game. "This young lady has agreed to donate her bones to one of the most prestigious collections in all of Europe."

"Oh my! How thoughtful of her!" Betty exclaimed.

"Perhaps you would care to make a small donation of your own?" Pierre asked, slowly rising to his feet. "You would make a *wonderful* addition to a doctor's office or a duke's study."

Betty took a moment to glance down at her arms and legs. "You really think so?" she asked, sounding flattered.

"But of course!" Pierre began inching his way toward Betty, making no sudden movements that might startle her. He was a powerful man, with big, broad hands that could have snapped a girl's neck in an instant.

"What would I have to do to make a donation? Will it hurt?"

"No, not at all! I will give you a little medicine to help you sleep. Then I will remove as much flesh from your bones as possible. The Dermestidae do the rest. I promise, you won't feel a thing!"

"Dermestidae?" Betty was slowly circling the room as she kept a careful distance from Pierre. She couldn't allow him to come within reach of her, but she was having trouble positioning the man so that his back was turned toward the door.

"The flesh-eating beetles. My brothers and I have been raising them in the catacombs. They're essential to every bone collector's work."

"Those cute little things eat meat?"

"They're voracious carnivores. They can pick a skeleton clean in a single night." Pierre was almost upon her. He was no more than a lunge away when Betty noticed Sidonia's whole body starting to tilt to one side.

"Looks like you might have tied that girl a little too tight when you propped her up against the wall," Betty noted. "She's about to topple over."

Pierre glanced quickly at Sidonia just before she crashed to the ground. He appeared conflicted for a moment but kept his eyes trained on Betty.

"Oooh, that sounded painful," Betty said with a theatrical wince. "Did you hear a crack too? I think she may have just broken something."

"I heard nothing," Pierre insisted. But when Sidonia groaned with pain, his whole body swiveled long enough for Marcel to rush into the room, a femur raised like a club. He hit the man at the base of the skull, but Pierre didn't fall.

"This must be our lucky day!" The enormous man laughed as he rubbed his neck. "Les Frères Corbeaux have never procured more than two full skeletons in a single day! And such fine specimens!" Judging Marcel to be the greatest threat, Pierre grabbed the boy's collar with one hand while the other moved toward his jacket pocket.

"Looking for this?" Betty held up a syringe. "What's in it, anyway? Is it the medicine you use?"

"Give me that, you fool!" Pierre growled, his patience finally exhausted.

"Come and get it," Betty told him.

Pierre threw Marcel to the ground and rushed across the chamber at Betty. As soon as he was within range, she tossed the syringe into the air. Pierre's eyes instinctively followed its path. His fingers had just made contact with it when the tip of Betty's boot swiftly found the beast's softest spot. Pierre doubled over in pain, and Marcel stepped forward to deliver a blow hard enough to put the man out of his misery for a few blissful minutes.

"Nice job. I'd say we make a pretty good team." Betty patted Marcel on the back as they stood over Pierre Corbeaux's massive carcass.

"You deserve all the praise," Marcel said. "How did you manage to pick his pocket?"

"I didn't. That was just an empty syringe. I found it in his bag."

"Fantastic!" Marcel exclaimed.

"Thanks! Here. I'll let you do the honors." Betty took out the duct tape and tossed it to Marcel. Then she pulled the gag out of Sidonia's mouth and began untying the Princess's ankles.

"What are *you* doing here?" Sidonia sneered at Betty. "Aren't you my cousin's friend? The girl from the Bannerman Ball?"

"That's right. I'm here to rescue you," Betty replied. "A person with manners might even say thank you."

"I'm supposed to thank *you*? If I hadn't distracted that monster, you'd be a pile of ground chuck by now. You should be thanking *me*. And I wouldn't be down here in the first place if it wasn't for your friend the evil elf. But trust me—I would have figured out a way to escape."

"Really?" Betty asked. "In that case . . ." She began to wind the rope around Sidonia's ankles once more. "Maybe we'll let you give it a shot. Let's see if you can escape before the beetles start nibbling on your pretty little toes."

"Don't you dare!" the Princess shrieked.

"Yeah, that's what I thought," Betty said with a laugh. Once Sidonia's legs were free, Betty helped the girl to her feet.

"What about my arms?" Sidonia demanded.

"Why don't we keep those tied for a little bit longer," Betty replied. "And now that I think of it, a little silence might be nice too." She shoved the gag back into Sidonia's mouth. "Are you about ready?" she asked Marcel.

Pierre Corbeaux was practically mummified in duct tape. Marcel had gathered the last of the man's tools and tossed them into the doctor's bag.

"Yes," he said, checking the clock on his cell phone. "It's a quarter past four. We should have just enough time to make it to the coliseum."

ChAPTER 32

One for All
and All for One

No visitor would have asked why the Darkness Dwellers called it the coliseum. Painted on the cavern's walls was an ingenious trompe l'oeil mural that made entering the room feel like stepping onto the stage of a Roman coliseum. A dozen arched doors circled the open space. It was hard to tell which of the doors offered a real means of escape and which were the work of a clever artist. But it wasn't hard to imagine that there might be a ravenous lion or trident-wielding gladiator stationed behind any one of them.

At least a hundred people had gathered inside the coliseum. Most were dressed like spelunkers or sewer scavengers—gray jumpsuits, black boots, and miner's hats. By 4:55 it seemed as if the search party was complete. Time was precious, and Etienne and Kiki hurried to their places at the front of the room. Standing atop wooden vegetable crates that Phlegyas had provided, they prepared to address their audience. Then three dust-caked individuals emerged through one of the entrances like battle-weary warriors stepping into the ring. Latecomers, Kiki assumed, until she realized one member of the unusual trio had her hands tied and a gag stuck between her teeth.

Their faces coated with a paste of sweat and catacomb dirt, the three interlopers might as well have worn masks. Two of them wove through the curious crowd, while the third trailed behind, pulled like a donkey at the end of a rope. The tallest of the group approached Etienne. In one hand he held a black doctor's bag.

"May I say a few words?" he asked.

"Marcel!" Etienne growled, hopping off his crate to confront his former friend.

"Betty!" Kiki exclaimed, following suit. "What are you doing here? Is that *Sidonia*?"

"I'll explain later," Betty said. "Just listen for now."

Marcel clambered on top of the vegetable crate that Etienne had just vacated. "We have the girl you came to rescue," he told the Darkness Dwellers. "Thank you all for your help, but the search party is no longer necessary."

"H-how did . . . ?" Etienne stammered.

"I will answer all questions when there is time," Marcel announced in a clear, confident voice. "Now you must follow my instructions. The Catacomb Patrol is on its way. Any members of the Darkness Dwellers who remain here in the coliseum will be arrested."

"How did the police find out about the meeting? Did you do something stupid again?" Etienne demanded.

Marcel could have concealed the truth, but he didn't. "I told my father," Marcel confessed. "I thought he would help search for the missing girl. But it seems Philip Roche only wants to see his face in the papers."

Etienne was red with rage. "I can't believe you—"

"You can say what you think of me when everyone is safe," Marcel interrupted him. "Right now, we don't have time to argue. The police will be here at any moment, and they will be coming from every possible direction."

Phlegyas and Verushka had been observing the confrontation from the edge of the crowd. Now Phlegyas stepped forward to intervene. There was no trace of anger in his voice. "If what you say is true, Marcel, then it is already too late. There is no hope of escape."

"There is if you trust me," Marcel replied calmly, speaking loud enough for the crowd to hear. "As you know, four tunnels lead away from the coliseum. Three have exits to the surface. You must all hurry toward the fourth, and wait where it reaches a dead end. I will give word when the coast is clear."

Etienne scrambled on top of the other crate. "It's a trap!" he insisted. "He's rounding all of you up!"

"The fourth tunnel is the only one from which the police cannot make an approach," Marcel attempted to explain. "Hide there, and I will do my best to send them to another part of the catacombs."

"Don't listen to him! He's a traitor!" Etienne shouted, but the Darkness Dwellers seemed unconvinced.

"Marcel isn't a traitor," Betty announced. "He made a mistake, but he wants to fix things. You'll see!"

"Whoever you are, you don't even *know* Marcel!" Etienne argued. "You don't know what he's capable of!"

"I think I know him much better than you do," Betty

countered, putting her hand on Marcel's arm. "And I've seen *exactly* what he's capable of doing."

Etienne pointed a finger at Betty while his eyes turned to Kiki. "Is *this* your friend—the one that you didn't want involved?"

Betty was stunned. "That's why you told me your plans had changed?" she asked Kiki. "Why didn't you want me involved?"

"I was trying to protect you," Kiki responded. "You're good at what you do, Betty, but missions like this aren't your strength. The fact that you've teamed up with a moron like Marcel proves my point. You want to look for the best in people—even when it isn't there."

"You seem to think that is a *weakness*, Katarina," Verushka spoke up. "Did you ignore the lessons I tried to teach you? A lack of compassion can be a fatal flaw."

"I'd be the first to admit that I'm flawed—but Marcel Roche is completely useless." Kiki hopped up on the crate where Etienne stood. "Leave now," she urged the Darkness Dwellers. "Split up into three groups. If each group takes a different tunnel, some of you may have a chance to escape to the surface."

One hundred eyes were glued to Kiki, but no one moved a single finger.

"Was there something wrong with my French?" Kiki muttered.

"What are you waiting for?" Etienne shouted in frustration. "Why are you still here?"

"I'm afraid you've never understood, Etienne," Phlegyas said. "We are Darkness Dwellers. Either all of us will be arrested . . . or none of us will. An organization such as ours would be useless if, in times of great crisis, it became every man for himself. We are not just a coalition of individual adventurers. We are a family that lives by one simple principal: *un pour tous, tous pour un.*"

The man put a grubby hand on the boy's shoulder. "When you brought your new friends to the tunnels, I hoped it was a sign that you would soon be ready to become one of us. Four years have passed since you abandoned your schoolmates—cast them aside because they'd made a careless mistake. You told me once that you felt betrayed, and I hoped you would realize that you can't *expect* loyalty. You must *earn* it. If you want people's hearts, you must be willing to give them your own. And if they hurt you, you must be strong enough to show them kindness in return. But I can see you don't know this yet, or you wouldn't treat Marcel as you do. You are very young, Etienne, and it seems as if you have a great deal to learn."

The moment his speech had concluded, Phlegyas was instantly absorbed by the crowd of Darkness Dwellers that had begun to evacuate the cavern. Every one of the members chose the door that led to the dead-end tunnel. Thirty seconds later, only six people were left behind in the coliseum. One was gagged, and others were speechless. In the silence, Betty could hear the hammering of heels on stone. It was five p.m. Philip Roche and the Catacomb Patrol were right on time.

"You, too, Etienne," Marcel whispered. "Please follow the Darkness Dwellers. Only Betty and I should be here when the police arrive."

Etienne could only nod. Phlegyas's words had struck him dumb.

"What are the two of you going to do?" Kiki demanded as the sound of boots grew louder.

"Trust us," Betty pleaded. "Take Sidonia and hide with the others. Marcel and I have a plan."

"*You* have a plan?" Kiki asked skeptically.

"That is *enough*, Katarina," Verushka scolded. "It seems you have a great deal to learn as well."

With their friends and Sidonia finally in hiding, Betty and Marcel were the only ones left to greet the policemen who flooded into the coliseum. Guns out, fingers on the triggers, a dozen officers surrounded the two young people standing in the center of the room. Philip Roche made a beeline toward his son, the confusion on his face quickly turning to fury. A woman with a camera followed two steps behind him. Just before she reached Marcel and Betty, she stopped and snapped a photo of the pair. Philip Roche had brought along a journalist to document his finest hour.

"What is this?" he hissed at Marcel. "Where are the Darkness Dwellers?"

"Who?" his son asked, his brow furrowed with confusion.

Philip Roche turned to the journalist with a phony laugh. "My son appears to be playing a trick on me," he said.

"That's your son?" The woman was all business as she scribbled a few words in her reporter's notebook. "Who is the girl?"

Right on cue, Betty broke into theatrical tears, and Marcel patted her on the back. "Go ahead. You can tell them," he assured her.

"My name is Betty. I was lost in the ossuary. Three men tried to kill me. Marcel saved my life."

"Where is the Princess of Pokrovia?" Philip Roche demanded, clearly uninterested in hearing the tale of an ordinary girl's brush with death.

"Who?" Marcel asked.

"There were men trying to kill you?" the journalist inquired, moving closer to Betty as if she'd just caught the scent of a juicy story.

"Yes," Betty whimpered.

"Their names are Guillaume, François, and Pierre Corbeaux, and they run an 'anatomical supply shop,'" Marcel informed the journalist, handing her the men's business card. "They're the ones who've been stealing bones from the ossuary. And according to their own records, they've kidnapped and murdered at least three people in the past few months."

"They were going to steal my skeleton!" Betty cried. "And put it in a powder room!"

"This is madness," Philip Roche growled. "I am terribly sorry. My son, Marcel, has a very active imagination."

"Your son also has *proof.*" Marcel handed the journalist the black doctor's bag he had taken from the butcher. "These are the Corbeaux brothers' tools. There's a journal inside that lists everything they've stolen from the catacombs—and the people who've been purchasing their gruesome wares."

The journalist rifled through the bag and pulled out Guillaume Corbeaux's leather-bound journal. Her eyes grew wider as she flipped through the pages. "How did you get this?" she asked in astonishment.

"I took it from one of the brothers. Right after I ambushed all three of them."

"After you did *what*?" Philip Roche sputtered.

"I ambushed them and bound them with duct tape. All three are waiting in the ossuary to be arrested," Marcel said. "Follow the man-eating beetles, and look for a room with a plastic tarpaulin spread out on the floor. They were planning to remove this girl's flesh and let the bugs clean her bones overnight."

"This is incredible!" the journalist proclaimed. "Grave robbers, murderers, and body snatchers working right here beneath the streets of Paris! It will be the story of the decade! And you, young Monsieur Roche, will be proclaimed a great hero."

"No," Marcel insisted, surprising even Betty. "I don't want my name to be mentioned at all. The credit can go to my father instead. He's the reason I first came to the catacombs. I wanted to be just like him. He deserves to be the man with his face in the papers."

It appeared that Philip Roche couldn't have agreed more. "All right, men," he called out, his chest puffed with pride. "We are needed in the ossuary!"

The police officers marched out of the coliseum, and the journalist hurried behind them. Philip Roche lingered behind for a private word with his son.

"You've done a great thing, Marcel," he informed the boy. "The Catacomb Patrol should be pleased to welcome you when you come of age. Who knows? Perhaps you'll grow to be a man like your father after all."

"I have no interest in being like you, Papa," Marcel

said coldly. "We both know you deserve no praise for protecting the catacombs."

The older man recoiled. "Then why did you want me to take credit for the arrests?"

"Because you're going to do me two favors in return. First, you're going to drop all charges against Louis Fitzroy. I want the detective released immediately. Then, you're going to forget anything you've ever heard about the Darkness Dwellers. And whenever they're mentioned, you will continue to insist that a group by that name does not exist."

"How dare you give *me* orders?"

Marcel took a menacing step toward his father. "Do as I say, or I will go straight to the press. I will tell every paper in Paris that you refused to investigate the atrocities that were taking place in the catacombs. More people might have died because you were too incompetent to take action."

"You would stoop to blackmailing your own father? Do you know what this will do to our family?"

"You may be my father, but that doesn't make us family," Marcel said. "I'll find another family someday. One that wants to have me as a member."

Marcel's father regarded the boy with contempt. "*Bonne chance,*" he said with a laugh. "Who would want *you*?"

The boy didn't flinch, and he didn't fight back. There was no need.

"You'd better hurry to the ossuary, Monsieur Roche," Betty said in a voice that was no longer tremulous. "You wouldn't want those beetles to eat the Corbeaux brothers before you manage to make the arrests."

Philip Roche shot the girl a curious look before he turned and raced away.

"I'm very proud of you," Betty told Marcel.

"I couldn't have done any of this without your help," Marcel replied.

"Yes, you could have," Betty assured him. "You just didn't know it."

Once the catacombs were quiet, the two young people hurried to the fourth tunnel and found it filled to capacity. The Darkness Dwellers were so tightly packed together that there wouldn't have been space for another soul. In fact, while Philip Roche's men focused on Betty and Marcel, the toes of Phlegyas's boots had been poking out of the shadows.

"You'll be able to make your escape now," Marcel announced. "The police have left for the ossuary. The tunnels that lead in all other directions are safe."

None of the Darkness Dwellers made a move.

"We couldn't help but eavesdrop, Marcel," Phlegyas said, speaking for the crowd behind him. "Is it true that you single-handedly captured three killers in the ossuary?"

"No," Marcel admitted. "Betty and I ambushed them together. I knocked one of the men unconscious, she beat up another, and the last one we both clobbered."

"How did you guys manage to subdue three men?" Kiki asked Betty. "Were they all unarmed?"

Betty merely smiled at the veiled insult. "They were carrying all the tools they needed to strip the flesh off of bones."

"They were planning to use those tools on your cousin," Marcel explained, pointing to the dirty, gagged Princess.

"Her skeleton could have ended up as a conversation piece in some rich man's house."

"And the two of you rescued her." The shock seemed to be too much for Etienne.

"I am not at all surprised." Verushka squeezed Betty's arm. "Sometimes the best soldiers are those who choose the right allies."

"Yeah, well, I'm not quite ready to hand Marcel a medal just yet. I bet he wants something—he just hasn't told us what it is yet." Kiki glanced over at her cousin. "Let's get Sidonia to the surface. She has a date with the police."

"Perhaps you can tell me what crimes she's committed?" Verushka asked.

Kiki stared at her guardian as if the woman had gone mad. "Kidnapping, attempted murder, identity theft . . ."

"And your proof?" Verushka inquired.

The truth seemed to hit Kiki right between the eyes. Now that she and Verushka were free, there was no evidence to back up her claims. The police were just as likely to arrest *Kiki* for kidnapping.

"Looks like it's time to move on to the next stage of my plan," Betty announced.

"This plan of yours has another stage?" Kiki asked.

"Of course," Betty replied. "And it's a *doozy*."

Chapter 33

An Offer She Couldn't Refuse

The next stage of Betty Bent's plan kicked off the next morning at seven a.m. It could have begun much earlier, but she needed her coconspirators to be rested and ready. Most of them hadn't caught a wink in days and a few were too exhausted to make the long hike out of the tunnels. So while Betty kept careful watch for flesh-eating beetles, the team camped out on the floor of Etienne's hideout. Sidonia demanded, but did not receive, a place on the couch. Verushka refused, but was given, the only comfortable bed in the catacombs. Etienne and Kiki curled up in a corner. Kiki tried her best to keep one eye fixed on Marcel, but eventually she, too, succumbed to sleep.

Yet even after a reasonable slumber, Kiki continued to grumble. She was still listing her many reservations by the time Kiki and Betty had crammed themselves under the bed of room 709 at the Prince Albert Hotel. It was an uncomfortable fit, even for someone as tiny as Kiki. Betty's ribs were squeezed between the box spring and the floor, and she worried that she wouldn't be able to breathe if anyone were to plop down on the mattress.

"I just don't trust that boy," Kiki mumbled.

"You should," Betty replied. "But it's good that you don't."

"Why?" Kiki demanded. She tried to shoot Betty a nasty look but couldn't manage to turn her head.

"Sidonia's not stupid. She knows you can't stand Marcel. You *were* pretty rude to him back in the catacombs."

"I reserve my manners for people who don't try to have their friends arrested," Kiki replied.

"You'd have forgiven him more quickly if you weren't in love with the boy he betrayed."

"*Excuse me?*"

"Shhh," Betty said. "I think I hear them outside the door."

The girls lay with their chins mashed into the carpet, peeking under the bed skirt as six shoes caked in catacomb dirt entered the hotel room. A large trunk that once served as a coffee table in Etienne's hideout was dumped down on the floor.

"Take her out quickly." The voice belonged to Verushka. "Kiki is waiting for me in the lobby."

The latches on the trunk were popped. The next thing Kiki and Betty heard was the sound of furious grunting.

"Now lift Sidonia out and put her in the chair. Good. Very good. Etienne, you may come downstairs with me. Kiki would like to speak to you, too," Verushka said.

"Marcel, you stay here and keep an eye on the prisoner. Do not let her stand up, and do not remove the gag. If she behaves like a brat, put her right back in the trunk."

Two pairs of feet disappeared from view. The hotel room door slammed. A few minutes passed. The girls under the bed could hear someone opening drawers and rummaging through Betty's belongings. Then Marcel spoke, his voice hushed and conspiratorial.

"If I take the gag out of your mouth, do you promise not to scream?"

"Mmuh mmuh!" the Princess agreed.

"Okay, then." There was a pause while Marcel untied the gag's knot. "There you go."

"Does this mean you're going to help me escape?" Sidonia asked in a sickly sweet tone of voice that was probably accompanied by a flutter of eyelashes.

"I think you have the wrong idea, Princess," Marcel replied. "You're not my type, and I'm not in the market for a girlfriend."

Sidonia instantly dropped the act. "Then what do you want from me?"

"I want to know if you're interested in making a deal."

"What kind of a deal?" Sidonia responded warily.

"I happened to be eavesdropping when you and Kiki were having your little spat in the catacombs. I heard your cousin mention some sort of cure. It sounded like the sort of thing that could be worth a great deal of money."

"Oh *that*," Sidonia said dismissively. "The elf claimed she had a cure for baldness. She wanted to trade it for the old servant's life."

"If I recall correctly, Kiki said that a friend of hers had

delivered the cure to Paris, and she told *you* it was at the Prince Albert Hotel. Well, this is her friend Betty's room. And look what I just found in Betty's suitcase."

"Is that it?" Sidonia gasped. "Let me see it! No, bring it closer so I can read the label!"

"I don't read much English," said Marcel. "But whatever is inside this jar looks disgusting enough to actually work. Your mother is bald, is she not? And forgive me for saying so, but your hair appears to be thinning as well."

"Really?" Sidonia sounded horrified.

"Looks like you left a bunch of it behind in the trunk," said Marcel.

"How much do you want for that jar?" Sidonia asked eagerly.

"How much do you have?" Marcel replied. "I'd like to leave Paris as quickly as possible. You heard what happened yesterday in the catacombs. There's no reason for me to stay here. My father despises me, and my only friend is in love with a girl I can't stand. But if I *do* decide to leave Paris, I intend to do it in style. So how much are you willing to pay to keep your pretty hair?"

"I would need to make a few phone calls to find out how much I can afford. . . ."

"No," Marcel announced. "If I wanted other people involved, I would make a few phone calls myself. I'm only offering the cure to you because your nasty little cousin nearly ensured I die childless. But there must be plenty of *very* wealthy people who would like to purchase a product like this."

"No, please," Sidonia implored. "Just let me think." A pause followed. "My mother has jewelry. She's right upstairs in room 836. I can't give you cash—but I *can* give you a fortune in diamonds and pearls."

"Fake," Kiki muttered under her breath.

They heard the sound of Marcel picking up the phone. "Room 836," he told the operator. A minute passed before he hung up. "Good. No one is answering the phone in your mother's room. Let's go."

"But I don't have a key," Sidonia said.

"We'll find a maid to let us inside."

"You'll have to untie my hands before we go anywhere," Sidonia insisted.

"Don't make the same mistake your cousin made, Princess. I'm not as stupid as I look," Marcel told her. "I borrowed a shawl from Betty's bag. We'll put it over your shoulders and no one will ever know your hands are bound. Once we're in your mother's room, you'll show me where to find the jewels. Before I go, I will allow you to phone her. Then I will leave you in the room with the cure. Your mother can liberate you when she returns."

"You know I can't wait that long! The elf will start hunting for me the second she knows I've escaped."

"I'm sure she will. And where's the last place Kiki would look?"

"I don't know," Sidonia said.

Marcel snorted. "Here at the hotel! You and your mother should lock yourselves in her room for a few days. You'll be perfectly safe as long as you're here."

"And leave my cousin free to do as she likes? She'll be on the first plane to Pokrovia! We can't let her get there!"

"You weren't planning to capture Kiki yourself, were you? Send someone *else* to hunt her down. Meanwhile, you and your mother can enjoy a little girl time. Give each other mani-pedis. Isn't that what ladies do?"

"Are you insane?" spat Sidonia. "I've never given anyone a manicure in my life."

"Then perhaps you could both give Kiki's cure a try. See if it does any good. Once Kiki is captured and the coast is clear, you'll be able to claim your throne. By the time you arrive in Pokrovia, you and your mother will both have full heads of hair. Does that scenario sound appealing to you?"

"If this is a trick, I swear I will have your head."

"Yes, well, you'll just have to take the risk and find out. So, what do you say, Your Highness? Do we have an agreement?"

★   ★   ★

The deal had been brokered, and Marcel made sure the door slammed loudly behind him. Kiki and Betty wriggled out from under the bed.

"Marcel did a great job, right?" Betty asked.

"Slightly better than average, I'd say," Kiki offered reluctantly.

"Do you think Verushka had enough time to slip into her maid disguise?" Betty asked. "The plan won't work unless she can let Marcel into Livia's room."

"I've seen Verushka hop into a costume and glue on a nose in forty seconds flat," Kiki said. "I'm not worried about *Verushka*."

"I *know* you would have preferred to take Sidonia to the police," Betty commiserated. "But Verushka made it clear why we can't do it today. All we have to do is keep your cousin and aunt in Paris for the next two days. That's enough time for you to fly to Pokrovia and get back to France with the proof that will send them both to jail."

"You're sure Sidonia and Livia are going to stay put in that hotel room for forty-eight hours? As soon as they hear that I've renounced the throne of Pokrovia, Livia and her spawn will know they need to skip town."

"Trust me. They're not going anywhere. You didn't see DeeDee's face after she'd sampled the cure. She just used a teeny, tiny bit and she looked like my neighbor's affenpinscher. There's no way Sidonia and Livia will want to be seen in public after they rub that stuff all over their heads. I told you—DeeDee had to go through five rounds of laser treatment just to get rid of her beard."

"Yeah, and your plan made perfect sense when I was too tired to think. But what's going to stop Livia and Sidonia from having *their* beards removed?"

"They'd have to leave the hotel."

"So?"

"I'll make sure that every paparazzo in Paris is waiting outside with their cameras ready."

"You really have thought this through, haven't you?" Kiki finally acknowledged.

"Does that mean Ananka might have sent the right girl to Paris after all?" Betty teased. "Are you trying to tell me you're glad I got involved?"

"Yes." Kiki grinned. "I am."

"And are you going to start being nice to Marcel?"

"Don't get carried away. I'll think about it, okay?"

Before Betty could ask for a promise, she and Kiki were interrupted by the sound of a key slipping into the lock. There was no time to run to the bathroom or slide back under the bed. The door opened and Amelia Beauregard appeared with a hotel manager and a policeman behind her.

"This is her room," Amelia Beauregard began to say before she realized it was occupied. "Miss Bent!" she exclaimed.

"Is this the young lady you reported missing?" the policeman inquired.

"I'm missing?" Betty asked.

"You've been gone for almost twenty-four hours!" Madame Beauregard exclaimed. "When I couldn't reach you or Detective Fitzroy, I phoned the police. I told them you were lost in the catacombs."

"I'm afraid there's been a misunderstanding," Betty informed the officer. "As you can see, I'm perfectly well."

"I'm terribly sorry," Amelia Beauregard told the policeman. "This is all extremely embarrassing."

"Yes, Madame," the hotel manager bluntly agreed. "I would imagine it is."

"Precious time has been wasted," the officer scolded the woman. "At this very moment, my colleagues are investigating terrible crimes that have been committed in the Paris catacombs—and you've had me hunting for an *inconsiderate* child?"

Amelia Beauregard merely nodded, too chagrined to speak. After the men stomped off, Betty attempted to break the ice.

"Madame Beauregard, I would like to introduce you to my friend Kiki Strike, otherwise known as Princess Katarina of Pokrovia."

Rather than shake the woman's hand, Kiki performed a perfect curtsy.

"How do you do, Princess Katarina," Madame Beauregard said. "I read in the papers that you've been visiting France, but I had no idea you were friends with my young assistant. Are you the reason Miss Bent was so eager to travel to Paris?"

"*Oui,* Madame. And you must be the person who lied in order to get her here."

Amelia Beauregard stiffened. "I apologize," she said.

The apology sounded insincere to Kiki, but Betty happily accepted it. "I forgive you," she said. "Though it *was* terrible of you to trick me. If you had asked for my help, I would have given it—especially after Detective Fitzroy told me you might not have much time left. I was very sorry to hear that you're ill."

"Ill? Wherever did he get *that* idea? I'm not ill, Miss Bent. I'm eighty-four years old. And I had no idea that Detective Fitzroy could be such a gossip."

"He's not a gossip. He is a very considerate man who wants nothing more than to make you happy. But *I* think you need someone to be honest with you for once. I don't believe Gordon Grant's body is in the catacombs. My friends in New York broke the code on the final message he wrote. Mr. Grant was writing to tell you that he was in love with another woman. Her name was Thyrza."

It was like watching a statue be hit with a wrecking

ball. Amelia Beauregard crumpled. Before she completely collapsed, Kiki helped her into a chair.

"I'm so sorry, Madame," said Betty, crouching down by the headmistress's side. "Maybe I was wrong, but I really thought you should know the truth."

"The truth?" It was a different Amelia Beauregard who looked up at the girl. "The truth, Miss Bent, is that Thyrza had yet to be born when Gordon wrote that message."

CHAPTER 34

Lili's Revenge

NEW YORK: SATURDAY, FEBRUARY 21

i f you're anything like me (and I hope you're not), then you often feel like you're stumbling through life like a tourist trapped in a pea-soup fog. And yet there have always been moments when the clouds have lifted, and I'm able to see the world with perfect clarity. Those brief glimpses usually help me locate the path I need to take. Occasionally, they send me running and screaming in a different direction. More often than not, I keep these revelations to myself. But I know other people experience such moments, because there happens to be a word for them: *epiphany.*

I think I can speak for four of my fellow Irregulars when I say that we all experienced an epiphany the night Amelia Beauregard called New York to tell me that Betty was missing. Suddenly, nothing else mattered aside from her safety. There was no more talk of Kaspar, cures, or purloined Prada shoes. We sat in silence amid the debris in Oona's bedroom, our phones in our hands. We texted the

French boy, we phoned the police, and we tried our best to contact the mysterious Darkness Dwellers. We cursed the speed of our Internet connections and our woeful attempts at French. Shortly after midnight, Oona was about to book tickets to Paris when we heard Iris gasp.

"*Le Monde* just published its morning edition online. Three men were arrested for murder in the catacombs last night. They were apprehended by a policeman named Philip Roche after their latest victim escaped. She's identified only as a teenage American girl named Betty."

"Why didn't I go to Paris instead?" Oona lamented.

"Poor little Betty!" DeeDee moaned.

"I've got a brand-new device with Beauregard's name on it," Luz snarled.

I was about to join the pity party when I remembered Kaspar. Not his perfect cheekbones or winning smile. I remembered something wise he'd once told me. Something I'd almost forgotten. "I think we're overlooking an important fact," I announced. "Betty's an *Irregular*. She's come face-to-face with murderers before. And according to the paper, that American girl *escaped*."

"Yeah, but . . . ," Luz started.

The time had come to take a stand. "I was the one who sent Betty to Paris. I take full responsibility, but I have a hunch it may turn out to be one of the best decisions I've ever made."

The four other Irregulars looked like they might break into tears or vomit in unison. But then Luz's phone beeped. DeeDee's buzzed. Iris's tweeted. And mine played a few notes of the *James Bond Theme*.

"It's from Betty!" Iris yelped.

"With Kiki. All is well. Everyone safe. Don't believe what you read. Will call ASAP."

When I finished scanning the text, I found four sets of eyes trained on me.

"You were right, Ananka," Oona marveled. I appreciated the sentiment, but I wished she didn't sound quite so surprised.

"So, what are we gonna do now?" Luz asked.

"Yeah, Ananka," DeeDee chimed in. "What's next?"

"Next?" It took a second to realize I'd finally earned the respect I'd been craving. "Well, I guess we should clean up this bedroom and get some sleep. We've got an evil twin to find in the morning."

There aren't many people for whom I'd have left the house that next morning. The temperature was downright Siberian, and the entire city was frozen solid. Long, sharp icicles dangled from the roof of Lili Liu's lair. Someone inside was making a terrible racket while the Irregulars waited behind a pair of overflowing garbage cans for the shed's occupant to emerge. We were cold and miserable, but we couldn't believe our good luck. Extra Place had been our first stop on the hunt for Lili, and it looked as if we might not need to search any further.

My phone had been vibrating nonstop in my pocket. Betty had called twice during our stakeout, and as much as I wanted to hear her news, I hadn't been able to answer.

"She sent a text this time," I whispered to the other Irregulars. "She needs to speak to me right away."

"Ten minutes," Oona pleaded. "If we miss Lili now, we'll never catch her again."

"She's out," DeeDee said. Dressed in her fur coat and stiletto-heeled boots, Lili was lugging a suitcase.

"Going somewhere?" Oona stepped out from behind the trashcans and grabbed her sister by the arm.

"Get your filthy hands off me or I'll scream," Lili growled.

"Go for it," sneered Oona. "We were going to take you to the police anyway, but I was hoping you'd like to meet a friend of mine first."

The five of us led Lili out of the alley. I suppose we should have expected more of a struggle. I know Luz was looking forward to an altercation, but Lili never attempted to escape as we walked all the way to Fat Frankie's diner.

The Irregulars slid into our regular booth. Less than a minute later, Fat Frankie stomped out of the kitchen with a chicken carcass clutched in one giant hand and a bloody meat cleaver in the other.

"Here he comes," Oona muttered.

"*That's* your friend?" Lili snickered. "I had no idea you'd discovered the missing link."

"Shut up!" There was murder in Oona's eyes. No one made fun of Fat Frankie in Oona's presence.

The diner's owner towered over our table. "I thought I told you . . ." Then the man stopped, his eyes flicking back and forth between Oona and her double.

"Hiya, Frankie," Oona said. "I brought my sister to say hello. She wants to pay you for all those meals she stole." Oona reached across the table and snatched Lili's purse.

"What do you say—will a couple hundred cover the food and a mind-blowing tip?"

"So it *wasn't* you I saw on the security tapes?" Frankie began to reach for the bills Oona had pilfered from her sister's wallet before he realized both of his hands were already filled.

"Nope."

I'd never seen someone Frankie's size look quite so stricken. "Oona. I'm sorry. I don't know what I . . ."

"I don't need an apology," Oona told him. "How were you supposed to know I had an evil twin? We've been friends for years, and I figure I still owe you for a few dozen hamburgers. So what do you say we just call it even?"

"That's not enough." Frankie set six menus down on the table. "Order up, girls. It's on the house today."

Oona took the offer as a challenge. "Go ahead, Frankie. Give us free food. I'll just have to leave the biggest tip your waiters have ever seen." She pulled several more bills out of Lili's wallet and slapped them down on the table.

Frankie chuckled. "You win," he told Oona. "As usual. I sure have missed you."

"D'you hear the man, Lili?" Oona asked Lili as Frankie shuffled away. "I always win."

"My name isn't Lili. It's not even *Lillian*. That's just what our father likes to call me. For your information, my real name is *Imelda*."

"Whatever, *Lili*. What did you do with my stuff?"

"I sold it."

"Where?" Luz leaned until her lips were only millimeters from Lili's right ear.

"I'm sorry, who are you?" Lili glanced briefly at the girl

sitting next to her. "And why are you dressed like some kind of grease monkey?"

"Luz is my friend, and you'll show her the respect she deserves!" Oona growled.

"Or *what*?" Lili replied.

"You think I won't beat you up just because you're my sister?"

"*Half* sister," Lili corrected.

"I *told* you guys they weren't identical twins," DeeDee muttered.

"My mother was an heiress. Yours was some pathetic little peasant," Lili said.

I grabbed Oona's left arm and DeeDee held on to her right. It took all the strength we could muster to keep Oona from hurling herself over the table at Lili.

"But you share the same father!" Iris still held out hope the family feud could end with hugs and kisses. "That means you have a lot in common."

"We have *nothing* in common," Lili said. "I inherited a fortune when my mother died. I've gone to the best schools in Europe. I graduated with top honors from L'Institut Beauregard in Rougemont. My friends are all either rich or royal. I am nothing like the girl who calls herself Oona Wong. I might as well belong to a different species."

"And yet you've been living in a maintenance shed on Extra Place," I noted.

"Certainly. Just to prove I could do it. You know, I never even knew I had a father until six months ago. Then one day, out of the blue, Lester Liu shows up at my school to claim me. He says he's been searching the whole wide *world* for me. I guess I must have been temporarily insane, because I bought his story for a couple of weeks. Until I realized that all he ever talked about was his *other* daughter. The brilliant one. The criminal mastermind. The one who'd tried to send him to jail. He treated me like a stupid little lapdog, but he actually *respected* you."

"Respected me? Lester Liu tried to murder me!" Oona nearly shouted.

"And you survived. Our father may hate you, but I bet he's more proud of you than ever. I actually *wanted* a father. I even stayed in New York after he was arrested. I requested permission to visit him in jail, but his lawyer told me not to bother. He said Lester Liu had no use for a soft, spoiled girl like me."

"Is that when you started harassing Oona?" Iris asked.

Lili didn't bother to look at Iris. She kept her eyes on her sister. "No, at first I just watched her. I couldn't figure out what was so *special* about her. So what if she'd eaten out of trashcans as a kid? Or broken a million laws before turning twelve? Or made her own fortune by the age of fifteen? None of that made Oona any better than *me*. I could do the same things if I wanted to. So I decided to prove it. And look who outmaneuvered the criminal mastermind. Everyone in Chinatown thinks Oona's a thief. All of her prized possessions have been stolen and sold. *I've* won the game, and now it's time for me to go home."

"Wow," DeeDee marveled. "You really are Lester Liu's daughter."

"I don't want to be anyone's daughter," Lili announced. "Or anyone's sister. I learned that lesson the hard way."

"Well, I think I've heard enough for now," I announced, slapping my palms down on the table. "We've got a lot of work ahead of us today. First, we need to introduce Lili to all of the shop and restaurant owners she's victimized. Then we've got to take her to the police so she can give them her full confession. You guys want to get started? I need to give Betty a call."

"That all sounds like fun," Lili said. "But I'm afraid I can't stay. I've got a plane to catch."

"You're kidding, right?" Luz snorted.

"Not at all," Lili replied. "But don't worry, you may still get a chance to visit the police today." She lifted her arm and waved to someone sitting at the counter toward the front of the restaurant. A woman rose and began to stroll toward us, a broad smile on her face. My stomach turned sour the moment I recognized her. It was Faye Durkin, Senior Vice President of Fem-Tex Pharmaceuticals.

"Are you ready for me, Miss Liu?" Faye asked.

"Yes," Lili said. "I think I've said everything I need to say to these ladies."

"What's going on?" Oona demanded. "How do you two know each other?"

"It's *such* a funny story," Lili said with a giggle. "I was following you, and Ms. Durkin was watching your chemist friend. We *literally* bumped into each other a couple of days ago."

Faye Durkin chuckled at the memory. "I mistook Miss Liu for a young lady who'd recently threatened me. She set me straight, of course, and then we put our heads together and planned this little party."

"You *planned* this?" Iris asked.

"That's right," Lili said. "I knew Oona would come looking, so I let her find me. I wanted to have a quick chat with my sister before I left for the airport. Now I must go." She turned to Luz. "Would you mind sliding out of the booth so I can be on my way?"

"Keep still, Lili. You're not going anywhere," I snarled.

"I appreciate the invitation, but there's really no need for me to stay," Lili said. "I've already seen the video Ms. Durkin is about to share with you."

"It's some very interesting footage from a security camera near Bryant Park," Ms. Durkin said, brandishing an iPhone. "It shows a girl slashing four tires on a black Mercedes-Benz."

For a second, I worried that Luz might faint. Her face was as green as her jumpsuit.

"I consulted a few acquaintances who work for the juvenile justice system," Faye Durkin continued. "It seems Miss Lopez is currently on probation. If she were convicted of a crime of this magnitude, she might be facing as much as a year behind bars."

"Oooh, such a thrilling story!" Lili exclaimed. "I'm so sorry I won't have a chance to see how it ends!"

"You're not leaving this booth, Lili." Luz refused to budge. "You aren't getting away with any of this. You're going to pay for what you've done to Oona. Even if it means I could end up being your cellmate."

For the first time, I saw a flicker of concern in Lili Liu's cold, calculating eyes.

"You'd really go to jail, Luz?" Oona asked. "Just to help me?"

"Hell, yeah!" Luz exclaimed, offended that she'd even been asked.

"Then please, let Lili go," Oona requested.

"What? No!" Luz insisted. "Absolutely not!"

"Yes, Luz," Oona replied calmly. "If Lili doesn't want a sister, that's fine. Because I already have six. I don't care what happens to that little she-devil sitting across the table—but I do care what happens to *you*. Now, Ms. Durkin. What would you want in exchange for that video?"

"Do you even need to ask?" Faye Durkin replied. "I want Miss Morlock's cure."

CHAPTER 35

The Wildest Girl in Manhattan

Whenever I found myself alone in Principal Wickham's office, I always examined the walls. It may have looked like I was admiring the photo gallery of Theodora Wickham's former protégés. But in fact, I was searching for evidence that a pull-down bed was hidden somewhere inside the wood paneling. There had to be one, I figured, because Principal Wickham rarely seemed to leave the school. Most of my fellow classmates were convinced that the principal spent her evenings and weekends watching footage from security cameras that were said to be hidden inside every classroom. They didn't understand that after fifty years at Atalanta, the principal's office *was* her home. And the girls in the photos that covered the walls were Theodora Wickham's family.

That Saturday afternoon, I needed to speak to the principal face-to-face, but it never occurred to me to pay a visit to her townhouse. When I reached the Atalanta School for Girls, the front doors were locked and the halls were dark. I forged through the boxwood bushes that lined the entrance and made my way to the east side of the building. There, three feet above my head, the principal's office window cast a warm golden light into the dark, dismal day. Cramming my fingertips and the toes of my sneakers into cracks in the masonry, I managed to climb far enough to sneak a peek through the glass. Before I could get a good look, the office window was thrown open, my fingers slipped, and I landed on the snow-covered ground with a wet thud.

"Ananka!" Principal Wickham exclaimed. "What are you doing? I thought you were the ghost!"

"So there really *is* a ghost?" I asked, thrilled to finally get official confirmation of one of the rumors I'd heard since kindergarten.

"Yes, but he hasn't given me a scare like that in ages."

I was dying to hear more, but I couldn't afford to get sidetracked. "Sorry I startled you, Principal Wickham," I said. "Something happened this morning, and I need your help. May I come in?"

The principal sighed. "Meet me at the entrance. I'll unlock the doors."

"Don't bother." I scaled the wall and tried to slip gracefully through the window, but my foot caught on the sill. I tumbled to the floor and rolled within inches of the principal's feet.

"You never cease to amaze me," she said with a shake of her head. Even on a Saturday she was wearing one of her tailored suits. "Why risk your neck like that when you could have called on the phone?"

"I have to talk to you about something serious. One of

the Irregulars is going to need a good lawyer soon. I was hoping you might be able to recommend one. I don't know anyone else I can ask."

"I'll look through my contacts and make a suggestion," the principal said, casting her eyes at the giant old-fashioned Rolodex that sat next to her desk phone. Twice I'd been lucky enough to get a quick glimpse of a card. The first contained the private number of a Supreme Court Justice. The second was the e-mail address of the first lady of France. "But just so you know, I'm going to do it for your *friend*. I'm not in the mood to be doing *you* any favors at the moment. Did you happen to hear that Molly Donovan has opened her own academy?"

I'd almost forgotten all about Molly.

"Yes, I was planning to drop by her house this after-noon," I fibbed. "I'll try my best to talk her into closing the academy before she holds any classes."

"You're too late. I spoke with Theresa Donovan this morning. I hear Molly gathered quite a crowd at her house last night."

"But how?" I yelped. "There was an ice storm! The meeting should have been cancelled!"

"Apparently, it wasn't. And the mothers of Amelia Beauregard's students have been sending Theresa Dono-van expletive-filled e-mails all morning. They're furious that Molly seems bent on destroying their daughters' expensive training. A few are even threatening to picket Mrs. Donovan's house unless she removes Molly from the institute at once."

"Do you think she will?" I asked hopefully.

"No. Theresa Donovan refuses to alienate her daughter.

They've had a complicated relationship for years now. And Mrs. Donovan doesn't know why it's so important that her daughter keep a distance from the institute."

The frustration that had been building inside me finally erupted. "I don't know either! If Molly is turning all of the zombies back into regular girls, what's the problem? And if there's some reason why Molly's in danger, why won't you tell me? And why haven't you told Mrs. Donovan?"

Principal Wickham's face was grim. "Because I *can't* tell Mrs. Donovan." This from a woman who always had a solution to any problem. I had never seen her so flummoxed. "I was hoping I wouldn't need to tell *you*. I have no evidence to support the suspicion I'm about to share with you, Ananka. Though I suppose proof would be easy to procure. But you'll soon see that it's not my place to get involved."

"You're *already* involved. Whatever the big secret is . . ."

"Molly is Amelia's granddaughter. Great-granddaughter to be exact."

"No." I dropped down into a chair. "It's not possible."

"Oh, I'm afraid it's very possible," the principal told me. "I've been fascinated by Molly Donovan since the first day she arrived at this school. I couldn't quite put a finger on it, but the red hair, the boundless energy—it all seemed terribly familiar. It wasn't until you mentioned Amelia's interest in Molly that I finally put two and two together. Molly is the mirror image of Amelia as a girl. And her unusual mathematical ability? *That,* if I'm not mistaken, must be a gift from her great-grandfather."

For a moment, I was confused. "Wait—are you talking about *Gordon Grant*?"

"Yes."

"The traitor?"

"I doubt we'll ever know for sure if Gordon really betrayed his country. That's one of the things that makes this story so tragic."

"But I still don't get it. Even if Molly is Amelia Beauregard's granddaughter, why are you so desperate to keep them apart?"

Principal Wickham pulled a framed photo down from the wall. Even from a distance I could tell the picture she had chosen was different from all the others. I rose from my chair to take a closer look. It was a black-and-white photo of a cocky young woman in a 1940s-style evening gown. Amelia Beauregard was standing on the stone railing of one of the bridges that span Central Park Lake. Her knees were bent, her arms formed a triangle above her head. She was preparing to dive into the water.

"This picture was taken in April of 1944. And yes, she jumped. Amelia was every bit as wild as Molly. Perhaps even more so. But by March of 1945, she had become the person she is today—cold, rigid, and formal. If you think the same can't be done to Molly, you're wrong. Amelia's father—the founder of L'Institut Beauregard—used his own daughter to prove the power of his method. He liked to boast that he had tamed the wildest girl in Manhattan." The principal tapped the photo with a finger. "You have no idea how much I miss this girl—how much I regret that I wasn't able to save her. She was my best friend, Ananka, and I won't allow her granddaughter to be destroyed the same way she was."

"But how could someone be destroyed in less than a year? What did her mom and dad *do* to her?"

"I don't know exactly what happened to her, but shortly after Gordon disappeared in France, Amelia's parents sent her to an asylum upstate to recover. They told everyone that their daughter had experienced a nervous collapse. None of us were allowed to contact her, but I had my suspicions even back then. In those days, there was nothing more scandalous than an unmarried girl with a baby. If you were rich, as Amelia was, you simply vanished for a few months. The girl would have her child, the baby would be put up for adoption, and the young mother would return home with her reputation intact."

"What if a girl decided to keep her baby?" I asked.

Principal Wickham regarded me as if I'd just stepped out of a time machine. "You have no idea how much the world has changed in my lifetime, Ananka. And I can't tell you how happy I am to hear you ask that question. You've grown up believing that choices like that are yours to make. I've worked my whole life to ensure that they are.

"But when Amelia and I were girls, we had far fewer options. Life could be very hard for young women who didn't play by the rules. Amelia's family would have refused to support her, and she had no means of supporting herself. She'd have been an outcast at the age of eighteen, and her poor child would have suffered as well. Perhaps with her family's help, Amelia could have kept the baby. But her parents were obsessed with appearances. And the fact that the child's father was a suspected traitor. Well . . ."

"You're saying Amelia's parents forced her to put her baby up for adoption so their fancy friends wouldn't shun them."

"All I know is that Amelia didn't come home with a

child. And when she got back, she was different. She was hard in the way only broken people can be."

"Why would she want to break Molly the same way? Why would she want to turn her own granddaughter into a prissy little zombie?"

"I honestly believe that Amelia thinks she would be doing Molly a favor. She doesn't want her granddaughter to end up suffering the way she did. Amelia's not being cruel. She's trying to be kind. She just doesn't know *how* anymore. And she will never admit that she and Molly are related. If she did, it would expose her as a hypocrite. Her institute would suffer. It might even be forced to close."

"Wow," I said, trying to absorb everything I'd just heard.

"Now do you understand, Ananka? Do you see why Molly must be kept away from Amelia?"

"Yes," I said. "I do."

"Then please. Go see Molly this afternoon."

"What should I tell her?" I asked.

"Anything but the truth," Principal Wickham said.

ChAPTER 36

What Happened to Amelia

Not far from Prince Albert Hotel lies the glorious Tuileries Garden. Once the site of a magnificent palace that housed France's kings and emperors, it is now a public park where all of Paris comes to promenade. Betty found Amelia Beauregard sitting on a green garden chair in the middle of a sandy path in the dark and deserted garden. The moon shone down on a white marble statue that appeared to have entranced the old woman. Perseus held the Minotaur by the horns. His right hand grasped a club, and he prepared to deal a fatal blow to the beast. Betty found another chair beside a fountain and set it down softly next to Madame Beauregard.

"Hello, Madame. I've been looking all over for you. Have you been here all this time?"

The headmistress showed no interest in polite chit-chat. "You can destroy me, Miss Bent. You know that, don't you?"

"Why would I want to?" Betty asked.

Amelia Beauregard snorted as though the answer should have been clear. "Because there's nothing people despise more than a hypocrite. I've spent my entire life teaching girls how to avoid scandal and ignominy. And yet I've been hiding a terrible secret for all these years."

"Thyrza is your daughter, isn't she?"

"She was named after the *Thyrza* elegies by Lord Byron. They were Gordon's favorite poems. That was the only condition I demanded when I was forced to give her away—that Thyrza keep the name her father wanted her to have."

"He knew about her?"

"Oh yes," Amelia said. "Before Gordon volunteered for the mission in the catacombs, he was allowed to visit home for a week. While he was in New York, he asked me to marry him. Our engagement was a secret, of course. My parents never would have approved. We planned to elope as soon as the war was over. Thyrza arrived just a little bit early. I wrote to tell Gordon that I was expecting, and he was overjoyed. Somehow he knew that the baby would be a girl, and he called her Thyrza from the very beginning."

"Where is she now?" Betty asked.

"Dead. She died in a car accident many years ago. When my own father passed away, and I came into my inheritance, I paid a detective to find her. I saw her once, but I never dared speak to her. She was such a lovely young woman, and I didn't want to burden her with my shame."

"Your shame? What's shameful about having a baby?"

"I suppose there's no reason for you to understand, Miss Bent. I was eighteen years old in 1944. My father

ran an etiquette academy. My mother was a Manhattan
socialite. An illegitimate child would have destroyed all
of our lives. Not only was I unmarried when the baby was
born, but her father was wrongfully believed to be both a
traitor and a murderer."

"Wrongfully believed? So the rumors aren't true? You
think Gordon was innocent?"

"I *know* he was," Amelia said. "Gordon gave his life to
save this beautiful city. I'm certain he's still here. Three
years ago, I was contacted by an author who was writing
a book about the liberation of Paris. He had discovered a
document that the Army had recently declassified. It was
a note Gordon wrote the day he disappeared. The code
he'd used had never been broken. The author wanted to
know if I had any idea what he might have written. Of
course I was horrified that the man had uncovered my
connection to Gordon, and I refused to assist him. But the
author was very persistent. He mailed a copy of the document to me. I instantly recognized the code Gordon and I
had used. It was a good-bye letter to me. When Gordon
wrote it, he must have suspected he was going to die."

"Why didn't you tell the author what you had discovered?"

"Because I was a coward. Because the note spoke of
Thyrza and it would have exposed my secret. But I wanted
the world to know that Gordon wasn't a traitor. I owed
him that much. So I hired Detective Fitzroy to search for
his body in the catacombs."

"I see," Betty said. "And that's where I came into the
story."

"Yes," Amelia confirmed. "But I want you to know something, Miss Bent. I didn't choose you because I thought you were weak. I'm afraid it was a much more impulsive decision. The day I met you at the cemetery, you were wearing a red wig. You reminded me of my daughter. My hair was that very same shade when I was young. Thyrza was a redhead as well. And so is my great-granddaughter."

"You have a great-granddaughter?"

"I do. And she inherited far more than my red hair. She's just as reckless and headstrong as I ever was. That's why I asked your friend to convince Molly to enroll in the institute. I want to keep her from following in my footsteps."

"Molly? Molly Donovan?"

"Yes. Do you know her as well?"

"Only by reputation," Betty said. "But Ananka thinks she's great."

"Miss Fishbein is very young. She doesn't understand that other people will not be amused by Molly's behavior. My granddaughter needs to learn how to act like a lady if she wants the world to judge her kindly. People can be incredibly cruel, Miss Bent. I want Molly to be as happy as she can be."

"Well," said Betty after a long pause. "It seems to me there are two ways you could try to make sure that your great-granddaughter leads a happy life. You could teach her how to behave like a perfect little lady. Or you could teach her to believe in herself—and tell her she shouldn't give a hoot what other people think."

"That's very naïve of you, Miss Bent. Unless one intends

to live alone in a cabin in the middle of the woods, it matters a great deal what other people think. They can make life terribly difficult for those who don't toe the line."

"Maybe I *am* naïve," Betty admitted. "But may I ask you a question? Even if it sounds a little bit rude?"

Amelia Beauregard sighed. "Oh, why not?"

"Do you think your life might have been happier if you had kept Thyrza?"

"That was never a possibility. There would have been a scandal. I would have been shunned, and my father would probably have been forced to close the institute."

"I didn't ask if your life would have been *easier*. I asked if it would have been *happier*."

Amelia Beauregard didn't respond, but the answer was written on her face. She gazed off into the distance as if another history were unfolding right before her eyes.

"And what do you think would make you happier now, Madame—being the headmistress of L'Institut Beauregard, or being a grandmother to Molly Donovan—even if she is a little bit wild?"

Betty said nothing more. She had asked two questions, and she knew Amelia Beauregard was still contemplating the answers. They sat in silence for almost an hour. Then somewhere in Paris, a clock began to toll.

"Madame?" Betty asked.

"Yes, Miss Bent?"

"I hate to disturb your thoughts, but I was invited to dinner with some friends at eight."

"By all means, please go. Don't let me make you late," Amelia said. "I will be fine on my own."

"I know you will," Betty told her. "But I was wondering if you'd like to join us. Detective Fitzroy is throwing a little party. And he's invited two boys who might be able to help us find Gordon."

Chapter 37

Betty Calls
the Shots

NEW YORK CITY: SATURDAY, FEBRUARY 21

L'Institut Beauregard was my very first stop after my chat with Principal Wickham at the Atalanta School for Girls. It was a quarter to three, and I hoped I might have a chance to catch Molly between classes. Tenth Street already felt like the front line of a skirmish. The north side of the block was held by a bevy of well-groomed, middle-aged women, while the south was patrolled by a battalion of reformed zombies. The girls stationed on the sidewalk outside the institute had left their headbands, pearls, and pumps at home. Molly Donovan's wealthy troops now wore custom-tailored uniforms in various shades of olive green. Many had accessorized with red berets and aviator sunglasses. Amelia Beauregard's academy was being invaded by the best-dressed army on earth.

I never made it as far as the institute's steps. My path was blocked by a blond girl dressed in chic fatigues. With her hair pulled back in a no-nonsense ponytail, I barely recognized Taylor Lourde, the girl who'd insulted me on my first visit to see Madame Beauregard. "Declare your allegiance and state your business."

"My allegiance?"

"Are you one of us or one of *them*?" Taylor pointed to the women who had gathered across the street. None of them appeared to pose much of a threat. Most seemed terrified to have finally encountered a problem that their money couldn't solve.

"Taylor!" one of the women cried out. "Sweetie? It's me, it's Mama! Please come home!"

The stony-faced girl ignored the plea.

"I'm just looking for Molly Donovan," I said.

"Yeah, you and everyone else," the girl responded. "Give me the password or get lost."

"Kiss my butt," I said, ready to push past her.

"Close enough." Taylor grinned. "Molly's not here. Her classes don't start until five."

☆   ☆   ☆

Fifteen minutes later, I was standing in front of Molly Donovan's house. A hand-stenciled sign on the door screamed, RECLAIM YOUR BRAIN! My finger was poised to press the bell when I realized I had no idea what I should say. Principal Wickham didn't want me to tell Molly the unpleasant truth. But I couldn't think of anything else that might convince the girl to surrender when she seemed so close to winning her war. I started pacing back and forth on the sidewalk in front of the Donovans' door, mumbling to myself as I composed arguments inside my head. A kid on a scooter paused to gape until his nanny wheeled him away. The doorman from a neighboring building stepped outside to keep a close eye on me. A cop car slowed as it passed.

My brain was about to explode, when I heard my phone ring.

"I've been trying to reach you for hours!" Betty exclaimed.

"Sorry," I groaned. "It's been a bit nuts here. So, you're really okay? How's Kiki?"

"We're both fine. Kiki leaves for Pokrovia tomorrow. We're all having dinner at a friend's house right now. Madame Beauregard made me leave the table to call you, so I only have a few seconds to talk."

"Madame Beauregard?" I could hardly believe my ears. "You're having dinner with that old bat after everything she's done to you?"

"Please don't call her an old bat."

"Oh my God—she's gotten to you!" I gasped. "She's turned your brain to mush! You've got to come home right now! That's an *order*!"

Betty's giggle made it clear that I'd overreacted. "My brain isn't mush, Ananka. Paris has been a pretty amazing adventure. I'll tell you everything later. But there's a reason I've been trying to call you all day. There's something you need to know. Molly Donovan is Madame Beauregard's great-granddaughter."

A trio of tourists nearly ran me over when I came to a dead halt in the middle of the sidewalk. "How do *you* know?"

"Madame Beauregard told me. It's a really sad story,

and I don't have the time to do it any justice. But I just want you to promise me that you won't say anything more to turn Molly against her."

"What? *Why?*" I asked.

"Just trust me, Ananka. Please."

I looked at the sign hanging on the Donovans' door. "I'm standing outside Molly's house right now. She's been leading a revolt at the institute, and my principal thinks Amelia Beauregard is going to have her for breakfast when she comes back from Paris!"

"She won't," Betty insisted.

"Betty," I said, trying to talk some sense into her. "I think it's great that you're so much nicer than the rest of us. I respect you, I really do! But believe me when I tell you that Amelia Beauregard doesn't deserve your sympathy."

"You've misjudged her, Ananka. We all have. Like I said, I wish I could explain, but we're in the middle of making plans. Four of us are going back to the catacombs tomorrow to find Gordon Grant's body."

"Okay, that's it," I huffed. "Now I *know* you've lost your mind. He's not down there!"

"Yes, he is," Betty said. "Kiki and Etienne think they may know where to find him."

"*Kiki* thinks Gordon Grant is in the catacombs?"

"Look, just wait a little while before you talk to Molly. That's all I'm asking."

"I *can't.* Luz is going to get arrested because we won't give the baldness cure to a crazy lady from a pharmaceutical company! And my principal will only help us get a good lawyer for Luz if I convince Molly to stay away from Amelia Beauregard!"

"Go ahead and give the pharmaceutical lady the cure," Betty advised. "That way you won't need a lawyer and you won't need to talk to Molly."

"What? You don't even know . . ."

"I know a lot more than you think," Betty said. "It doesn't matter if the pharmaceutical lady gets the cure. She's not going to want anything to do with it in a couple of days. Trust me."

For a moment, I wondered if I was really speaking to Betty Bent. The girl on the other end of the phone sounded remarkably cool and confident.

"Really?" I asked. "You really think we should give her the cure?"

"Yep. Then go find Kaspar. Tell him we're going to have a new graffiti project for him before he goes back to school."

What she'd asked was too dangerous. I couldn't allow myself to be tempted again. The last time I'd seen Kaspar my willpower had failed me, and Oona had almost died. "I don't know about that, Betty. Maybe you should call him and tell him yourself."

"When? I'm going to be too busy looking for Gordon Grant. Besides, I thought you liked hanging around with Kaspar."

"Yeah, well, there's something you should know, too," I confessed.

"That you have a crush on Kaspar?"

"Did Iris tell you?"

"Iris? Of course not. I'm not dumb, Ananka."

"And you don't mind?"

"Why should I? I trust you. Now I *gotta* get off the phone. Like I said, we're making plans for tomorrow."

"Good luck," I mumbled, feeling like a criminal who'd been captured, then released on her own recognizance.

"You, too!" Betty chirped.

As I dropped my phone into my pocket, I heard a voice behind me.

"Ananka?"

"Yeah," I said, spinning to face Molly. Now that I knew Amelia Beauregard's secret, I could see it. Molly was the spitting image of her great-grandmother.

"I thought it was you! Some guy down the street just called to say there was a weird kid lurking outside my door. He thought it was one of Mommy Dearest's stalkers. So are you here to try to shut down my academy? Or do you just enjoy creeping out my neighbors?"

"Neither," I said.

"Then what do you want?"

I thought for a moment, took a deep breath, and said, "Nothing."

"Oh," Molly replied. "Well, I know you didn't ask, but it's all going really well. About half the girls from the institute joined my academy last night. But we decided to postpone classes until we liberate the rest of our comrades."

"I saw a bunch of your troops outside the institute," I told her. "Cute uniforms."

"I know, right? I never thought I'd turn out to be such a trendsetter."

"I'm happy for you, Molly," I said. "I should go."

I'd started walking away when Molly called out again. "By the way, I talked to my mom."

I stopped.

"She said my grandmother, Thyrza, was born in 1945. She couldn't have been the floozy who stole Amelia Beauregard's boyfriend. Unless the dude was a *serious* cradle robber."

And that's when I remembered Gordon Grant's coded message. *I never believed I could love anyone but you. Thyrza has proven me wrong.* I no longer needed an explanation from Betty. I knew *exactly* what had happened. Amelia's fiancé wasn't a traitor. He'd figured out that he was going to die. The note he sent was a good-bye letter to the love of his life and the child he would never have a chance to know. And the Beauregard Method wasn't responsible for turning the wildest girl in Manhattan into a proper young lady. Amelia Beauregard had died inside the day she'd lost everything that she loved.

I glanced back at the redheaded delinquent who'd never felt at home in her family, and I realized Betty Bent was right. No two people on earth needed each other more than Molly Donovan and her grandmother.

※   ※   ※

While I was taking a painful stroll in Amelia Beauregard's shoes, Betty was rushing back to join the dinner party in Detective Fitzroy's dining room. Gathered around a small table were Kiki, Verushka, Etienne, Marcel, Amelia Beauregard, and their host. Everyone looked on as Madame Beauregard instructed Verushka on the proper use of escargot tongs.

"You worked for a royal family, but you've never eaten escargot?" Amelia Beauregard inquired skeptically.

"No," Verushka replied, picking up a knife by the side of her plate. "But I could spear a snail with a dagger from the other side of the room."

"That sounds like a much more practical skill," Amelia Beauregard admitted. "Perhaps you'll teach me someday?"

"It would be my pleasure," said Verushka. "But now I must learn how to capture this mollusk." She set down the knife, opened the escargot tongs, and tried to clamp down on a shell. The butter-covered sphere shot straight across the table at Kiki, who caught it with a lightening-fast flick of her wrist.

"Fantastic!" Betty's employer exclaimed, clapping her hands with delight. And for the most fleeting of moments, Betty caught a glimpse of the girl Amelia Beauregard had once been.

THE FISHBEIN GUIDE TO . . . PERSONAL STYLE

It wasn't all that long ago that a young lady was expected to wear a dress, hat, gloves, and pantyhose whenever she appeared in public. (Gloves can be quite useful, of course. But pantyhose? Can you *imagine*!) Those were dark days, indeed. Fortunately, twenty-first-century ladies may wear whatever they like. Which means you have the opportunity to develop what's known as *personal style*.

Being stylish isn't the same thing as being fashionable. True trend-setters don't *follow* fashion. They do their own thing—and let other people follow *them*.

Refuse to Be a Follower

If you want to have personal style, you first need to know who you are. Are you the kind of person who craves attention? Or would you rather fly under the radar? Do you prefer loose-fitting clothing that will let you deliver a good kick when necessary? Or do you think a three-inch stiletto heel is the best defense a girl can have? Let *your* personality and *your* lifestyle determine your fashion choices. What's right for your best friend (or the ladies at *Vogue*) may not be right for you.

Say the Right Thing

As we've discussed in previous books, your clothing can communicate a great deal. Make sure it's saying what you want it to say. If your grandmother is a biker chick, wearing your favorite leather pants to her latest wedding could say, "You're my hero." If she's a member of PETA, those same pants might say, "I can't stand the sight of you."

Forget the Rules and Trust the Mirror

Any follower of fashion knows there are lots of "rules." Redheads shouldn't wear red. Curvy girls shouldn't wear stripes. Older ladies should burn their bikinis. More often than not, these "rules" were developed to grab your attention and sell magazines. Forget them. Try on anything and everything that catches your eye. Then take a good look in the mirror. Do you like what you see? Does it make you feel good? Can you sit down in it? Will the color make you look like a corpse? Is that what you're going for? Trust your own eyes.

Learn How to Sew

I envy anyone who's handy with a needle and thread. It's a very useful skill. If you know how to sew, you can create the perfect wardrobe from scratch—or alter store-bought clothes to fit perfectly. You can also stitch up wounds in emergencies, add a few secret pockets to your clothing, make your own mummies, or whip up a disguise at a moment's notice.

You Don't Have to Play the Game

If you would rather hang out in an orangutan habitat than a shoe store, go for it. The fact is, some people would rather not waste their time thinking about clothes. I always try to be nice to these people. One day they'll be running the world.

The Secret Ingredient

Whatever you wear, wear it with confidence.

CHAPTER 38

The Original Darkness Dwellers

The next morning, Betty wolfed down a croissant and scrambled to meet her French friends at the abandoned Metro station on the Boulevard St. Martin. They walked along train tracks and then through the tunnels for what felt like miles and miles. When at last Etienne pointed his finger at a pile of rubble, Betty's spirits sank. The rock heap didn't look particularly promising. They had seen several just like it on their way to the site. The catacombs were ancient, and their walls were prone to crumbling. Even the most seasoned cataphile wouldn't have paused to investigate.

"I've passed by this spot a hundred times. Are you certain this is the right place?" Detective Fitzroy asked.

"I can't say for sure that we'll find anything," Etienne replied. "But this is definitely where Phlegyas told me he first discovered the name."

"It's going to take a lot of work to clear this rubble," Betty noted.

"Yes, we'll be lucky if we finish by midnight," Etienne grumbled.

"Then we should get started right away!" Marcel sounded relentlessly chipper. But his high spirits were no match for Etienne's bleak mood. The dark-haired boy had been unusually quiet at dinner the previous evening. At first Betty wondered if he might still be smarting from Phlegyas's scolding. Then she observed the first of many hushed and heated exchanges between Etienne and the pale little princess seated beside him. Betty's fellow guests must have noticed them too. Everyone knows it's terribly rude to whisper when other people are around. It must have taken tremendous restraint, but even Madame Beauregard managed to hold her tongue.

One by one, the four underground laborers hoisted the stones, then placed them in a neat pile along the tunnel's wall. Every rock they removed seemed to have a hundred more behind it. As Betty worked, she inched her way over toward Etienne until they were working side by side. He was far too preoccupied to notice her presence.

"You're worried about Kiki, aren't you?" she asked.

The boy fumbled a heavy rock and quickly hopped back before it crushed his toe. "Excuse me?"

"That's why you're in such a terrible mood, isn't it?"

"I offered to fly to Pokrovia with her, but she didn't want me along."

"It's going to be a very dangerous trip," Betty said. "Livia and Sidonia are out of the way, but Sergei Molotov will still be searching for Kiki."

"All the more reason that she shouldn't have gone alone!"

"Kiki doesn't want anyone else to get hurt. She didn't even let Verushka travel with her this time."

"But I'm not a sixty-year-old with a bad leg!"

"Don't be fooled by appearances," Betty advised. "Bad leg or not, that sixty-year-old could kick all of our butts."

"Still . . ." Etienne shook his head and said nothing more.

Betty refused to let the conversation conclude. "Did Kiki tell you why she went to Pokrovia?"

"There's something hidden inside the royal palace. Kiki's mother had evidence that Livia Galatzina was trying to kill her. If Kiki can find whatever it was that her mother hid, she might have enough proof to put her aunt in jail."

Betty laughed. "You should feel flattered. There aren't many people Kiki would trust with that much information. But she still didn't tell you the whole story."

"What do you mean?" Etienne demanded.

"Can you imagine what it's like to lose someone you love?" Betty asked. "It must be terrible. I mean, just look what it did to Madame Beauregard. Both of Kiki's parents were murdered. And she's almost lost Verushka— *twice.* Her friends have been drugged, kidnapped, wrapped up like mummies and left for dead. So let's face it . . . The throne of Pokrovia has almost claimed the life of every person Kiki's cared about. *That*'s what the trip to Pokrovia is about. It's not really about revenge anymore. Kiki's is trying to protect the people she loves. And that's why she made you stay here in Paris. She couldn't risk losing you, too."

"You think Kiki cares about me?" Etienne asked.

"She'd be crazy if she didn't. Where else is she going to find a boy who's just like her?"

Etienne's grin lasted all of two seconds. "I'll feel better when she's back."

"So will the rest of us," Betty told him.

Once again, Betty's words had worked magic. The atmosphere brightened a bit, and Etienne attacked the rubble with renewed energy. As the hours passed, there was little talking—just grunting and panting as thousands of stones were removed from the pile. The workers were hungry, exhausted, and covered head to toe in dirt. But it was hard to tell if any real progress had been made.

"May I ask what you're doing?" Phlegyas was perched on a pile of rocks behind them. Betty wondered how long the man had been watching.

"Phlegyas!" Etienne looked embarrassed. "You remember Marcel and Betty. And this is Detective Louis Fitzroy."

"Ah, yes!" Phlegyas held out a hand to the detective. "I enjoyed reading about your adventure in the catacombs. I've been looking forward to meeting you for years now."

"I'm terribly sorry," Fitzroy told him. "Had I known more about the Darkness Dwellers in those days, I never would have reported your secret cinema to the authorities."

"No need to apologize," Phlegyas assured Fitzroy. "There are many secrets still left in the catacombs. In fact, it looks as though you may be attempting to uncover one right now."

"Yes, but I'm beginning to think there's nothing here to be found," Etienne admitted. "We've been slaving away all morning, and we haven't made a dent in the rubble."

"If you tell me what you hope to find, perhaps I can be of assistance," Phlegyas said.

"We're looking for a body," Marcel said.

"And what do you plan to do if you discover one?"

"I'm not sure," Etienne admitted, glancing over at Betty. "What *are* we going to do if we find him?"

"We'll reunite him with the woman who's loved him for sixty-five years," she said.

"Amelia?" Phlegyas said, taking Betty by surprise. His eyes danced at the sound of the headmistress's name. "I never *dreamed* she might still be alive! She must be quite old by now."

"How do you know about Amelia?" Betty asked.

"Come." Phlegyas rose to his feet and walked to the far edge of the rubble. "You will never get in that way." He stopped in front of a large rock. "I started visiting the tunnels when I moved to Paris to attend university. One day I stopped here to eat my lunch. I set down my sandwich, and a rat popped out of a hole in the rocks, grabbed my food, and scampered back inside. I wondered if there might be something behind the rubble, so I aimed my flashlight into the hole and discovered a hidden cavity. I tried to find a way inside, but I couldn't do it alone. So I brought four friends with me the next day. We worked for over a week, until we had created an entrance. When we left, we hid the entrance behind that rock. If you like, we can move it now."

A single person could never have budged the boulder. It took the entire group of five to roll the rock just a few feet to one side. When they'd finished, they found themselves peering into a small chamber.

Dusty surveillance equipment had been arranged on a desk. The old-fashioned black boxes featured a complicated array of knobs, dials, and counters. Wires led from the machines to a small hole bored into the ceiling. Five wooden crates functioned as makeshift filing cabinets. Each was filled with yellow paper that would have disintegrated if touched. Across from the desk, a long wooden box lay positioned against a wall. Draped over it was a piece of black cloth embroidered with the Darkness Dwellers' logo.

"When we uncovered the room, we found an Englishman inside. He was half buried under the rubble. He seemed to have perished in some sort of explosion. We freed his bones from the rocks and built a coffin for them. But we left everything else exactly as we found it."

"Why did you assume he was English?" Betty asked.

"There was nothing in the room to identify him. He had a gun in one hand, but his clothes were the hand-stitched rags of a working man. There was a photo of a girl in his pocket. The picture looked to be from the 1940s, around the time of the war. It had been signed on the back, and Amelia is not a common name here. In France, we would call her *Amelie*. We also found this when we began to move the man's bones. It must have been with him when he died." Phlegyas took a Zippo lighter from his pocket and handed it to Betty. Inscribed in the metal was the Darkness Dwellers' logo and two lines in English:

THE DARKNESS DWELLERS
Defending the Bowels of Paris

"Maybe the man was English. Maybe he was a Frenchman who spoke English. But whatever his nationality, I've always felt certain that he died protecting Paris and the catacombs. My friends and I were so inspired by his sacrifice that we started an organization to continue the man's work. We called ourselves the Darkness Dwellers as a tribute to our anonymous hero."

"His name was Gordon Grant," Marcel said. "And he wasn't British. He was an American. But other than that, you were right. He gave his life to save Paris."

"And Amelia?" Phlegyas asked. "I could tell from the photo that she was a fascinating girl. I've been half in love with her for ten whole years."

"Would you like to meet her?" Betty asked. "She's waiting back at our hotel for news. I know she'll want to thank the man who's kept Gordon Grant's grave undisturbed for so many years."

"Oh, but he hasn't lain undisturbed," Phlegyas said. "Not at all! Monsieur Grant has had hundreds of visitors over the last decade. Whenever the Darkness Dwellers initiate new members, we bring them here so they can pay tribute to our true founder. He is what we all aspire to be."

"Back in America, they think Gordon Grant was a traitor," Betty said. "He was the leader of a small group of spies, and all of them were murdered. When Gordon's body wasn't found, they assumed he'd fled Paris with the German army."

"Monsieur Grant isn't the only hero in the catacombs who has been mistakenly labeled a traitor," Phlegyas noted with his eyes now on Marcel.

"Me?" Marcel turned to see if there might be a more qualified candidate standing behind him. "I'm not a hero."

"You all are," Phlegyas said. "You and Miss Bent saved untold lives when you captured those bone-stealing fiends in the ossuary. Etienne risked his neck to save a rather unpleasant girl who was lost in the tunnels. And Detective Fitzroy did his best to protect the Darkness Dwellers, despite the fact that he's never met any of us."

"How did you find out about that?" the detective asked.

"I have my sources," Phlegyas replied with an enigmatic smile. "You're all heroes, but only one of you had to fight his own father in order to do the right thing."

Marcel blushed and stared at his feet.

"I heard what you told him," Phlegyas continued. "You said you hoped to find a family that would want you as a member. I've spoken with the other Darkness Dwellers. We would like to be that family."

"You're m-making me a member?" Marcel stammered. "But you never accept anyone under eighteen!"

"We are happy to make an exception in your case," Phlegyas said.

Betty was about to squeal with delight when she saw the boy shaking his head vigorously. "No," Marcel said. "I can't join without Etienne. If it hadn't been for him, I would never have made it into the catacombs. I'll wait until we're both old enough to be Darkness Dwellers."

"I was hoping you would say that," Phlegyas said. "We would like to extend an invitation to both of you. And to

Detective Fitzroy. Miss Bent would make a wonderful addition as well, but I believe she may have another city to protect."

"Thank you, though," Betty said. "I'm honored."

"You're very welcome. Three new members in a single day! We must celebrate! But first, Miss Bent, when will you introduce me to the woman I've been waiting a decade to meet?"

Chapter 39

The Metamorphosis

PARIS: MONDAY, FEBRUARY 23

> *Good manners must be mastered in one's youth.*
> *By a certain age, bad habits become impossible*
> *to eliminate. In my experience, teaching a grown*
> *woman to behave like a lady is like casting a pig*
> *in the role of a princess. You can put a diamond*
> *tiara on the animal's head, but you'll never fool*
> *your audience. Once we reach adulthood, we are*
> *who we are. For better or worse, there is simply*
> *no going back.*
> —Amelia Beauregard, *Savoir Faire*

Not long after the events I've described, the secondhand-book world found itself in a frenzy. An anonymous collector was offering five hundred dollars for copies of a common etiquette manual. Most thought the offer seemed too good to be true, but after thousands of books had been bought and paid for, a New York journalist decided to investigate.

He identified the mysterious collector as none other than Amelia Beauregard. She was determined to purchase and destroy every last copy of her very own masterwork, *Savoir Faire*. When questioned, Madame Beauregard was unusually blunt. She told the reporter that she'd discovered that her manual contained information that was both unreliable and dangerous. Asked to be more specific, she identified several passages, including the one I've copied above.

"I was eighty-four years old when I became a new person," Amelia Beauregard was quoted as saying. "You're never too old to change."

Betty Bent was on hand to witness the transformation. The day after she discovered the location of Gordon Grant's coffin, Betty and Verushka guided Amelia Beauregard down to the catacombs. While they journeyed through the tunnels, the old woman wore an unreadable mask. Her face showed no sign of the emotions she must have been feeling. When they reached the small chamber that held Gordon's coffin, Amelia ventured inside alone. Verushka and Betty waited at a distance for their companion to emerge. More than three hours passed before Betty began to worry that Amelia hadn't come to say goodbye—but to join Gordon Grant in the afterworld. She tiptoed to the chamber's entrance to take a quick peek. She found the headmistress sitting on the ground beside the coffin.

"Come in, Miss Bent." The woman glanced up at the girl. Amelia's eyes were ringed with red, but she didn't seem sad. She looked as though she had finally found peace. "Would you mind giving me a hand?"

"I'm sorry, Madame," Betty said as she helped her boss to her feet. "I wasn't spying this time. I just wanted to—"

Betty's explanation was cut short when Amelia Beauregard wrapped her up in a heartfelt hug. "Thank you," Amelia said.

"You're welcome," Betty replied.

And that was it. There was no going back. In the hours she'd spent in the tiny chamber, Amelia Beauregard had become someone new.

✴   ✴   ✴

Amelia released the girl and checked her watch. "Oh dear! I hope I haven't made us late for the party!"

"I don't think the Darkness Dwellers will mind one bit," Betty said. "You're their guest of honor."

They found a cavern furnished with the longest table Betty had ever seen. It was set with china and silver on loan from Etienne's family. Dozens of candles lit the scene. Every member of the Darkness Dwellers was in attendance, and they were dressed in their finest clothes. For some that meant ball gowns and tuxedos. Others wore their cleanest T-shirts and jeans. Everyone rose when Amelia Beauregard entered the room.

"The Darkness Dwellers are honored you could join us this evening, Madame." Phlegyas seemed spellbound.

"Amelia," Madame Beauregard corrected him.

The woolly-haired man broke into a smile. "*Amelia.* We have something we would like to give you. This has been our organization's most prized possession for many years. But now we know it belongs to you." He presented her with a rusty Zippo lighter.

Amelia beamed when she read the inscription on the metal case. "I *knew* this must have been what you found! I had the lighter engraved myself. It was the last joke Gordon and I ever shared. I can't tell you how much pleasure it brings me to see this, but I'm afraid I can't keep it." She returned the lighter to Phlegyas and addressed the entire crowd. "Please accept it as a token of my appreciation. Thank you for taking such good care of Gordon."

"We are happy that Monsieur Grant is finally going home," Phlegyas said with a bow.

Amelia shook her head. "Now that I've had some time to consider the matter, I've decided that Gordon's home is in Paris now. His parents have been dead for many years. He never had any brothers or sisters. I am the only person left in America who ever knew or loved him. Soon I will be gone, too. I would like him to remain with the people he's inspired to do so many good deeds."

The Darkness Dwellers responded with a standing ovation.

"This is indeed a banner night!" Phlegyas announced. "We have never had so much to celebrate! Three new members and two wonderful gifts from our guest of honor! As soon as the two youngest Darkness Dwellers arrive, the festivities shall begin!"

Amelia shook a hundred hands while Betty and Verushka found their seats at the table. Once the greetings were over, Detective Fitzroy was waiting to help the headmistress with her chair.

"I've been thinking," he said once he had her ear. "If

the truth about Monsieur Grant were known, it could inspire all of Paris. In the hands of a good reporter . . ."

Betty expected Amelia Beauregard to balk. A reporter might uncover facts the woman wasn't ready to share. But Amelia seemed quite fond of the idea.

"You're right, detective," she agreed. "It's time the truth was finally told. *All* of it," she added with her eyes on Betty.

"Are we sure we know what really happened down here?" Betty asked. "Gordon Grant didn't betray his men. He died protecting the catacombs. But we don't know much more than that, do we?"

"I've spent sixty-five years of sleepless nights in the catacombs with Gordon and his spies," Amelia said. "One thing is for certain. There *was* a traitor among the original Darkness Dwellers. Someone rigged the tunnels with explosives, but that man wasn't able to finish his work. Gordon must have discovered the plan and realized the danger he was facing—otherwise, he wouldn't have had a reason to write a farewell message to me. I think I've pieced together the rest of the story as well. I have no hard evidence, of course. But when I was a girl, I was a fan of Sherlock Holmes and he always said . . ."

"*'When you have eliminated the impossible, whatever remains, however improbable, must be the truth,'*" Betty quoted.

"Good work, Miss Bent! Well, my theory may sound improbable, but at least no one can say it's *impossible*. As I just mentioned, I think Gordon found out that someone was planting bombs in the catacombs. So he sent his most trusted colleague to the surface for help. Unfortunately that man—the one who was carrying the coded letter addressed to me—lost his way in the tunnels and eventually died of thirst.

"The traitor must have gotten nervous when a member of the team disappeared. Perhaps he decided to act sooner than planned. He ambushed three of the Darkness Dwellers, but Gordon probably put up a fight. They must have been near the surveillance room at the time. Somehow one of the bombs exploded during the struggle, burying Gordon in the rubble. But the traitor didn't get away, either. He died without seeing his plan to fruition."

"Who do you think the traitor might have been?" Detective Fitzroy inquired.

"I know better than to make accusations. But if I were investigating the crime, I would pay close attention to the man Gordon shot."

"Wasn't he the American engineer?" Betty asked.

"His name was Joseph Hanson, and he was a nasty little man. Even before the team left for the catacombs, someone had started spreading rumors that Gordon was involved in a dangerous love affair. Perhaps Joe had planned to frame Gordon all along."

"Your theory does make a lot of sense," Betty said.

"Yes," Amelia replied. "But as I mentioned, there's no evidence to support it."

"If all fingers were pointed at Monsieur Grant at the time, perhaps no one bothered to investigate the men who'd been murdered," Louis Fitzroy said. "A good detective might be able to uncover solid proof that Joseph Hanson wasn't who he claimed to be."

"And would you be able to recommend such a detective, Louis?" Amelia inquired mischievously.

"I believe I know the ideal man, Madame," Fitzroy replied with a smile.

"Then by all means, investigate. Any information you uncover can be handed over to the press. But before any article is published, I will need time to contact my family. Aside from that, my only request is that the location of Gordon's grave remain secret."

"Are you sure you don't want to take him back to the Marble Cemetery?" Betty asked. "That way, you wouldn't need to travel so far to visit him."

"My dear, I don't need to visit Gordon," Amelia responded. "He is with me all the time. *'To me there needs no stone to tell, 'T is Nothing that I lov'd so well.'*"

"That's the poem from the cemetery," Betty said.

"It's one of the *Thyrza* elegies," Amelia said. "I've spent so much time mourning my fiancé and our daughter that I forgot that there's a bit of both of them still left in Manhattan. So—what do you say, Betty—shall we catch a flight home tomorrow? I believe there's someone waiting for you as well."

"I'd say that sounds fantastic," Betty said. "But I should stay in Paris until I know Kiki won't need me."

Her last few words were drowned out by the sound of applause. Etienne and Marcel had arrived at last. They circled the room, thanking their fellow Darkness Dwellers. When Etienne reached Betty, he took the seat by her side.

"I spoke to her."

Betty didn't need to see the boy's face to know it wore a smile.

"I suppose that's why you're late to your own party? And?"

"The announcement is tomorrow. Marcel and I will be waiting outside the Prince Albert Hotel as you asked."

"I'll call the paparazzi as soon as I'm on the surface."

"Excellent!" Etienne said. "Now if you'll excuse me, there's something I must do."

The boy got up from his seat and waited patiently for the crowd's attention. When the cavern was quiet, he began his speech.

"As many of you know, our friend Kiki Strike was unable to attend this party. But she asked me to make the following toast. I'm delighted to have been given the honor." He paused for a moment. "When Marcel and I were invited to join the Darkness Dwellers, we could hardly believe our good fortune. But eventually, we realized that *luck* had nothing to do with it. Remarkable things have taken place in Paris over the past few days. Lessons have been learned. Old loves have been located. Criminals have been captured, and justice has prevailed. Friendships have strengthened, and new ones have formed. All of this may look like serendipity. But the truth is, a single person is responsible for all of these miracles. No one else could have accomplished so much in so little time. And she only had to thrash Marcel *once*." Etienne waited until the laughter subsided. "So please join me in toasting Mademoiselle Betty Bent—one of the few people I've met who's brave enough to be *nice*."

Chapter 40

Stunning Developments

Paris: Tuesday, February 24

Stunning developments out of the Eastern European nation of Pokrovia tonight. Princess Katarina, the only child of Princess Sophia, the beloved royal who was murdered fifteen years ago, has returned to her native land for the first time since her parents' deaths. Long believed to have perished with her family, Princess Katarina has submitted to genetic tests that have proven beyond doubt that she is, indeed, the true heir to the country's throne.

It is a throne that the princess says she has no intention of claiming. In a press conference earlier today, Princess Katarina stood beside the Pokrovian Prime Minister and announced her support for the fledgling democracy. "There will be no more queens or kings in Pokrovia," she said. "This land should belong to its people."

*And in a shocking turn of events, the young
princess ended the press conference by declaring
that she had solved the mystery of her parents'
murder.*

The video cut away from the television news anchor to
footage from the press conference that had taken place on
the steps of the royal palace of Pokrovia. Kiki stood on a
step stool behind a podium. Her white hair was swept up
in a chignon, and she was dressed in a simple, elegant
black coat. Her ruby earrings sparkled in the sunshine,
and some talented makeup artist had given her cheeks and
lips the color they lacked in real life. She looked very
much like a princess. Perhaps not a *human* princess, but a
princess nonetheless. She held a pink diamond ring up in
the air. The camera zoomed in on the magnificent jewel.

*"Many people in Pokrovia will recognize this
piece of jewelry. It was my mother's engagement
ring. She wore it every day. In fact, she took it off
only once—to have the band inscribed with a
secret message—a message she wanted discovered
in the event of her death. The ring was missing
for fifteen years—until I found it in the possession of my aunt, Livia Galatzina. The band
contains a set of directions. Those directions
recently led me to a secret compartment in my
mother's old chambers. There, I discovered a note
and a security tape. That tape clearly shows Livia
poisoning a meal that had been prepared for my
family. That first attempt on my parents' lives did*

not succeed. Unfortunately, Livia's second attempt did. It has been many years since my parents were murdered, but it is never too late for justice to prevail."

Less than an hour after these accusations were made, Princess Katarina survived an attempt on her own life. Shots rang out as she left the palace, the bullets narrowly missing the diminutive royal. A man was captured fleeing the scene. Lending further credence to the princess's claims, the assassin was revealed to be a man by the name of Sergei Molotov. A former member of the Pokrovia Royal Guard, Molotov has been in the employ of Livia Galatzina since the former queen's short and disastrous reign.

Police in France arrested the remaining members of the Pokrovian royal family at a Paris hotel. Livia Galatzina's daughter, Sidonia, was also taken into custody. In yet another bizarre twist, the two had been hiding in a hotel room for days, trying to combat the side effects of an untested hair tonic. Paparazzi photos captured two fur-covered females being taken away in handcuffs. According to those on the scene, at least one photographer was overcome by the sewage-like odor that followed in the Pokrovians' wake.

"Thanks for finding an American news report on the Internet," Betty said. "There are some things you need to enjoy in your native language."

"Marcel has the photo you requested as well," Etienne informed her.

"I'm not sure I got a good shot. My eyes started watering from the stench. Do you think this will suit your purposes?" Marcel asked, holding out a picture of Livia and Sidonia. Both of them were covered in hair.

Betty took the photo and nearly collapsed in a fit of laughter. "It's *perfect*," she cackled.

"One of the guys at the hotel told me Sidonia clogged every drain in the bathroom trying to shave the stuff off," Marcel said. "I'm truly impressed, Miss Bent. You knew exactly what would happen each step of the way. You played your cards brilliantly."

"Yes, the first part of your plan has been a triumph," Etienne agreed. "And from what I've heard, the next stage is equally ingenious. You have a gift for mischief, mademoiselle."

"Thanks," said Betty with a twinkle in her eye. "I just wish you both could be in New York for the grand finale."

"We'll be scouring the *New York Times* for news every morning," Marcel said. "But you must call with all the juicy details that the papers won't publish."

"I promise," Betty said, embracing the two boys.

"I will miss you," Etienne said.

"He will," Marcel confirmed with a wicked grin. "Though I suspect he may miss one of your friends even more. He was heartbroken when Verushka said she was going home so soon."

"Marcel!" Etienne exclaimed, turning beet red.

"You have the hots for Verushka?" Betty teased. "Kiki is going to be very upset when she finds out that you've fallen for an older woman. If I were you, I wouldn't tell her when she gets here."

"Gets here?" Etienne asked. "Isn't she flying straight back to New York?"

"Verushka, Amelia, and I are flying to New York. For some reason, Kiki wants to stay in Paris for a while."

Chapter 41

A Picture's Worth
a Thousand Words

The buzzer rang just before four p.m., and five girls jumped. Oona hurried to her living room window and peered down at the sidewalk below.

"It's Kaspar," she said. "Looks like he's lugging a whole bunch of stuff. Someone should go down and help him bring it up."

"I will!" I volunteered. Maybe my enthusiasm made my fellow Irregulars nervous. Maybe a couple of them shared a look of concern. But I didn't notice a thing.

"Hey, Kaspar," I said when I reached the bottom of the stairs. "Let me grab one of those bags."

"Is Betty here yet?" he asked eagerly.

"No, but she should be arriving any minute now. She's coming straight from the airport. I bet you're looking forward to seeing her."

"I haven't been able to sleep since she booked the flight. I hope I get a kiss before I pass out on the floor."

A few days earlier, those very same words might have broken my heart. Now they made me smile. The moment Betty had told me she trusted me, I somehow knew I deserved it.

DeeDee met us at the door of the apartment.

"Are those your graffiti supplies?" she asked Kaspar, wringing her hands. "Do you know what Betty wants us to do with them?"

"Nope," Kaspar replied.

"I hope she's got a good plan!" DeeDee was so anxious that she couldn't stand still. "We gave Faye Durkin the cure two days ago. I've started working on a hair-removing ointment just in case she makes some poor person try it."

"Relax," Luz said from the sofa. "Betty knows what she's doing." It was the first time that sentence had ever emerged from Luz Lopez's mouth.

"She's here! Betty's here!" Iris shouted from the window. "I'll go carry her things."

"No, Iris," I ordered. "Let *Kaspar* do that."

"If you say so," Iris said with a wide smile on her face. "You're the boss, Ananka."

Ten minutes later, Betty and Kaspar finally joined us. It was hard to tell if they were both blushing—or just out of wind from carrying two enormous suitcases up three flights of stairs.

"Geez, Betty," Oona said, eyeing the luggage. "Did you bring half of France back with you?"

"My stuff is getting dropped off at my house," Betty said. "These are for *you*. I heard you were robbed while I was gone. I had a little bit of time yesterday to do some shopping, so I picked up a few new outfits I thought you might like."

"In Paris?" Oona gasped.

"What'd you do? Raid a souvenir shop at the airport?" Luz droned, but everyone chose to ignore her.

"I was really sorry to hear about Lili," Betty told Oona.

"Lili? Lili *who*?" Oona joked as she gave Betty a giant hug.

"Maybe you should consider giving your sister another chance," Betty advised. "I seem to remember that you were a pretty tough nut to crack too. And I know we're all glad that we didn't give up on *you*."

I'd never thought of it that way, and I could see that Oona hadn't either.

"It sure is nice to be back," Betty said after the rest of us had finished smothering her with hugs. "So, what do you say? Are you guys ready to get to work?"

I kept my eyes on Betty as the Irregulars crowded around to hear her plan. She hadn't changed a bit, I decided. The poised, confident girl who'd just arrived in New York was the same sweet, sensitive soul I'd sent off to Paris. The only difference, it seemed to me, was that Betty Bent no longer wanted to be anyone else.

"*Please* tell me you know how to get the cure from Faye Durkin," DeeDee pleaded.

"We're not going to bother getting the cure back," Betty said. "We're going to make that pharmaceutical lady regret she ever wanted it in the first place."

"How are we supposed to do *that*?" Luz asked.

Betty flipped the latch on her handbag and took out a photo. "We're going to launch an advertising campaign for

Fem-Tex Pharmaceuticals. I've already found the perfect spokesmodels."

Even DeeDee burst into laughter at the sight of Livia and Sidonia Galatzina covered in thick, matted fur.

"Kaspar can help us paper the whole island with posters," Betty continued. "We'll use that image. I figured the ads could say something like, 'The latest advance in hair care. Brought to you by Fem-Tex Pharmaceuticals.' No one's going to want the cure after they see one of our posters."

"Oh my God, that's brilliant!" I exclaimed.

"Yeah," agreed an awestruck Iris.

Oona started fidgeting like a five-year-old with a full bladder. "I gotta make a phone call," she suddenly announced.

"Who are you going to call?" I asked. "We're all here!"

"My broker! I'm going to short Fem-Tex stock! We'll make a fortune!"

Only Luz remained skeptical about the plan. "I think it's a really smart idea, Betty," she said. "But there are only seven of us. We'll need a whole army if we're going to put posters up all over town."

"Fortunately, I know just where to find an army," I informed the group. "You guys get started. I have to go see Molly Donovan."

Betty pulled me to one side. "We should have a chat before you go," she said. "I never got a chance to tell you the whole story."

"You don't need to," I told her. "I know what happened to Amelia Beauregard."

☆　☆　☆

I waited on the stoop of L'Institut Beauregard with a framed photograph clutched to my chest. Judging by the students who marched past me, Manhattan was now a zombie-free zone. I listened as the latest gossip passed from girl to girl. Madame Beauregard had returned from France, and Molly Donovan's troops were eagerly awaiting an epic showdown. A few of them seemed to believe it might even get bloody.

I had one chance left to stop Molly's war, and I prayed the picture I'd brought would do the trick. If I failed, a girl and her grandmother might remain mortal enemies. And Principal Wickham would lose the last of her dwindling faith in me. That afternoon, I'd visited her for the first time in three days and found her preparing for a visit with Amelia Beauregard. The principal had decided to confront her old friend face-to-face, and it took a full hour to convince her to remain on the sidelines.

At ten minutes to five, Molly Donovan marched down Tenth Street, surrounded by a legion of supporters. The day she'd been waiting for had finally arrived. And Molly seemed to smell victory in the air.

"Are you here for the show?" Molly asked when she saw me. "Beauregard is back just in time to see the freaks take over the finishing school. I heard she's going to be addressing the entire student body tonight, and I've got something real *special* planned for the occasion."

"Can I talk to you first?" I asked. *"Alone?"*

"I'm a big girl, Ananka. I don't need you to warn me that what I'm doing is dangerous."

"I'm not here to warn you," I said. "I just want to show you something."

"Give me two minutes, guys," Molly told her comrades. "I'll meet you inside."

"Thanks," I said with a sigh of relief.

"I was serious, Ananka. You've got two minutes. That's *it*."

"That's all I need." I gestured for Molly to sit beside me on the stoop. Then I handed her the framed photo I had taken off Principal Wickham's wall.

Molly grinned. "Who's the girl? I like her already. Did she really jump in the lake?"

"Yep. Just like you would. In fact, you and this girl have a lot in common. She even looks a bit like you, wouldn't you say? I know the photo's black-and-white, but I've heard her hair used to be as red as yours."

Molly wasn't grinning anymore. "What are you trying to tell me?"

"This girl is your great-grandmother. You think you're a freak of nature? A mutant? A mistake? You're not. You're *exactly* like your great-grandmother. And all those math skills you don't like to talk about? They came from your great-grandfather. He was a mathematics prodigy just like you."

"How do you know all of this?" Molly demanded. "And why are you telling me now when I'm about to go into battle?"

"Because you're about to meet your great-grandmother for the very first time. Her name is Amelia Beauregard. She wasn't Thyrza's rival. She was her *mother*."

"No!" Molly jumped up as if the stoop had been set on fire. "No, no, *no*, Ananka!"

"It's true. Hopefully, Madame will tell you the rest of

the story. But please promise me you'll listen to what she has to say. It might be different from what you're expecting to hear."

For the first time since I'd known her, Molly Donovan looked terrified. "Does my mother know about this?" she asked in a whisper.

"No," I said.

"What am I supposed to do?" Molly asked.

"Be brave," I told her. "And try to be kind."

"If I go see her, will you promise to wait for me?" Molly asked.

"I'll be right here," I assured her.

✸   ✸   ✸

To this day, I don't know exactly what was said in Amelia Beauregard's Wedgwood-blue office. But I do know it took forever to say it. It was almost eight o'clock by the time Molly plopped back down beside me with her red beret in her hands.

"Well, that explains a lot," she said.

"Still convinced you're adopted?" I asked.

"I never really thought I was adopted," Molly admitted. "There were a million photos taken the day I was born. I just couldn't understand what happened after *that*. I thought someone must have dropped me on my head when I was a baby. Or maybe I ate a bunch of paint chips or something. I know this will sound weird to anyone who's actually seen us together, but I always felt really bad for my mom. I knew I'd never be the perfect daughter she deserves. I didn't want to disappoint her, so I figured it was better to keep my distance." Molly looked shocked to hear her own words. "Wow. I think I just made some kind of breakthrough. Maybe I should call all my old shrinks and demand a refund."

"So, now you know why you are who you are."

"Yeah. I'm not sure why it makes me feel so much better, but it does. My mom was always sad that she never knew her mother or grandmother. They were the only two people she really wanted to meet. Now I've found one of them, and I'm exactly like her. Maybe I won't turn out to be such a disappointment to my mom after all." Molly paused, and her eyes widened. "Oh, God—can you believe I almost destroyed my own grandma? You kept trying to stop me, and I wouldn't even listen!"

"Does this mean you're finally going to shut down your academy?"

"Nope," Molly said. "Beauregard doesn't want me to. She said it's the sort of school she would have wanted to go to when she was my age. She asked me to keep running it until the institute reopens next semester."

Now I was surprised. "Madame Beauregard is closing down the institute?"

"Temporarily. She's decided to retire so she can spend more time with me and Mom. But the institute will reopen in a few months with a new headmistress. She says she has someone special in mind. I think the lady's name is Verushka. They met in France."

"Verushka *Kozlova*?" I sputtered.

"That's the one," Molly confirmed. The name meant nothing to her . . . *yet*.

"What else did Madame Beauregard tell you?" I asked.

"Everything," Molly said. "Way too much to repeat.

Besides, you probably know it all anyway. She just wants me to grow up to be the person I was meant to be. I guess she never had that chance."

It's hard to feel lucky for things you've always taken for granted. But suddenly I knew just how fortunate I was to be growing up in twenty-first-century New York.

"I guess that's it, then," Molly announced, interrupting my thoughts. "My war is over. But it sure was fun while it lasted."

"How many troops do you have at your command?" I asked.

"I dunno. A hundred, maybe?"

"They might get restless if you don't keep them busy," I said.

"Sounds like you've got something in mind," Molly said. "Are you saying there might be another opportunity to fight the forces of evil?"

"Yep," I said.

"Then my army of freaks is at your disposal. But first, I have to go home and talk to my mother. Grandma says she'd like to meet her."

Chapter 42

The Snodgrass Guide to Being a Lady

The *New York Times* later called it "one of the top three guerilla ad campaigns of the twenty-first century." A few savvy observers noted similarities to an earlier campaign in which giant squirrels demanded rights for all animals. For days Fem-Tex Pharmaceuticals was the talk of Manhattan. With the help of Molly Donovan's army, the Irregulars had plastered the entire city with posters. Every ad featured the same image of two hair-covered Pokrovian criminals and the following message:

THE LATEST ADVANCE IN HAIR CARE
BROUGHT TO YOU BY FEM-TEX
PHARMACEUTICALS
FOR A FREE SAMPLE,
CONTACT FAYE DURKIN, SVP

The company's stock price plummeted the morning after the ads went up. Faye Durkin got the boot, and

Oona Wong made a killing. The Irregulars immediately started spending her fortune. It took several days and many thousands of dollars to restore Oona's reputation around Chinatown. I doubt most of the shopkeepers and restaurant owners really believed that Oona was innocent. But they found it in their hearts to forgive her as soon as she presented them with envelopes stuffed with cash.

The afternoon Oona made peace with the last of Lili Liu's victims, she invited the Irregulars over to celebrate. Thanks to a previously scheduled appointment, I couldn't stay long. But I stopped by Oona's house to offer my congratulations—and to bid farewell to Kaspar, who was finally returning to art school. When I arrived, our hostess was missing. Wherever she was, Iris must have been with her. The two girls still bickered incessantly, but they'd become as inseparable as conjoined twins.

Without them, I was the fifth wheel at the party. I didn't want to disturb Betty and Kaspar, who were cuddled up on the sofa. And I couldn't understand the conversation DeeDee and Luz were having. All I gathered was that DeeDee was working on a hair-removing ointment, and Luz had designed some new equipment for her lab. Rather than learn about nozzles, hoses, and valves, I wandered into the kitchen to find Mrs. Fei. She was busy at the stove, and for once the goo bubbling away in the pots smelled absolutely delicious.

"Hey, Mrs. Fei. You making some medicine?" I asked her.

"Yes. Very powerful stuff," she responded. "Makes everybody feel better. In English, you call it *candy*."

"Candy? Who are you planning to treat with it?"

"A girl who spent Chinese New Year in a shed when she should have been here with her family."

"You're sending candy to *Lili Liu*?" I lowered my voice to a whisper. "Does Oona know about this?"

"It was her idea," Mrs. Fei replied.

"Hey!" Oona burst through the kitchen door. "*There* you are, Fishbein." She acted like she'd been searching the city for me.

"There *I* am? Where have *you* been?" I asked. "You're late to your own party."

"Iris and I were picking up a present for you. Come see what it is!"

When I didn't respond fast enough, Oona practically dragged me out to the living room. There, making small talk with Kaspar and Betty, was a boy I'd never seen before. A gorgeous brown-haired boy with glasses, who looked like a cross between a Roman statue and a young Indiana Jones. Iris rushed up to me.

"What do you think? Isn't he cute?" she whispered.

When I realized what was happening, I nearly bolted for the door. "Oh my God. *Iris!* I was kidding about kidnapping a boyfriend!"

"We didn't *kidnap* him, Fishbein," Oona said with a roll of her eyes. "We met him on Doyers Street. He was boring a bunch of people from Boise with a lecture on the Chinatown gang wars."

"The gang wars aren't boring at all!" I argued. "Do you know how many people were murdered on Doyers Street?"

"Exactly!" Iris squealed.

"We thought he was leading a tour group, but it turns out our new friend, Hector, just likes to 'share,'" Oona said.

"What's wrong with that?" I demanded. "I do the same thing!"

"Exactly!" Iris squealed again.

"We told him we have a friend who knows more about New York history than he ever will. We said we could prove it, and he accepted our challenge."

"Prove it, prove it!" Iris was jumping up and down.

"I can't do this right now. I'm meeting Molly Donovan in ten minutes!"

"Geez, Ananka, no one's asking you to elope. Just go over and say hi!"

☆ ☆ ☆

The four words that had been bouncing around in my head accidentally popped out of my mouth the moment I met Molly Donovan on the corner of Broadway and Houston. The two of us had been asked to tea at L'Institut Beauregard. My mother had been invited as well.

"I have a date," I told her.

"Cool," Molly said, apparently unaware that my news should be shocking. "Is he cute?"

"*Yeah,*" I said as if I couldn't quite believe it.

"You gonna tell your mom when we see her?"

"I'll think I'll wait until after we have tea. Any additional stress could prove fatal right now."

Molly cackled. "Your mom's really that nervous?"

"She spent the whole morning ransacking her closets for the perfect outfit and muttering to herself."

"Talking to herself? Is that normal for Fishbeins?"

"'Fraid so," I admitted. "It's kind of a family thing."

"Well, we can always go back and grab *my* mom,"

Molly offered. "If she can soothe the savage beasts that sent their kids to the institute, she can have Lillian Fishbein relaxed and ready in no time."

It wasn't a joke. Even her daughter now admitted that Mrs. Donovan had been born with special powers. The morning after Amelia Beauregard failed to shut down Molly's academy, the furious, frustrated mothers of Manhattan had gathered outside the actress's home with picket signs and bullhorns. Thirty minutes later, the ladies were chuckling over cocoa with the impossibly charming Theresa Donovan. An hour after that, they were touring their daughters' new finishing school and eagerly accepting souvenir T-shirts emblazoned with the slogan RECLAIM YOUR BRAIN.

"Wow, Molly. Are you *actually* volunteering to spend time with your mom?" I asked.

"Yes, well, I'm trying to be nicer to the poor dear," Molly said in a perfect imitation of Amelia Beauregard's crisp accent. "Mother *is* the black sheep in the family, after all. I even agreed to go to Europe with her this summer. Grandma's going too. She's accepting some big award from the city of Paris. By the way, did you read that newspaper article I sent you?"

"Of course not," I said. "It was in *French*. But Betty told me your great-grandfather was finally declared a hero. Must be nice."

"It is. I just wish that double agent guy was still around. I'd teach Joseph Hanson a thing or two. Even his daughter thought he was a snake. She ratted her dad out the first time Detective Fitzroy phoned her. Of course, she *could* have mentioned something a little bit earlier."

"Yeah, well, at least she came clean in the end," I said, just as I laid eyes on my mother. "Must have been hard walking around with a secret like that for so many years."

Lillian Fishbein was standing outside L'Institut Beauregard, studying the building as if it were an enemy fort. She looked uneasy but she didn't seem scared.

"Mom, I'd like you to meet Molly Donovan."

"So, you're the legendary Molly," my mother said. "Ananka tells wonderful tall tales about you. One of my favorites had something to do with a pig rodeo."

"I won second place at the Boreland Academy Games," Molly said.

"It was *true*?" my mother asked in astonishment. "You really ride pigs?"

"Not as often as I'd like," Molly said. "I'm back at the Atalanta School for Girls, and Principal Wickham says there's nowhere on the Upper East Side to keep my prize sow, Ananka Jr. So I'm having her sent to my mom's house in Southampton."

"I *see*," was all my mother could offer.

"So! Are you ready?" I asked her. "I've heard one should try to be punctual when summoned to the head-mistress's office."

My mother didn't budge. "Are you sure this is absolutely necessary, Ananka?"

"No," I admitted. "I have no idea why Madame wants to see you. I'm only following orders."

Molly led the way through the halls of L'Institut Beauregard. The zombies were gone, and workmen had taken their place. A flower-arranging classroom had been refitted for survival skills instruction. The room in which girls had once learned to curtsy had been transformed into an archery range. Everywhere we looked, pastel-colored walls were being repainted and pretty carpets ripped up.

"Orders of the new headmistress," Molly explained over her shoulder. "She says the color pink gives her migraines."

My mother nodded scientifically. I had a feeling she would be thumbing through psychology books later that evening, trying to diagnose our redheaded tour guide.

When we reached Madame Beauregard's office, we found it relatively untouched. Several boxes filled with martial arts equipment sat against the wall. I recognized a Japanese pole weapon that belonged to Verushka Kozlova's personal collection.

"Molly! Ananka!" A lovely, bright-eyed woman in an emerald green dress jumped up from the loveseat where she'd been sharing a pot of tea with Principal Wickham. After she gave us both a hug, she held out a hand to my mother. "Thank you for accepting my invitation, Mrs. Fishbein."

"My pleasure, Madame Beauregard," my mother said, though we could all see it was anything *but*.

"Please. Call me Amelia. Come, have a seat. You already know Theodora, I believe."

"Yes. Hello, Principal," my mother said, trying to figure out how I'd gotten Theodora Wickham involved in this strange scheme.

"What do you think about the renovations, Lillian?" Principal Wickham inquired. "Soon the institute will look nothing like the one you remember."

"No," my mother responded. "It won't." We all waited for more, but my mother had nothing more to say.

"Our new headmistress has wonderful things planned for the institute," Amelia Beauregard said. "Have you met Verushka Kozlova?"

My mother's head spun around toward me. I wouldn't have been surprised if it had kept on spinning. "Verushka Kozlova?" she whispered. "She's real?"

"Yep," I said. "You'll meet her on the first day of classes."

Amelia Beauregard clapped her hands together with excitement. "So does that mean you'll be enrolling at the institute, Ananka?"

"All of the Irregulars are planning to take classes here. We still have a lot to learn from Verushka. Which reminds me . . ." I reached into my back pocket and pulled out a check. "We want to start a scholarship fund in Gordon Grant's name."

Amelia Beauregard took the check. "One hundred thousand dollars! Oh, Ananka! This is an incredibly generous gift!"

"Woo-hoo!" yelled Molly.

"Where?" my mother croaked. "Where on *Earth* did you get all of that money?"

"After we put up those Fem-Tex ads all around town, Oona made a fortune betting against the company's stock," I said, trying to explain.

"Your friend *Oona*—the pretty girl who always picks the lock on our front door—she made a hundred thousand dollars on the stock market?" My mother collapsed against her chair's cushions.

"The Irregulars have made tons of money before," I pointed out. "Remember the Reverse Pied Piper?"

"Yes, but . . ."

"Yeah, I know. You and Dad didn't want to believe that 'Ananka's Story Hour' could be anything other than fiction."

"I just never imagined that my daughter . . . So the stories were *all* true?"

"I can vouch for most them," Principal Wickham said. "And I've never once doubted the others."

"But Ananka is only *fifteen*," my mother blurted out.

"I didn't expect you to sound quite so shocked, Mrs. Fishbein," Amelia Beauregard announced. "When I discovered the identity of Ananka's mother, it all made perfect sense to me. Lillian *Snodgrass*'s daughter would be capable of *anything*."

"You remember me?" my mother gasped when she heard her maiden name.

"How could I forget you?" Amelia asked. "You were the only girl I ever expelled. And as I recall, you were *fifteen* years old at the time. Even back then, I was *very* impressed."

"Oh, this is going to be *good!*" Molly was bouncing up and down in her seat.

"What did my mother do?" I asked, hoping I wouldn't keel over from all the excitement.

"Lillian Snodgrass was a very quiet girl who never called much attention to herself. None of the institute's instructors ever suspected she'd been spying on them for a full semester. She must have followed each teacher for days, waiting to observe an embarrassing moment. Then she snapped a picture for posterity."

"You know how to tail people?" I asked.

My mother shrugged and kept her mouth shut, but her devilish smile said everything.

"That wasn't the end of it," Amelia Beauregard continued. "When Lillian finished documenting the lives of the institute's teachers, she focused on her classmates' parents. Some of the wealthiest women in Manhattan were photographed with their skirts tucked into their pantyhose, their fingers up their noses, or their arms around other ladies' husbands."

The memories were too much for my mother. She broke into a fit of laughter. "I was just trying to prove that no one is perfect," she insisted.

Even Amelia Beauregard couldn't keep a straight face. "And I believe you succeeded. The photographs were bad enough, but the book you wrote to accompany them was . . . how shall I put this . . . ?"

"Possibly the greatest book I've ever read," Principal Wickham finished the sentence.

"I believe my good friend Theodora is right," Amelia Beauregard said. "And I've reached the conclusion that every young lady deserves a copy of her own. Unfortunately, I had most of the books destroyed thirty years ago. Fortunately, my friend Theodora managed to save one. I have a feeling the author's daughter will enjoy it."

Principal Wickham pulled a small paper book from her handbag and passed it to me. I glanced down at the cover and fell off my chair when I read the title.

THE SNODGRASS GUIDE TO BEING A LADY

"You're a very lucky girl, Ananka," Amelia Beauregard informed me. "You turned out to be *just* like your mother."

THE FISHBEIN GUIDE TO ... MAGIC WORDS AND MORE

The single most annoying phrase in the English language is, "What's the magic word?" Even as a toddler, I cringed when I heard it. I'm a little more mature now, and I've come to believe that words *can* be magic. Whatever you want, there's a secret combination of words that might help you get it. (In case you're wondering, very few of these words will be four letters long.)

There are three things you can use to address any challenge: Your brain, your fists, and a few magic words. The trick is figuring out which should be put to work first. I used to be in awe of quick-fisted types, but experience has taught me that they often waste energy punching when a simple *please* would do.

Here are a few Fishbein tips for getting what you want . . .

Make Politeness Your Plan A
How many successful spies, detectives, or adventurers are *rude*? Very few. (In fact, I can't think of a single one.) They're not all wonderful people—but they're smart enough to know that curses, sneers, and insults won't get you anywhere.

Be Ready with Plan B
Sometimes sweetness only goes so far. Know what your next step will be if the people you're dealing with need a little more *convincing*.

Know Who Deserves Politeness—and Who Deserves a Swift Kick in the Pants (or Worse)
There are several kinds of people around whom you should never mind your manners. These include kidnappers, adults who don't keep their hands to themselves, or anyone who seems like a threat to your safety. Should you encounter such individuals, do not think twice about screaming, thrashing, or kicking them in their most vulnerable spots.

Build a Network of Associates
It's a simple fact—and the secret of every great detective. People to whom you've been helpful are more likely to give *you* help when you need

it. And it doesn't matter who you are—one day, you're going to need some assistance. You don't need to be best friends with all of your associates. Merely offer people your respect and do them a good turn if you have the chance—and you may be surprised to discover how willing they are to help you out of a jam.

Be Courageous Every Single Day

You don't have to battle man-eating rats to show you've got guts. Defend the innocent and the weak. Stand up for your own beliefs. Challenge your mind and your body. Don't take the easy route. Refuse to be anyone other than yourself. Sleep with the light off. (Okay, I'm still working on that one.) Don't expect other people's respect. Earn it. You'll find its far easier to get what you want.

Don't Let Anyone Make You Feel Inferior

One of the greatest women who ever lived once said, "No one can make you feel inferior without your consent." Never, ever give that consent.

CHAPTER 43

And They All Lived
Happily Ever After

So now we must conclude our tale of two princesses. How did you expect it to end? With wedding bells and "happily ever after"? Well, I won't promise "happily ever after." And as for a wedding . . . you've got to be kidding. (Kiki probably just vomited at the thought.) Fortunately for those who like to keep things traditional, I *can* promise bells.

At eight a.m. on Sunday, May 3, the bell of St. Maurice rang for the first time in a century. The regulars at the sidewalk café below the tower glanced up in astonishment. The bell's sonorous tone—both melancholy and hopeful—bypassed the brain and delivered a message straight to the soul. It was, everyone agreed, the most heavenly sound they'd ever heard.

Two young people sat at the same café with newspapers open in front of them. Many of their fellow patrons must have recognized the famous couple the moment they'd taken their seats, but no one dared invade their privacy. When the bell of St. Maurice began to toll, the dark-haired boy peeked over his copy of *Le Monde*, and his pale companion set her *New York Times* aside. They grinned at each other across the table. In the bell tower high above them, a tall blond boy swung from the rope like a jubilant chimp.

"Mission accomplished. What shall we do next?" Etienne asked Kiki. "Any ideas?"

Kiki took a sip of her café au lait. "I don't know."

✦   ✦   ✦

Even by Kiki Strike's standards, March and April had been busy months. There were countless royalty-hunting reporters to evade. Hundreds of bones to return to the ossuary. Dozens of Les Frères Corbeaux customers to capture and escort to the Paris police.

And of course, there was the trial of Livia Galatzina to attend in Pokrovia. The evidence against the former queen proved so overwhelming that arguments lasted less than a week. Kiki was in the courtroom every single day—with her handsome French boyfriend by her side and her mother's pink diamond ring on her finger. When the guilty verdict was read, the victims' only daughter was allowed to address the court and the heavily veiled defendant. As cameras flashed, Kiki thanked the jurors and the people of Pokrovia, but she had no parting words for her aunt. Instead, she shocked the whole world by publicly requesting that mercy be shown to her cousin Sidonia. The girl deserved a chance to change.

Later that afternoon, Kiki was spotted delivering a mysterious gift to the reform school where her furry cousin was being trained for a life as an ordinary (if extraordinarily hairy) girl. The brightly wrapped box held a tube of an ointment called Morlock's Hair Today, Gone Tomorrow.

"You have ONE chance, Sidonia," read the card inside.

✦ ✦ ✦

"What do you mean, you don't know what's next?" Etienne scoffed. "There must be another adventure for us here in Paris. France is filled with villains!"

"You're right," Kiki said, her eyes skimming across page C-4 of the *New York Times*.

Sometime around the middle of April, Kiki had taken to purchasing a copy of the American newspaper each morning. When asked, she claimed she was keeping up to date on the scandal surrounding Fem-Tex Pharmaceuticals, but Etienne could see there was far more to the story. Kiki missed Verushka Kozlova and her fellow Irregulars. After three months in Paris, it was time for her to go home.

Something on page C-4 had grabbed Kiki's eye. She pinned the paper to the table and traced a headline with one finger. Etienne's heart sank when he saw the excitement in her eyes. Adventure was beckoning Kiki from across the Atlantic.

"I'll miss you," he said.

"Miss me?" Kiki looked up and arched an eyebrow. "Your school lets out in a month. Have you ever smelled New York in the summer?"

"I can't say that I have," Etienne replied with a laugh.

"Then you're in for *quite* a treat."